D1250611

*Dark Road
Home*

Also by Karen Harper
and available in Beeler Large Print

Black Orchid
Circle of Gold

Dark Road Home

KAREN HARPER

Middletown Library Service Center
786 South Main St.
Middletown, CT 06457

FEB 99

BEELER LARGE PRINT
Hampton Falls, New Hampshire, 1998

Library of Congress Cataloging-in-Publication Data

Harper, Karen (Karen S.)
   Dark road home / Karen Harper.
     p. (large print)   cm.
   ISBN 1-57490-135-4 (alk. paper)
   1. Large type books. I. Title.
   [PS3558.A624792D37 1998]
   813'.54—dc21   98-5877
                                          CIP

Copyright © Karen Harper, 1996
All rights reserved.

Without limiting the rights under copyright reserved above, no part of this publication may be reproduced, stored in or introduced into a retrieval system, or transmitted in any form, or by any means (electronic, mechanical, photocopying, recording, or otherwise) without the prior written permission of both the copyright owner and the original publisher of this book,
Signet, an imprint of Dutton Signet,
a division of Penguin Books USA, Inc.

Published in Large Print by arrangement with
Penguin Books USA, Inc.

BEELER LARGE PRINT
is published by
Thomas T. Beeler, *Publisher*
Post Office Box 659
Hampton Falls, New Hampshire 03844

Typeset in 16 point Adobe Caslon type.
Printed on acid-free paper and bound by
BookCrafters in Chelsea, Michigan

For Don
for everything,
including sharing with me
the simple treasures
of Ohio Amish country.

Dark Road
Home

CHAPTER ONE

May 9, 1993
Maplecreek, Ohio

SOME SAID YOU CAN'T GO HOME AGAIN, BUT Daniel Brand was bound to do just that. He pulled the U-Haul behind the house, where no one would spot him from the road. Starlight grayed the black of early night when he turned out the headlights and killed the engine. He sat for one moment, gripping the steering wheel. His stomach knotted at all there was to face and do here. Starting right now.

He climbed down, stiff and sore from the long drive, waging war with himself for calm, even for courage. His new house, like his new life, was an old one, but he'd make it right, make everything right from cellar to roof, inside and out. He was taking his life's biggest step forward by taking many steps back.

He unlatched the back doors of the truck and yanked them open. From the dark cavern loaded with his meager possessions, piles of wood, and handmade furniture, he dragged out his toolbox and flopped it open on the grass. He strapped on his leather tool belt, jammed wire cutters, screwdriver, metal snips, a claw hammer, and needle-nose pliers in the pockets. Pulling on leather work gloves, he grabbed a saw.

He scraped his tall stepladder out, hefted it next to the back porch, and jerked it open. With his flashlight wedged in his belt, he climbed to the porch roof, then to the steeper shingled roof of the house. He hunkered down next to the tall television antenna and began to

1

work.

In five minutes he had cut the antenna loose. He shoved it over the side. It crashed two stories down, shuddered, and lay still.

Next, he dug at the nails and metal bands securing the two old lightning rods, but did not toss them over. They would fetch a good price as antiques at the Saturday morning auction in Pleasant.

He gazed at the plain, clean roof line with relief, for it would publicly declare his commitment to all who rode by. Sweating in the cool breeze, Daniel thrust aloft the rods like trophies of his victory. He had conquered himself; he had come home.

Slowly, he lowered the rods to his knees and gazed down from his precarious perch. The dark bulk of the U-Haul waiting to be unloaded was his last link to his previous life. He had snapped the radio off once he crossed the state line from Indiana, right in the middle of that bouncy-beat chorus he loved in "Achy Breaky Heart." He didn't mind giving up country music for good, he tried to convince himself. After he turned the truck in tomorrow, he'd never drive again, either.

The only lights he could see were from Verna Spriggs's Sewing Circle Shop and its second-story living quarters across the field. Two large farms, his own family's and his sister Emma's in-laws', lay beyond his lot line, but kerosene lanterns could never be spotted from here. No traffic on the road, nothing but star speckles overhead until he watched the full moon, big as a ripe peach, roll over the hilly horizon. It was a stunning sight, but he had things to do.

The knot in his stomach yanked tight again as he scooted crab-like from the roof, to the porch, and descended the ladder. He laid the lightning rods in the

2

grass. Under the clay pot where Emma said it would be, he found the key. He unlocked the creaky back door and went in. The interior smelled of vinegar, lemon, and soap; Emma had written that she and her girls would have it spick-and-span for him.

He turned on no lights and never would here—not the electric, anyway. Tomorrow he would disconnect it and have the wires pulled soon, the ones for the telephone, too, for he hoped to bring a good, plain woman here, one he could trust and, hopefully, someday love.

In the empty living room, the thick soles of his work boots sank into what Emma had described as fairly new wall-to-wall carpet, *thick and green as grass, you won't believe it, Dan.* He flicked off the flashlight and stood silent. But even in the dark, he saw pairs of white, fancy, ruffled draperies at each window like graceful ghosts bowing to a partner for a dance. He yanked them all down and hurled them in a corner.

Tears burned Brooke Benton's eyes as she listened to her niece Jennifer's closing to her bedtime prayer to "please tell my mommy I still love her. Especially because it's Mother's Day. And good night, God. Amen."

Brooke bent down to kiss the child's forehead.

"You know," Brooke said, "God has a very good memory, so maybe you don't need to remind Him of that every night, because then both of us just start crying."

"Yes, but *she* used to forget things sometimes. When she was sick, I had to tell her some stuff again and again. So I'm asking Him to remind *her*," Jennifer insisted in her seven-year-old's logic that often amazed

3

Brooke.

"Come on now. It's hit the hay time, as Mrs. Spriggs says," Brooke urged, plumping up her pillow and trying to make her voice light. "That Monday morning school bus will be here bright and early, Jen."

"I guess Daddy would be mad at me for going to bed late, don't you think?"

Brooke sank back on the edge of the four-poster bed and gently stroked Jennifer's hair. "No, I'm sure he'd understand that we were just having fun. I told you he's not mad at you for anything."

Frowning, the petite, blue-eyed blonde looked away to arrange her two dolls, leaned against the other pillow. They were totally mismatched: the small, molded plastic, adolescent Skipper doll had been Jennifer's mother Melanie's years ago; the soft, faceless Amish baby doll, named Nettie, was a recent gift from her friend Susie.

"I know," Jennifer said, her voice shaky with exhaustion and emotion, "that Daddy's not mad at me because Mommy died. That wasn't anyone's fault but cancer."

"That's right" was all Brooke could manage, but even then her voice broke. She still stroked Jennifer's hair; the child sighed and turned onto her side to cuddle into her deep down pillow. After tucking the sheet and quilt around Jennifer's thin shoulders, Brooke rubbed her niece's back, went out, and snapped off the light. A floorboard creaked loudly, but it would take a bomb to wake Jennifer once she fell asleep in this pretty haven of her room.

The bed, pillow, quilt, the rag rugs on the floor— Brooke thought again how this old but vibrant house and store below were just like their owner, Verna

4

Spriggs. Brooke missed her, but it had been her suggestion that Verna seize the chance for a long visit to her son's family in Maine. And immersing herself in Verna's duties made her feel useful as well as safe and sane again.

Brooke went downstairs to the big quilting room where she and Jennifer had been practicing line dancing with a videotape called *Country Dance Time*. Learning the Elvira and the Tush Push to the lilting, rhythmic tunes was one of many shared activities that bound them closer. Tonight Jennifer had gotten so into it, she seemed to temporarily forget her troubles, too.

Brooke pulled the quilted cover off the TV again—for when it was not in use, they kept it draped in deference to the Amish who came here—and rewound the tape to lesson one, the grapevine step. With the sound turned low, in her jeans, T-shirt, and beat-up boots, she did the grapevine around the room—step, behind, step, kick—while she straightened the quilts for sale on their circular revolving racks, retacked price cards for pieced wall hangings and table runners on the pegboard display, and aligned booklets and supply boxes on shelves. Monday morning would come too soon for her, too.

The two group quilts in progress—a Courthouse Steps and a Drunkard's Path—stretched on their separate rectangular frames needed no tending, for the Amish women who stitched them always left things immaculately ordered. Her only real Amish friend so far, Emma Kurtz, who oversaw things, made certain of that.

But Brooke noticed some scraps under one quilt where Emma's youngest, Susie, and Jennifer had been playing house on Saturday. She crawled under to pick

5

those up. The vacuum didn't reach clear under here, anyway.

She jumped when she heard a knock—and on the back door at this hour. Her heart thudding, she scrambled out from under the quilt, then calmed herself as she snapped on the kitchen light and walked to the back door. This was not the city, she scolded herself, and he—or them—couldn't possibly find her here. It was probably just an Amish person wanting to use the phone.

She peered out through the window and smiled in relief Emma's eldest child, Katie, age eighteen, who came with her to quilt if she was not tending the house or her siblings, stood there with three others. Holding Katie's hand until the door opened was Gideon Stoltz, Maplecreek's blacksmith's son, whom Brooke knew Katie had been dating. Behind them stood two other young people about Katie's age whom Brooke did not know.

"Your lights, we saw them still on," Katie said. "Stop by with Gid anytime for an ice-cream bar, you said— that Ha—Hagens . . ."

"Häagen-Dazs. Yes, please, all of you, come in."

"This is Cora Troyer, my best run-around friend, and this is her come-calling friend, Ezra Yoder," Katie told her, blushing ever so slightly under the freckles speckling her cheeks and pert nose.

The girls removed their black shawls and bonnets, leaving their white starched *kapps* covering the back of their heads. All Amish women wore their uncut tresses parted in the center and swept straight back in a hidden knot. Katie's green eyes looked huge behind her wire-framed glasses, especially because her dress was emerald green. How much she looked like Emma, even the

6

glasses, Brooke thought, warmed by the fact these four had come to visit. It showed her acceptance in the community was growing, even without Verna, whom the Maplecreek Amish had known and trusted for years.

The boys did not remove their straw hats, nor do more than nod. No *pleased to meet you's*, and Brooke knew to expect no *thank you's* or even a *good-bye*. For such polite pleasantries were deemed "fancy" or "prideful" by the Plain People, who tried as best they could to live separate from what they called worldly folk. At least, that evidently did not mean avoiding an outsider named Brooke Benton or the rich ice-cream bars that were her worst edible indulgence.

"Now, each of you choose what one you'd like," she prompted after she had trooped them down past shelves of fabric bolts into the back basement storage room and lifted the heavy lid of Verna's old chest freezer. Most of it was filled with food stored here for Katie's family, who bartered home-baked bread and canned goods for its use. Brooke had taken to keeping her storehouse of chocolate ecstasy down here so she wasn't tempted every time she got an ice cube from the kitchen.

When the four of them just stared down into the swirl of frosted air, Brooke prompted, "Let's see, we have Heath Toffee or Snickers Ice-Cream Bars, you know, like frozen candy bars. Maybe you should all try a different one and compare."

She should have known they'd all take the same kind so as not to look special or individual. They selected Häagen-Dazs as, she surmised, the ersatz name sounded German to them. Upstairs, she gave them napkins and pulled five chairs from around the quilting frames into a circle.

"Any day now my Uncle Daniel will come home and

7

be your neighbor," Katie offered in the silence as paper wrappers ripped and crinkled open. "Clear from Goshen, Indiana."

"Your mother told me he bought the old Whitman place across the field," Brooke responded. "I hear they had modernized it."

"Mm," Gideon said with his mouth full. "If he's really back to join the church, he'll have to convert it back. The black sheep comes home. Daniel Brand could tell us how to have a good, long *rumspringa*, I bet, yeah."

Cora said with her mouth half full, "The running-around time our young people have to try different things in life—even in the world—that's *rumspringa*. To see if we really want to commit to being Amish."

"The whole church will be glad to have Uncle Daniel home," Katie picked up her original topic. "My grandfather Jacob, especially."

"I'm sure it is hard for the bishop to have his own son living away from the family and church," Brooke said.

"In church this morning, Grandfather talked about it. But just now, heading home from a hymn sing, that's where we were," Katie explained, licking her chocolate instead of biting into it. "By midnight I'm supposed to be in the house—what you English called a curfew, Miss Brooke."

Gideon scooted his chair slightly closer to Katie's as she spoke. "His own buggy, Ezra has one, too, for courting, but it broke an axle, so tonight we came together."

"I'm so glad you did. I know how much Katie likes ice cream, and I told her she hadn't lived until she'd had a Häagen-Dazs."

They nodded, and Brooke realized how silly it must sound to hear someone English, as the Amish called

8

non-Amish, claim an ice-cream bar made any sort of difference in one's life. In just a few years these four would probably be committed to their church, married, and rearing families. And here, at age thirty-one, she had done none of those big, life-shaping things.

"A lot of fun gadding about," Ezra said, "like telling riddles. Know how to double your money real easy, Miss Brooke?"

"No, but I wish I did," Brooke replied, willing to play straight man to these very straight kids. Their wholesome naïveté always struck some strange chord in her.

"To double your money real easy, just fold it in half," Ezra said, then had to dive for his ice cream to keep from losing a huge chunk of chocolate. As they all laughed, Brooke noticed that Ezra sported a forbidden wristwatch and all four of them wore Reebok running shoes.

"The English—well, I don't mean you and Mrs. Verna—got the wrong idea about Plain People," Katie declared when she saw Brooke looking at their feet. "Like we're sticks in the mud or something. Our own fun, we have plenty of that, and we've been around a worldly place or two, uh-huh."

"I'll bet you have," Brooke managed, fighting to keep a smile from her lips.

"Promise you won't tell my mother?" Katie asked, leaning forward in her chair. Brooke didn't want to know something taboo she couldn't tell Emma. But what could this bunch possibly have done bad?

"I won't tell," she vowed.

"That dinosaur movie, we saw it in Pleasant," Katie whispered.

"*Jurassic Park*? I wouldn't let Jennifer see that."

9

"Real scary," Katie said, almost gloating while the others smiled. "People screamed right out and everything. We dressed English, we saw it, and *fressed*, too."

"Fressed?"

"Eat a lot, it means, almost as bad as gluttony," wide-eyed Cora put in with her mouth full of the last of her ice cream. "Like at the last table at the wedding, after hours of eating."

"Like now, for sure," Ezra said and waved his empty stick with a flourish. "And, Miss Brooke, real good I been watching that dancing on the TV over there. Barn dancing, we know how. That kind we could learn, too, I bet."

"Oh, I forgot I left it on," Brooke said. "I guess I could teach you the grapevine step, if you're sure it's OK." She looked at Katie for confirmation. But Katie only stared at Gideon over the last, licking good bit of ice cream. Brooke caught the charge of intimacy that crackled between the young couple. Amish girls might not be allowed to flirt, but Katie was doing fine with her come-calling friend with just two huge green eyes and a pink tongue on cold ice cream.

"Sure, it's OK," Gideon said.

Brooke ran the tape, and they all mastered the first step. Her guests seemed to enjoy its repetition and the fact everyone did the same thing. Brooke had seen that Amish cooperation, not good-old American competition, was what the Plain People believed in and taught their children.

As the tape went on to the next dance, the four young people frowned as they concentrated on the more complicated Tush Push steps. But no one balked at the double hip right, double hip left, right-left-right hip swings that pushed Amish tushes every which way. "Now, go ahead," the woman's voice-over on the tape instructed, "and dance in a straight line with or without a partner. And remember, though everyone does the same steps, you can put in your own personality!"

Out of the corner of her eye—was it a feeling first, a funny foreboding?—she glimpsed a man's face at the window. She jumped, stopped, spun to stare. Nothing. Had she imagined it? That she was being watched again? And out here in the country?

At first, the kids went right on. Her heart beat harder than the music; her palms began to sweat; a pulse pounded low in her belly. So fast, even here, it came crashing back—the fear and frenzy of losing control, of maybe losing—everything.

Brooke Benton had fled to Maplecreek because she had been tormented by some demented stalker after one of her court cases—a very high-profile one—blew up in her face. The abuse began with hate mail; she felt followed, then pursued; she feared for Jennifer more than herself, and that was bad enough. The bastard broke into her condo and played horrible pranks she feared would escalate against them. After the fallout at work, too, she'd been so certain she and Jennifer would be safe out here in rural Ohio among the peaceful Amish, since only one trusted friend back home knew where they'd run to.

Now she felt like an idiot standing stiff while everyone else stopped, then stared at her. When the front doorbell rang, she sagged in relief. She was here, sheltered in rural Maplecreek, far from home and harm.

"Miss Brooke, you all right?" Katie asked.

"Yes, fine. The doorbell just startled me."

In the front part of the shop, Brooke peered out

11

through the bay window they used for a display area. A tall man, a rough-hewn-looking stranger, in jeans and sweatshirt stood at the door.

"Mrs. Verna?" he called out and knocked.

Brooke opened the door. At the sight of Brooke, his high forehead furrowed to crush thick brows over night-dark eyes. His hair looked shaggy and windblown, shorter than the Maplecreek Amish to-the-collar length. Worn jeans hugged narrow hips, and his faded, cut-off-at-the-shoulder sweatshirt read JOHN DEERE. For one moment she wondered if that was his name, before she remembered it was a farm equipment company. He had very tanned, muscular upper arms and broad shoulders, but overall, he looked rangy, even a bit gaunt with circles under his eyes and hollows under his high cheeks, shadowed by beard stubble.

"Where's Verna Spriggs?"

"She's away to see her son, and I'm taking care of things for her."

"Taking care of things, so I see."

"If you were looking through the window, you had no ri—"

"Katie!" he called.

"Uncle Daniel?" the girl called, hurrying down the hall with her friends behind her. "You're back!"

Katie hugged him, and the other kids greeted the man delightedly—all in a rush of Pennsylvania Dutch German dialect the Amish used among themselves—while Brooke stood there feeling left out and very annoyed. Why had Daniel Brand been looking in the window and who was he to criticize her, even indirectly? Hadn't he refused his Amish church vows and taken off to live with some liberal group? If he blamed her for the kids being here late and dancing, that wasn't fair.

12

"And this is our friend—Mother's good friend—Brooke Benton," Katie was saying. "A *maidal* she is and used to live in the city, but here now with her niece, like a daughter to her," she explained in English as Daniel Brand's hard brown eyes examined Brooke again and did not soften. Brooke knew that *maidal* was the word for spinster, and once again, as if she could read the man's mind, she knew he did not approve of her living in Maplecreek, especially next door to him.

"Very good to us, Miss Brooke is," Katie went on. "And a lawyer she used to be, too, a woman lawyer."

"I can see she's a woman, Katie, but a lawyer?"

It annoyed Brooke that they talked about her as if she weren't here, and she wished Katie hadn't tried to help again. The Amish mistrusted lawyers for scriptural reasons, but the way he glared, Katie might as well have announced her to be a mass murderer.

"It's obvious everyone's glad you're back, Mr. Brand," Brooke said. "Thank you for dropping by to let us know."

"I came to ask if I could use Mrs. Verna's phone. I'll pay for the call, of course."

"Of course. There's one on the wall, right inside the office here." She snapped on lights ahead of him, only too glad not to have to stand in the hall and be examined like some rare piece of forensic evidence. She was used to having the Amish use her phone; they left a quarter next to it for every call, just as they insisted on paying mileage if she ever drove them anywhere in what they called taxi service.

"This is long distance to Indiana," he said, looking at the phone now and not at her. "I'll leave two dollars, and you can tell me if it's more."

"That's fine," she said and rejoined the kids in the

13

hall. The girls had gone back to get their bonnets and shawls, the boys their straw hats they'd removed dancing, though they didn't put them on. But they were so quiet now that she heard Daniel Brand's deep voice tell someone he had arrived safely.

Emma had said her brother had never married and had come home to settle down and start a family. Brooke pitied the woman of choice. And because of Katie and Emma, she felt bad that she did not care one bit for him, though she'd learned the hard way that her assessment of a person's character could be wrong.

As Daniel joined them in the front hall, he clapped his hands once and said to her guests, "You *yungie liet* better get on home if midnight is still the time. I just saw a clock on the wall in there—or we could consult Ezra's watch. All four of you came in that one courting buggy, huh?"

"Cozy as can be, yeah," Gideon dared with a grin while Ezra just shuffled his feet and beamed. "You never learned the Tush Push dance in your *rumspringa*, either, I bet."

"The Tush Push?" Daniel asked, turning to Brooke. She just rolled her eyes behind the kids' backs as he frowned at her again. "You do know what it means to push a tush, don't you?" he asked.

"No," three of them chorused while Cora nodded, but evidently chose not to dare a definition.

"It means get out of here now or else!" he told them with a low laugh.

He opened the front door and pushed both boys out with a little knee shove on their rears. Giggling, Katie darted away before he got to her. Gideon caught on at once to Daniel's definition of a tush push and reached back to give Katie a little spank on her fanny with his

14

straw hat. Still laughing, she flipped her shawl in his face, then grabbed Cora's hand to pull her out of Ezra's reach. Despite their lighthearted cavorting, Brooke just stared. It was evidently all right for Daniel Brand to have fun with them, but not for her.

Putting on their bonnets and shawls, the girls waited under the front pole light while the boys went around in back for the buggy. Unfortunately, that left Brooke and Daniel, and he was studying her sideways, his eyes going up and down her body. If he thought he'd come back here to re-Amishize himself, she was tempted to tell him, he'd best start by not staring at an English woman in a worldly way. But worse, she'd been out here in the boonies away from normal civilization longer than she thought if someone like this man could intrigue as well as irritate her.

Now, still staring at her, he opened his mouth, then closed it, compressing it into a tight line. He shifted his weight; his glanced wavered. "So my sister Emma's a friend of yours," he said.

"Will you try to send her away, too?"

"I didn't mean it like that. They needed to go home."

She wanted to accept his halfhearted apology, but, in more ways than one, he had ruined her evening. You might know that the first Amish person she had not liked lived right next door, even if there was a wide, hilly field between them.

"Excuse me, but I'm going to bid my guests goodbye," she said, grateful the boys had brought the buggy around. She left him standing in her doorway and went out.

When the four young people piled inside, Brooke reached up to shake their offered hands, an unusual concession they had evidently decided to offer her. She

15

was very aware that Daniel came out and stood just behind her in the night shade of the biggest maple on the front lawn while she was bathed in light. She sensed more than saw his disapproving presence there, his narrowed eyes on her back—on her tush, darn him, when, of course, Amish women were so completely covered and draped. A car went by slowly on the road as if someone were lost and looking for a turnoff, but she concentrated on the kids.

"Real good Häagen-Dazs and dancing!" Katie called to her as Gideon snapped the reins and "giddyapped" the horse. Brooke caught a last glimpse of them, all crowded in on the single seat, the girls sitting on the boys' knees. The steel-rimmed buggy wheels crunched gravel. Katie's face, smiling, stuck out the side window, as pale and round as the moon above. From the house lights, the orange safety triangle reflected on the back of the buggy. Two very distinct lanterns dangled there, one a quaint kerosene lamp that glowed silver; the other, battery-run, flashed bright red. The clippety clop of the horse's hooves and the kids' chatter drifted away on the sweet night air.

"I'd best be walking back home," Daniel muttered behind her. "I only glanced in the window because I took the cut-corner across the field and passed the window heading for the front door. I looked in, and it was hard to miss. Good night," he added and started up her driveway, evidently to his path across the field.

From under the big tree where he had stood, she watched him go, listening to his long-striding footsteps on the gravel, then the silence. So, she thought, he knew it had annoyed her that he had peeked in the window. Maybe that's why he had even bid her a worldly good night. Daniel Brand might be Maplecreek

16

Amish, but the remnants of the outside he'd evidently seen and rejected clung to him yet. A car roared by on the road, but her attention was riveted on Daniel. An interesting study, that man.

Daniel stretched his strides through the thick mix of grasses in the hay field. You might know he'd come home, he thought, to find a worldly woman with a fancy, sharp tongue—a city lawyer, no less—living next door. And she was blond and shapely and dressed to flaunt all that. He couldn't believe Emma had let Katie get close to the so-called Miss Brooke just because she ran the Sewing Circle and was her temporary boss. The first time his big sister gave him her "I told you so, brother" look about anything, he'd take her to task for her own mistakes and misjudgments. Unlike most Maplecreek Amish, he knew the real lures and bait that waited to hook a man out there m the world.

Brooke Benton's face faded to that of that other blonde, whose name should have been Delilah. He slowed, breathing hard, then, feet spread wide, halted on the top of the hill. He clamped his hands under his armpits and stood scowling at the moon, remembering putting his hands all over the other woman's breasts and bottom. Her hands slid so skillfully over him, too, though he did not need that to make him want her—and then came the violence and pain.

He walked slower on the downward side with the pale shape of his house growing in the distance. On Sawmill Road down the rise, a big triangle of automobile headlights snagged his gaze. The car ate up the road fast. Over the top of a hill it seemed to soar, then plunge. At the bottom, a screech of brakes shredded the night air for what seemed an eternity. The

17

headlights swerved. He tensed, then jumped. A crash. A quick crunch of metal, canvas, fiberglass. He felt the field shudder; his legs trembled, for he knew—he feared—what it was.

Brooke turned to go in the house when she heard a muted explosion. It vibrated the air, or was she still trembling? Her first thought was of Jennifer. She ran into the silent house, listened for her voice, then stepped back outside. Someone's kerosene storage ignited? A tank at the gas station in town blew?

Walking out beyond the halo cast by the pole lamp, she squinted to peer into the night. She could see nothing down the road, but it was hilly and disappeared over the first rise and plunged to a hollow before the hill at the old Whitman house—now Daniel Brand's. Then she remembered that car going so fast past the house after Daniel had walked away. The sound—perhaps the car had hit a tree.

She stood indecisive for one moment. Then she tore back to the house and, from outside, closed the door behind her, hoping, praying Jennifer would not awaken, and if she did, not think her aunt had deserted her as she feared her mother and father had.

Then Brooke realized it would help to have a light to see if anyone was hurt. If it was far down the road, she could get there faster by car. Then she thought of the buggy, slower than a car, so fragile. Where would the buggy have been on the road in that little time?

She yanked open the front door she'd just closed, darted into the house, locked the door, and ran upstairs, listening for Jennifer. Grabbing her purse, she dug for the car keys as she ran back down, panting, panic drowning her, worse than she'd felt when her own life had been in danger.

She ran out the back door. Since Verna's car was stored in the small garage, Brooke's sat out. Her hands shook so hard, she dropped her keys. She fumbled for them, got in, started the engine, turned on the headlights. She ignored the buzzer from her unhooked safety belt as she backed up, turned around, then roared down the drive.

But on the road, she turned on her broad beam brights and crept. The buzzer went silent; she could only hear the thud of her heart out here.

It could not be, she thought, not those four smiling kids. Not Emma's pride and joy, not Katie. And they had been out late because they had been to see her. If anything bad had happened, surely the Amish community, let alone Daniel Brand, would hold it against her.

If—anything—bad—had happened, that litany kept tormenting her as she crested the hill. Tears rolled down her cheeks; she blinked them back to see and hunched over the steering wheel. Surely, that awful crash would bring others, but this road was surrounded by Amish farms set way back, and no one drove anything faster than a buggy—a buggy like that courting one the kids were in. Then, too, it was late, so late, at least for rural Roscoe County. She glanced at the clock and blinked to clear her vision again. Ten after midnight. Maybe it was right of Daniel to hustle them away, because Katie and Cora would be late for their curfew, if—anything—bad—had happened . . .

And then she saw scattered bits of buggy strewn along the two-lane road. The red lantern still flashing, flashing along the grassy berm made a scene from hell illumined even brighter by her headlights. It was a

19

terrorist bomb blast site—the evening news from some war-torn, primitive place. Broken glass glittered against dark asphalt. The bulk of the dead horse, a twisted white body on the pavement, whose? Daniel bent over someone on the do-not-pass double yellow stripe on the road. She sucked in a sob; her hands clenched the wheel. She sat immobilized for one moment gasping for air until Daniel looked up into her headlights, and she saw tear tracks reflected on his face.

She hit her wanting blinker in case anyone else drove up. She fumbled for her car phone, turned on the dome light, punched 9-1-1. Somehow she talked, told the woman on the line the horrible things. As soon as possible, she said. Help soon.

Brooke's legs shook so when she got out that there might as well have been an earthquake. The metal ridges of her keys bit deep into her palms as she hurried to lean over the first body—Ezra, lying in a black pool of oil—no, blood. The whole scene smelled of burned rubber, the acrid, coppery scent of blood, the staggering stench of death. She crunched glass, stepped over a broken piece of wheel.

"Ezra's dead," Daniel announced the evident from ten yards farther down the road. His voice broke. "Cora's in the ditch to your right."

Brooke went to her, knelt in the thick grass. The girl was looking back over her shoulder in a grotesque position, her eyes open to behold the night, her long hair fanned loose, her skirts twisted under her to expose white thighs. Her shawl dangled from a bramble bush behind her. Brooke did not even feel for a pulse. She wanted to cover that quiet, sad face with the shawl or even the girl's hair, but attorney instinct told her not to move anything at the scene until the police came. Still,

20

she pulled the shawl from the briars and quickly covered Cora's legs.

"This is Gideon, gone, too," Daniel said when she came out of the ditch. Daniel looked stunned, maybe in shock. "But Katie," he said. "I don't see Katie. Katie!"

Shaking, panting with an almost animal fear, Brooke started down one side of the road while Daniel thrashed along the other. "Where's the car that hit them?" she called to him as she sloshed ankle-deep through low water in the grassy ditch.

"Took off!"

But her despair at the deaths stabbed so deep that her rage at the hit-and-run barely fazed her. Still, her voice of reason recited, this was not an accident scene but a crime scene. A murder site with no witnesses, no suspects. But evidence, horrible evidence everywhere. She felt numb. She fought down the urge to throw up and went on, trying to stay calm no matter how loud Daniel howled Katie's name.

Then, up on the rise above the ditch a good sixty feet from the buggy, in the distant glow of mingled moonlight and headlights, Brooke saw something pale—an apron, a prayer cap?

"Here! She's here!" she screamed and clawed her way up the little rise beyond the ditch. She bent over the girl. She looked so young like this, without her glasses. She looked so much like Emma. Katie, lying still, so still. But breathing. Breathing!

"She's alive! Alive!" she shouted as Daniel ran across the road. He fell to his knees so hard beside Brooke he almost bounced her back into the bramble bushes beyond.

"Yes, thank God. Alive!" he exulted.

"I called the squad. They said they'd be here soon.

We have to cover her, not move her because of possible back and head inj—"

"It will take them too long to get here," he interrupted. "We've got to take her in."

"In? In where? Maybe they'll even send an emergency helicopter that will be faster to get her to a city hospital. It's dangerous and illegal to move an accident victim!"

"Listen, city lawyer," he ground out and yanked Brooke to her feet as he stood, "she might be dead when they get here. We'll take your car to the county hospital in Pleasant. I'm going to lift her, so try to steady her head." He bent, grunted, lifted her.

Brooke was aghast at his daring and determination. She tried to keep up with his long strides and hold Katie's head as it bounced against his shoulder. She was as limp as Jennifer's Amish doll, and, thank heavens, unconscious. But how would this man feel later if he had hurt her more? She felt the warm, sticky blood on her hand and wrist and saw it came out from Katie's ear. And the back of her head was soft—too soft—where she tried to cradle it so it wouldn't bounce against his arm. At her car, she scrambled to open the back door so they could slide her in.

"Ride with her in back," he ordered. "Give me the keys."

The keys, she thought. She'd had them, but where were they now? Then she realized she held them in her left hand, her fingers frozen around them. She extended them. And then they were bathed in new headlights, heard a voice, saw new warning lights blinking behind Brooke's. A car door opened, then slammed.

"What got hit?" a man called out in English, then repeated it in German, maybe when he saw the broken buggy.

22

Brooke knelt on the narrow back floor of her Toyota and took Katie's hand; Daniel slammed the door and got in to start the engine. Was he not going to stop to talk to the man? But he backed up and called out to him in German. She heard him give his name and hers, the names of the four victims, but couldn't follow what else was said.

Another vehicle, a pickup truck, drove up from the other direction. At least, Brooke thought, there would be someone here to guard the scene—and the bodies— from both sides. Daniel didn't wait, but backed up again, not using the rearview mirror, twisting his body with his arm on the back of the seat to look behind them. His fingers snagged and pulled strands of Brooke's hair, but she didn't move. He seemed to hover over her and Katie. She could hear and feel his ragged breath, though he was looking beyond them as the car climbed the moonlit hill backward.

She noted Katie's limp arms had gone rigid in a strange, angular posture. She still breathed, though so shallowly and irregularly that Brooke had to keep touching her to be sure. She put two fingers against Katie's neck to keep track of her pulse there. She tried to remember any testimony of doctors who had been at the scenes of crimes or accidents; this was all she could think of to do. She would have given years of her life to have Emma here for Katie now instead of her. The Amish refused to recognize Mother's Day, but what a horrible day for this to happen.

Daniel continued to back up the car, far down the road with warning lights still blinking to turn around in her driveway. She thought then of Jennifer alone in the house.

"I can't just leave Jennifer."

23

"That man was Paul Hostetler from the other side of town. He's going to bring Katie's folks to the hospital and have someone tell the other families and get someone to watch your girl."

"Thank you. She—at least she sleeps hard and long."

"How is she?" he asked, and she knew he meant his own niece. Brooke's despair deepened, for this was to him as if Jennifer lay here, injured, maybe dying. But Katie had to live, she had to!

"She's breathing. I can feel her pulse," she said, afraid to tell him about the spreading blood.

They seemed to be moving so slowly, even though she craned around to glimpse the lighted speedometer once and saw it read sixty-five. Katie's pulse, already erratic, slowed, slowed.

Every few minutes Brooke assured Daniel that Katie still breathed. Besides, they said comatose people could hear voices, so, however unconscious she looked, maybe Katie could hear her. Her voice shook, though she began to talk steadily to her.

"You're going to be all right, Katie Kurtz. We'll take care of you. Your Uncle Daniel is here. Your mother will come soon, your father, too. You're going to be all right, you have to live, have to be strong, Katie."

When she paused briefly once, Daniel began to speak to Katie in German, his deep voice rough with emotion, but almost crooning. It washed over Brooke as if to soothe her frenzy. If things could only be different, if he could be speaking kindly to her and if only Katie still had that trusting smile . . .

After an eternity, Daniel pulled up at the EMERGENCY side door of the small county hospital and ran inside, shouting for help. Brooke reached up to click on the dome light again. Katie looked pasty pale.

When an orderly and a sleepy-looking nurse appeared rolling a noisy gurney and opened the car door to peer in, Brooke informed them, "She's breathing shallow, and her pulse is jumpy and slowing. Her head is soft, back, lower left, about the size of my palm. She's bleeding from her left ear. Her arms went stiff about fifteen minutes ago."

The surprised-looking orderly said, "OK, lady, good work."

"Is there a surgeon on staff or at least on call?" Brooke asked.

"Dr. Woo-Lun will be here in a minute," the man told her.

Brooke's hands shook, but when they reached in to slip a foam collar around Katie's neck and slide a headboard under her and tape her forehead to it, Brooke helped while Daniel stared in the window. Both Brooke and Daniel helped support Katie while they slid her out; then the three of them outside the car lifted her onto the gurney.

"You're not her mother?" the nurse asked, peering back into the car.

"No, but this is her uncle. He can sign for anything until her parents arrive. And the Amish don't have insurance, but they'll pay."

"Amish, is she? Didn't realize it with her hair loose. Yeah, we know they pay," the nurse said.

When they wheeled Katie away with Daniel running beside, now holding her hand, Brooke tried to rise, but she seemed frozen in place. Her legs bent under her had gone completely numb. She felt terrified and trapped. That woman who had called 9-1-1, that tough-as-polished-acrylic-nails attorney, as the senior partners had called her—she had been through a lot, been so

25

afraid, but never like this.

Brooke Benton bent over her sticky red hands clasped in her lap, and sobbed.

CHAPTER TWO

EMMA KURTZ JOLTED AWAKE IN HER HUSBAND'S arms, bumping his chin with her head. "Mm, sorry."

"Bad dream, Em?" Levi murmured and cuddled her closer.

She slitted her eyes to see pale moonlight spilled across the quilt. "I—I don't know," she whispered, straining to hear.

"Just a jet going over again, maybe. Big Red's not howling."

You might know, she thought, he would think of a jet. She'd seen him halt the five horse-hitch plowing the middle of a furrow to watch any plane go over, *verboten* though they were. And here he had dared to lecture Daniel about cars before he left, more than their father, Jacob, had. Oh, how she prayed Levi, as well as her dad, would patch things up with Daniel when he came home.

"No strange sounds now," Levi whispered, his beard tickling her bare neck. "You done worrying, so I can sleep?"

"No. At least the children are too big to be falling out of bed anymore. I don't think Katie's home yet."

"What do you expect in *rumspringa*, my little mother hen, hm? Gid Stoltz is a good boy, so don't worry. Just down the lane smooching like we used to, that's where they are."

"Not with Ezra and Cora along. Those two haven't

26

been paired off long like Katie and Gid, *rumspringa* or not."

Emma tried to rise, but her long hair was caught under Levi's shoulder. She tugged free and rose, then padded across the polished floor, took her shawl, and whirled it around her shoulders over her long white cotton nightgown.

"All right, all right," he groused and sat up, rubbing his eyes, "a look around, I'll do it. But we can't sit up like croaking frogs on a moonlit log waiting for them."

Their Irish setter Big Red began to howl outside. Emma's hair prickled along the nape of her neck and sheer dread shivered up her spine. She ran to the window lifted halfway for spring night air, thinking surely she would hear the buggy on the lane, however much that would not disturb Red. She clutched a knot of shawl and gown between her breasts and bent low to press her face to the screen. Moonlight silvered everything outside. She gasped.

"What?" he asked as he hurried up behind her.

"See, a car coming fast down the lane and at this hour!"

He squeezed her shoulder and turned away. Half hopping, half walking, he pulled his pants on under his nightshirt and went out the bedroom door. She heard him thudding down the hall, down the stairs. Fear cramped her belly; she scraped the window higher but could not hear words over the engine running, just men's voices in German, quick, perturbed.

She stripped off her nightgown and yanked on undergarments laid out for her predawn rising. She fumbled for her dress, closing the front of it with straight pins by feel as she ran downstairs. As Levi turned back inside, she stopped several stairs above him.

A pale patch of moonlight stretched his shadow across the polished wooden floor.

"What is it?" she demanded. "Not Katie—"

"A car hit the buggy on Sawmill, then took off."

"Not Gid's buggy?"

He nodded, his face in darkness. He came to the bottom of the staircase, his hand gripping the banister. "Bad hurt, some, but Katie's at the hospital in Pleasant. Daniel arrived tonight and took her in. Your English friend was there, too. That's Paul Hostetler in the car," Levi went on, starting upstairs, as if he were afraid to look at her. "He's going to take us in, get folks to tell the others."

"How's Gid?" she asked as she started up beside him to tell Leona to watch the younger ones. When he did not answer, she turned to grab his arm. "Tell me! The others?"

"All gone, God take their souls," Levi whispered. She gasped and gripped his arm so hard he flinched. Then they leapt at each other, holding tight, swaying on the steps. "We gotta go, Em," he said, but only clamped her harder to him. "She'll be all right. She didn't live when the others died just to leave us now."

Emma thrust him away. "I won't lose another one so soon, not Katie, not her!"

In five minutes they were bumping along the back lane toward town, for Paul Hostetler said they could not get past the site of the crash on the road. Beyond Maplecreek, when they turned onto the highway into Pleasant, they saw the rescue squad rush at them, then past them. No siren, but blinding, blinking bloodred lights. Huddled in the backseat, Emma and Levi gripped each other's hands in silent, desperate prayer.

28

*   *   *

When Brooke got hold of herself, she sniffed hard and blinked to see. Crying always blurred her contact lenses beyond belief. She half dragged, half lifted herself up off her bent legs, which had gone to sleep, and hobbled out to lean against the trunk of the car, where she flexed and massaged her leg muscles. Beyond, red light from the EMERGENCY sign stained the closed glass doors to the Roscoe County Hospital.

She wanted to go in to see how Katie was doing, but would Daniel want her there? Should she wait out here for Emma and Levi, try to prepare them for how bad Katie was? If Daniel had left the keys in the ignition, she should move the car. And she must call home, be sure whoever was staying there—had she even left a door unlocked?—would assure Jen she had not left her if she woke up . . . if only Katie would wake up!

She looked in the open front door of her car and saw the keys and her purse there. After ransacking her purse for a tissue, she blew her nose, but still could not breathe through it. She moved the car, locked it—for even in a little place like Pleasant, fears died hard—and went inside. Although she needed to use the women's rest room, she walked through the empty lobby to the vacant reception desk, then peeked through the double doors beyond.

She saw Daniel down the pale green hall, his elbows against the wall, his head in his hands. She wanted to respect his privacy, but she had to know how Katie was . . . if Katie was . . .

Wiping away tears black from running mascara, she edged through the doors and started down the hall.

"Mr. Brand—Daniel?"

His head jerked around; his features looked crumpled,

29

blurred. "I was going to come find you. They say she's bleeding internally, head and here," he said, hitting his head and flat belly. "They're prepping her for surgery. That Chinese doctor is hard to understand, but I think he said something about an emergency helicopter to Columbus or Cleveland, but then decided it would take too long. They phoned some other doctor to help."

"Maybe a specialist on call. They'll save her. Surely, you did right to bring her in fast. We didn't even see an ambulance."

"If it's still the volunteer township one, it will take a while," he muttered, slumping back against the dingy wall. With thumb and index finger he rubbed his eyes under a deeply furrowed frown. "What does their rush matter if they just have corpses to rescue? I wanted to stay with her, but they said we should wait in there." He nodded toward an unlighted room labeled FAMILY. "I can't bear to have to tell Emma and Levi this," he choked out.

She wanted to touch his shoulder, comfort him, but she stood unmoving just inches away. "Yes, it will be so awful for their families. Especially Emma, to have to face Katie hurt, after losing her little son. She isn't over that yet."

"I could tell from what she didn't say in the letters, more than what she did," he admitted and heaved a heavy sigh. His dark eyes narrowed to squeeze out a tear he brushed away with the back of his hand.

"Daniel, I know it's the kids being with me that kept them out late and—"

"Don't think like that," he interrupted and glared at her. "Things like this are all part of God's plan, though I sure can't see how. If it's anyone's fault, it's that coward who hit them. Probably didn't so much as get his big bumper dented," he added and his voice broke.

He smacked both fists on the wall behind him so hard she jumped. "And don't think you're to blame, either," he added, "because *I'm* the one who kicked them out of your place, or they wouldn't have been on the road then."

She saw now the reason he didn't—couldn't—blame her. If he did, he must blame himself, too. Silence stretched between them; she felt totally drained. She tried to recapture that tiny flare of fury she'd just felt— for justice, even revenge. Three counts of aggravated vehicular homicide and one count of aggravated vehicular assault, the indictment would read—if Katie lived. If and when the local police or the highway patrol or whoever had primary jurisdiction here located the hit-and-run criminal, she could testify; she'd love to prosecute the culprit. Even when she didn't close her eyes, she kept getting flashes of those twisted bodies on the road, the shattered buggy, and that red safety light, blinking, blinking.

Still leaning side by side against the wall, they jolted upright when a bell rang. The orderly appeared from down the hall and seemed surprised to see them in his path.

"They haven't started quite yet, but they'll do everything they can," he assured them. "She's on the table, just waiting for the surgeon on call to assist Dr. Woo-Lun. If you'll wait in there, I'll just see who . . ."

Brooke saw Emma's white face peer through the distant door; then she and Levi rushed down the hall. The orderly had the good sense to stand aside.

"Dan. Dan!" Emma cried, and hugged him hard. "How is she? Thank God you could help her, be with her!"

31

Levi stared blankly at Brooke as if he didn't really see her, as if she should not be here. He shook Daniel's offered hand. When Emma stepped back from Daniel and Levi put his arm around her shoulders, Emma reached out to take Brooke's hand, and she pressed Emma's hard in both of hers.

"Two doctors are going to operate," Daniel explained as they leaned toward him, listening intently. "To stop her bleeding. Internal—head and abdominal." Then, he glanced at Brooke and added, "Brooke held her hand. We talked to her, told her you'd be here, that she would be all right."

"But she was unconscious the whole time, so she's not in pain," Brooke added. "Hopefully, none of them knew what happened. They were so happy, having such a good time. Emma, I'm so sorry. But she's young and strong, and she has to be all right. They stopped to see me—the four of them—for ice cream, and Daniel came to use the phone . . ." she tried to explain, but she couldn't go on.

And then, Brooke felt ashamed again, for Emma held out her arms to comfort her.

In the buzzing crowd of family and friends, Emma, seated on a slippery plastic couch, noticed the foreign man in the doorway of the waiting room. He wore scrub pants, shirt, cap; almost the same green color, she thought, as the new dress Katie had worn tonight. Emma could see her now, smiling, sailing out the door this very afternoon full of expectation with a wave and a smile. "Don't worry about a thing, Mom. We won't be out too late . . ."

But now, Emma feared, it might be too late, as it had been for baby Eli. Mothers sensed these things somehow, and she could not bear it, not again. Not Katie, her firstborn, who had been not only a daughter, but almost a younger sister, a second mother to the other children, her salvation through hard times lately when Levi did not understand. Not Katie, that sweet, God-graven image of her younger, happier, better self.

Levi noticed the doctor, too, for he stood and helped Emma up. She saw the big-faced clock read 4:45 A.M. Her insides felt frozen; her voice would not come when she must be strong.

Dr. Woo-Lun, who they had learned was actually a foreign medical graduate from China, hesitated at the door. He was obviously taken aback to see the room packed with people. They had been arriving as the word spread, and they managed to get car rides into Pleasant. Others, of course, had gone to the homes of the three dead young people to help their families. The men wore hats, the women bonnets, all black-garbed. Perhaps the doctor thought, Emma realized, they were already in mourning, for his narrow eyes widened and he stood there uncertain. She and Levi started toward him. He evidently recognized only Daniel, for he walked to him while everyone hushed and made a path.

"These are Katie's parents, Levi and Emma Kurtz," Daniel said and put a hand on Emma's back. She held hard to Levi's hand, but leaned gratefully against Daniel's strength. Brooke stepped back and pressed a hand hard to her mouth, as if she, too, sensed what this man would say. That was exactly what Emma wanted to do, to keep from crying out against it all. Even more, she wanted to scream herself awake in Levi's arms back in their bed and end this nightmare.

Emma's father, Jacob Brand, the local bishop who had led a long prayer earlier, and her mother, Ida,

33

hovered close as did Levi's family. But all Emma wanted was Katie, all she wanted was to hear what she somehow knew she would not hear.

"I regret to tell this," the doctor said and cleared his throat. "The young woman died during surgery—trauma to the brain, internal bleeding, very bad. Perhaps a blessing. Maybe she never regain consciousness, never recover. So very sorry. Two doctors tried, but it too late, probably too late the moment those young people hit."

The room was absolutely silent and absolutely stifling. Accept. God's will. Be strong, Emma tried to tell herself. She opened her mouth to say something as Levi and Daniel propped her up. But her thoughts only crashed into a white blank wall.

Brooke grabbed for Emma when she saw her faint, but Levi and Daniel kept her from pitching forward. The doctor called, "Mrs. Linard, Mrs. Linard!" as if he could operate on a dying woman but not tend a fainting one. But he helped them lay Emma back on the floor before he went out, while Brooke and Emma's mother knelt to hold her hands. Mrs. Brand fanned her daughter's face with her apron.

The big-shouldered nurse pushed in and cracked an ammonia capsule under Emma's nose. Her head jerked; her eyes flickered open. Brooke could see her remember; her eyes filled with tears, which spilled down into her ears.

"She's awake now," the nurse announced the obvious, "but leave her there a few minutes before you help her up. I'm needed back in the OR."

Suddenly, for the first time in all this, the righteous anger that had propelled Brooke through many a case and trial stoked her strength. She was angry at this nurse

34

and at the doctors who had not saved Katie. It had taken them too long to start; that foreign doctor didn't know what he was doing; they'd never even seen the other doctor—medical malpractice at its worse.

She felt fury at the person who had hit the kids, at herself for keeping them up late, dancing no less, something she had found herself admitting to these people tonight as though she had to make a public confession to them. And she was furious with Daniel Brand, who had peeked in her window, interrupted everything, and who no doubt blamed her—blamed all worldly English people, for all she knew—no matter what he said. And she was exasperated at these quiet, passive people for accepting all this without one normal human murmur of denial or accusation.

When they got Emma on the couch, sipping water, surrounded once again by family, and the deep buzz of solemn solicitations hummed in Brooke's ears, she went out and leaned against the wall in the hall, then slid down it to sit on the floor. She had washed her face and hands earlier, but saw her shirt, jeans, even her boots were covered with dirt and bloodstained. Dare she hope that was one reason the Amish stared and not just the fact she was in jeans and a T-shirt that said AMERICAN BAR ASSOCIATION? It hit her then that, whether or not they thought that referred to lawyers or liquor, they could not possibly approve of her.

But, Brooke admitted, she did not feel part of this patchwork of extended family of Emma's, however kind they were to her. They even called Emma by a different name, Levi Em. Since so many of the local Amish had the same first names, they often used the husband's name to differentiate women. Brooke thought it was ridiculous to refer to a woman by her husband's name, as

35

if she had no identity beyond her relationship to him. It was one thing if a wife carried her husband's last name, but must she change her first name, too? And Levi, of the Levi Em union, didn't like Brooke or trust her, probably no more than Daniel did.

Nor could Brooke stand seeing the sad but stoic faces in there anymore. She almost wished they'd shut her out instead of saying they were grateful for all she'd done for Katie. They'd promised to pray for Brooke, too, when it was Emma who needed that. She could not bear it that Katie, sweet, shy Katie, who had blossomed so beautifully just hours ago with Gideon, her friends, with Daniel, with her, was dead now—a murder victim as far as Brooke was concerned, while the Amish said it didn't matter who did it and that they forgave whoever hit their young people!

"Excuse me, ma'am, but are you with the Amish group?" a woman's deep, commanding voice asked. Expecting the nurse again, Brooke looked up to see a trim brunette, beautifully coiffed and attired in a mauve business suit, holding a notepad and a microphone that read EYEWITNESS 12 NEWS. A man with a Channel 12 camera perched on his shoulder stood farther down the hall, fussing with his equipment.

"Don't turn that on—the camera or the mike!" Brooke warned, and stood up. "The Amish won't be interviewed or filmed, you know."

"I realize that, but we've come clear out here in the chopper and obviously scooped the other stations. We could do an interview where we blur a face and even scramble the voice. But you're not Amish, so if you'd just give us a quick statement, then we can do the doctor before we go out to the accident site."

"No!" Brooke cried, not sure what of all the woman

36

had said she was protesting. "No statement. A tragedy occurred, and I'm sure you'll honor the Amish not to intrude here."

"Intrude? Look, lady, the American public has a right to know. People are fascinated by the Amish, let alone by any human tragedy. Besides, we can help publicize what's known about the hit-and-run vehicle, help catch the guilty party. Don't you want to see justice done? Channel 12 could spearhead a huge drive for funds to help with hospital bills or the funerals, because I know the Amish refuse to carry insurance."

During that spiel, Brooke realized she recognized this woman from a Columbus station that was a network affiliate. She supposed, no matter what she said, everything would be in living color on central Ohio's TV screens tomorrow. But she wasn't going to help them pry into Maplecreek's privacy. Besides, all she needed was for this so-called investigative reporter to realize who and where she really was. She had probably escaped recognition so far only because she looked like a holy horror out here in the boondocks instead of a once up-and-coming, now disgraced criminal lawyer at the court building or in the interview room at Stedman & Rowe.

Brooke turned her back on the woman and went to the door of the waiting room. Standing on her tiptoes, she motioned to Daniel, who saw her over the hats and bonnets. He frowned, but he came.

"I'm going with Emma and Levi," he said, "to see Katie—her body. But I don't want you to have to drive back alone."

Before she could explain, he saw the woman and the cameraman. "I thought," she told him low and fast, "you'd be best to head them off before they get near the others. But they mentioned they could do a drive for funds if it would help. I told them absolutely no coverage, but she won't listen. And please don't give them my name, either, as I'm going to try to keep the police from giving it out."

When Daniel lifted one eyebrow at that, she blurted, "I just don't want to be quizzed or quoted on this, any more than your people do."

"Good. I'll handle this. But the police report will be another thing."

When Daniel came out and took the media people down the hall, Brooke stepped back into the waiting room and closed the door. She explained to Bishop Brand who was outside, and he warned everyone else. She could hear Daniel's voice through the door, stern, insistent. The woman's was sharp and strident—and then gone. Brooke peered out. Daniel was speaking to a police officer, but the reporter and her cameraman had evidently retreated at least as far as the lobby.

Brooke knew Daniel was right about the police, for they had to be talked to, no matter how much she dreaded it. She could only hope that they would agree to allow her to stay under the protection of Amish privacy, too. She could not afford to have her Columbus stalker trace her and Jennifer through the media. Exhausted, she walked toward the men on legs that no longer seemed to be there. She had a headache, but not the kind that dragged her down. It made her feel so light and floaty she hoped she would not faint as Emma had.

"Sheriff Barnes," Daniel told the stocky, middle-aged man, "this was the second person on the scene, Miss Brooke—ah, Benton. Like me, she's totally exhausted. If we could talk to you tomorrow—I mean, later today. We both live on Sawmill Road on either side of the accident site."

"And the young woman who died here is—was—your niece, Mr. Brand, that right?"

"I'm afraid so. I haven't been living in Maplecreek for years, but just returned last night—to this. Have you found the person, the car?"

Brooke was amazed Daniel asked. It was obvious the Amish did not care if they ever knew, except maybe to pray for the killer by name. But Daniel seemed to belong in both worlds—and in neither of them.

"Not yet, but we will. Anyone breaks the law in Roscoe County answers to me, as you may recall, my boy. That suit you, too, being interviewed later, Ms. Benton?" Sheriff Barnes asked. "My deputy on call's out at the scene to oversee the highway patrol boys, who always show up, with or without an invite. So I'll be following up with you two. Patrol boys ask you for a statement, tell them whatever you have to, but I'll be top dog handling things."

Brooke watched him scribble something in his small notebook, then squint up to study her. She stared back; the man looked like former President Lyndon Johnson with his droopy eyelids, big ears and nose.

For the first time tonight she became appalled by her bloody appearance. Through her exhausted mind flashed the picture of Jackie Kennedy in that bloodstained pink suit, standing stunned while the new president was sworn in on the plane from Dallas. Jackie had refused to change the suit because she wanted people to see what *they* had done to Jack. And part of her—the old Brooke—felt that way, too. She'd like to call the TV people back and make a statement about Katie and her killer, but she could not risk it. Maybe Daniel was not the only one being pulled two ways.

39

"I said, that all right with you, Ms. Benton?" Sheriff Barnes repeated, tipping his hat back with one finger.

"Yes, that's fine."

Ordinarily, Brooke would have asserted herself, told the man she was a criminal lawyer, understood police procedure, and would be willing to testify or assist under any circumstances. But she—this new Brooke she sometimes didn't know—did not want her name and address given to the press, and she hated having to deal with the police. When she had needed them in her personal life, they had failed her and Jennifer badly.

"If you don't mind, Sheriff Barnes," she added, "like the Amish, I'd rather not have my name released to the press. I may be the only non-Amish person involved, but I really can't presume to be a spokeswoman for them."

"Like I told Mr. Brand, I'll do what I can, ma'am, but public record, Freedom of Information Act and all that, you know."

"Not if it's vital information in an ongoing criminal investigation where it might help to keep some evidence privileged," she insisted. "What I mean is, perhaps some of this will be at your discretion."

"You got that right. I only hope these news hounds keep that in mind. Them and the patrol boys," he muttered and shook his head so his jowls bounced.

After the sheriff wrote down her address and phone number and said he'd be out to talk to her later, Daniel steered Brooke down the hall. "The sheriff told the TV folks to wait out in front, and there will be other gawkers, I bet," he said, his voice edged with bitterness. "You can't trust reporters or writers. Anything unusual for the Amish brings them in—barn raisings, even funerals, like we were part of some special zoo."

40

Their eyes met and held; she could see her reflection in the deep pools of his eyes. She felt a strange closeness to him, a need to help him, a desire to be touched, to throw herself into his arms to comfort and be comforted. She tried to seize that glimmer of emotion, but if he glimpsed it, too, he shut her out as he looked away. The feeling was over, gone—foolish. There was nothing else to share or say.

But when he took her arm, her elbow tingled as if she'd hit her funny bone there. He guided her past the waiting-room door where she thought she would go in to say good-bye to Emma.

"Where are we going?" she asked when he steered her on.

"Before I go with Emma and Levi—they actually have to identify Katie when the coroner comes—I want you to go home. Amos Mary Lapp—that's my cousin—has already gone out this back exit to wait. She'll go home with you. Then she's going to walk to Kurtzes to tell the other children what happened."

He shoved open the door marked EMERGENCY EXIT ONLY, but Brooke guessed every door in this wing could be marked that. A sturdy, middle-aged woman she did not know stood with her shawl wrapped around her in the chill, predawn air.

"Brooke, this is Amos Mary." When Brooke did not budge, he gently pushed her out the door. Brooke almost told him she didn't have her keys, but she saw her purse hung over her shoulder. She felt so disconnected from herself now, maybe like in those out-of-body experiences in which people claimed they floated just a bit above, looking detached down at everything. But, however exhausted she was, body and mind, she could not feel detached.

41

"All right, thank you, Mary," she said to the woman whose face was hidden by her deep bonnet. She wanted to say something to Daniel in farewell, in consolation, but no words seemed adequate for what they had been through. "Thank you for taking care of—things," she said to him, and her voice caught.

"We tried. We tried, but we didn't." He turned away to let the door snap closed behind him.

CHAPTER THREE

JENNIFER STRETCHED HERSELF AWAKE, THEN rolled onto her back, keeping her eyes pinched shut. First thing each morning, she ran her tongue over her teeth—part baby and part big ones—to see if any more little ones were loose. Nope, but they sure felt uneven with gaps and not smooth and pretty like Aunt Brooke's. Even through closed lids, she saw the room was too light. What day was this? Did she have to go to school? Then she remembered.

Oh, no, it was Monday, and the bus would be here soon to take her into Pleasant, because Aunt Brooke said the Amish school in Maplecreek wasn't right for her. But maybe they both overslept, and the bus came and went without her.

She rolled over to look at her Beauty and the Beast clock and saw it was nine o'clock. Really late! They had done all that fun dancing, and it had made them both too tired to get up on time.

She scooted off the bed and grabbed her clothes from the chair. Aunt Brooke always made her put them out for a school day, but she'd rather just pick them in the morning. Mommy had not been so planned-ahead like

Aunt Brooke.

But as she wriggled out of her pajamas and into her underwear, she heard noises outside, like cars, voices, a horn. She peeked out her side widow between the curtains.

"Oh-oh," she said when she saw a lot of cars going slowly by. "Customers, and Aunt Brooke is missing them if she's not up."

Holding her skirt and top, she ran down the hall and listened at her aunt's bedroom door. First of all, it was funny that it was closed. Jennifer heard Aunt Brooke on the other side of the door say, "Yes, I'll let you know. And thanks for the advice. Yes, it's just terrible. I feel horrible about it. I'll do what I can. Bye now."

Jennifer stood silent. That must have been Daddy on the phone. Probably saying he did not want her back, that she made him feel terrible, that Aunt Brooke should try to keep her, do what she could with her. She thought she would get sick, just like she did when Daddy left. When she turned away, the door opened behind her.

"Oh, Jen," Aunt Brooke said, "I was just going to wake you."

"Was that Daddy on the phone?" she asked, turning back.

"No, or I would have called you double-quick. Are you crying, sweetheart? Come in here," she insisted and pulled her into her room. The bed was made, and she had on nice clothes, but her hair and her face looked kind of messy.

"Jen, I was talking to Mrs. Spriggs on the phone. I had some bad news to tell her, and now I have to share it with you, too. But it doesn't have anything to do with our family, not your daddy or anything, I promise."

43

As she talked, Aunt Brooke took her clothes from her hand and knelt to dress her like she was a baby or something.

"What?" Jennifer asked, still feeling afraid, even if she was glad that wasn't Daddy saying he didn't want to talk to her or see her anymore, ever again.

"It's about Susie's oldest sister, Katie," she told her as Jennifer's head popped out of the shirt.

"She made us snickerdoodles last week and pushed us on the swing in Susie's yard."

"Jen, sweetheart, there was a bad car accident on the road last night when you were asleep. A car crashed into a buggy with Katie and three of her friends in it."

"I would have heard it."

"You know you sleep through fireworks. You didn't even know Mrs. Schmitter came to stay with you for a while. Now, just listen. The driver of the car took off, but Katie and her friends died. So Susie and her family—Mrs. Kurtz, all of them, Susie's daddy, too—are very sad. I know you understand how that feels to lose someone real close you love, Jen. That's why you're staying home from school today, because—because there are people out in front who are just poking around, and I don't like that. If you'll help me, we'll fix some food for Susie's family and go see them to let them know how we're mourning with them . . ."

Jennifer figured out what "mourning" meant when she saw her aunt's lips shake and tears jump to her cheeks. She felt really sad for Aunt Brooke, but especially Susie. Yes, she knew just how it felt when death took someone away.

"I'll help you and Susie, too," she promised, holding her aunt's hands as they both sat on the floor. "I'll help you like you always help me."

Somehow that made Aunt Brooke cry harder. Jennifer patted and rubbed her back the way she sometimes did for her. "You see, Jen," Aunt Brooke finally said, blowing her nose, "before the accident, the four of them stopped here last night for ice cream and stayed awhile learning the same dances you and I were doing earlier. When they got hit, I went to the hospital with Katie and her Uncle Daniel, and the doctors tried to help, but she died anyway."

"Even doctors can't fix some accidents and real bad cancer. It's not your fault. So those people out in front don't just want to buy things or learn how to make a quilt?"

"I closed the shop for two days. Mrs. Spriggs—said it was all right," she said and sniffed, rubbing under her eyes with the tissue. "Since I saw the wreck, I have to talk the police about it, too."

"They might tell we're here! That person might find us again!"

"No. No!" Aunt Brooke said and put her hands on Jennifer's shoulders, holding her out with straight arms. "I'll take care of that. I'm sure we're safe here. Now, go get on some shoes, wash up, and we'll have breakfast. And, Jen, I don't know what I'd ever do without you."

"If this mess don't beat all," Daniel's father muttered as another car passed the buggy and a woman leaned out the window on crossed arms to gawk at them. The old man quickly hid his face with his black broad-brim hat and spoke from behind it. "*Ach*, even now, can't they just leave us be?"

Daniel marveled that his father's voice was not angry, only agonized. He admired his fortitude when he felt like flipping them the finger—something he had never

45

done, but he had a buddy in Goshen who had honed it to a fine art. Daniel supposed he should follow his father's lead and at least turn his head, but he just stared back.

"From the license plates," Daniel observed, "it looks like most of these folks are our Roscoe County neighbors. Wait till the city people come swooping in."

Despite deep despair over the accident, Daniel was beginning to feel at home today, eating breakfast at his parents' table, dressing Amish, riding in the family buggy to help his father invite the few extra people to Katie's funeral who would not know to attend. With four funerals in a tightly bound community, Bishop Brand had been in on the early-morning decisions to hold Katie's and Gideon's services on Wednesday since there were fewer out-of-state mourners to be contacted and brought in. Cora's and Ezra's people had some far-flung relatives, so their services would be on Thursday. It was tradition to hold a wake in the home of the deceased before the funeral was preached there.

When a videotape camera sprouted from the window of a passing van, Daniel, too, covered his face with his hat while the horse pulled them on. The automatic pilot feature of a buggy was one advantage of a horse instead of horse power, he thought. Another—ordinarily—was that passengers had time to look around to enjoy the scenery. No blur of crops or wildflowers, no slamming into deer, possums, woodchuck—or people.

His father spoke from behind his hat, picking up their earlier conversation. "Providence that you came home when we lost Katie, my son. Under other circumstances, I would kill the fatted calf. The Lord giveth and the Lord taketh away."

They replaced their hats on their heads as they passed

Daniel's new home with the unloaded truck still sitting in back. Daniel saw his father nod when he evidently noted the curtainless windows and lack of television antenna and lightning rods. Daniel wished he'd had time to deal with the electric and phone wires that swooped in from poles like some sort of intravenous tube lifelines.

He turned toward his father. "I've learned the lesson of my life, Dad. I'm here to settle down and give back. I know it will never be recompense for Katie's loss, but—"

A car horn blared behind them, as if they were blocking the road. The horse didn't startle any more than Jacob did, but Daniel jumped and had a good nerve to turn around to at least motion them to pass. But he got hold of himself and sat still.

His father, whose square jaw and flinty eyes were part of Daniel's heritage, nodded and patted Daniel's knee, either for his vow to change his ways or his impassive acceptance of the ass behind them who leaned on the horn again. The nod and touch were great comfort. For Jacob Brand was a man of much work and few, but powerful, words—except when he preached in church, which had fallen to him by lot to keep all church ministers from pride.

Except for a quick smack or two over the years, it was the wrath-of-God gaze and the steely voice that had controlled the Brand brood, all seven of them, that is, until Daniel's defiance and departure. His last argument with his father would make damnation on Judgment Day pale by comparison, he thought. At least he had not joined the church before he left, or he would have been shunned, too: Emma could not have written; no one would have so much as spoken or eaten with him

47

when he returned. The Bible might decree forgiving seventy times seven, but once he took his vows soon, at age twenty-eight, about ten years late, he could never go back to the world. He knew he'd get no second chance to come home, not with Bishop Brand and, therefore, not among the Maplecreek Amish he loved and had missed so much.

In the morning light, Daniel noticed more lines in his father's weathered face, more silver hairs in his beard and hair than when he'd left eight years ago. He wondered how dark his own beard would grow in when he was baptized soon, very soon.

As they approached the accident scene, cars crawled, even slowing the buggy. Some people were on foot, too, staring, pointing where the dead horse had been dragged but not hauled away yet. Cameras clicked and whirled not only at that horse, but at the fine retired harness racer that pulled their buggy. Orange police cones dotted the long, snaking skid marks, forcing both lanes of traffic to drive on the berm. The investigating officers were gone now, but yellow plastic tape, probably broken by people ducking under it, fluttered forlornly where wreckage had been strewn.

Once Daniel saw what else they were gaping at, he averted his eyes from the police chalk marks in the crude shape of bodies on the pavement and the dark stains that had been young Amish blood. Sheriff Barnes had told him this morning his deputy had to remove scattered bits of buggy to the gas station in Pleasant, because visitors were carting them off as souvenirs.

When his father pulled into the Sewing Circle drive, Daniel saw a CLOSED sign on the door, but several cars were parked in front anyway. He wondered if Brooke Benton had guests calling on her the way their own people were doing with the Amish, or were these the cars of those walking on the road?

"Go around in back, Dad," Daniel urged, and Jacob clucked the horse farther down the drive. They climbed out, and Jacob threw the reins over the hitching post. Brooke pulled the door open before they knocked. She looked so different—feminine but covered in her denim, ankle-length skirt, red-and-white striped, long-sleeved blouse with an unbuttoned denim vest. Her shoulder length, honey-hued hair was swept up in a kind of topknot that spilled a lot of pieces—*struvvles*, the Amish called the wayward strands. But it looked good on her. He had to admit that she had an intriguing face: oval with wide-set eyes, soft mouth but strong nose and determined chin. Still, right now, she looked fragile and her swollen, bloodshot eyes showed what she had been through. Those eyes—sky blue in daylight this close— widened, evidently in surprise to see him in broadfall black trousers, light blue long-sleeved shirt, suspenders, and broad-brimmed hat he'd borrowed from his older brother, Mahlon.

"Good morning, Bishop Brand, Daniel," she said. He could read on her face then that she wished she had said something but "Good" morning. Nervously, she wiped her hands on the dish towel she held.

Her little blond niece, seeming shy, came out and stood close to her during introductions. Daniel could not help but admire the two of them, similar in coloring, if not temperament. A touching little picture they made in the morning sun at their back door as if waiting for a husband and father to come home. He had already glimpsed this soft side of the woman lawyer, who had argued with him and taken command with the hospital orderly, the TV reporter, even Sheriff Barnes.

49

When she'd cried over Katie, he had wanted to hold her, though he knew that was a trap he could never be caught in again.

In the short, awkward silence, when his father just stood there, Daniel said, "Levi Em and the whole family wanted to ask you to Katie's funeral Wednesday—nine o'clock in the morning."

"I'm honored. Since your—I mean, the Amish— children will be there, I heard—Verna told me—would it be all right if I bring Jennifer?"

"Of course. Lots of children will be there. For us, death is part of life."

"For us, too. Jennifer lost her mother last year." The girl put her arm around her aunt's waist and just nodded, big-eyed.

Daniel felt the impact of that right in his belly. He wanted to say something kind to them, but his father beat him to it.

"Sorry we are for your loss, too."

"Thank you, Mr. Brand. I really didn't mean to bring that up at a time like this. Would you like a cup of coffee or some cinnamon rolls?" she asked, pushing the door open behind her. Daniel's nose twitched at the crisp, mingled aromas.

"No," he said, wanting both to dislike her and comfort her. "We have to go to town to ask others."

"I didn't mean to delay you. I'm sure you have a great deal to do. Daniel, I was wondering if it would be all right, today or tomorrow, if I called on the other three families."

"Yeah, good." He felt instantly, deeply touched, not only that she cared enough to do that, but that she consulted him for advice instead of his father, whom the Amish asked for help in decisions.

"And Jennifer and I," Brooke went on, "plan to walk to Emma—Levi Em's—house this afternoon with some food. I want her to know how very much . . ."

Her voice drifted off; Daniel saw her eyes dart, her head turn. Someone peeked around the back corner of the house, and he knew how she reacted when someone watched her secretly. A stranger emerged, then two of them in shorts and T-shirts. The man said to the woman, "Told you they came round back here, Judy."

"May I help you?" Brooke asked, and walked closer to them as if to block their view of the men and Jennifer. "The shop is not open today."

"Just wanted to see some real Amish close up," the woman explained loudly, as if Daniel and Jacob were not even present. Jacob turned away, retrieved the reins, and climbed up in the buggy. Daniel knew he should, too, but he stood his ground.

"And wanted to see a buggy like the one got hit," the man said as he walked to the back of the square vehicle and patted it hard enough to rock it. "I told you, honey, these homemade things are really flimsy and unsafe, especially painted black and running around after dark."

Daniel clenched his teeth and fists. Did these people dare to imply the blame lay with the kids who had been hit? He hoped—he even prayed—that he would not lose his temper in front of his father. He forced himself to walk around the horse to the other side of the buggy and climb in.

"Leave that buggy alone!" he heard Brooke say when it bounced again, after he got settled. He craned his neck to see she had advanced on the invaders. "Can't all of you out there on the road just give grieving people— and that's all of us around here—some privacy?"

"Look, ma'am, the Mrs. and me didn't mean any

harm."

"Then, get off this property right now!" Brooke backed them up, pointing with the dish towel still in her hand while Jennifer stood silent, with her little fists on her narrow hips by the back door. Daniel could just imagine Brooke berating someone in court, backing them into a corner like on those old Perry Mason reruns he'd seen in Goshen where the guilty party finally stood up and screamed out, "I'm guilty. I admit I did it!"

"How would you like it," Brooke was demanding, and he could see his father hung on every word, though he didn't make a move, "if people came poking around in your backyard? Can you imagine someone saying, 'Oh, we just wanted to see some real Presbyterian people close up?' or 'Let's just trespass in this backyard and get close to some real Catholics and see how they grieve and have a funeral.' I said, get off this property!"

Daniel fought to keep his mouth from turning up as his father glanced askance at their avenging angel and snapped the reins. The guilty had turned tail and were clear back to their convertible in front of the shop before the buggy rolled out onto the road.

"Are you ready, Jen? Come on!" Brooke called upstairs and, once again, rechecked the plastic snap-lids of the containers in the picnic basket. She kept losing her train of thought, going over and over how much Daniel resembled his father, how much his just wearing Amish clothes had seemed to change him. He had been soft-spoken and mild-mannered. He'd passively allowed those people to insult everyone when she was certain he would have acted differently just yesterday. Oh, come on, Brooke Benton, she told herself. Forget Daniel Brand. It was Emma she had to care for now, and that did not include caring about her black sheep brother.

She and Jennifer went out the back door, for, with the growing parade of cars, they could not have easily walked the road to the path through the field that led more directly to the Kurtzes' farm. She had spoken with Sheriff Barnes on the phone and asked him to do something to control the press of people, but he said he had enough worries planning how to "guard" four funeral processions this week.

She had answered some preliminary questions about the accident over the phone and agreed to speak with him tomorrow, even to visit the accident site with him. He had warned her again that when "the highway patrol boys" contacted her, she must not tell them anything she didn't tell him. Evidently, the local police and the patrol were waging some sort of turf war "here'bouts," even though she knew Ohio police jurisdiction laws specified that the patrol could not help investigate an accident unless permission was given by the local authorities.

She lugged the basket with the sloppy-joe filling and potato salad; she had never made either in such huge quantities. When she'd gone down to get the ground beef from the basement freezer, she had lost control again, standing there, remembering the kids. Unbelievable it was just last night they had all chosen the same treats. As petty as Häagen-Dazs and dancing seemed now, the four of them had been happy, so happy in their last hour.

Jennifer walked beside her with the boxes of peanut-butter cookies and brownies in her school backpack. For the first time, Brooke noticed it was a lovely day. She really enjoyed walking out through the small woodlot and by the pond on the fringe of the Kurtzes' farm. She had given up jogging when things went wrong back in Columbus—partly because Jennifer could not keep up—but maybe she'd have to begin again. Before yesterday, she had felt safe here in Maplecreek with its surrounding haven of hills.

"You want to see pollywogs in the pond?" Jennifer's high voice interrupted her thoughts again. She was touched the girl had been content to stroll along this far without a word. "All us kids who play there call it Pollywog Pond."

"I guess we have time."

"Isaac and Andy showed us where the pollywogs hide out," she said, almost conspiratorially, referring to two other Kurtz kids, ages fourteen and twelve. Emma's children had stretched from eighteen-year-old Katie to seven-year-old Susie—and, of course, the baby she lost and had told Brooke she would never forget, even if she hadn't even known him.

"And guess what Isaac dared Susie and me to do," Jennifer said, "even if the Amish aren't s'posed to make dares?"

"Tell me."

"He dared us to catch and kiss a pollywog, but we call them tadpoles at school!"

Brooke smiled, but her facial muscles actually hurt.

"Did you do it, Jen?"

"No, but I told them the story about how the princess kissed the frog and it turned into a prince. Susie thought it was pretty awesome, but the boys said pollywogs turn to frogs but frogs don't turn into anything. Then they splashed us and ran away."

They set their burdens on the grassy skirt of the small, sun-dappled pond and sat while Jen showed her the flitting tadpoles in the golden shallows. Brooke sat

and leaned back on her hands to watch a swallow—
Emma said they were the ones with forked tails—skim
the pond, dipping its bill in to drink. It was so peaceful,
almost solemn, here today. Brooke watched the ripples
Jennifer made with her wrist circling out, out.

"Let's go, Jen. We'll want to be back home before
supper."

They walked around the edge of the precisely plowed
field that already sprouted blades of green corn. This
one was hemmed by hedgerows instead of wood or wire
fences, but some of the adjoining Kurtz and Brand fields
had solar-powered electric fences to keep cows in.
Compromise and ingenuity were Amish traits for
certain, she thought as they walked by the little phone
shanty on the lane where tourists sometimes tried the
door in vain, thinking it was an enclosed farmer's stand
or public outhouse.

The Amish made some bargains with the world, such
as phones being permissible if they were only for
emergencies and kept outside their homes. For some
liberal groups, electricity passed if it could be generated
somehow on-site so it didn't link the Amish to the
outside world. And Emma had told her that Amish
women now used plastic spray on their stiff white *kapps*
instead of starch. She sighed as they cut across the long
yard that stretched toward the cluster of houses, the
mammoth barn, and outbuildings beyond.

Most large Amish farms in Roscoe County had at
least two houses, usually linked by a covered walkway.
The larger one belonged to the farming family; the
smaller they called the *gross daadi haus* or the grandfather house. It was the retirement home of the
patriarch, a much better form of social security, Brooke
had to admit, than so-called rest homes or retirement

55

centers. Emma and Levi had lived in the big house here for years already, Verna had said; but on the Brand farm, the second-youngest son, Mose, and his wife, Mose Susan, lived in the *daadi* house, and Bishop Brand still did the majority of the farming from the big house. When Mose really took over—or had a third child— they would exchange houses.

"Looks like they've got lots of company besides us," Jennifer observed as they saw the line of buggies along the lane.

"Friends visit and do all the work for the grieving family, Jen, not to mention so many of these families are related. That's why I wanted us to bring some food, so we can feel part of the neighborhood and show all of them we really care."

Despite visitors, Brooke saw that clothes still flapped on the long line in the breeze. Two straight rows of early onions, a fringe of asparagus, and elephant ears of rhubarb filled one end of Emma's neatly disked and immaculately weeded garden. That evidence and the lack of lightning rods on the roof were the best ways to tell an Amish house at a glance, along with signs that read NO SUNDAY SALES.

When they had walked past the buggies—for the three other times Brooke had been here, they had gone in the back door—the screen door pushed open. Susie stepped out, barefoot, with her older sister, brown-haired, plump Leona, behind her.

"Kindly of you to come, Miss Brooke," Leona said, and hurried to take Brooke's basket while Susie greeted Jennifer. "In the dining room, most are," she said, "waiting for Katie in her coffin to be brung from the undertakers in Pleasant."

"Oh, I see."

"And upstairs with some family, Mother is, but she'll be so glad to see you, uh-huh. You'll be coming to the funeral tomorrow, I hear. Pleased you're coming, very."

A huge knot caught in Brooke's throat. Leona was fifteen, but had obviously now stepped forward to help her mother, and to take, if that were possible, Katie's place. Inside, Leona unloaded the food, turned it over to the women working in the kitchen, and took the cookies Jennifer offered with a hug.

Four women bustled about, cutting bread, laying out cold meat slices, pickles, and cheese on platters. Brooke knew two of them, including the Brand cousin, Mary Lapp, her companion home from the hospital. Emma had brought the other woman, Sam Anna, to quilting. They nodded and, amazingly, spoke to Brooke about the good growing weather as Susie and Jennifer whispered and Brooke waited Leona's return with Emma. When Jennifer asked if the two of them could go out and sit in the porch swing, she let them, though she felt very alone waiting here.

Despite the people and piles of food, the kitchen seemed so spacious and uncluttered to Brooke. But it was filled with delicious aromas. Besides the food, she could smell that tart lemon soap mingled with the pantry smells, dried dill and mint, garlic and onions, coffee waiting to be ground.

The two other Amish homes she'd seen in the month she had been in Maplecreek were similar in size the Amish held their church services, weddings, and funerals, too, in their homes, so the rooms had to be large and able to be emptied to put in pews. No doubt it took the men just a few minutes to carry out the big table and the beautifully carved oak cupboards here.

But amid white walls and bare, shiny wood, there

57

were splashes of color, too: pink paper napkins neatly folded down over the edge of kitchen shelves; colored china plates in the oak hutch in the corner; marigolds and nasturtiums popping from red-painted tin cans on the windowsills; and four picture calendars and several hand-embroidered quotes on the walls.

The saying Brooke could see from here read, "*Work makes life sweet.*" She thought for one moment of her own life's work and what had become of it—at least for a while. Here she was running a rural quilt and sewing-goods shop instead of practicing criminal law in a booming metro area. But she had been burned doing that, believing so intensely in her clients, and it had shaken her world. Her eyes and thoughts focused fast when Daniel's big form filled the doorway.

"I just wanted to tell you," he said, and his deep voice made the women quiet and look up before they bent back to work, "that Father and I were grateful for how you handled those people this morning. And I, before we speak of it no more," he said as he stopped across the big table from her, "want to say the same for your help last night with Katie."

She nodded, her hands gripping the back of a chair. She wanted to say so much to him, but he had chosen such a public place and terrible time that words would not come. Again, she was struck by the change in him. He was controlled and calm, no longer challenging, his intensity seemed contained, though something flickered yet in each dark eye for her, and she felt that flash of heat and light deep in her belly.

Could a change of clothes or place so transform a man? He was looking down at the food on the table now, but the brunette next to him with the heart-shaped face was staring at Brooke. Evidently, having nothing else to say, Daniel rapped his knuckles once on the carved chair back and left the room.

Emma came in right behind Leona. Brooke saw her friend's steps were no longer brisk; her gaze not piercing, even through her thick glasses. "Brooke!" was all she said as they clasped hands.

"Would you like another cup of that sage tea for your headache, Levi Em?" the watchful brunette asked.

"Maybe later, because it helped," Emma said and gently guided Brooke from the kitchen. Brooke thought Emma's face looked like pale porcelain, perfectly composed, but ready to shatter. She squeezed her arm. "They're bringing her home soon," Emma whispered, "and I want to show you something." She led Brooke down the hall, bypassing the side room where a group of men evidently waited for the hearse from Pleasant or the food from the kitchen. Brooke could hear women's and children's voices from upstairs.

"Here," Emma said and walked Brooke into the front room, where stood two sawhorses, a quilting frame, and Daniel. "We're going to put the coffin on the sawhorses, so Dan's going to move the quilt to make room for the mourners and the service. He said you'll be here."

"Yes" was all Brooke could manage with the knot in her throat. For it wasn't the surprise of mere sawhorses awaiting Katie's coffin that snagged her gaze, nor even Daniel Brand as he seemed to study the partly completed quilt on the frame he was evidently planning to dissemble. For beneath his big brown hands stretched the most beautiful quilt Brooke had ever seen, pieced together in a Wedding Ring design.

With it, Emma had far surpassed her other masterpieces, which she always insisted were just everyday, practical items. The pattern was a rare one for an Amish woman for two reasons: this quilt was a worldly design, and the Amish did not exchange wedding rings. Yet Brooke had never seen the pattern so beautifully expressed.

The quilt was done in calm creams, leaping blues, and glorious golds. It reverberated radiance and intensity, but also seemed serene, restrained. From the window under which usually sat Emma's treadle sewing machine, sun spilled across the endlessly interlocking circles of the pattern. The entire piece awaited its border and the elaborate hand quilting that would adorn it.

"Perfect to lay her out here, in the room where she helped me stitch this quilt," Emma said. "Now I'll have to finish it alone. We joked about making one like it for her and Gid. But for Dan, we wanted this one. Planning that last day to play matchmaker for him when he got back, that we were."

"Not now, Emma," he said. Brooke saw his tanned face flush as he unscrewed the last clamp and carried the big quilt from the room. She saw the frame itself rested on four ladder-back chairs, beautifully shaped and carved.

"Barbara Yoder, a widow," Emma whispered, "with dark hair, fixing the meat tray in the kitchen. Dan's run-around friend she was once, years ago."

The pretty, watchful woman, Brooke thought. A totally unwanted and unbidden pain slashed at her through her joy in the quilt and her numbness of grief. Now that the quilt and Daniel were gone, she felt the room had become plain bare floors and walls. Yet the encompassing fabric of these Amish lives—love of family and friends like those solid circles—was still here.

And it was that awareness that made her decide two very different things. Not only would she make this challenging Wedding Ring quilt for herself, but she must do something far more important. Though she feared risking her privacy and offending her Amish neighbors, she was going to do anything she could to help find who killed the Amish kids and bring that criminal to justice.

Brooke startled when Emma squeezed her arm and whispered, "I'm taking those pills again, the ones the doctor gave me when little Eli died."

"Prozac? I thought Levi threw them out."

"Sh! Only what he found," she admitted with a little shrug. "Not many left. Just to help me get through. Important we just get through this week, Levi says, and get all this behind us."

Brooke knew from her own experience—as surely Emma did, too—you didn't get such things behind you. Thoughts of Melanie were with her and Jennifer after six months, and memories of her parents, though they'd been gone for years. She knew Emma's arms were still longing for the little son she'd lost. When she saw out the window a long gray hearse driving slowly up the lane, she excused herself before they brought Katie in, home at last.

CHAPTER FOUR

"EXACTLY WHERE WAS IT ALONG HERE YOU stopped your car when you saw the wreck?" Sheriff Will Barnes asked Brooke the next morning as he slowed his crimson car emblazoned ROSCOE COUNTY SHERIFF. Both license plates read simply: SHERIFF. She could imagine what this vehicle looked like with its bright bar lights flashing.

61

"I'll have to get out near the scene, then walk back until it looks right," she told him, peering out the rolled-down, passenger-side window. "Since it was so dark, all I can tell right now is it was at the bottom of this hill."

He pulled over on the narrow, grassy shoulder where she indicated and hit his flashers. The police car still blocked part of the lane and others had to go around him. Brooke had suggested they walk the short distance from her house to draw less attention, but she was starting to see he liked to be at the center of things. She also saw he did *not* like any sort of suggestion from her, whether because she was a civilian, an outsider, or a woman, she was not sure.

They got out of the car and thumped their doors closed. He produced his notebook and flipped it open, then fished in his plastic-lined pocket for a ballpoint pen. " 'Course it wasn't really *so dark* that night, was it, Ms. Benton?"

Her explanation caught in her throat when, just beyond him, she saw for the first time the smudged silhouettes of the bodies. Everything looked so different in daylight. Neon-yellow police tape waved almost festively along the fringes of the road. Even from this distance, she could see the depression in the blowing grass where the dead horse must have lain.

Memory stabbed her—sharp, fierce, bloodred. That safety light, blinking, blinking on the bodies. The terror, her trembling, the desolate yet furious look on Daniel's face, the lost ones on Cora's and Katie's.

She drew in a long, slow breath. She saw the sheriff scrutinize her with his pen poised, as if she were some hostile witness he could not wait to trip up on her testimony. Steadying her legs and her voice, she began to explain why she had parked her car here. He hurried after her, taking notes.

"Pretty dangerous to stop at the bottom of this steep grade," he interrupted.

"I was hardly thinking about my safety. Where would I have pulled clear off? I hit my warning lights. And," she added, so he didn't think she was avoiding his earlier question, "no, of course it wasn't really *so dark* that night with the full moon, the blinking lantern, and my headlights. But it *seemed* dark to me when I drove out here. But this is definitely where I stopped my car."

"Maybe it *seemed* dark to the driver who hit them, too," he muttered.

She ignored a blue van that slowed to gawk at them and the police car. "Sheriff, the driver of the car that hit those kids could not only see a triangle reflector on the back of the buggy but, a kerosene lantern *and* the blinking red light. I certainly didn't mean to imply the driver's visibility was impaired or—"

"No, 'course not. Only, there's two sides to this, see."

She turned to face him squarely. The man's bulk loomed large to block the morning sun so she didn't have to squint at him. "You don't mean to imply those kids might have been at fault?"

"Naw, I'm just figuring all the angles of what some local folks been thinking. Four teenagers—even Amish ones—packed in that one-seat courting buggy and out so late, on their own *so dark* Sabbath night. Where the bodies got thrown suggests the girls were on the boys' laps. That your recollection?"

"Yes, that's true. Ezra's buggy had a broken axle, or the four of them would not have been together. Still, you realize, from the way the wreckage was strewn, they were over as far as they could get in their lane."

"You got a real sharp mind, Ms. Benton, sure do. Specific facts and then real fast conclusions from that."

She decided to ignore the sarcastic undertone. "Then, please keep in mind, Sheriff Barnes, if I can do anything to help—"

"Why, you're helping me right now, sure are. By the way, 'bout the lights on the back of the buggy. Them old kerosene lanterns they all use get real smudged from being bounced along, then don't throw much light, you know."

"No, I didn't know, because the one Gideon had hanging on the left side looked clean and bright to me. As you said, it was a courting buggy, and I'll bet the boys keep those immaculate. And, I repeat, they had a battery-run red safety light that blinked, hanging on the right side."

"So Daniel Brand told me, too."

"Then, when you trace and arrest the suspect, whether or not the Amish can be convinced to go into court, I will." She hesitated a moment, realizing what such public, publicized testimony could mean for her and Jennifer, but it had to be done. "I'll testify," she went on, even more decisively, "that, besides the reflective triangle and the glowing Amish lantern, I saw that bright red light fully operational when the buggy pulled out of my driveway *and* at the accident scene, even after that monster plowed into them."

"OK," he said, holding up his hand with the notebook as if to ward her off, "got that all down. You know, the victims might not even have had so much as that slow-moving-vehicle triangle if the Amish had gotten their way. Stubborn ones next county over claimed back a few years in court—through a lawyer, that is—that the state shouldn't make them put those warning signs on their buggies. Too fancy they called them." He snorted. "They know damn well when a buggy meets a car, the buggy's gonna come out on the losing end. There's been bad bust-ups before and will be again, though maybe not with four kids and a hit-and-run. It's like them lightning rods they refuse to have on their roofs. If the place catches on fire, it's just God's will and we'll all get together to rebuild it even better," he said, shrugging and shaking his head.

Brooke was shocked at the man's apparent prejudice. She could not believe that the sheriff in this area evidently sided with those who disliked the Amish. But he had said something else that really caught her attention. She turned away, crossing her arms to grip her elbows in her hands.

"I'm surprised to hear you say they've used the courts," she told him, frowning at the accident scene and remembering Daniel yanking her to her feet with the words, *Listen, city lawyer*! She hoped Sheriff Barnes had not delved into her past, but she had to know about this. "I thought the Amish hated lawyers," she added, hoping she sounded merely curious.

"They do. Only now and then, they're forced to tangle with the system. Back in '72, they got legal rights to have their own schools. An attorney somebody hired for them went clear to the Supreme Court in Washington to win that. Point was, they didn't even let their kids go beyond eighth grade. See why some people think they're crazy?"

"Yes—some people," she admitted, turning back to meet his gaze. Despite her growing dislike of this man, she steeled herself to try to make him an ally instead of an enemy. "But how fortunate that the Roscoe County Amish have some influential neighbors who recognize and admire their many good traits and will step in to champion their causes—like you, Sheriff Barnes."

"You got that right, 'long as people remember who's in charge around here and keep their place. But if I hear one more Amish tell me they render unto Caesar—I'm their Caesar around here, see?—and then refuse to testify or file so much as a complaint when I ask 'em to, 'cause it's their Christian belief, I'm gonna puke."

Or toss them to the lions, Brooke silently finished his comparison for him. Controlling her growing frustration, she spent the next fifteen minutes walking him through what she had done that night, how she and Daniel had rushed from body to body. She admitted she had covered Cora's legs and then, her voice breaking again, where she had found Katie before they moved her. She explained about Paul Hostetler's fortunate arrival and pointed out where he had parked. She did not know who drove up afterward, but it turned out to be people the sheriff knew and whom his deputy had already questioned. Off and on, he nodded, asked another question, took more notes. She admitted she didn't even notice at first that there was no car at the scene to have hit the buggy. She told him that she was going to have the backseat upholstery in her car replaced rather than just trying to cover the bloodstains.

"Daniel Brand was a stubborn fool to move that girl," he said. "If he wasn't in the victim's family, and them Amish and all, a big city lawyer like you would have sued the socks off him."

Her head jerked up; her nostrils flared. So he did know she was a lawyer from Columbus, but then, he had been talking to Daniel. She wondered if the sheriff had done another investigation to learn the circumstances of her failure and her flight. What if he

66

told everyone around here—Daniel—about that? Perhaps she should regard the man with more respect, however much she resented his attitude.

But, she thought, if Sheriff Barnes was going to call her a big city lawyer, and make it sound as much of a condemnation as Daniel had, perhaps she'd just start acting like one around here. A clever, careful one, who always began by disclosing and discrediting the credentials of any smug opposing expert witness. Besides, she needed to change the topic back to the one that the sheriff obviously favored.

"I can tell you've had years of experience with investigative and police procedural work, Sheriff."

"Been elected to seven terms." He removed his broad-brimmed hat to wipe his brow with a handkerchief that sported his initials in bold letters. "Started as the only deputy here'bouts. School of hard knocks, that's my alma mater, best there is. I don't care what those prissy police academies and college criminology courses teach these days. No big-time crime around here, and that's the way I'm keeping it. Things go 'long just fine and dandy here till outsiders come barging in."

She knew it was another warning to her, but she decided to play as dumb as he probably thought she was. "You mean these tourists and gawkers?"

"I mean the highway patrol prima donnas, who should just keep their new radar cars out on the interstate looking for speeders and leave Roscoe County to me!" He slapped his hat back on. Though another car coming up behind them evidently interrupted whatever he intended to say next, she sensed it could have been, *"And the worst outsiders are invaders like you who barge in by living here!"*

Brooke was tempted to tell him how much more

professional, even informative, she had found the two highway patrol officers who had called on her earlier this morning. They were going to reconstruct the accident, something she had benefited from numerous times to prepare for a trial. They had said she could certainly inquire about their findings later, but she'd wait, she thought now, to ask Sheriff Barnes for that same consideration. The way he was glaring at her, perhaps it was just plain luck that the car edged them apart.

A low-slung jade green sports car, the make of which Brooke couldn't name, slowed to a stop, then idled, purring, between them. She recalled a case where the criminal kept hanging around the scene where he had shot a man to death, so she decided to memorize the license plate. When she stepped around the sleek front grillwork to see it, she saw it was easy to remember—IDZRVIT. The brazenness of "I deserve it" on a car like this didn't surprise her.

The driver was a handsome, prematurely gray man of about forty in a golf cap who leaned a tanned elbow out the window and asked, "I see this is the spot, officer. Got any leads?"

"Police business. Move on now."

"A pity," the driver observed, dangling his sunglasses out the window, "what happens when the present hits the past, isn't it? These poor Amish keep getting a wake-up call to join the real world, but they're fatally deaf. Judas Priest, I just heard on the radio that the charity fund for the accident families has reached over sixty thousand so far, but I bet they'll take that modern, worldly money, won't they? Have a good day!" He waved the sunglasses once more out the window as the car hummed up the hill. The last thing Brooke noted about him was that the pavé diamond ring on his left hand glared in the sun.

"Smart-ass son of a bitch," Brooke heard the sheriff hiss. "One more question I gotta ask, Ms. Benton," he called out as she, too, waved and turned to walk home. "Any chance those four kids been drinking? I told the coroner no need to test for it and didn't bother the kids' families with it, but I gotta ask."

She walked back toward him. At least the man had shown some sensitivity, but then, even if the kids had been drinking, the wreck was *not* their fault. "Absolutely no chance they were drinking, Sheriff Barnes. They had just come from a hymn sing. They had nothing but an ice-cream bar at my place and were with me almost an hour. I smelled nothing on their breath, nor saw any behavior whatsoever to indicate anyone had been drinking. They weren't high on anything but youth and love of life. Though, I suppose, considering our evidence, drinking might be something we could consider for their killer if—"

"*Our* evidence?" he drawled. "*We* might consider? While ago, you said you refused to admit the driver was in any way impaired!" He flapped his notebook at her and pointed at it with his pen. Then, as if to apologize for his outburst, he added, "I guess old habits die hard, huh, Ms. Benton? 'Spose you're used to having a say in investigations and all back home and just forgot where you are now."

She wished she could have bitten her tongue for her slip—and bitten this man's head off. But finding the killer meant more to her than pride or anger. And, at least, it was completely clear how much help she could expect to get from this man if she was forced to begin her own investigation.

69

"As I said, I just want to help, Sheriff."

"You've done all you're gonna," he intoned ominously as he pocketed his pen. "Come on now, and I'll give you a lift back to Verna's," he said as he opened the passenger door for her.

"No need, thanks. I'm going back another way." She started home again, glad to get away from him and the accident scene. She wanted to call on the families of the other three kids today before Jennifer got off the school bus at three-thirty. And, now that she couldn't count on Sheriff Barnes, she had a lot of thinking to do about how she—Caesar's decrees to the contrary notwith-standing—was going to proceed.

When the police car disappeared, Brooke cut up into the field that stretched between the Sewing Circle and Daniel's house. She wanted to see exactly what view he'd had of the road when the accident occurred. When this week was over, she intended to interview Daniel, for, unfortunately, he was the only—if distant, if Amish, if stubborn—eyewitness to this *so dark* crime.

Brooke had decided to break her own first commandment: *Thou shalt tell no one but your best friend in Columbus where you are living now.* She dialed Columbus area code, her hand shaking, telling herself she was doing the right thing.

After all, Jake Kaminsky had always been loyal and discreet. He hadn't been able to ID or catch her stalker, but he'd made her feel a whole lot safer by just being there for her. And, before his accident, he'd been one of the top Columbus Police Department crime-scene technicians.

"Kaminsky here."

"Jake, believe it or not, it's Brooke. Long time, no

talk."

She heard him suck in a sharp breath. "Brooke! I—I can't believe it. I've been so damned worried about you. Over four weeks without one word, lady!"

"I'm sorry for the way I left, but it had to be quick and quiet. The police weren't helping, and I have Jennifer to worry about, too."

"Yeah, but you're talking to Jake here. Where the hell are you? You really OK? Anything I can do?"

As she explained things to him, including the small-town sheriff with the big attitude problem, she felt better already. Jake always sounded so take-charge, so sure he could solve a case and make everything come out right.

"Of course, I'll help you look for clues at the scene," he said. "And no, you're not paying me. Plus, no worrying about me telling anyone here where you are, you hear me. But I assume you got somebody taking care of things here in town."

"Yes, a friend at the firm."

"Not that pompous pain-in-the-ass, McCarron? Tell you the truth, Brooke, I had that guy high on the list of possibles for what happened to you and the kid."

Brooke frowned out her bedroom window at the wind-tossed maple leaves, seeing Ray McCarron's classically handsome face. Ray had definitely *not* been pleased to only assist her in her last case, because he was used to being Mr. Stedman's fair-haired boy. At least Ray didn't take the brunt of the blame—though he'd acted as if he had—when everything exploded.

"No, not Ray. Elizabeth Crandle's been sending all my mail and caring for the condo. Besides, you and I both know half the city of Columbus hated me. I think taking the time and trouble to harass and stalk me is

71

way down on Ray's transparent agenda to make partner at any cost. Jake, I wanted to call you so much before I left, but I didn't feel I had the right to involve you anymore, especially long-distance. And now here I am, calling you for help . . ."

"We're friends, Brooke, and that's that. You been with me in tough times. I told you before, I'm there for you anytime, including first thing tomorrow morning."

"No, Jake, listen. The funerals are tomorrow and the next day, and that will even bring more gawkers to the accident site. Saturday afternoon I've got help so I can leave the shop to have time for us to visit the scene and so I can show you around."

"Yeah, I'd like to see your safe haven. Saturday then. And, Brooke, we'll get the bastard that killed those innocent Amish kids, I swear to you, we will."

For the first time, she really believed they would.

The day was overcast as Brooke parked their car at the end of the long line of black buggies outside the Kurtz farmhouse for the funeral. At regular intervals, the Amish women's black bonnets and shawls draped the white porch railing.

Brooke had dressed the two of them formally, but simply, she in a navy blue and white suit, and Jennifer in a sailor's-style dress so their colors matched. Jennifer must have been bothered by the black-draped railing, too, because she whispered, "Hope they remember we're not Amish so that's why we didn't wear black."

"They'll remember we're not Amish," Brooke said only as they held hands and went in the front door.

The girl clung close in the crowd inside, no running off with Susie. They saw the women were in their normal garb of dark-colored dresses with pinned aprons

72

and white capes, stiff prayer caps perched on their heads. The unmarried girls wore brighter hues or pastels. The men, in their Sabbath best, wore fine, specially tailored wool outfits in black, from broad-brimmed hats to frock coats. The boys were miniatures of the men but for their warm-weather straw hats.

When Brooke and Jennifer entered the front room where the coffin was displayed, Brooke saw—or felt, she was not sure—Daniel's dark eyes on her. He stood talking to several other men in the corner and gave no nod or tilt of head of recognition or greeting.

"Come on, Jen," she whispered. "Let's pay our respects."

They joined the line of mourners moving toward the coffin, where Emma, Levi their children, and close relatives stood. Brooke regretted to see, as they approached, that the plain pine box was open, hinged halfway back to show Katie's face from the shoulders up. Brooke had been trying to remember her as she had been at the house, chatting, smiling, not still and white as she was on the road and in the car. And Brooke worried for the first time that, perhaps, she should not have brought Jennifer.

"Welcome, my friends, and Katie's, too," Emma said and hugged her, then Jennifer. Levi nodded, frowning, but by then Brooke had noted, he was not only frowning at her but at everyone. Over Levi's shoulder, she saw Daniel now stood on the far fringe of the family group. Whatever she had planned to say in comfort to Emma flew right out of her head, and she jumped when Jennifer, peering over the edge of the coffin at Katie's profile, spoke.

"She still looks like you, Mrs. Kurtz. I look like my mother, and that's nice, I think."

73

"For sure, Jennifer, I think so, too," Emma said, staring intently at Katie. "Like a piece of myself up in heaven already instead of being left behind . . ." she began before her voice caught, and she lifted a handkerchief to her mouth. When Levi didn't budge to comfort her, Emma's mother stepped in before Brooke could. Some other women edged closer, so Brooke tugged Jennifer on in the line.

"Did I say something wrong, Aunt Brooke?"

"No, you said something just right, sweetheart." She was going to take her aside to explain before the service began, when a tall, spare, older woman stepped from the cluster of relatives and motioned to Brooke. In the room of shorter, stouter matriarchs, her somehow familiar face commanded attention. Although Amish women looked plain with their hair pulled straight back and no cosmetics, this woman's countenance looked, though glazed with grief, almost regal.

"Emma and Daniel's mother, Ida Brand," she said in a soft voice. She touched Brooke's hand, then placed a piece of paper in it. "A statement from the families of the deceased—all four. You would deliver it to those in charge of things, if you would."

"To Sheriff Barnes?"

"*Ach*, no. To the folks at Pleasant People's Bank and the television station that is calling for all that money to be sent. Kindly grateful for the concern we are, but we can care for our own. The money should be returned. Or maybe given to the county hospital for—another doctor. To be left alone by the English, that's all we ask. No earthly blame we feel, and the attention is burdensome to us, very much."

"I see. I am sorry. Yes, I'll pass it on," Brooke promised, hoping the stay-away part of the message—

74

delivered by Emma and Daniel's mother—was not also directed toward her. Or had her interview with Sheriff Barnes made her paranoid?

"Good," the woman said with a nod as she rested a hand on Jennifer's shoulder but stared earnestly at Brooke. "A strong voice to keep outsiders away, my husband says you have." She stepped back into the ring of relatives, so Brooke took Jennifer to sit on a back bench to await the start of the service.

"You'll have to sit on the other side of the room, you know," a male voice said. Brooke looked up. She didn't recognize the man, but the fact he was not dressed Amish immediately narrowed the possibilities.

"Paul Hostetler?" she asked and stood to shake hands.

"I wasn't sure you'd remember me after everything that night," he said. After a hearty handshake, he thrust his fists in his new-looking jeans with which he wore a shirt, tie, and brown suit coat. He was stocky, sandy-haired, and thirty-something with a boyishly handsome face. "But what I mean about not sitting here," he added in a whisper, "is it's the men's side. And I hope you're ready for two to three hours of High German. They speak Pennsylvania Dutch dialect everywhere but in church services."

"You know a great deal about them."

"I grew up around them."

"At any rate, it was fortunate you found the accident, especially when you live clear across town, Daniel said."

He looked past her now, as if he were studying something on the blank wall. "I work late shift at the Swiss cheese factory. It was such a nice night with the full moon and all, I just felt like a drive before I went home. I used to know Dan before he left, raised a bit of a ruckus with him more than once," he admitted to her and looked at her again. "You ever hear their saying, 'The wilder the *rumspringa*, the stricter the adult'?"

"No. Meaning Daniel will be a strict adult now?"

"Could be. My dad always used to say the Amish know how to handle their *rumspringa* rowdies, but it's the ones who think too much that cause them problems. That's Dan, I guess. He was real smart, but a fence-jumper, like they say. When I talked to him a few minutes ago, he made me think he'll be as straight as his old man now."

Brooke nodded as she glanced at Daniel. "Do you have a family, Paul?" she asked, forcing her attention back to him.

At that, to her surprise, he turned away. "Yep, wife, two kids. See you around sometime," he said over his shoulder and walked out without another look back.

Jennifer leaned her head against Brooke's shoulder as the service went on until everyone rose for the slow singing of two hymns. They sounded like Gregorian chants to Brooke, especially because no one sang separate parts, however different the voices were. After the congregation sat to creak the wooden benches, Bishop Brand preached in sometimes sonorous, sometimes sweeping tones, followed by two other speakers. Brooke could understand nothing, and found herself, even sitting, feeling dizzy and shaky under Daniel's intense gaze.

Or, she told herself, the likelier scenario was that Daniel was actually staring at Barbara Yoder, who sat two rows ahead of her, the pretty widow whom Emma evidently had picked out for him. Surely, he was really studying Barbara, planning to marry her perhaps, to no longer be a "fence-jumper." Fine. More power to him.

76

She tried not to so much as look at Daniel again, but sometimes, she couldn't help herself.

Daniel Brand was not only mourning the loss of his niece, but the loss of his resolve. Today might mark a glorious home-going to heaven for Katie, but it was a terrible homecoming for him. True, he tried to preach in his own inward sermon, his return had brought joy to his people to help soothe their loss of their four young folk. But he had to get hold of himself or he was still on the highway to destruction.

For he could not stop looking at, thinking about, being fascinated by Brooke Benton. Sweet, willing Barbara Yoder, now sitting right in his view, had smiled and spoken to him, invited him to visit her family for dinner, and here he was still surreptitiously staring at a slim, worldly woman he wanted no part of. And it had even annoyed him to see Paul Hostetler talking to her earlier. Someone had said Paul was cheating on his wife with a red-haired English divorcée down the road a mile or two. Evidently, Paul Hostetler had not yet become a good family man any more than Daniel Brand had.

With iron resolve, Daniel forced his thoughts back to the singing. But the once familiar words of the hymn, printed small in the *Ausbund* hymnal, blurred before his eyes, still sore with lost sleep and tears. For Katie, Cora, Gideon, and Ezra—and for his own lost youth. Worse, this building anger that he thought he had released still coiled cold and cruel inside him.

He glanced straight across the coffin at Emma. He still felt closer to her than to his brother and sister nearer in age to him, for Emma, four years older, had been a second mother to him in his early years. More than once she had teasingly called him her first baby. It cut deep that Emma was in such agony over Katie.

But he had to admit she appeared to bear up surprisingly well. Perhaps she was drained from exhaustion or from bridling that inherently runaway temperament of hers that they shared. But she'd always been better at reining it in than he had. Even that first time he had been forced to know she could be hurt and—if he wanted to be Amish—he could not help her the way he wanted.

Emma had been thirteen that spring day, so he must have been all of nine, thinking he was a man since he'd plowed a furrow alone—while Dad and Mahlon watched from the fence, of course. But he'd had a sour stomach that day from eating too many green apples on top of lunch and, in his excitement to control the five-horse hitch, he'd puked and been sent home. He'd caught up with Emma, where she'd been dawdling, carting the lunch pail and water bucket back to the house. And it was a blessing he came along, sick stomach, weak-kneed or not, because a big-finned Ford Fairlane with two English boys cruising the back lanes looking for trouble had found her, too.

"Hey, Amish gal, never been kissed, I bet," Daniel recalled hearing as the two got out of their car. They left the doors open, the engine running, and had Emma backed up against the hedgerow fence. Emma had kept her silent courage, but they blocked her way from flight.

"That's my sister! Leave her alone!" Daniel spoke for her and started to run, ignoring the cinders that cut his bare feet along the berm of the road.

"Your sister, huh? She got a boyfriend, 'cause I'm real int'rested in a date!" the bigger boy, the car's driver said. "And since you Amish is nonresisters—yellow-bellied cowards, we call 'em—'gainst the war in 'Nam, where my brother is, I'm just gonna take a real nice, nonresisted kiss from this gal, even if she barely got any tits to touch."

The other boy guffawed as the lout dared to yank Emma's burdens from her hands; he pulled her forward for a rough kiss.

Daniel's fury turned everything bloodred. All the church's teachings—turn the other cheek, love thy neighbor, do no violence, all those pictures of the martyrs who died for the faith rather than recant or resist—exploded in raw rage.

"I said leave her alone!" he shouted, but he knew better than to just use his fists against overwhelming odds. He darted for the open car door on the driver's side and stared at the amazing array of equipment inside. A wheel, levers, meters, more than in the old Ford pickup he'd ridden in. But still, he reasoned, it must work the same. The big machine he had so longed to touch, to ride in and drive, loomed open to him like a new world.

But Emma needed him.

He yanked a lever back, turned the wheel, then jumped away as the car began to move. The boys yelped, cursed, and chased their car as it headed down the slope of hill and nosed into a tree. Daniel grabbed Emma's hand, and they ran cut-corner across the plowed field for Dad.

"I would have hit them, wanted to hit them, even kill them," Daniel kept saying to the panting Emma as if he had to confess. When he finally dared a look at her, she was red-faced and not just from the run.

"Look," she said, grabbing his other hand to halt them, "what happened back there we got to tell. But don't you ever tell you wanted to hit them, not any of that. You hear me, Daniel Brand? But what you done to help, I'll never forget, never, 'cause it was just like David and Goliath, and you won!"

They carried Katie Kurtz to her rest in the Shekinah Amish Cemetery on the windswept hill with a fine view of the valley. The mile-long funeral procession of buggies made Brooke realize the size of the crowd, for mourners had also sat in other rooms with the overflow from the main house preached to in the *daadi haus* and even the barn. She estimated there might be as many as four hundred attenders, and everyone was expected back at the house for dinner afterward, before many would go to Gideon's funeral this afternoon. "*Komm esse*—come back to eat," she and Jennifer had been told numerous times after the service.

Although she saw special duty officers, some in cars, some on noisy motorcycles, the men under Sheriff Barnes's command could not keep all the spectators at a distance. Cameras clicked or whirred all along the way, especially as the open-bedded, horse-drawn hearse went by. The procession passed the accident site; there Brooke was doubly grateful she and Jennifer had been asked to ride in the backseat of a buggy, for her tears would have blinded her and she could not have driven on. But as the ride continued, the sway and rattle of the buggy, the cropping of the horse's hooves and jingle of the harness lulled her, calmed her some.

Yet when they emerged from the buggy in the cemetery, she saw some outsiders had managed to scramble for spots on the nearby hill. Then, as she held Jennifer's hand and the breeze ruffled her skirt and hair, she felt it:

That distinct, primitive feeling of being watched, not

just by a curious crowd, not just as the Amish were stared at. That old feeling of someone glaring at her, waiting, wanting something evil. The creeping sensation she'd had the times they drove into the garage at home when she was sure they'd been tailed but couldn't see anyone behind. That feeling she had gotten even at work, walking through the maze of secretary desks, all eyes on her, past office doors to her own. Her skin prickled all over the way it had after she knew someone had been in the condo, the way she felt when she had opened mail or been in an elevator with strangers she didn't know.

She jerked her head around and squinted into the distance. Dark silhouettes of strangers on the hill, some with elbows sticking out, people probably holding binoculars to their eyes. Now, she thought, gripping the girl's hand, she really knew how the Amish felt. That was all it was, surely. She felt such empathy for these people that it had thrown her back into the past where she was threatened. That was all this feeling really was.

"You all right, Aunt Brooke?" Jennifer asked, looking up at her.

"Yes, sweetheart. Sure."

They clustered around the open grave as the final words were said and the coffin lowered by wide leather straps into the ground. The men who had carried Katie up here, where three other gaping graves awaited the later burials, began to shovel soil onto the closed coffin. At first, the earth made cruel, hollow thuds, then softened, surely, Brooke prayed, as sharp pain must.

She looked for Emma, but could not see her. She glanced at Daniel, his head bent low across a sea of black hats and bonnets. Finding no solace, giving none, she stared up at the pearl gray sky. But instead of

81

comfort, that other agony swooped at her, clawed her, the loss of Melanie, so young, so dear. Quickly, Brooke knelt in the soft grass to clasp Jennifer tightly in her arms.

CHAPTER FIVE

"PLEASE, CAN'T WE GO ACROSS THE STREET INTO the blacksmith shop and see the horses?" Jennifer asked, plucking at Brooke's sleeve as they traversed the narrow aisles of the Maplecreek General Store. "I want to see if they have one that looks like the Pi."

Jennifer had seen a videotape of the old Elizabeth Taylor movie *National Velvet* about a girl and her horse, the Pi, and horses had instantly become the love of her life. She was getting as bad as the tourists every time an Amish buggy went by, but because of what pulled the buggy, not who was in it.

"Jen, we'd just get in the way. Saturday is the farmers' busiest day in town. Besides, I'd rather not go into Mr. Stoltz's blacksmith shop," she admitted, and stopped rolling the grocery cart to look down at the girl. "The truth is I don't want to face him again right now, so soon after his son's funeral."

"But he said it was OK his son was at our house."

"He did, but we have to get back to the shop so we can see how Mrs. Lapp and the girls are doing." Besides, she thought to herself, *facing Daniel Brand will be quite enough for one day.* "Tell you what," she added when she saw the girl's expression droop, "we can stop at Susie's house after our errands, and you can see the new colt they have there."

"It's cute, but it's gonna grow up to be a big, sandy-

82

colored field horse to pull stuff, just like the others. It's not ever gonna be a real fast jumper, like in *National Velvet*."

Hustling her along, Brooke didn't give in this time as they ran their other errands in Maplecreek. No wonder the child was looking for a horse from a movie here, for at first the tiny town had reminded Brooke of a western movie set—harness shop, blacksmith, old-fashioned-looking Dutch Table Restaurant, even a sawmill. But the gas station and two small bed-and-breakfasts, not to mention a smattering of gift shops that sold both tasteful and trashy Amish souvenirs, anchored Maplecreek firmly in this world. The town sat four square at the intersection of the Roscoe Township and Sawmill roads—and at the crossroads of past and present, the ideal and the real.

Pumping her own gas, Brooke filled the car's tank. They headed toward home with Jennifer twisting around in her seat belt at every buggy or field horse they passed. But Brooke craned her neck, too, and slowed the car on the edge of town when she went by the old Victorian mansion that local people called Melrose Manor. Sturdy brick graced with tattered arabesques and arches of peeling wooden trim, it seemed to her a grand relic of the gracious but muted past. The third-story dormer windows stared out languidly, like eyes luring passersby to peek inside. Brooke wanted to but never had.

Her friend at church, Marnie Girkins, who owned the Valley View Bed and Breakfast in town had admitted she'd give anything to own the place and fix it up for a B and B. Marnie said that the Melrose family had owned much farmland here in the early days of Amish settlement. As the family, like their house, faded, the Melroses sold off their fields and meadows to the Amish. Eventually, the last old widow died and no children came back to claim the place. The house had been sold, resold, rented, and now stood vacant. A FOR SALE sign displayed a 614 area code phone number to call—a real estate agent in Columbus. Brooke drove on faster.

They stopped at the Sewing Circle to unload their groceries and check on how Mary Lapp was doing overseeing the staff of four Amish women today, a task Emma usually did. Everything was fine, but then it was only nine-thirty; few were in the shop, for the tourist crowd would begin to swell late morning Brooke missed Emma, who had said she would be back next week, and, after all, only a few days had passed since Katie's funeral. Levi Kurtz might have gone right back to his farming and chores, but this time, work might not be Emma's salvation in her loss. Yes, Brooke thought, she would definitely go to see Emma after this necessary stop at Daniel Brand's house. At least she was looking forward to Jake's visit this afternoon.

But her stomach fluttered at the thought of having to face Daniel. She both anticipated and dreaded that. But Verna had been pleased to hear he was back and had insisted Brooke order some of his quilt frames and quilt racks for the Sewing Circle. She said he had been a talented woodworker before he had left for Indiana to be apprenticed to a master furniture craftsman, so he must be fabulous now. *Fabulous*, a strange word for Daniel Brand, but—

"Aren't we going now, Aunt Brooke? I put the cans away in the pantry, and I'm ready."

"Yes," Brooke said, "but first come help me reshelve the fabric for my quilt."

84

"Which ones, 'cause you keep changing your mind."

"The very last I showed you. I'm sure these are *the ones*."

Unable to sleep the night of Katie's funeral, Brooke had spent hours walking the aisles of yard-goods bolts displayed downstairs: pastel and primary colored solids, calicos, ginghams, paisleys, plaids, batiks, bandanna prints, blossom sprigged ones, and lush Americana or English flower prints. She had selected her fabrics that night—then changed her mind the next day. And the next. Verna's advice to customers kept ringing in her head, but it only confused her more: "When you choose fabrics, ask yourself, 'do I really like this? Does this seem right to me?' "

After many choices and re-choices, yesterday she had chosen six richly hued, coordinated colors of plain or flowered fabrics for the wedding rings. She picked two others for the joining squares, one a solid that would serve for the bright border, too. Finally, she found the flower-sprigged eggshell background to make the design and other colors spring forth. Her palette of hues in the rings would be roses and azures with touches of white and gold. She was quite sure she was on track at last, but she didn't want any mistakes or regrets.

She was certain—fairly certain—that these latest choices would be just right, because they—as Emma said—sang to her. As with her earlier selections, she had been carting them all over the house to arrange them in various orders in different window light to imagine them in the quilt. It was a whole new daunting but thrilling experience for her. The only thing was, she needed to get the gumption, as Verna would put it, to actually cut them up into the necessary pieces, and begin to arrange them, and then there would be no turning back.

They walked into the big workroom where the two Amish women who had arrived early bent over to whipstitch the bright blue border of the completed Courthouse Steps quilt. Verna had told Brooke on the phone last night that it should be priced at eight hundred dollars. A lot of money, but, Brooke had thought, how could you put a price on a unique, handworked quilt from these unique Amish women who came together to create their art? Yet, to their way of thinking, it was simply another household item, "for use, not for pretty."

"Good morning, ladies," she greeted them as they both looked up and nodded. "I just realized I left the fabrics for my Wedding Ring quilt in your way on the cutting table if you get to starting that new Barn Raising design today."

"So you're doing curves and circles," Fanny Bauman said. "A task, for sure, but all the pieces will go together if you're careful. Real bold colors and prints you picked."

"I thought the blend of them will look lush—kind of Victorian," she told them, her arms full of six bolts while Jennifer picked up the last two. Brooke wondered if women who had never gone beyond the eighth grade knew what she meant by Victorian. The Amish never wore nor used patterned materials for their own clothes or quilts, for only plain would do. For some reason she wanted their approval of her choices, but then, her tastes were hardly theirs, and she had to learn to accept that. Besides, in describing her fabrics as Victorian, she realized that her quilt would be perfect on a four-poster in the Melrose mansion. Its cream background would accent the gingerbread trim outside the house, which needed so much work to be repaired and painted.

"A lot of work, a Wedding Ring," Sara Bauman, Fanny's sister-in-law, said. "But if you hit a snag, Levi Em or any of us will lend a hand."

Grateful anew for the kindness of these people, Brooke thanked them. But at the last minute, she decided not to replace these bolts in the stock downstairs and they carried them to her bed upstairs. She'd get the template pattern and cut out the pieces as soon as possible.

Brooke's insides clenched when she and Jennifer drove by the accident site on the way to Daniel's house. The police tape was gone, the chalk marks were washed away, but not the memories. Long, swerving skid marks had burned a brand into the road. The timing of Jake's visit seemed good; with his help she'd begin her own investigation and just hope the Amish didn't hold that against her.

In her phone call yesterday to the patrol boys, as Sheriff Barnes always called them, she had been told the matter was under "continued investigation" and would be until a "successful conclusion." Evidently, their "accident reconstruction squad" had even been out after dark to "hypothetically reenact the crash on-site" to see what information they could derive from that. "However, Ms. Benton, conclusions cannot be released at this time because the patrol is officially assisting the county sheriff's investigation, which has primary jurisdiction of disclosure . . ."

And Brooke knew how far she would get asking Sheriff Barnes for information. She could, she thought, wait a bit longer, trusting the authorities would find the killer, but she knew trails grew quickly cold. She had learned the hard way not to rely on the police, but above all, this crime was not going to be filed or fade away, not if she could help it.

And that was why she made a phone call and took a drive to Cuyahoga County south of Cleveland yesterday to follow up on it. She knew it would probably be a wild-goose chase to try to trace the man in the sports car with the IDZRVIT license plate, but she was desperate to follow every lead. Besides, he had seemed so brazen and callous, and if a man had money for a car like that, he could surely own a bigger vehicle, too, one that could have blasted a buggy to bits.

So she had phoned her longtime contact at the Bureau of Motor Vehicles in Columbus, who used to help her on investigations. She learned that particular vanity license plate had been registered to a Kenneth T. Champion of Cuyahoga County just south of Cleveland, so she had gone to question him at his home, and finally located him at his car dealership. But this Ken Champion was not the man she'd seen driving the sports car, and although he hadn't wanted to talk at all at first, she finally finagled an explanation:

"Right, that's one of my personal cars, but I wasn't driving it that day. I leased it to a guy just passing through."

"Just passing through from where?"

"Out west, he said."

"A guy from somewhere out west who just happened to want to drive down to Amish country, so you let him use your personal vehicle?"

"I said lease, not use. The guy fell for the car and the license plate amused him, that's all. People with dough like that get their little whims, I guess."

"Have you ever had anyone lease a car who had a wreck with it and brought it back damaged, wanting to just pay you to have it repaired privately?"

"No way I'd be a party to anything like that! Look, Ms. Benton, if you're on some sort of fishing expedition about that Amish hit-run, I can't help you. I'm a businessman, and this guy offered me big bucks—cash up front and a security payment that could almost replace the car. I do things by the book, but you think I'd have this big car dealership if I didn't take advantage of breaks that come my way?"

Breaks that come my way, Brooke mused. That's exactly what she needed if she was ever going to get anywhere in finding the killers of those kids.

She gripped the wheel tighter as she pulled in Daniel's driveway. When she saw him leaving the big building behind his house—she could not tell if it was an oversize garage or a small barn—she was grateful they would not have to knock and actually go in the house. She could give him Verna's orders from the car and be on her way. What a coward she was being, but she had actually dreamed about him staring at her, blaming her, even though he had said he didn't.

"Oh, Aunt Brooke, look! I can see a horse in there, a brown one, just like the Pi with a white face, too!"

Before Daniel could approach the car, the child was out and racing toward the building. "Jennifer, you can't just . . ." Brooke cried.

Daniel did an about-turn to go after Jennifer. Brooke sat in the car, passenger door gaping, motor running. "Damn it!" she said, hitting the steering wheel. She yanked out the ignition key to follow them.

She peeked in the building and saw it contained piles of planks, a long workbench, some tools, partly finished furniture, bundles of hay, a horse in a single old stall— and Daniel with one foot propped on a bale of hay and

Jennifer halfway up the stall rails, leaning over the top to pet the horse. The smell of sawdust and hay, wood and horse, made Brooke want to sneeze, so she pressed the side of her index finger hard under her nose.

Daniel wore the standard Amish work clothes for this area: broadfall denim trousers; a white, long-sleeved shirt rolled up to show tanned forearms; and suspenders stretched in a Y across his broad back. The pattern of the suspenders, like the length of the hair and the width of the hat brim, were ways to differentiate one Amish order from another, if you knew how to read the signs. But with Daniel, Brooke wasn't sure about any of the signs. His straw hat was cocked at too bold an angle for any Amish man.

"She's not a jumper but a harness horse, Jennifer," he was saying, his voice filling the air. "Her name used to be Queen Bess, but I'm just going to call her Bess."

"But there are fences and hedges around here, just like in England. I'll bet Bess could learn to be a great fence jumper."

Paul Hostetler's words about Daniel at the funeral came back to Brooke: *Daniel was real smart, but a fence-jumper, like they say . . . one who thought too much and rebelled . . .*

As if he sensed Brooke's silent presence, Daniel turned his head to look at her. Two shafts of sunlight poured through twin windows about his head; sunbeams and dust motes swirled to make it seem everything was slowly spinning inside, as when you shook one of those plastic snow scenes.

"Your new buggy horse," Brooke said to break the spell of his stare.

"Got her at the livestock auction in Kidron last Thursday. I'm getting delivery of the buggy—a double-

90

duty surrey for a family or deliveries—this weekend. Jennifer," he went on, looking back at the excited child, "Bess is a filly—a female horse who used to be a harness racer in New York State. She's a trotter with a mile-eating gait, but she'd only stop if she came to a hedge or fence. But now she's retired from her kind of racing, she's going to get me around and help me deliver my furniture if folks don't drop by to pick it up."

"We didn't come to buy furniture but some smaller stuff for the shop," Jennifer said, as if to prompt Brooke.

"Yes, that's why we're here. Verna has asked me to place some orders for quilt frames and racks."

"For store displays or for sale?"

"Both. She said you'll build a big name for yourself here, so we'd better get some before your prices go up."

He walked toward her, blotting out the background, making the open space seem to shrink around him. Despite Daniel's friendly tone, his eyes were narrowed, his lips tight, his stance stiff.

"I don't want to make a name for myself. That's prideful. Want to see a sample, though, so you know what you'll be getting?"

"Sure, I guess so."

They pried Jennifer off the stall rails and headed for the house when they heard a child's high voice calling Daniel. Brooke saw him startle and turn—and then she knew. Like her, he was still on edge from memories that would not let him go from the night of the accident. Maybe, she thought, like her, from other, earlier things, too.

"Oh, it's Susie and her friends," Jennifer announced before Daniel or Brooke spoke. "Can we all pet Bess? I wish we could go for a ride."

"You cannot go for a ride," Brooke said, "and you

can't be bothering Bess with a lot of noisy kids."

"They sound noisy to you?" Daniel challenged as the five scholars—as the Amish called their school-aged kids—walked up. Only Susie greeted Jennifer while the others nodded.

"Come on, *Shusslick*, you can play Andy Over with us," Susie said to Jennifer. "Uncle Daniel has the best roof—real steep—so the ball comes over it faster."

"Can I, Aunt Brooke?"

"Yes, go ahead." When the kids went off toward the house to split into two teams, she said to Daniel, "If you don't mind my asking, what does *shusslick* mean—what Susie called Jennifer?"

He surprised her with a fleeting smile. "It's a term of affection," he said and motioned her toward the house again. "It means someone who hurries too fast and trips over her own feet."

"Or *his* own feet?"

His gaze dropped down her body to her feet. "If the shoe fits, wear it," he said and held the back door open for her.

Daniel showed Brooke his furniture samples in the living areas of the first floor, arranged like a store showroom. She ran her hand along the satiny stretch of almost every piece she passed; she could not resist touching them. Sturdy tables, cupboards, lithe rocking chairs, all in bold, golden grains of oak from subtle to rich hues. She saw smaller pieces she longed to own, like jelly cupboards and pie safes. The items resembled other handmade ones she'd seen for sale in Amish country, yet they were unique, too, as if he'd put his special stamp—his strength and rough hewn grace—on every piece.

"I love this hutch," she said.

"That's white oak. I work to make the joints invisible

by matching the dominant grains. I avoid nails—dovetail joints and glue and dowels hold pieces together. Here—I do make cedar dowry chests, too, good for storing linens and quilts."

The sweet, clean scent of the beautiful chest he opened invigorated her. But it was the hutch she especially adored with its four doors and beveled glass windows—and a price tag of $2150.

"It must take you many hours to make such a useful but attractive piece by hand," she observed.

He nodded and tapped his knuckles on the sleek surface of a drop-leaf table. "Handmade doesn't mean I don't use some tools," he explained. "They're not electric, but air-pressure-powered ones." He reached for a pocket calculator, another compromise with progress she'd seen other Amish businessmen make. "I'll have everything set up by next week," he went on, punching the buttons intently, "and then hope to have a workshop out back by wintertime. Here," he added, pointing into the corner, "are the kind of quilt racks Mrs. Verna wants."

They talked numbers, prices, delivery dates. He told her no down payment until he delivered the first batch. Besides giving his calculator the attention now, he jotted numbers on—ironically—a yellow legal pad like those that used to be her constant companion. She eventually realized there was nothing to sign, no order form, only his word and hers, like an exchange of vows.

"So, that about does it," Daniel said. He kept a tabletop between them because his hands were actually tingling with the urge to touch Brooke Benton. He gripped his calculator so tightly his fingers cramped. Unfortunately, she was making him feel proud of his work again and that was not good, not for a man who had told his father just this morning that he would take instruction and join the church this autumn at the traditional after-harvest time.

"Daniel," Brooke said, evidently missing his hint she should leave, "I was wondering if you would tell me in detail what you saw from the hill the night of the wreck." She turned to face him squarely "I know it was dark and happened so fast, but you could just describe what you told the highway patrol and the sher—"

"No! It's over. I've let all that go now, and you must, too, if you want to live here, be accepted among us. You've seen it's not our way to carry on the quest for revenge."

"It isn't revenge, but justice! There is a big, big difference. I know you believe justice belongs only to God, but where would we be in this country that allows individual beliefs—like those of the Amish—to flourish, if people can just trample on—crash into others and get away with it? The laws that lawyers help to uphold are some of the same ones given by God, Daniel, the Ten Commandments and more. I have to do this—"

"You don't! You're an *auslander*, so—"

"Oh, I can translate that one, I'll bet," she said, hands on her hips. "An outlander, an outsider."

He kept the table between them because she made him feel like doing all sorts of crazy things. "That's right," he said. "An outsider, who'd better leave worldly police business alone, lawyer or not from Columbus, or wherever else you've been!"

"Daniel, this discussion has nothing to do with my past—or yours." She was gesturing, pacing now. "I'm just asking you, please, to at least tell me what you saw that night. I don't trust the police to take care of

94

things—*that's* what I've learned talking to Sheriff Barnes and the highway patrol, let alone in Columbus or 'wherever else I've been.' "

"I tell you what," he said, his voice much too loud. "I'll explain all about what I saw that night when you admit why you didn't even want to give your name to the media or—I could tell—talk to the sheriff at the hospital."

"I'm not some escaped felon. But then, I guess, even if I were, I'd be safe from being turned in by you because you just don't believe in getting involved no matter what or who is lost or threatened. *Do you?*"

"That's not it at all. And I don't need your help or advice on how to act. I'm home, I'm Amish—and I'm not your neighbor by choice, Miss Brooke Benton. I'll see you get the things Mrs. Verna ordered."

He turned away to make another unnecessary note on his yellow pad, hoping she felt dismissed. He let her walk out, heard her call her niece and drive off, her wheels spitting gravel.

Behind her house, Emma flopped flat on her back in the grass where she had been gathering dandelion greens for Levi's favorite salad. She stabbed her cutting knife into the ground and left it there in arm's reach.

She wished she could faint again, just tumble into oblivion, as she did at the hospital that night. Lying here, snagged between earth and sky, she stared straight up at the vastness of her pain. Nearby—somewhere— her three-year-old nephew, Sam, played horse and buggy. His snorts and whinnies blurred with birdcalls as she frowned at the masses of clouds overhead.

She knew the grass might stain her cape and *kapp*, but she didn't care. Didn't care if she ever did another load of wash, or fixed this salad for dinner, or cleaned, or quilted. Not without Katie. She felt so down, heavy, so tired, now that she had run out of those pills. It wasn't that they lifted her, but that they cradled her from slipping into the void of black despair. She wished the turf and soil would gasp open and swallow her as it had Katie last week. Yes, then Levi wouldn't look at her that way, as if she was not strong enough to accept God's holy will for His taking their firstborn so soon after the lastborn.

Without getting up, she reached for the knife and stabbed the grass again and again until little Sam came to stand over her, staring down curiously. With a huge sigh, she sheathed the knife in the turf again. The boy looked like a giant to her with his head in the clouds. He had lost his straw hat somewhere. Twine still trailed from his mouth since he had been the horsie, crawling on all fours, pulling the cardboard box he now toted under one arm. When he saw she was all right—what did he know?—he went off to leave her studying the sky again.

She sat up, opened her mouth, and tried to claw at the ropes she thought gagged and bound her there, keeping her cries inside, keeping her pulling her load. But there were no ropes in her mouth, no twine.

Emma put her head in her hands, pressing her palms hard against her temples to hold her thoughts inside. And her screaming pain.

The moment Brooke got out of the car with Jennifer at the Kurtz farm, she could see something was wrong. The place looked so still: no wash flapped on the line, no Emma or Leona greeted her, no one peeked out the window of the *daadi haus*. Susie, of course, was over at

Daniel's, but for the first time Brooke realized it was strange that the girl would be free to go with friends this early in the work day. Emma's boys, Isaac and Andy, were probably in the fields with Levi. But it was almost dinnertime and, as she peeked in through the back screened door, she saw no one and no preparations for the big midday meal.

"There's a little boy out back," Jennifer said, peering around the side of the porch. When they walked behind the house, Brooke saw Emma sitting slumped in the grass with her head in her hands.

"You play with him a moment and let me talk to Mrs. Kurtz," Brooke said, and gave Jennifer's shoulder a soft shove to send her toward the boy.

Brooke walked slowly toward Emma, noting a white plastic colander and a kitchen knife jammed in the ravaged grass beside a tumble of dandelion greens she must have been cutting. Her heart thumping, Brooke bent to pick up and pocket the knife.

"Emma? Are you feeling sick?" she asked as she sat beside her and gently touched her arm.

"Didn't hear you at all," Emma said, lifting a dry face, when Brooke was certain it would be tear-stained. Emma looked strange, too calm, distant. Her voice was softer than usual. "So much to do—fix dinner, put up some rhubarb preserves, get everything ready for the Sabbath." She started to rise before Brooke tugged her back.

"Where's Leona?"

"She could go to town with her brothers, I told her, because Levi wanted to get the last cornfield planted. A list of things to get he gave the boys. If they were going clear into Pleasant, I would have gone with them."

"Why is that?"

"I—I know I can tell you," she said, but kept avoiding Brooke's assessing stare. "My prescription for pills renewed, that's all. To burden Levi with it, I don't want that. I'm glad you stopped by, uh-huh."

"I just came to see how you were doing. Emma, I don't want to get between you and Levi on these pills, but—"

"But you could get some for me, if I just phone in the need for more," she said, suddenly gripping Brooke's hand in both of hers. "Or from the shop someday you could take me, because I'm coming back to work Monday." She seemed to deflate with a huge sigh. "Just look at these greens wilting. The sun's nearly straight up, and I don't think I started dinner."

"You don't think you have? Come on, then. Jennifer and I will help you before Levi or the kids come back. I would have come sooner if I had known you'd be alone. Usually, there are so many here."

"Saturday, you know," she said with another sigh. "On errands, everyone. Even Levi's folks visiting over town. Susie's with some friends. And," she whispered, seeming to shake herself even more awake from wherever she had been, "to be alone once in a while, I like that, uh-huh. Tonight, for supper, everyone will be here, Dan, too. He'd say I was pushing too hard or I'd ask Barbara Yoder."

Brooke had nothing to say to that. She watched Emma regather the dandelion greens' evidently not missing the knife. Brooke noted she was startled to see Jennifer playing with the boy, as if she had forgotten he was here and needed to be watched. Brooke's hands clenched tighter around the handle of the knife in her pocket instead of giving it back.

"Speaking of Daniel," she ventured, "Verna had me

stop by to order some quilt racks and frames from him. And, Emma, I've decided that I'm done doing that practice nine-patch quilting and I want to make a quilt like the one you—you and Katie—were doing, that beautiful Wedding Ring. I've picked the fabrics, too."

She was sorry she had mentioned it the moment it was said. Whereas talk of quilts usually snagged her interest, Emma looked sad again. Her usually clear eyes magnified by her glasses hazed over before snapping back.

"On Monday, I'll help you trace the pattern. But it won't be easy, a Wedding Ring—I think you know that by now—not with all those twists and turns to sew down flat and a design that interlocks."

"But I'll have you to guide me," Brooke said, trying to sound cheerful as she linked her arm through Emma's.

"And we'll trade that for a trip to Pleasant," Emma countered as they shooed Jennifer and little Sam inside ahead of them. "Oh, would you look at that clock and the macaroni and cheese not even started!"

"Just tell us what to do," Brooke said. Because Emma seemed normal now in her kitchen bustle, Brooke rinsed the knife while she washed her hands and slipped it in a drawer.

In the next fifteen minutes, she grated a huge hunk of cheese, sliced a cold meatloaf and two loaves of oatmeal bread, dished out rhubarb sauce, and made lemonade from a homemade powdered mix. Emma cooked up a big kettle of macaroni, made the sweet-and-sour bacon dressing for the dandelion salad, and produced two brown sugar pies she said Barbara Yoder had sent over. Jennifer set the table and amused little Sam.

When Brooke took a swig of the lemonade to be sure it was strong enough, she spewed it out into the sink.

"Oh, no!" Emma cried. "Too sour?"

"Ick! Sorry, but—it's awful."

Emma took a sip of the concoction. "That," she announced with the first smile Brooke had seen from her since Katie's loss, "is the cornstarch. Side by side they were in the cupboard, I must admit."

"Oh, if Levi would have tasted that . . ." Brooke said, grabbing for a glass of water to wash her mouth out.

"Then, I would have told him things aren't what they seem," Emma responded as she moved away to give the macaroni another quick stir.

At least, Brooke thought, Emma had smiled and was back to being in control of her chores. Brooke's heart lifted more, even as she and Emma had a stiff debate over whether or not she and Jennifer would join the family for dinner. Brooke finally convinced her they had to get back to the shop since Amos Mary wasn't used to being in charge of the salesgirls. With the children, they strolled out onto the porch. They could see Levi driving the five-horse hitch back down the lane with the family buggy right behind. The oldest boy, Isaac, was at the reins, and he waved importantly. Everything looked more normal to Brooke now, and she hoped Emma would continue to act that way.

"So you stopped to see Dan," Emma said to catch Brooke off guard, while Jennifer hefted little Sam to let him look in the window of the car. "Did he seem some better or poorly?"

At that, Brooke regretted she had goaded Daniel. After all, he was in mourning, too. "Better, I guess," she said. "Pleased with his new horse."

"Used to love horsepower, Dan did, but in cars, before he went gay."

Brooke jerked back so hard she banged into the

screen door. "Went gay?" she gasped. "Is that what—why he—why he left? With him—I—never guessed."

"Oh, dear," Emma said and smiled again, then burst out laughing so hard tears poured down her cheeks. "You—you are thinking I mean—well, see, another fence between us and the English—your worldly language. 'Gone gay' means he rebelled. You know, left for the world." Emma wiped tears away with the back of her hand. "Old-time talk, I guess, but that's our way. And you were afraid it meant—oh, no, *that's* not Dan's problem, and never was!"

Brooke felt her face flame crimson, even as relief flooded her. For one moment she had actually thought—that that big masculine man—that man who made her feel so aware of herself, feel so deeply was—really gay—worldly gay.

"Oh, n-no, s-sorry," she stammered, "and *please* don't ever tell him how I misunderstood."

"I won't tell anyone," Emma promised from behind her apron as she wiped away her tears. Her face had suddenly gone serious, even stern now. "Levi, Dan, my father—no one would find it one bit funny." And then a shadow seemed to descend over her again. Her smile and color faded as Levi nodded and pulled the team into the barn. Brooke squeezed Emma's hand and hurried Jennifer into the car. They pulled out, waving at Emma, then to the three children coming home with Susie in the buggy.

"Jake, I'm so glad to see you!"

"Same here, for sure, lady!" he told her, his deep voice gruff with emotion. They stood awkwardly smiling at each other outside his van in the crowded parking lot of the Sewing Circle, then hugged. She looked great to him, at least, not so thin or haunted as right before she fled.

"Come on in," she said, tugging at his hand. "Jen's visiting a school friend's house, but I'd love to show you the place."

"Packed with females shopping or sewing?" he said in mock horror, squeezing her hand back before she pulled gently away. He shoved his hands in his neatly tailored slacks that looked so dressy out here. "Naw, maybe later. Let's get to business. Come on, climb into the 'Burgundy Baby.' "

He quickly walked around the front of the dark red van to open the passenger door for her. He had to hitch himself forward a bit each time he thrust his right, artificial leg forward, but Brooke knew better than to ever call attention to it or try to help him do something. She climbed up into the seat and kept her gaze straight ahead, even when he had to pick up his leg and lift it into the driver's side before he could get in.

Jake Kaminsky thought the world of Brooke Benton. For a guy lucky enough to be sent home in one piece from 'Nam after working with land mines, he'd never expected to lose a leg on the job, pinned between two vehicles while investigating an accident in his own safe suburb of Worthington, Ohio. When he had been offered the magnanimous choice of a damned desk job or dead-end disability retirement by the Columbus Police Department, Brooke won his lawsuit for him against the city. The two-million-dollar settlement had at least let him set up a private injury and accident investigation office, mostly working for lawyers or insurance firms.

"How's your father doing lately, Jake?" she asked him.

"Good as can be expected with his heart trouble," he

told her. His dad lived with him, which was a good thing because the old man wouldn't have made it just on his Social Security checks with the cost of his heart pills, plus he didn't drive anymore. Her asking was another sign, he thought, that Brooke Benton really did care.

"So, other than this tragic hit-run, how's life out here in the boondocks?" he asked as he turned the van around, then headed out the drive.

"I've been relatively happy—Jennifer, too, though she's still adjusting to losing her parents."

"Poor kid. I know how much she means to you."

"Turn left here."

"I figured left, 'cause I didn't see anything the way I came in and you said this road."

"This doesn't feel like the boondocks when you're here, Jake," she said, turning slightly toward him. "Just different, very much alive and vital. Special. It grows on you."

"Sounds like the place is seducing you. Haven't found a Prince Charming with hay in his hair and cow crap on his boot soles, have you?" he teased with a grin.

"Nary a Prince Charming in sight around here," she said, shifting, then fidgeting in her seat as the vehicle climbed the hill.

"Now, don't tell me where the site is, and let me guess from what you told me," he insisted as he felt the old juices pumping. He used to thrive on digging up clues so the prosecution could nail someone just from the evidence left behind at the crime scene.

His stomach gave a little pitch as they crested the hill and started down. "I see skid marks below, long ones. This is it, right, Brooke?"

"Yes. This is it."

As ever, Brooke was amazed at what Jake could deduce from a scene, though she had explained to him where everything—and everyone—had been thrown by the impact.

She admired how he looked so in charge in his spit-polish shoes, militarily creased slacks, and crisp, long-sleeved white shirt open to show his bull neck. His sharp blue eyes occasionally darted to her as he went about his business. She supposed if things and times had been different—except for his Rush Limbaugh politics and rampant chauvinism, both of which he usually managed to gloss over so they didn't argue—they might have been closer than friends.

But her unease grew at his nerve to block off a bit of road with orange plastic cones. She hadn't expected him to make such a production of it. Sometimes he impatiently motioned vehicles around—buggies, too. She hoped no one told Sheriff Barnes in time for him to catch them like this and prayed the Amish would not turn against her when they saw someone taking another look at the scene. Still, this was worth the risk, so she stood stoically where Jake told her along the berm and took notes he called out to her as he traced the skid marks with the long-handled Rollatape wheel.

"Forty-three and one half feet of skid. No chatter marks until the last four feet, five inches. They probably weren't even pumping the breaks at first. I'll bet they were at least partway down the hill before they saw the buggy, no matter what you say about the lanterns and a reflector triangle. Then they had too much momentum to even get skip marks on this first thirty-nine feet, one inch of skids. Got those measurements?"

"Got them, boss."

"The swerving indicates too much speed, too. Unless

they just plain panicked, I'd guess they were not familiar with the road and were afraid to just drive off it to avoid the hit when, at the end, the car swerved right into the buggy. And it seems the kids got over as much as they could, for all the good it did them. Now," he went on, whipping out a pocket calculator, "if I take my handy-dandy formula for computing speed from distance and width of tire marks . . ."

"Does the width of tire marks indicate size or type of car?"

"Not good enough tread marks here to indicate something like, say, Goodyear or Sears. But these marks show approximate speed—the tire was really flattening out to try to grab the asphalt when they finally did hit the brakes. It looks like," he said, squinting to see the readout on his calculator window in the sun, "that car crested the hill doing fifty to fifty-five. And as for assured clear distance, a driving test would be needed to tell when they could see the buggy."

That was a mental note she need not make. Somehow, she was going to do her own buggy reconstruction and driving test. That might tell her whether or not the driver must have been drinking or was otherwise impaired.

"Why do you always say *they*?" she asked him.

"Figure of speech. It's sexless. Obviously, there was only one driver, but it's real possible on a full-moon night like you said, sweet country air and all that, the driver could have had someone with him—say a lovely lady. Maybe one who distracted him until it was too late to stop. Plus, even as slow as we were going, my stomach pumped coming over the hill, like on a roller coaster, and some people like to accelerate for that brief free-fall feeling."

105

"You're right. I've done that for Jennifer over some of the smaller hills, and she always squeals in delight."

He leaned against the back of his van, his big shoulder close to hers. "But since there probably weren't kids aboard at midnight, it might have been a joyride," he went on. "I mean real joy, like the driver was high on life or just plain in a great mood, because something wonderful had happened."

"And if he—they—were celebrating something, having a few drinks could play a part."

"Sure. You always gotta figure in the possibility of demon rum when you see something like this, Sunday night or not. And if they had it in their big car—maybe a van—they probably dumped their beer cans or whatever, first chance they got."

"So it really looks to you like a big vehicle? It couldn't have been a smaller one, maybe a sports car going at a high rate of speed?"

"No way, not with the distance between these tire tracks. You got a particular sports car in mind?"

"Not anymore. I've got to realize that a trained lawyer does not a trained private investigator make."

"That's one reason you need me."

She grinned at him. "And I am grateful—at least enough to spring for a big country dinner for you at the real fancy Dutch Table Restaurant in town."

"Oh, no, you know better than that. I'm buying. I'm still living off the interest of 'our' two million, you know, even though I pick up enough little jobs to keep from going off my gourd. You know," he said, at last picking up the cones from the road, "after I drop you off tonight, I think I'll stop at that gas station in Pleasant. See if the good ole country boys there still have the broken buggy stored so I can get a fleck of that red paint

106

you said the newspaper mentioned. I still got my ways to get a spectrum analysis on it, 'cause that will tell whether the hit car was new or old, GM or Chrysler or Ford. Then, I'll be back here with a full report soon as I can."

"Jake, I don't expect you to be driving more than two hours out here. Please, just call. See, the thing is, your being here with me here on the road at the scene—and anything else you or I do about solving this crime—is going to make the Amish very edgy, disapproving."

He grinned a bit lopsided and shrugged, though his eyes held hers. "Like you said, the warmth of the place does grow on you."

"They're wonderful people, Jake, but you've just got to understand their ways. And you've done so much for me already. I really do appreciate it."

He stepped closer to squeeze her shoulder. "I told you, Brooke, all you gotta do is call, 'cause that's what real friends are for."

CHAPTER SIX

EARLY SUNDAY EVENING, DANIEL STARED DOWN at the envelope in his hand. In Brooke's neat, unadorned handwriting it said simply, *Daniel Brand*. He had just returned from supper at Emma's when Paul Hostetler had dropped it off. That alone annoyed Daniel, though Paul had his wife, Norma, with him. They had stopped, even though it was a Sunday evening, to get some material at the Sewing Circle, they said, and Brooke had sent this note over. Since none of the Amish could be phoned, that in itself was not unusual. Yet Daniel had quickly explained he was making the shop some quilt racks, so it must be about the order Brooke had placed.

And it annoyed him that people had seen Brooke yesterday—he heard about it more than once at church this morning, too—with some sort of ununiformed investigator at the accident scene, making a public study of it when he'd told her to leave things alone. Now, just when he had talked himself into steering clear of her—again—here was this note. Biting his lower lip, he tore it open.

Daniel, as you yourself suggested, I will trade my confession of why I am in Maplecreek for your account of what you saw that night. I'll meet you on the hill before dark. Yes, it's that important to me.

Thanks, Brooke

He could almost hear her voice as he read it. And in the last sentence, she was already arguing with him again, and he yearned to answer back. But he wadded up the paper and sailed it into the kitchen wastebasket. He sat there, frowning at his fists, then smacked them on the table, went over to fish the note out, and smoothed it open to study it, creases and all.

Brooke Benton was brave and seemed honest, he told himself, staring at the evenness of the strokes of her pen, the curves, and the graceful tails of the y's as if he were a handwriting expert. And she was determined—even stubborn—just like him. He believed that she sincerely cared about Katie's loss and what she called justice. She wasn't on some crusade because she felt guilty about having Amish kids to her place that night. She really liked and admired the Amish and was only curious about them in a friendly way. It wasn't that she wanted to mix in with Amish ways because she was nosy or looking for some sort of spiritual answers in her flight

108

from the world out there. But she sure had run from something, something he suddenly, desperately wished he could soothe away for her.

He grabbed his hat and coat and banged out the back door. He walked around string stretched between stakes that marked the perimeter of his future cabinet shop and display room. When the lumber arrived from the sawmill, the Maplecreek Amish menfolk would help him build it in a sort of barn raising. With a soft whistle so Bess knew he was near, he started uphill.

He wished he could roll back the calendar so that Katie and the kids would still be alive. Wished he could roll it back months, so he would never have known Tracey Stevens. Back years, so he would be a settled man now, with shop, wife, family, the welcome yoke of responsibilities.

He stopped on the crest of the hill as twilight licked up the valleys and treetops embraced the last golden rays of sun. He saw Brooke stood just below him, almost on the very spot where he had seen the accident, looking steadily, maybe hopefully, toward him, waiting for him. His heart thudded as he stretched his strides to meet her.

From a distance, Brooke watched Daniel's approach; his feet thrust through the blowing tangles of tall grass. Emma had said this was a hay field this year, which Levi had planted for animal feed, a jumble of clover, alfalfa, and timothy with some invading weeds and wildflowers, to be harvested in early June. It had always seemed to Brooke a friendly field with songbirds bobbing on milkweeds, serenading their neighbors with their songs.

But now, Daniel's long, lean body shot a jagged

shadow on the hill, making the field smaller. His speed, his very presence devoured the space between them, as if he kicked down a path straight toward her.

She steeled herself against his arguments and anger, even his continued refusal to help her. To her amazement, he doffed his hat perhaps, she thought, so if someone looked up from the road they would not be certain an Amish man spoke privately with an English woman in blue jeans. When he came close, she saw he looked around as if to ensure they weren't being watched. Maybe she had miscalculated to suggest this public meeting place rather than one of their homes. He stopped five feet from her.

"I thought you'd bring Jennifer. I know you don't like to leave her."

"She's making cookies with Mary—Amos Mary—who's taken Emma's place at the shop this week. I must admit I only told Mary and Jennifer I was going for a long walk. And you're right that I don't like to leave her. Since her mother died and her father never sees her, it helps her if we're close. It helps me, too."

"You probably didn't want her to hear what you have to say."

Brooke was surprised his voice was encouraging, not accusing. "It isn't that," she said, repeatedly brushing a stray wisp of blowing hair out of her mouth until she hooked it behind her ear. "Jennifer knows just about everything I've decided to tell you, though I don't want her living through it again in any way. I couldn't bear it if she suffers anymore, especially because of me, let alone what happened before." She knew she couldn't be making sense to him. How she wished this was all over, her explanation and his.

"Are you certain you want to tell me? I won't hold

you to it."

"Yes. And I know you will keep your word. In Maplecreek, only Verna knows the real reason I'm here, not even Emma. I'm only hoping when you hear all of it, you won't blame me for what happened to the kids down there."

When she pointed shakily toward the accident site, he reached out to clasp and lower her hand in his. She dared not look into his eyes. His skin felt warm, his fingers strong, his palm calloused.

"I've been curious about you," he said as they stood on the windy hill, shoulder-to-shoulder, holding hands. "I want to understand why someone like you is really here."

She glanced at him but stiffened her legs to keep from toppling into his arms for comfort and support and more. Would he run then, or, with that look lighting his eyes, would he have held her? Her voice came out much too breathy: "I, too, about you. Do you want to sit down?"

To her relief and dismay, he released her hand. Yet she felt he still touched herd sensations tingled up her arm and down into the pit of her belly. It scrambled her thoughts even more, for she wasn't sure where to start. But she knew now that she had wanted to tell him not only so he would describe the accident to help her solve it, but because though she wasn't sure why—she *needed* to tell him.

She gripped her hands around her bent legs as he settled beside her, sitting Indian style cross-legged with his hat on the grass. Only their height on the hill let them see out of the blowing, rusting grass to the road below. It seemed silent, even as a red-winged blackbird stared at them, bobbing on a tall piece of grass, then

111

flitted off into the sky. All the beginning lines she'd rehearsed had flown, too, as if she'd never planned a plea bargain before, never memorized an opening statement to a jury.

"I guess," she began, "if I were going to hold something back, I'd just tell you I'm here because Verna Spriggs had been kind to my sister, Melanie, the last few years before she died. They were mostly long-distance friends, but Melanie loved to visit here. She had always adored doing all sorts of handcrafts and needlework, but she gave them all up when she discovered quilting on her first visit to this area. Her dream was to have a store like the Sewing Circle someday. Before Jennifer was born, Melanie had been an elementary teacher, as our mother had been. My father," she added, "was a criminal lawyer. Talk about following in someone's footsteps . . ."

When he said nothing, she went on, "Anyway, when Melanie died, she left her quilts to Jennifer and me—and one to Verna, who came to the funeral. Verna and I hit it off right away, and she said—more or less tongue-in-cheek, since I told her I could hardly thread a needle—that if I ever wanted to visit or needed a change of pace, I should come take quilting lessons at the Sewing Circle. But Verna, Melanie, and the quilts are not really why I'm here. You see, in a way, I'm really—hiding out."

She dared to turn again and look directly into his eyes. His irises looked so dark they melded with his pupils. In the deepening dusk, his face was all shadowed planes and angles, as if carved from his own oak. She sensed in him a strength of someone else who had suffered, yet come through. She felt his curiosity, compassion—even desire, and she was no longer afraid

112

to tell him why she wanted to avoid the media and the police.

"You see," she said, clearing her throat, "as a criminal defense attorney these last seven years, I've been used to dealing with—even using—the police and the media. It comes with the territory. So did my ambition, the fierce need to succeed in my job. I know that's so different from how you think and live. When Melanie died painfully and young and Jennifer came to live with me, I began to realize I was too driven, but then, before I could change my life, everything just exploded . . ."

"Here's to many more national TV appearances after victories in court!" Elizabeth Crandel said and tapped Brooke's coffee mug with hers in salute. "It's fabulous for the firm as well as you!"

An elegant and statuesque blonde of fifty-five, Elizabeth accidentally tipped over a framed photo of Jennifer, which Brooke rescued and righted even as they drank the toast. "I may be the real estate law queen around here now," Elizabeth went on, crossing her long legs and smiling down at Brooke, "but I evidently remembered enough of my earlier criminal law days to mentor the city's premier up-and-coming criminal defense attorney!"

"I don't know what I would have done without you these last two months of this trial—especially since I had Jennifer to worry about, too."

"I know, kiddo. There are all kinds of trials."

"Yes, but Jen's a joy and I didn't mean otherwise. And now that I'm out from under this case, I have to find more time with her. I thought things would get better right after the decision, but it's been worse. Elizabeth, what I really want you to know is that things would not have come out this way without your support and advice these last seven years, especially in this men's club called Stedman & Rowe," Brooke whispered with a dramatic glance at her closed office door. "Your advice was invaluable and your senior partnership proved to me the glass ceiling can be broken around here—if one is willing to commit oneself to the utter joy of eighty-billable-hour work weeks."

"If you didn't run home right after work every night lately, we could grab something better than this office coffee," Elizabeth said, sliding her derriere from the desk and twisting her trademark pearls with a crimson-lacquered fingertip. "Just like we did in the old days when you were green as grass. You know," she said lowering her voice, despite the fact the office door was closed, "Lord Myron assigned you to me because it wouldn't be *kosher* to have an attractive, single young associate working under one of the men, however much you needed to learn from them. I guess we showed Ray McCarron you could handle the big case he had his eyes on."

They shared a little laugh. Mr. Fast-track McCarron had made it all too obvious he didn't think she could handle all the publicity and pressure that went with the Kistler case. He'd sat second chair to her like a vulture—if a handsome, suave one—just waiting for her to crack up or turn to him in tears to ask him to take over. He'd even tried putting a move on her, as if getting intimately entangled with him was what she needed to get her through, but she's managed to make him keep his distance.

Brooke told Elizabeth she'd take a rain check on the formal celebration; she felt amazed anew that the usually astute Elizabeth seemed not to hear her whenever she spoke about her dedication to Jennifer. But then, without losing Melanie and gaining Jen, she herself would probably have been just like Elizabeth over the years, successful, of course, but wed only to her career.

When Elizabeth left, Brooke surveyed her small, windowless, cluttered kingdom. She regretted she had not told Elizabeth her decision that she must work part-time for a while, since Jennifer was still so disturbed by the loss of her parents. But it was probably best Brooke ask—tell—Myron Stedman, the managing senior partner, first. As she tried to stoke her courage for that task, she got up to straighten the frames on the wall and then her desk. The matched wooden wall frames displayed her Juris Doctor degree from Buckeye State and the cross-stitch piece with the Shakespeare quote Melanie had done for her at law school graduation: *The first thing we do, let's kill all the lawyers.* Brooke forced herself to file those memories and attacked the desk.

The chaos here always made her think she might drown in stacks of paper. Thank God, she was internally organized. She got a good laugh whenever she saw a movie where a lawyer had a cleared, gleaming desktop. Now she aligned, rearranged, filed, and tossed memos, briefs, pleadings, case files, reams of her own notes on the People of Ohio vs. Kistler both in her own handwriting on yellow legal pads and transcriptions typed by her secretary, Liz. She left the pile of newspaper clippings for Liz to laminate and file. Flipping through the congratulatory notes, she put them with the things to be saved. The Kistler case had been covered on Courtroom Cable TV, and after its conclusion, Brooke had appeared on both local and national interview shows, via remotes from TV studios here in town, so faxes had come in from far and wide.

115

Rodney Kistler might have been a loser in life, Brooke thought, but she had proved beyond a reasonable doubt that he did not abduct and rape the daughter of one of the popular assistant football coaches of Buckeye State University. In a city and state where college football was the state religion, that was no mean feat. Unfortunately, that meant the culprit was still out there somewhere, when people wanted to have the case closed and the streets safe. Brooke hoped the police caught the right man soon, but for now, justice had been done both for Rodney Kistler and to her criminal law career.

Waiting for her appointment with Mr. Stedman, Brooke returned a few messages, committed to two more interviews, then took a call from Mr. Stedman's secretary that he would see her in his office at five-twenty. No, Brooke thought, even this big win was not enough for Myron Stedman to walk down the hall to speak to her informally.

The next call came while she surveyed her time log, where she, like the other rank-and-file associates recorded their billable hours. Her services had been worth one hundred fifty dollars an hour these past months, but that might as much as double now, at least until people heard she was going to be a part-time lawyer for a while.

She punched her secretary's button, then the phone line to take another call, amazed to hear who was on the other end. "Judge Prescott, hello," she said to the eminent judge who had presided over the case. Marshall Prescott was a big, brusque man with a glowering gaze that could make both opposing counsels consider not objecting to anything. Behind his back, attorneys called him Old Ironsides and not because he resembled the crusty lawyer Raymond Burr had once played on TV. Old-guard, unflappable Judge Marshall Prescott resembled in gunpower and the wide wake he cut the historic battleship *Old Ironsides*. The rumors that the man had a sense of humor in private life was universally rejected as ungrounded hearsay.

"Caught you on Larry King's show last night, counsel," the sonorous voice said. "Other than the time that little earpiece fell out and snagged in your hair, good job."

"That means a great deal, coming from you, your honor."

"Appreciated the compliments you gave the presiding judge, yours truly—and for the fact you didn't call me Old Ironsides on national TV."

She grinned, uncertain whether to laugh or not. The man must be meaning to make a joke. "I always thought the 'old' part of that was unfair anyway," she dared to say. She jumped as he guffawed into the phone. Wait until she told some friends about this call!

"Listen, counsel, just wanted to say, for a young attorney . . ."—she was almost certain he had wanted to say, "for a young *woman* attorney," because it was no secret he was from the old school—"you did a fine job overall. I guess we both held our own on the court TV coverage, the prying media liberals. I've got to admit the pro-victim publicity with even the local sportscasters and football fanatics mouthing off prejudiced a lot of people. But the poor girl on the stand just couldn't convince the jury that the accused was the hooded man who had her eyes taped the whole time. Not with that strong closing argument you had."

Brooke gripped her pencil so hard it snapped in two. "I feel *really* bad about the victim, your honor, but that doesn't mean a man who collects guns, bought some duct tape, and has a raspy voice is guilty, no matter what kind of a husband or father he's been in the past."

"I guess neither of us had better bank on good seats in the stadium from here on out, if they so much as let us through the hallowed portals. You think Myron's going to reward you with a partnership for all the good publicity you got the firm?"

"I don't dare to hope. You know as well as I do, but for a few of us younger, token maverick associates, it's a *very* conservative firm."

"I hope you mean that as a respectful compliment, counsel. But tell you what—I'm going to remember your name and McCarron's, too, if I do decide to run for senator." Before she could answer, he hung up.

Brooke sat holding the receiver, staring at it for a moment. So it wasn't just rumor about Prescott's political aspirations; did he mean state senator or congressional? She—and Ray McCarron—had obviously helped Judge Prescott get the wider audience he needed to be able to run for office, probably to build a bigger war chest. And she should have known the word conservative was holy ground to Judge Prescott. "But no," she said aloud, "Lord Myron's not going to give me partnership when he hears I want my afternoons free and the summer off."

She punched the number of Ray's extension and told him what the judge had said. "Hot damn!" he exploded. "Do you think he means it about using us if he runs and makes it?"

"Who knows? If he's got a politician's heart, are we supposed to believe anything he says anymore?" she contended, but she was thinking, *Your first step toward being attorney general of the known universe, Ray.*

After that call, she'd put her head in her hands, staring down at the embossed letterhead stationery on her desk. How proud she had been when she had first been able to use it: *Stedman & Rowe, Attorneys at Law. Criminal Defense, Civil Litigation, Estates, Real Estate.* It had not been her father's firm, but one he had told her once he greatly admired. She wasn't sure how long she sat there, feeling drained, exhausted.

She jolted at the loud rap on her door. It opened before she could respond. Myron Stedman stood there with Ray McCarron behind him and others pressing in. Had she missed her appointment with Stedman? She glanced at her clock; no, it wasn't barely after five. Her first feeling was elation: the grand old man had come to her cubbyhole after all! Her next thought was that they were going to burst in with a surprise party, but no, something was very wrong.

"Haven't you heard?" Mr. Stedman demanded. "Hasn't anyone called?"

"About—what?" she said, rising, her eyes darting to Ray's face, then Elizabeth's behind him.

"It's all over the five o'clock news!" the usually staid, circumspect Stedman shouted. "Your esteemed client Rodney Kistler has just abducted some woman and is threatening her life, and the police have him trapped behind a building five blocks from here!"

"What happened then?" Daniel prompted when she stopped talking and just frowned into the gathering dusk. "Especially to your client and his hostage?"

"Police sharpshooters—the HIT Team, they're called—tried to take him out. They have an excellent record, but—you might know Kistler jumped at just the wrong time and they—they accidentally killed him and

119

his hostage, with one bullet no less! On *Live at Six News*, of course, which then made all the networks with me starring in the role of scapegoat for getting him off. Daniel. I actually believed that man was innocent! I fought to free him, so what happened was my fault! I have the rape and public degradation of one woman and the death of another to carry around for the rest of my life!"

He reached for her hand again. "And everyone turned on you, so you left Columbus for a while, thinking at least it gave you time for Jennifer."

She gripped his hand. "No, I didn't run then. The firm gave me my half days, all right—actually, gave me a month's paid leave before they took me back half days. The media had a feeding frenzy on my—my mistake. The police more or less hinted that the next time I asked for one of their expert witnesses or an officer to testify for a client, they wouldn't be exactly thrilled about helping me. But then it got so much worse."

She held tightly to his hand as she began to talk again.

YOU WOMEN'S LIBBER FEMINIST BITCH DYKE LAWYER! YOUR BLEEDING HEART GOT THAT BASTARD MURDERER FREED SO HE COULD KIDNAP AND KILL AGAIN. IT SHOULD HAVE BEEN YOU. TIT FOR TAT, IT JUST MAY BE YOU.

A CONCERNED CITIZEN

Stopped for a red light en route to pick up Jennifer at her suburban school, Brooke stared for the hundredth time at the photocopy of the note. It certainly stood out, even among the torrent of hate mail she had received.

120

She had the copy only because the police had the original for their investigation of whoever was menacing her. But there was no way to trace the original. Maybe, the police psychological profile consultant had said, it was sent by someone at least over forty, since the terms "women's libber," "bleeding heart," as in bleeding heart liberal, and "tit for tat" belonged to a certain past era, but that was the extent of the help from them.

"Good work, detectives!" she muttered and stuffed the note back in her purse one-handed while she drove. "That narrows it down to only about five hundred thousand possible suspects! Thank God, Jake's willing to help, because you're not."

"You real sure," one officer had said when she'd finally gotten him to the condo, "this isn't something the kid did for an early April Fool's Day joke, Ms. Benton? You're sure someone's been in here, but you admit there's no signs of breaking and entering, nothing out of place but the sugar's switched with the salt, the vegetable shortening with your face cream?"

"And the mouthwash with the nail polish remover, which I took a good swig of!" she'd told him. "No, it's not some prank Jennifer and I have been playing on each other. I think you understand, lieutenant, that neither of us has been in the mood for pranks lately. It's obvious that someone is harassing and menacing me, and I'd like to request a stakeout on my condo and car."

"I'll see what my supervising officer says, Ms. Benton, but with all the serious crimes lately—like abductions and killings in broad daylight right downtown—I'm sure you realize we may be a bit short-handed."

Brooke glanced again in her rearview mirror, scowling at the car behind that had stayed entirely too close all the way up Tremont Road. She knew she was getting paranoid, but after her car had been so cleverly moved last week to a different place in the mall parking lot than where she'd left it—looking untouched, no sign of forced entry, no fingerprints, as if she had just forgotten where she'd put it—she'd almost taken up smoking again to calm her nerves.

But she didn't, wouldn't. Not with all the latest news on secondhand smoke since Jennifer had been living with her. She cursed and hit her brakes to keep from banging the car ahead of her. "You stupid idiot!" she yelled, though he couldn't hear her and she knew it was her own fault.

Her own fault, the words haunted her. In a way, she supposed this harassment was her own fault. Why had she not seen through Rodney Kistler? She should have pleaded his case out, gotten him some help, made certain he was detained or committed. She was usually a good judge of character.

Worse, besides her fear of Jennifer's being hurt by some vengeful nutcase, besides being too terrified to let the child play outside, besides her loss of sleep, all this had made her question the very bedrock ethics of any defense lawyer: your client is right and you must defend said client to the utmost of your resources and ability, or the whole American legal system is doomed. But she had hurt the system—hurt herself—her employer, everyone—by so ably and passionately defending a damned guilty man!

She was gripping the wheel so hard her hands cramped when she pulled into the line of mother-manned cars waiting in front of the elementary school. When the dismissal bell rang, she scanned the groups of kids bursting from the building.

Brooke breathed a sigh of relief when she saw

Jennifer hurrying toward the car. She couldn't help but worry that some of this would fall on Jen, but at least her last name was Reynolds and her teacher and principal had been very helpful in keeping the girl's relationship to Brooke quiet.

"Look, Aunt Brooke," she called out before she reached the car, "a drawing of my favorite animals we did in art!"

Brooke admired the rainbow crayoning of Jennifer's two exotic pet angel fish, which her father had given her last time he passed through. "This is very good, sweetheart. I can even tell which is Barney and which is Arnie."

Jennifer chattered about her day on the way home, thank heavens, seemingly untouched by the odd events that plagued her aunt. Or maybe, Brooke thought, after losing both parents in different but dreadful ways, nothing else could compare.

But Jennifer quieted as Brooke stopped the car in the driveway of their condo unit, opened the garage door with the remote, then looked inside from where she was. Unfortunately, Jake had to be in Cincinnati today and hadn't been able to drive by. Nothing seemed amiss, but then nothing outside ever did. They pulled in, piled out; Brooke made sure the door to the attached condo was locked before she unlocked it. Quickly, she checked the closet before Jennifer hung up her coat, then walked through, scanning things, darting upstairs to look under beds and peer in closets with her illegal can of mace poised, which she tried not to let Jennifer see. When she turned to head downstairs, the girl's voice floated to her.

"What're we having for supper, Aunt Brooke?"

It took Brooke a moment to remember, but she pictured the day-by-day menus she had posted on the

123

refrigerator door. "Salmon that's still in the freezer," she called down, "so I'm glad you mentioned—"

Jennifer's scream cut her off. Brooke thudded downstairs to see the child pressing her nose to her aquarium. "They're gone! Barney and Arnie! Oh, no, maybe they got abducted like those girls Mr. Kistler took! I wanted to show them this picture, but what's this stuff?"

Brooke hurried across the room and bent down to peer into the slightly murky water. Two salmon fillets floated in the aquarium amid little castles and water wheels Jeff had bought for his daughter to soothe his conscience.

"But where are Barney and Arnie, Aunt Brooke?"

Sugar switched with salt, Brooke thought. Crisco in her face cream jar, nail polish remover with mouthwash. And fish fillets with—

She ran into the kitchen and yanked the freezer open, then almost gagged as she took the frozen angel fish out and got them into warm water in the sink. When they did not revive, she cried right along with Jennifer. And realized the invader of her home and her life had now hurt the one she most wanted to protect.

"You should have changed your locks," Daniel said.

"I did. After the first incident, I got deadbolt locks and a security system, too, but unfortunately, the second illegal entry that got the fish was the day before I got them installed. And I had a friend with crime-scene training, who frequently drove by, to do some stakeouts. Jake, the man I just mentioned."

"The same guy who almost blocked traffic on the road yesterday because you asked him here to look over the accident scene?"

It was a simple, calmly stated question, but Brooke heard the anger—or maybe just frustration—in his tone. "Daniel, I know you and the Amish don't approve, but I have to do something. *I have to!*"

He heaved a huge sigh and hit his fist on his knee. "So, did you find who was tormenting you?" he asked. "Maybe the intruder was not the one who sent the note."

"Yes, I realize that—and so did the police," she admitted, grateful he had not protested her pursuing the hit-and-run more. Maybe, deep down, he wanted her to keep after the killer. "Anyway, I didn't leave town then," she went on. "I was still unwilling to move because Jennifer was just getting used to me, to the condo, her school I wanted her to have that stability, until I saw it wasn't possible. I know this sounds so melodramatic, like some B-grade Hollywood flick, but, just after I started feeling better about the condo being safe—when we were coming out of a movie theater in a mall one evening—a large, late model car with tinted windows tried to run us down."

"What? And then took off, like here?"

"Yes," she said and shook her head in disbelief even now.

"So you are thinking . . ."

"The thing is, after that, we left town so quickly and carefully. But somehow, what if this madman—or woman—traced me here somehow and tried something even worse? Remember that car that went by slowly when the kids were getting ready to pull out of the driveway that night, as if someone were looking for something? I was standing under the light in the front yard then. What if that person saw me—even maybe through tinted windows—thought I got in the buggy,

125

too, circled around, came back, then intentionally . . ."

Daniel put his arm around her, and she gratefully leaned against him. Her shoulder fitted perfectly, her arm molded against his hard ribs. She shuddered with remembered fear, but also with the sweetness of his embrace. He held her stiffly at first, one-armed, like a buddy, then encircled her so she leaned into the muscled strength of his chest and thigh.

"Have there been signs someone's found you here, was watching you here?" he whispered, turning to her, his mouth, so close to her temple his breath stirred her hair.

"No. And only two people from Columbus I really trust know where I am." The moment was so precious that she did not want to tell him more, not now at least. Not about the final threat that had sent her fleeing, the blood. Later, she would tell him, for he knew enough now to understand.

"Just as you're not the one who kidnapped those women, you're not to blame yourself for those kids' deaths," he insisted, squeezing her shoulders once before he released her. "That car going by when you were under the light was probably coincidence, not a pattern. Still, I see why you were upset I peered in your window—and why you want to find the hit-and-run driver."

"Daniel, it's for those kids—for justice, I said—and not just my own past—that I have to dig into this, even if it flies in the face of Amish belief. I hope you can understand—even help me."

She saw her passion reflected in his face. "How? If I can do something, without betraying the man I must be—must become here . . ." His voice trailed off, then got stronger. "All right. I'll tell you what I saw the night of the wreck."

She listened intently while he explained why he thought the hit-and-run vehicle had been a big car: the breadth of the headlight beams, the slant of the taillights, and the way the car crested the hill. He was certain it was not a pickup or a van. No, the buggy lights weren't visible from here, but his angle was from above and lateral, and the red blinking lantern hung on the far side. His terror at the sound of the squealing brakes could have made him think it went on longer than it did. He felt he could not fairly estimate the time it took the car to try to stop or its speed. He was certain that one headlight on the car had been broken in the wreck, and not just because of the shattered glass on the road. When the car had driven away, its single beam was askew.

Brooke could tell he had rehearsed what to say, whether because he could then get it over with sooner, or because he had explained it all to the authorities before, or because the memory haunted him, she was not sure. He said he could not judge whether the driver had been drinking, because the swerving could have been from trying to stop a heavy vehicle coming down the hill. He did, however, given her one opinion, which in court, would have been stricken from the record as having no foundation:

"The person who hit them was a coward, but a bold one." His voice was angry now, barely leashed. "I know that sounds contradictory. But he hesitated only one moment before backing up and driving around and away. Maybe he didn't even know bodies had been thrown off the asphalt, but he sure could see the two boys when he drove right around them and fled. Like I said, a coward, but a bold one. Like me with you," he added those last four words so quietly she wondered if she had imagined them.

An awkward silence stretched between them. She was so tempted to press her advantage, to perhaps lean into him again, to come closer. But she saw that he struggled yet with himself; they sat so close and yet she felt a wall between them. Her voice was shaky when she spoke, but she saw his relief to be back to business.

"Could you answer something else, Daniel? Don't you think it's strange that Paul Hostetler came upon the accident so late at night when he lives on the other side of town? He should have been heading home after his shift, but he told me he was just taking a ride, enjoying the moonlight. He says you used to run around together. Does his explanation sound flimsy to you?"

"You can't suspect him. His car wasn't a bit damaged, and he arrived too fast to change vehicles. And then to go and face Emma and Levi right away like he did . . ."

"A coward but a bold one, you said. Besides, I intend to follow every lead."

"I heard," he said, frowning, "that Paul and his wife had some troubles and he has a woman friend around here."

"So he could have been going to see her?" she prompted. "Do you know where she lives?"

"Yeah, it's just down Sawmill, not more than a mile beyond the accident scene. But it still doesn't prove anything, and he did drive up to help us from the other direction."

"But maybe that wasn't his car. What if he accidentally hit the kids, drove on by to his girlfriend's where he was headed, told her, hid his car, borrowed hers. Then, feeling guilty, came around the back way to help when he wouldn't be blamed. He knew where the back lanes were when he drove Emma and Levi to the hospital."

"That's pretty far-fetched, but I suppose the sheriff could check to see if he has a big car and if there's been damage or recent bodywork on it. But when Paul stopped by my place with his wife the other day, there was nothing wrong with his car."

"A blue Dodge Intrepid—fairly new, if I recall," she said, to Daniel's obvious admiring surprise. "But that could have been his second car. Even out here, lots of families have two cars, just as the Amish have more than one buggy. Besides, at Katie's funeral, when I merely mentioned his family, he got very touchy and stalked off. And then a few days later—on a Sunday, no less— he just happened to show up at the Sewing Circle with his wife, as if he wanted me to think everything's fine between them, just in case I'd hear about his woman friend and where she lived, I suppose."

"Yes, but the way you're piecing this together is just— so—"

"Circumstantial. Do you know this friend of his?"

"No. I hear she's divorced and lives alone now on an old place that had the fields sold off to the Bontrager family. Down past the Stottlemeyer farm, where they're due to have that big farm auction next month. It's listed in the newspaper." He hesitated a moment as if pondering something. "Brooke, have you seen the recent *Maplecreek Weekly*?"

"You mean the article about Sheriff Barnes saying he'll solve the tragedy now that he knows he's looking for a red car because of paint smears on the buggy? That can't be much help, even if they type test the paint. Besides, how many people in this area, including the sheriff himself, drive red cars?"

129

"He gets a new one every year, has as long as I can remember. Sometimes he even drives the old ones—minus the big badge painted on the side and the bar lights—for his private car."

"I only hope," she said, "the illustrious Sheriff Barnes checked all the local repair garages and dumps in case the killer tried to ditch the car in question."

"Probably," he said. "And I'll bet he's reading the 'For Rent' pages, too. When an English farm goes under—like the Stottlemeyer place—like my place before I got here—outbuildings, even barns sometimes sit vacant. So a local person would know where to stash a damaged car for a while. Before I moved to Indiana, a ring of Cleveland car thieves hid hot vehicles around here until they could move them out, and Sheriff Barnes put a stop to that."

"I see," she said, both surprised and grateful for this lead. And his help gave her hope that, just maybe, if she was careful, she could later convince him to help her get a mock-up buggy to reconstruct what the car's driver could see when he came over the hill. "Daniel, I thank you for that hint about vacant barns as well as the eye witness account."

"But I didn't mean you should go poking around in old buildings," he added quickly. "I just mean it's what the sheriff is probably doing."

She was careful not to ask him the last question that burned in her. Did Paul Hostetler's girlfriend have an outbuilding on her place where a car could be hidden? She was going to personally find out as soon as she could.

They stood, almost simultaneously, and she brushed grass off the back of her jeans before she saw he was watching intently and stopped. "Daniel, I am grateful."

130

"I told you I am, too—for your help keeping outsiders away and helping me with Katie that night."

"Yes. I—I loved her, too."

Darkness embraced them; night sounds swept by. Daniel took one step forward and tipped his head sideways and tilted her chin up. She stopped breathing.

"Sometimes, I think," he whispered, "we are not so far apart."

His mouth touched hers once, tentatively, as if she might fight him. Then gently, comforting, tasting. Again, firmer, bolder.

Though startled, she responded instantly, softening her lips to fit the curve and command of his. She held to his hard-muscled upper arms to steady herself, then slid her palms flat to his shoulders, then his upper chest. Through his shirt she felt his chest hair and warm skin, the solid body. They seemed to breathe in unison.

Too soon, it ended. He held her elbow a moment, then stepped back.

"I won't say I'm sorry," he whispered, "but we—I—shouldn't have done that. Go on back now. I'll watch you until you get home. I can see you against the lights of your place."

She wanted to say more—*do* more. But she nodded and set off, afraid at first her feet might not be under her. But they moved; she swung her arms to keep her balance through the grass.

All the way she felt his touch, his kiss, his eyes. It was both comforting and deliciously disturbing, not at all like that sensation of being watched by—by the other. She became aware of her walk, the swing of her hips, her inner thighs brushing gently together.

Just before the lighted driveway, she turned around to wave, but by then the silhouette of hill supported only sky.

CHAPTER SEVEN

THE NEXT MORNING, A GRAY, RAINY ONE, BROOKE separated Verna's morning mail into two stacks on her desk in the office: the bills and business items Brooke would tend to and the pile waiting for Verna's return.

But her thoughts were elsewhere. Because she could hardly drag Jennifer along late last night, she had not yet gone to check Paul Hostetler's girlfriend's barn down the road, and she was itching to. Tonight Jen had a birthday dinner at a school friend's house in town, and she'd be on her own for a while. It was obviously best done after dark when the Amish—especially Daniel—would not see her. She hoped the rain stopped by then.

She went back to the big, busy workroom where she had been tracing her quilt pattern pieces and overseeing everything. The rain had evidently kept the customers down, even for a Monday morning, but eight quilters were busy on two projects. As far as she could tell, her Amish workers were not holding it against her that she had been seen surveying the accident scene with Jake. Or maybe they were just pleased to have Emma back. Unfortunately, it was Emma herself who was the problem this morning.

She was everywhere rearranging, fussing, criticizing. It was so unlike her. Brooke had thought Emma would be more quiet, even depressed, but she seemed only high-strung and shrill, especially for an Amish woman. After she'd asked Brooke to treat her no differently because of what had happened, she was making

132

everyone sullen as well as sad.

"Now, Brooke, you've heard Verna in her beginning classes," Emma scolded her the second time today. She leaned over Brooke's shoulder and reached down to tip her tracing pencil at an even greater angle toward the clear plastic template around which Brooke outlined her pattern pieces "Care now will mean good results laters, uh-huh, it will. But scissors straight up when you cut these pieces. Be sure no slant or the growth factor will creep in, or it will be a mess when you put it all together. Aaron Anna," she called to a quilter way across the workroom, "don't lean over the quilt that far or you'll hurt your back again! Don't you know it's time to roll it on that frame?"

Busy hands stopped; everyone looked up, eyes wide and nervous. The two customers stared, too.

"Emma," Brooke said, "could you help me with something in the back room for a minute?"

"For a minute. Getting something done out here, that's what I want to see. Things been falling apart while I was gone, that's sure," she told Brooke as she followed her.

In the small storage room, Emma stood, looking out the single window at the rain while Brooke closed the door behind them. "Falling apart is maybe what I want to talk about, Emma. You don't think you came back too soon, do you? I mean, we really missed you, but you seem—oh, Emma, I don't mean to put you on the spot, but it isn't helping you to be back, I can tell."

Emma turned to face Brooke; her eyes looked hazy, but not teary. "Nothing is helping me, that's sure. But being back here is the best. For everything to be right here, that's all I want."

"I appreciate that, but you're usually not so—"

"Falling apart—like you said. Then, can you taxi me into Pleasant later, you think?"

"Pleasant? To the doctor?"

"With more pills I'll be fine, just to get through."

"Prozac? Have you talked about it with Levi?"

"No wonder I can't keep calm!" she cried, smacking her palm on the sash of the window. "Yourself it was, Mrs. Verna, too, showed me thinking for myself. You two don't ask a man for this and that."

"Emma," Brooke said, feeling she was dealing with one of Jennifer's passionate if illogical outbursts when she was far too tired, "Verna and I are not married, and not to an Amish man who rules the roost."

"A man's place is the head of his household, but problems of his own, Levi has. Why should he have to worry about everything for his Levi Em?"

"I do believe it's good even for married women—even Amish women—to make some of their own decisions, Emma. But if you're feeling so desperate to get these pills, Levi should know that you need help and—"

"Desperate? Need help? Good hard work and more faith in God's will for taking Katie, that's all I'm needing!" She leaned her fists on the sill and bowed her head. Her shoulders slumped. Gently, carefully, Brooke put a hand on her back.

"I want to help, Emma."

"Just to see the doctor I'll stop by, like he said, to get the prescription refilled."

"If you're seeing the doctor first, that's good. I didn't mean to criticize."

"Good," Emma declared, straightening and turning to make Brooke's hand drop away. "Criticizing, enough of that I get somewhere else. And I thought we were friends."

"We are. I treasure our friendship."

To that, Emma only nodded' Brooke saw no tears, no real emotion on her face as she turned away, opened the door, and went back out into the room. Now Brooke stared out the rain-streaked window.

If Emma would see the doctor, she reasoned, perhaps she should take her into town. She could drop her off, deliver Jennifer to her party, then bring Emma back here before she drove out to check that barn. But maybe she'd just better observe her a little longer to see if she was even going to make it through the entire day without being taken home for rest.

Brooke went back to tracing and stacking her pattern pieces, but she watched Emma until she disappeared into the front room. She seemed quieter now, though she kept more to herself, which wasn't good, either. The pills had helped her cope before, Brooke thought, and the doctor had evidently insisted that she see him before he renewed her prescription. It was the doctor's duty to be certain Levi knew and to see to it that Emma was warned about side effects and counseled if need be. Besides, Emma's father was the bishop, who watched over the entire Amish flock, and she was close to her mother. Between the doctor, her family, and large Amish support group, Emma would surely receive the help she needed if she became dependent on Prozac. Brooke aligned her paisley pieces and went to find her friend in the front room.

Emma was just finishing up with a customer, so Brooke stood in the hall for a moment, rearranging pattern booklets and the fanned-out displays of quilted placemats on the narrow table. Yes, Emma seemed more her old self now—as if, after the tragedy—she could ever be that self again.

Brooke studied Emma's intent face, fair complexion, and her sturdy form—though she'd noticeably lost weight lately. It had struck her from the first that she and Emma were the same height with the same coloring—could almost have been sisters—though their appearances certainly varied beyond that.

Brooke had been slimmer, Emma plump, but now, with Emma's weight loss, that difference was disappearing. Brooke's pale brown hair had been through many lightening treatments, from streakings to full colorings, but nothing had ever tampered with Emma's completely natural tresses. Emma's soap-scrubbed skin, sprinkling of freckles, and pale-lashed eyes never felt a touch of cosmetics, while Brooke wore eye makeup and blush so she wouldn't look anemic or washed-out. Brooke's contact lenses allowed her to keep glasses off her face, unlike Emma's wire-rimmed, Coke-bottle, thick specs that Brooke remembered all too well from her elementary and junior high school days.

The Maplecreek Amish kept mirrors in drawers to be used for a quick peek each morning to assess neatness, while Brooke had grown up agonizing in front of mirrors over her glasses, her braces, her body. The Amish had plain, loose fitting, solid-colored clothing, but Brooke had to admit that the time, effort, and worry saved by Amish women was worth something. In their society, they would never be judged by externals alone. In some ways, at least, weren't the Amish really valued for themselves and, therefore, more independent and free from rules, customs, and demands than worldly women? But Emma bore her burdens now, and she wanted so to help her.

When Emma's customer went out with her sacks dangling as heavily as her swaying silver earrings,

Brooke went over and touched Emma's arm. "I'll take you into Pleasant later," she told her. "In case you need to make an appointment, just use the phone here to see if the doctor can fit you in this afternoon."

Emma's eyes widened, then misted as she gripped Brooke's hand.

That evening Brooke's windshield wipers swished, swished as she leaned over the steering wheel to read names on mailboxes through the blur of rain. She would have to pick Jennifer up by eight in Pleasant, but this couldn't take long. The continued rain had allowed her to risk coming in the early dusk, just after she dropped Emma off. She only hoped Emma had told Levi where she'd been and that she was back on her Prozac prescription. Brooke felt relieved, at least, that she had seen the doctor, and that should help. Maybe, Brooke thought, if whoever killed the kids could be caught— Amish forgiveness aside—that would help Emma to go on.

Finally, Brooke passed the mailbox painted MILLER. She tapped the brake pedal to slow even more.

Good—the barn could be seen from the road and looked deserted; the place didn't have a garage, so she would not have to check that, too. She drove on and turned around in the next distant driveway. Then she started slowly back.

She had learned a lot about people living on Sawmill Road when she'd dropped Jennifer off. Sally Neff, Jennifer's friend's grandmother, who was helping with the party, had been Maplecreek's rural mail deliverer for years. When Brooke intentionally mentioned she didn't know people who lived farther out from town on Sawmill, Sally had recited them in order, including,

"Rhonda Miller, whose husband up and left her with a house and barn on two acres she's like to up and sell to the Amish someday, like other old homesteads up that way."

"Rhonda Miller," Brooke said as she pulled the car into a farmer's lane before a closed gate to a field, "I'm going to up and visit your barn to see if your lover is hiding a damaged red car there." Brooke had also learned that Paul Hostetler—"Who liked cars and got a new one 'bout every year"—did indeed own a red car.

She turned off the wipers, lights, and engine. Despite the rain on the car and the distant rumble of thunder, it seemed so silent out here. When she got out, even with her umbrella, her slacks and jacket were soon soaked by blowing rain. Still she bent the umbrella into the breeze as she walked back along the road past the Miller house and barn, then ducked through the crumbling, split-rail fence. As she bent through the rails, one foot landed on an unseen bottle on the other side. It rolled. She went down on one knee, soaking it, sitting spread-eagle hard on the rail, her umbrella snagged in the fence.

"Ouch! Damn!"

At least she had not turned her ankle. Still trying to keep somewhat dry, she rolled the rest of the way through and pulled her umbrella after her. Two identical liquor bottles lay here.

"Stupid Americans! Booze and litter even out here!" she muttered.

She hated it when people just tossed things out of cars. The bottles looked so out of place here, Scotch no less, Glenbrae brand, which she had never heard of, with a bagpiper on the label. The one she'd fallen on looked sealed and partly full. She wouldn't mind a good slug of something to feel dry and warm out here right now herself, but not something anyone else could have been drinking.

She kicked the offending bottle so it clinked into the other and went on, surveying her broader surroundings. The vast stretch of fields here, as Daniel had said, belonged to the Stottlemeyer farm, which would be auctioned off—contents of the house and barn, too—next month. Brooke knew how important buying that land was to local Amish farmers, like Levi Kurtz, so their sons could settle and farm in this area without having to move west and break up the essential community of families and church.

Now she had to watch her footing through slick, uncut grass to give the house and its driveway a wide berth. Hoping Rhonda Miller did not keep big yard dogs as many families out here did, Brooke plunged on, straining to hear barks, planning if she were spotted or stopped to say she was just out walking on the old Stottlemeyer place and had been caught and confused by this rain. As long as they didn't notice she had a flashlight protruding from the pocket of her jacket, that little cover story would surely do. But she didn't want to use a light outside the barn unless absolutely necessary. She could still see a few feet ahead of her if she went slowly.

She held her breath as she looped back to the faded red barn, then sidled around its perimeter, looking for a door not facing the house. She had noted lights glowing inside the narrow house, and two cars—neither of them red—in the driveway, one a blue Intrepid. How ironic that Paul was also paying a visit. Still, just because he committed adultery hardly meant he'd committed vehicular homicide. But she had been burned by defending her last client with such a defense: even if he abused his wife, it didn't mean he would kidnap and rape a woman, she'd argued, more fool she.

Besides, if Paul had hidden a wrecked car here—one headlight had been broken in the crash and there must be more damage than that with the paint scrapings on the buggy pieces—he could have moved the vehicle long ago. She mustn't get her hopes up.

Her flashlight poised, Brooke unlatched a tall side door. She saw it slid on a track instead of swinging. Protesting with creaks and groans as she shoved it, it gaped wide enough to let her in. She froze, listening, but no sounds came from the house or within the barn.

Damp, stale smells assailed her as she shook and shut her umbrella, then stepped in. She slid the door closed after her; her stomach knotted, for now she had become an intruder. That really bothered her, but she had to know if there was a car hidden here.

Gray daylight and blowing mist filtered through the high loft door set ajar where they used to haul in hay. This place felt almost old-fashioned friendly, she tried to convince herself, with the rhythm of rain on the roof and walls. She clicked on her flashlight and swept the beam around the deep, quiet cavern of the interior.

Milking stalls, old cracked crocks, bare dusty floor, a feeding trough. A roll of old carpet and one of barbed wire, rusted rakes and hoes, a refrigerator crate, a green Toro lawn mower. She slowly shuffled farther in, suddenly angry with herself for playing this long-shot hunch. Daniel was right that it would be too fast, too difficult for Paul to hit those kids, then come down here, change cars, and race back to help. Besides, Paul had seemed friendly and candid; he had actually sought her out at the funeral. She felt like a scolded kid again with her too active imagination, her Nancy Drew

140

detective books she used to devour, the forbidden police shows she watched with her dad. This was a wild-goose chase and—

A shrill hiss careened at her; air fanned her face. She ducked and covered her head. A bat? Something bigger? The flashlight flew, hit, and rolled under the trough, plunging the barn to blackness but for a halo at her feet. Brooke dropped to her knees, reaching way under, feeling for the flashlight. She had to get down on her stomach to rake through deep dust, cobwebs, and something else.

"Ugh!"

She sighed with relief when she retrieved it. Grimacing, she furiously wiped mouse droppings off her hand onto the rag hanging over the lawnmower handle. Her series of sneezes from the dust echoed. She held the flashlight between her thighs to blow her nose, telling herself she must keep calm. However hard her pulse pounded, nothing here would harm her.

She played the beam upward and saw the source of her surprise: a blinking owl with a white, heart-shaped face sat on a nest wedged between two beams, tearing something red and wet apart to feed open-billed little ones. She shuddered again. It must have flown in through the loft door above. Assuming it would not attack, hurrying now, thinking of picking up Jennifer soon, she began a purposeful circuit of the barn.

She stubbed her toe on a bag marked "Cement." She went around it, skimmed the beam of light everywhere. She jumped when a raccoon skittered away, scolding. Then she stopped and stood aghast but triumphant.

In the farthest, back corner, draped with dark tarp, rested a large vehicle of some sort, no doubt a car. And her light caught a patch of exposed crimson surface, shiny as blood out there on the road that night the kids were killed.

Her heart thudded harder to match the distant thunder. Her mind raced ahead to what she must do next. Call Sheriff Barnes from her car phone. No, she didn't know his number. Drive into town to find him, get Jennifer, come back out here with him. He would have a fit if she just phoned the highway patrol. She'd phone Jake tonight, too, and thank him for all his help. Her luck had changed. This hunch about Paul Hostetler had been a good one!

She held her breath as she lifted the piece of tarp off more of the red trunk or hood. To think she had found the car that killed Katie, all of them, but she could not tell what part of the chassis she was looking at. Had it been disassembled because it was wrecked or could be secretly stored easier?

She shoved the tarp back farther, and her beam snagged block letters: RIDE THE TILT-A-WHIRL! FUN AT THE ROSCOE COUNTY FAIR! Under her foot was a piece of track that was also part of the amusement ride. Just beyond, on the slick red surface of this single car, a painted clown face stuck his tongue out to laugh at her, but it was hard to see because tears blurred her eyes like rain.

CHAPTER EIGHT

AS IF TO MAKE UP FOR A RAINY, SLOW—AND BLUE— Monday, the Sewing Circle was full of tourists by late morning the next day. Although Brooke's Amish staff always became quieter as outsiders made the bells on the front door and the antique cash register ring, the place itself got noisier. At times, snippets of conversation erupted from the purposeful hubbub, but unless someone was trying to question one of the salesgirls or the quilters about the accident, Brooke let most of them just roll past her.

"Oh, Dorothy, aren't those Christmas hangings just cute as a bug's ear? I know it's over six months away, but . . . Do you believe this one is nine hundred dollars, Kelly? What do they think this old farmhouse is, Neiman Marcus? . . . Don't tell me the Amish aren't rolling in money at these prices, I don't care how tacky they dress . . ."

So it caught Brooke's attention at once when the front display room she was overseeing went suddenly still but for a few hushed whispers, including, "Look, Mom. That can't be Ann-Margret, can it? *Here?*"

Brooke looked up to see a stunning, green-eyed, thirtysomething redhead, flanked by two tall men, just inside the front door. The woman instantly commanded the room, though she didn't try to. It was hard to look away from her vibrant coloring and perfect features.

The statuesque, shapely stranger was wrapped—one could hardly say merely dressed—in an aqua, raw silk shirt and stonewashed jeans unlike any Brooke had ever seen. Instead of studs on the pocket corners, tiny silver stars held the material together and glittered from the belt loops. The belt itself was set with nuggets of turquoise in silver settings. Other than a watch, she wore no jewelry except her natural beauty—a goddess almost unadorned. That is, no jewelry Brooke could see until the woman lifted her left hand to brush back her wavy, shoulder-length hair and gave an inadvertent flash of a diamond chunk almost the size of an Amish watering trough.

She spotted Brooke behind the counter and made her way toward her. Shoppers parted like the Red Sea for Charlton Heston. One of her escorts hovered near the door, eyeing customers, but managing to look very uncomfortable. Dressed in jeans and checkered shirt, he reminded Brooke of the Marlboro man caught at a bridal shower. The other man, in tow behind the goddess, was at least twenty years her senior, but he wore his age well. He had an alert, open face framed by silver hair his thatched eyebrows and gun-barrel gray eyes accented. But for pale circles where his sunglasses had been he was very tanned.

"Hi, there," the goddess spoke in a whispery voice instead of peals of perfect tones Brooke expected. "You in charge here?"

"Yes, hi," she said, extending her hand over the counter. "I'm Brooke Benton. How may we help you?"

"I'm int'rested in starting an Amish quilt collection, and I've been reading up on it. Oh, Ms. Benton, this here's my husband, Hank, and over there's our driver, Mitch, and I must admit we're strangers here, but enjoying every minute of our visit to your area. And I'm Kiki, Kiki Waldron. Here, I've got a card in case some of this will have to be on special order instead of what we can buy today. You all do mail things out, don't you?"

"Yes, we do quite a custom-order business, though not usually as far away as"—Brooke glanced down at the embossed vellum business card with surprise—"Las Vegas. However did you happen to find our little shop, Mrs. Waldron?"

"Oh, you just call me Kiki, please. I mean, everyone does." She turned to her husband. "Now that you know right where I am, Hank, how about you and Mitch go ahead with your business and pick me up back here in an hour or so—if that's OK with you, Ms. Benton."

"Brooke. Yes, of course. I'd be glad to show you around."

By the time Brooke took Kiki back to view the quilts in progress, the noise level was almost back to normal, however hard women still stared, worse than men would have. But as unearthly as Kiki Waldron's beauty was, Brooke found her very down-to-earth.

"I just adore country things," Kiki said; "I mean, real pioneer Americana country, not those little howling coyotes or plastic cactus or forty-dollar Kmart quilts and Indian blankets where I'm from."

"I know what you mean. Amish souvenirs are either treasure or trash."

Brooke wondered why a woman literally as well-heeled as this—snakeskin boots peeked from under the star-studded jeans—had been shopping at Kmart, but then, from the way she talked and her endearing lack of shrewdness and subtlety, Kiki must have an interesting past. Brooke tried again, this time more indirectly, to cross-examine her about how she ended up here, of all the Amish quilt shops in this area.

"Have you been going from shop to shop to compare quality or cost, Kiki? No problem, since a lot of shoppers do."

"Not if they were as pressed for time as we are here. Kind of found you like a blind hog finding an acorn. That's the story of my life, in a nutshell—well, didn't quite mean it like that," she said with a little laugh at herself. "It's just Hank says that Lancaster County over in Pennsylvania, which most people think of as the real heart of Amish country, is just too touristy to bother with these days—you know, like flashing neon signs that say PLAIN COOKING—and we heard Ohio's got the biggest number of Amish now in the country and is still kind of untouched but with lots of tourist int'rest, being kind of between Columbus, Cleveland, Pittsburgh, and all. We had to wait fifteen minutes to get breakfast in town, and Hank's not used to that, no way. He hates waitin' for what he wants."

"You should see Maplecreek on weekends," Brooke told her. "We've even got people coming in from all over by the busloads."

"But that's good—for business, right? Oh, I just love that one!" Kiki cried, staring up at the Bear's Paw double-bed quilt hung on the wall. Brooke steered her over to the two huge revolving racks of folded quilts. "Do you need Southwest earth tones?"

"Oh, just show me everything!"

Kiki continued to amaze Brooke as she selected six quilts from the first rack, three from the second—little gifts for friends at home, she explained, not ones she wanted for her collection. She placed custom orders for five for herself, pointing out patterns she wanted and describing the colors in a breathy but entirely serious Jacqueline Kennedy whisper while Brooke jotted down her specifications.

"And if they are everything I'm sure they will be, I'll be ordering more," Kiki concluded as she and Brooke loaded down three Amish girls with the quilts to be wrapped. Brooke recognized four by Emma in the selections, so Kiki did have a fine eye for quality, even though wisps of insecurity kept blowing through her conversation and she kept twisting her chain-link watch on her slender wrist as she spoke.

"Wait till Mitch sees he's got to get all this in our rented car and then in the Lear. I always travel light—

Hank says he's proud of me for that—but he's like to tan my hide when he sees all this. Now, how long a wait for these custom quilts, you think?"

"Many Amish women make one a month in the winter, but there is a waiting list. I'll have to glance at how long it is right now. And if you want a particular quilter, as some collectors do . . ."

"Oh, will you just look at that quilt in there!" Kiki interrupted and darted through the open door into the back storage room. Brooke quickly followed to see she referred to Emma's unfinished Wedding Ring Quilt, which lay over an ironing board. Emma had brought it here for help to get it quilted and bound, for she could not bear to do it by herself now. But Brooke had heard her tell two others she wanted it done soon so she could give it to Daniel and Barbara Yoder as soon as they were published in church.

Brooke knew what "published" meant—an announcement of an engagement. Daniel Brand was making certain his feet were firmly planted on the path to Amish eternity by planning to take an Amish wife, and you couldn't do that until you were baptized. But, strangely, besides making her feel so sad, it made her love for this quilt even more poignant, because its beauty would someday grace Daniel's marriage bed.

"Oh, it's just gorgeous!" Kiki said, touching it tentatively, then tracing a completed section of quilting with her fingertip. "This one doesn't look quite done, but how much does it cost? I'd pay anything to have it. It's that Double Wedding Ring design."

"They just call it Wedding Ring around here. But it's not for sale."

"One thousand dollars—would the maker take that?"

"Kiki, it's an heirloom gift for—the brother of the

maker. And it was partly stitched by the woman's daughter who died recently, so it's very special."

"Oh, sorry. I see. In that wreck down yonder everyone uptown was talking about?"

"Yes."

"What a tragedy. But I would like one real similar, maybe even by the same quilter," she told Brooke as she led her back out into the main room, where the plastic-wrapped quilts awaited, stacked by the front door. "Believe me, I've learned the hard way in life you just wait for the things that are really good to come along."

Brooke's eyes met Kiki's uptilted, jade green ones, and they agreed without a word or nod. Her fingertips touched Kiki's glossed nails as she took her credit card and rang up the total, which included one-third down for the custom-made quilts. Wait until she told Verna about this sale and paid the consignment fees to the quilters. Emma alone would have hundreds of dollars going home with her today, so that ought to cheer Levi up.

"Now, whatever are you doing here in Amish country?" Kiki asked Brooke the same question she had tried to ask her.

Brooke shrugged and sighed. "I'm a lawyer from the big city who just got stressed out, and decided my niece and I could use a breath of country air," she said as she handed back the card and the receipt. "Here, let me give you the card for the shop, but I or Verna Springs, the owner, will be in touch with you about the progress of your quilts."

"And I'll want more, I'm sure I will, if"—her voice came even quieter as her husband stuck his head back in the door and she fluttered her fingers at him—"Hank does not lay down the law about it. I've got plans for them, I'll tell you that. And before I'm done, I swear I'm going to do his office walls in them instead of all those awful painted cow skulls on blowing sand, too."

"We'd better help them with those quilts," Brooke said and came around to lift one from the stack Kiki pointed out to the amazed men.

"All those, darlin'?" Hank Waldron asked. "What in the world . . ."

And then Brooke realized who Hank was. Hank Waldron of Waldron World Entertainment Enterprises—WWEE on the stock exchange—the conglomerate a recent article in *Time* magazine said was the Disney empire's biggest challenge. Waldron owned luxury hotels, amusement parks, and who knew what else nationwide. She recalled something Elizabeth Crandel had said about Waldron doing a possible buyout of some Ohio Seaworld parks, or was it dealings in Cleveland with the Rock Music Hall of Fame or something?

But she wasn't going to say anything. All of a sudden, Brooke knew more about Kiki: the beautiful, second—or third—younger wife and the gap of experience and deluge of gossip that must entail. She sympathized with this obviously self-made woman more than Kiki would ever know. But this was Kiki's show today, and she had no intentions of ruining that for her by recognizing her husband's power or fame.

"It's been a pleasure to meet you, Kiki," Brooke told her as the men muttered darkly. They filled the trunk and one side of the backseat and floor with plastic-coated quilts, a stack of them seat-belted in place so they wouldn't slide. Brooke noted they had no luggage, so it must be stored elsewhere—or had they simply flown in for the day just to buy quilts? It appeared

Mitch really was their driver, though Brooke wondered now if he wasn't their bodyguard, too. She fought back a grin: a bodyguard in Maplecreek?

"It's been great to do business with you, Brooke," Kiki returned the compliment as they shook hands. "I'll be in touch." But Kiki's green eyes lit as she spotted something over Brooke's shoulder. "Oh, aren't those beautiful display racks!" she exclaimed and made straight for Daniel Brand, who was unloading quilt racks from the back of his new, shiny buggy across the parking lot. She followed Kiki toward him.

"Are these for sale here, Brooke?" Kiki called back over her shoulder.

"Well, yes," she admitted, "but the shop hasn't even paid for them, so—"

"Oh, I'll pay this man directly, if that's all right, sir."

"If Miss Brooke agrees," Daniel said with a nod.

Brooke said nothing for a moment. Daniel's stilted formality sounded so strange after what they'd shared. She felt the impact of reality: in the eyes of everyone but themselves, he was only an Amish craftsman she had hired, a neighbor. And the Amish knew he would become betrothed to Barbara Yoder soon. Suddenly, she felt annoyed, at him, herself—at the mess she'd made of her theory that Paul Hostetler might have been involved in the wreck. And now, Daniel stood like a tree trunk with his arms at his sides, his expression deadpan when she knew he studied Kiki for his own silent critique, just as he often did her.

"If Mr. Brand can make the shop some new ones soon, fine," Brooke told Kiki.

"Well, they're just beautiful!" she said and smiled up at him.

Brooke wondered how he handled all that wattage

150

without so much as a smile, nod, or blink, as if he had indeed short-circuited. She watched Hank Waldron pay Daniel cash for two racks, then waved to Kiki as they pulled out in their big car with its Cuyahoga County Ohio license plate.

Brooke helped him carry the rest of the racks into the shop. "Daniel," she said, keeping her voice low, "I'm moving ahead with my investigation of the wreck, and I was hoping you'd at least advise me—"

"I can't. I don't know anything else. Besides, pursuing this could be dangerous for you, tracking down a no-doubt desperate killer, even one who just drove a car."

"I'm only going to restage the wreck in similar conditions. All I wanted was for you to tell me where I can get the back of a courting buggy like the kids were in. But, never mind. I can ask around, get one myself, even if that tips others off to what I'm doing and turns more Amish than you against me."

"Brooke, I'm not against you, believe me. I just wish," he said as he finally looked into her eyes at the door to the shop, "you didn't live here, so close and all."

She had nothing to say to that. And, though she was sure he didn't mean it, when he carted his burden through the screen door, he let it swing back in her face.

Kiki kept her eyes on the rolling meadows, tended lawns, bright gardens, and fertile fields as they drove toward Maplecreek, then Pleasant. How restful, how hopeful the soft greens and twisting streams and fringes of spring forests. Imagine a place that really showed the seasons and had this much variety. What a pretty spot for people to visit. Sometimes at home, the man-planted beauty of precisely placed palms among clipped shrubs in pebbled yards, all fed by spewing sprinkler systems,

151

just sapped her strength. Here, she could breath cool, fresh air with the promise of moisture in it.

She tried to soak in everything she saw—until just beyond Pleasant when they passed a run-down-looking trailer park called Enchanted Acres.

She closed her eyes to shut it out, seeing not this sign but the one that read HAPPY HAVEN. She always felt queasy when the past sneaked up to slap her in the face like that. Putting her hand out to steady herself, she snagged the plastic wrapper on a quilt and drew back. The feel of it was like the torn tan plastic couch they had in the tiny, cluttered living room of the trailer. It brought back everything cheap and tawdry and torn from her past. And all that reminded her she was Hank Waldron's trophy wife and that—just as her dad had deserted her mother—Hank had left his wife for a Vegas showgirl.

"I said, you asleep back there, darlin'?" Hank asked and turned around, his arm along the back of the seat as he spoke over his shoulder. "I'm missin' sittin' next to my girl, but Mitch doesn't need that tower of quilts sliding onto him while he's driving. These poor people don't need another accident around here."

"I know. It's just terrible. But I'm awake, Hank."

She smiled back, loving him, wishing that some others approved—especially Hank's heir-apparent, her stepson, Garner. And friends of Hank's well-connected first wife, Anne, and the boards of the art museum, the symphony, and the planning committee for the Desert Gold Charity Ball, where "Queen" Anne still held sway. Just because Kathleen Buckland Waldron had come from nowhere, been a showgirl at the Trop, and sold real estate shouldn't mean she couldn't make some cultural contributions befitting the wife of one of Las

Vegas's—the country's—biggest business moguls.

Why, years ago, Hank had worked his way up, too. And it bothered her deeply that Hank never talked business with her. If only she could show him she was worthy to be part of things! If only she could be more like that lady lawyer back there. Why, Brooke Benton didn't go on vacation but just got in on a whole new business career with those gorgeous quilts. A busy tourist area like this could probably handle several shops like the Sewing Circle, and help employ the Amish, too. How she wished she could be a patron of something or other, just like Hank's first wife.

But for now, she guessed that Clay and Matt, her younger brothers she'd reared in a trailer court like that one back there, would still be her charity work. Hank had recently appointed them to the special projects division on WWEE, so maybe she'd just bounce an idea off them. Heaven knows, those two owed her. And they loved her—they'd have to help.

"Just an hour to that corporate airport where the Lear should be waiting, Hank," Mitch's voice interrupted her agonizing.

"If we can get off the ground with Kiki's newest passion loaded on the plane," Hank said and reached back to squeeze her knee.

Playfully, she slapped his hand. "You're my oldest and only passion," she told him and laughed. Hank chuckled, but soon went back to talking to Mitch about the new pro basketball team he now owned.

By kerosene lamp, Daniel Brand banged and ripped away on his custom-tiled kitchen floor late into that night. He ground the blade of the knife into the joints to score them, then chipped the grout away. He chiseled

153

and broke each piece of tile to get it out, then attacked the mortar bed beneath it. It was a horrible, grueling job, but it suited his mood.

He stopped only for lemonade from the big jar Barbara had sent home with him this evening when he'd had dinner with her and her parents. With fierce concentration, he began to work in the remaining corners of the floor, blasting at the ceramic pieces with his hammer. The craftsman part of him regretted the destruction of the bright sunburst pattern pieces, but they would not do in an Amish home. Nor could the tiles be salvaged to resell at auction, because they were just too hard to get up otherwise—and it just had—to be done.

He carted the rest of the rubble outside to add to the pile beside the back door. Bit by bit he would haul the pieces away when he made deliveries so as not to weigh Bess down too much. Leaning against the house, he sucked in a chestful of sweet night air. The stiff northwest wind felt good, cooling his sweat that had made ceramic and grout dust stick to his skin. He felt drained, but at least he would sleep tonight And hopefully, not just lie there, both wanting Brooke Benton and wishing something would make her leave Maplecreek so she did not tempt him so much.

When she finally fell into bed, Brooke realized she had made a mistake. For the first time since the accident, she had been so frustrated she had eaten a double-chocolate Dove Bar and washed it down with iced tea. It was the first ice cream she'd touched in days since she always pictured the Amish kids downstairs, eating ice-cream bars for their last meal before their executions, so to speak. Now, when she was exhausted from this day, she had foolishly pumped her body full of caffeine and could not sleep.

She tried to pray herself to sleep the way Jennifer sometimes seemed to. Since the unfairness of Melanie's death, Brooke's faith had wavered, but here in Amish country, prayer always seemed possible. She said a too hasty amen, then just stared at the moon spilling across the foot of her bed, mingled with the yard light from outside through the drapes she'd left slightly open. That was another of the good, wholesome things about country living: fresh air and no fear of anyone looking in windows, at least not second-story ones she didn't hesitate to leave cracked open. She's heard some of the Amish didn't even lock their doors at night.

Then, through the swish of leaves outside, she heard a crack and a pop as the light through the window dimmed. What a time for the yard pole light to go out, she thought, just as she heard another sound. Deep, droning, slightly distorted, like a cassette tape when the batteries run low—a man's voice! But it was fairly loud; she did not have to strain to hear.

"Woe unto you, ye lawyers! For ye lade men with burdens grievous to be borne, and ye yourselves touch not the burdens . . ."

She gasped and froze. What? Who? It sounded tinny, mechanical. Maybe it was through a megaphone—a loudspeaker. For one moment, she even considered that she might be dreaming, that this was a nightmare and not reality. No, it was both.

Jennifer! She slept so soundly and at the back of the house, but she'd have to check on her. The voice came again.

"Woe unto you, lawyers! For ye have taken away the key of knowledge; ye entered not in yourselves, and them that were entering in ye hindered."

The impact of the words registered now. She slid out of bed, fumbled for her glasses, and crouched to peer out the front window without being seen.

Through the shifting leaves of the front maple trees, she could glimpse a form from the waist down, apparently a man, legs slightly spread. His moonstruck shadow cast before him revealed more, the silhouette of an Amish man with the straight-cut trousers and jacket, broad-brimmed hat pulled low. It was a head-on shadow, not a profile, so she could not tell if he was bearded. He threw a long shadow, seemed quite tall, maybe as tall as Daniel.

She tried to force fear away to focus more clearly. He had recited Old Testament-type curses against lawyers, obviously against her. "City lawyer!" Daniel had called her. She knew she had to check on Jennifer, but she knelt there, transfixed. Her heart pounded, her legs shook under her.

"Woe unto you, lawyers! Laying wait for him, and seeking to catch something out of his mouth, that they might accuse him!"

Yes, she saw now in the shape of shadow that the man held a bullhorn of some kind. She should race down, turn on the porch lights if he hadn't ruined them, too, see him, confront him. But she stayed put, shuddering, half wrapped in the drape, stunned as the message sank in.

"*Geh weg, Weh. Geh weg, Weh!*" the voice kept repeating, evidently in German now, and then, even as she stared wide-eyed at the shadow, it was gone.

She darted out into the hall. Grateful she heard no sound from Jennifer's room, she tore downstairs, hit the porch lights, ducked low to see if the man was still out

156

there. Nothing, unless he was hidden behind a tree trunk. Had he left? Could he have gone around the house? Would he try to get in? She could call the sheriff, but if the man were gone, she could report it tomorrow. Besides, she'd called in the police before when she had nothing to show, nothing she could prove, and what good had it done her?

Then frenzy froze her and she stood panting, pressed against the wall. Somehow, her Columbus stalker had found her! Elizabeth had accidentally told someone; Jake had let something slip. But no, she trusted them. Or could Mr. Stedman have insisted Elizabeth tell him where she was living? Or could that slick Ray McCarron have wheedled it out of Elizabeth? Even though she knew Ray was a snake, he was a very seductive one and Elizabeth was always one to go for men like that. Then Brooke recalled Ray had used Jake's services before, too—and she herself had recommended him. Somehow, somehow, her tormentor—whoever he was—had found her here and dressed like an Amish man so she wouldn't know.

She darted around the first floor of the dark house, peeking out each window, holding her breath to listen at the doors, hearing only the tick of the workroom clock, the wind outside, her own panting. Quotes from the Bible, that's what the voice had recited, and then the German.

Or was it really someone Amish? she thought. They were peaceful people, but they were people. After the mess she'd made of things here—keeping the four teenagers out late, then flaunting her investigation of the wreck in public—surely, the Amish didn't want her here. She knew Levi didn't like her and Daniel's father would want her gone, too, and he had a deep, sonorous

157

preacher's voice. Even Daniel himself had said just today, he wished she didn't live here. But no, *no*, surely it wouldn't be any of them.

Her heart still thudding, she tiptoed back upstairs more than once to peek in and listen to Jennifer's even breathing. A miracle and blessing the child slept so heavily. Brooke got dressed, went back down to keep a vigil where she could protect the house better. She grabbed a quilt from the revolving rack and made a nest in the corner of the workroom floor for herself, armed with a rolling pin, a kitchen cutting board with a handle, and a butcher knife. She wished she'd bought a pistol at home, but she never would have known she'd need it here, even if she'd owned one. Besides, she feared and hated them; she had seen the havoc they wreaked.

She sat bolt upright, wrapped in the quilt, gripping the knife, until dawn stained the sky bloody red.

CHAPTER NINE

AT SEVEN-THIRTY THE NEXT MORNING, BROOKE put Jennifer on the school bus, then checked to see the big yard light had indeed been broken. She even found the stone that had probably been tossed into it. She hurried back in the house and phoned Elizabeth in Columbus before she left for the office.

"I can't believe it!" Elizabeth cried when she told her about her unwanted visitor. "No, kiddo, honest to God, I told no one where you are, not Mr. Stedman, not Ray, my secretary—not my own mother."

"As Amish as the man looked, despite what he said, it's not like them. And I don't know what would be

158

worse—that Columbus maniac finding me here or the Amish actually hating me that much when they're so forgiving of a multiple killer."

"Brooke, I'm so sorry. Is there anything I can do? Are you going to call Jake for help again?"

"I can't ask him to protect us like before. It would ruin things for Verna and me if I had a live-in man here."

"I—I just thought of something. Kind of a long shot but I had a big stack of your mail in my office last week. I mean, I usually package it at home, but I was in a rush."

"And someone saw you with it—saw the package after you addressed it to me here?"

"I—I really don't think so, but it was on my desk when I got called to Lord Myron's office. But my office door was closed and Penny was sick that day, so I didn't even have a secretary popping in—or guarding the door."

"So someone could have seen it. Elizabeth, I just don't know what to do."

"Oh, one other thing, something really off the wall, I suppose. That *Live at Five* TV reporter, Brian Broward—the one who was like a leech in the aftermath of the Kistler mess—has called twice to ask if I knew where you were for a follow-up interview."

"That bastard will do absolutely anything for a story! At least it was an anchor from the other station who interviewed me after the accident here, and she didn't recognize me. But Brian Broward's a friend of Ray McCarron's, isn't he?"

"Takes one to know one with those two. Ray wants to be attorney general someday and Brian's probably only shooting for Dan Rather's job. But all this, kiddo—the stuff on my desk, Broward's phone call—it's probably nothing, because your late-night caller sounds like he had to be Amish . . ."

When they said good-bye, Brooke felt no closer to an answer—any answer. But she still had an hour before her staff arrived so she checked to be sure all the doors were locked and hurried over the hill to talk to Daniel. Perhaps he'd have an idea about who her uninvited guest could have been.

She hurried so fast she got a stitch in her side. She forced herself to take slower strides as she approached his back door, trying to get her breath back. The door stood open, and she could see through the screen that the inside of the kitchen—the floor at least—looked a mess. So that was the cause of that pile of rubble.

She heard Bess whinny from the back building and realized he was probably out there. She strode to the open double door. Daniel's back was to her as he hefted a grain sack.

"Daniel, I need to talk to you!" she called to him.

He jumped and dropped the sack; Bess shied. He spun to face Brooke as grain spilled from the sack to bury his bare feet. His unbuttoned shirt displayed dark chest hair that swirled to a point below his navel and disappeared into his jeans, held up now by narrow hip bones and not suspenders. Stubble shadowed his chin and lean cheeks to hint at the dark, thick beard he would grow once he was married in the Amish church. He had probably just washed his face, because damp, curled tendrils of hair clung to his forehead and temples. Bleary eyed, he didn't look as if he'd slept well.

"Don't you know not to sneak up on horses and men who haven't had their breakfasts?" His frown testified to the fact he did not intend a joke. He patted Bess's flank

160

hard—slap, slap—to calm her before he bent to gather handfuls of feed in his hands and heave them so hard into her trough that some bounced to the floor again.

"I'm sorry, but I need to talk to you about a late-night visitor I had."

"Who?" he asked, scooping grain.

"A tall, Amish-looking man whose face I couldn't see. He stood in the front yard and recited biblical curses against lawyers through a bullhorn. Specifically," she went on, as he stood and gaped at her, "my mystery visitor thundered, 'Woe to you, lawyer!'"

"Is Jennifer all right?"

"Thank God, she slept through it. I—I didn't tell her this morning because I can't bear for her to go through all that again—like at home. She's felt so safe and content here."

"You must have been terrified. But who around here would do such a thing?" He walked partway toward her, then stopped, hands clenched stiff at his sides, legs slightly spread. She could tell he was fighting to keep from opening his arms to her. And if he had, she would have run straight to him. Instead she sat on a bale of hay just inside the door and told him everything she could recall about her visitor. As she spoke, he came to sit on the edge of the bale, leaning forward, away from her, elbows on his spread knees, head down to stare at his clasped hands. His jaw tensed as she talked.

"That's terrible," he said. "I can't believe—can't think who here would do that, even if everyone knows you're investigating the accident. It's not our way."

"I realize that. The thing is, it could be the man from Columbus again. He's clever. If he knows I'm here, he could cover his tracks by dressing Amish, though this man *sounded* Amish, too."

161

"Wait here a minute," he said, then added as if she would argue, "will you just wait here a minute?" She nodded, though once he was gone, she wished he hadn't left. He was back shortly with two glasses of orange juice and a Bible under his arm. Though he'd shoved the shirttail in his jeans, he had buttoned his shirt only partway, and he was still barefoot. She took the glass of juice he extended, then rested it on her knee while he sat beside her.

"Drink," he ordered. "You look shaky, and it will help." He edged closer to her on the hay, making it move and creak, as she took a sip. Flopping the big, well-worn Bible open, part on his knee, part on hers, he flipped pages and pointed. "The man's curses are from the book of Luke. See, here, here, and here."

She bent over the big Bible. "You've underlined those sections."

"I underline a lot that interests me. Lately, lawyers interest me."

Their eyes locked and held. Just as, she admitted to herself, lately Amish furniture makers interested her. Even when they were helping each other, working well together, this man absolutely scrambled her emotions. He was frustrating and fascinating, naive and knowledgeable. Surely, it was just that he was so different from any man she'd ever known, she assured herself. That was the attraction—even through the pain and frustration of dreadful events lately.

"As for that German phrase you say the man kept repeating," Daniel went on, "it sounds like *geh weg Weh*, which means 'go away, pain, go away, woe.' Amish mothers sometimes recite it when their children are sick."

"Oh, great," she said as he closed the Bible and put it

aside.

"But you and Jennifer are all right, and she didn't wake to have it frighten her, that's the good news."

Brooke nodded and they sat silent for a moment, while Bess shook her head and shuffled through the layer of hay and the grit of spilled grain in her stall. Daniel downed his juice and put the glass on the floor.

"I know I shouldn't be here alone with you," she said. "I don't mean to endanger your relationship with Barbara Yoder, your parents, or Emma. And I don't want the Amish here turning against me anymore than against you."

"You know," he admitted with a shake of his shaggy head, which looked rumpled from his pillow, "maybe Maplecreek just isn't the safe haven either of us wanted." She longed to smooth his hair with her hand, but she didn't move.

"You keep mentioning your past," she said quietly. "I told you why I'm here in Maplecreek. What really brought you back?"

He heaved a huge sigh. "I left Goshen because I was involved with an English woman, blond, bright, clever."

As he told Brooke a generalized, sanitized version of the story, he saw it all again in the stark, shameful detail of reality:

Tracey Stevens had careened into his life like that car down the dark hill. A freelance writer from the Indianapolis newspaper doing a series of articles on the Amish of Goshen, she evidently decided he would be the perfect person to illustrate how not all Old Order Amish stayed faithful. But Daniel blamed himself, too; he did not resist and then even encouraged her advances. She'd helped him, too, for under the pen

163

name of "Amish Andrew," he had written several articles for *Carpentry Crafts Magazine,* and she gave him some pointers and proofread his stuff. But the thing was, she was so seductive, so sweet with that scent of perfume that got even stronger when she stood there and began to shed her clothes for him that evening in the dimly lit Land O' Goshen Motel.

"Come on now, Daniel. It takes two to make this happen. I don't think I'm the only one overdressed for what we want here."

As he slid his suspenders down and unbuttoned his shirt, he could not take his eyes from her blond beauty; he had to touch her again. All the times she'd wet those lush lips with her tongue tip, crossed and recrossed her silken legs so her skirt slid up, the times she'd taken his arm to press it to her breasts, and blown in his ear in the workshop to make him grab her—all that strung a man tighter and tighter until he was ready to snap.

He pulled her to him even as she spilled herself from her bra and raked his shirt open, snagging her nails in his chest hair. Her forwardness, her hunger, surprised him, so unlike Amish girls he'd smooched with and touched. But nothing he believed in mattered now if he could have Tracey. They hadn't talked about it, but they'd make a life somewhere, and he'd support her, and she could do her pieces for the paper at home with the kids. He clamped his big hands around the soft globes of her bottom to lift her hard against him, while her fingernails scratched his back right through his shirt. To his amazement, she parted and lifted her legs to clasp his still-clad hips as if she could ride him like a stallion.

"I knew you could be like this, not so self-controlled," she whispered in his ear and licked him there.

"Marry me, Tracey! Say you will. I've been so torn so

long about my future, but if you . . ."

He almost dropped her when a knock pounded on the door.

"Tracey, you there?" a man's voice shouted. "Let me in, bitch, or I'll break it down!"

To Daniel's horror, Tracey squirmed from his grasp, stepped away, and unlocked the door. A balding blond man stood there, out of breath, but obviously for a far different reason from Daniel.

The man exploded into the room. "Think I wouldn't find the address of this place on your desk?" he roared, and leaped at Tracey to slap her so hard her head snapped back and she fell to the floor.

"Wait!" Daniel shouted and jumped the man as he dared to kick Tracey's hip so hard she curled up and rolled against the wall. "Who are you?"

"Don't tell me she gave you the 'I'm single' line!" the man roared, shoving Daniel back. He hauled Tracey to her feet. "Yeah, no wedding ring again, huh?" He slapped her again so her hair spilled over her face, down to her breasts in a curtain. "I'm her husband, lover-boy, that's who I am," he shouted, not looking away from Tracey. "Hey, who you got here this time, bitch, one of the Beatles with that haircut?"

That froze Daniel for a moment. He saw he'd been doubly deceived and stupid. He'd believed her, wanted her. But he could not bear to have her beaten by this brute. Daniel jerked the man away from her, pinning him against the wall.

"If you're her husband, take good care of her, not bad!"

"Let go of me, you son of a . . ."

Daniel yanked him forward, then slammed him into the wall again. Fury at Tracey, at himself drowned him.

Never do violence, he heard a voice, but he shut it out. He'd shut out all the other *Do not's* lately.

But his newest surprise, his next reward for his utter naïveté, was when Tracey leaped against him, pummeling his back and shoulders, screaming, "Let him go, you bastard, let him go!"

Shocked, Daniel did just that, gaping at her.

"Chuck," she sobbed, on her knees, clinging to the man's belt even as he began to unbuckle it, "I wasn't going through with it. I just wanted you to show you still cared, that you'd come for me—please take me home, please take me back again, punish me, I deserve it, but please take me right here on the floor, then . . ."

Disgusted to his damaged soul, Daniel grabbed his hat and coat, and walked out. Walked the seven miles back to his apartment, vowing never to be taken in again by any woman, vowing to really go home again where he would be safe from such temptation and degradation. In Maplecreek, such intimacies would not be brutal in a motel, but tender in the privacy of a home.

Finally, he finished the halting, brief explanation he'd given Brooke, and looked to see her reaction.

Brooke watched Daniel move a little pile of sawdust and hay around with his toes. She realized what he had admitted had cut him deeply. For most men, an unfortunate entanglement with a woman would be a lesson learned and left behind, but for Daniel Brand, Amish born and bred, however he clung to remnants of his rebel past, she saw it still loomed large. And it helped to explain why he had been so hard on her at first.

"Daniel, I'm sorry about what happened. Besides, you—you have Barbara Yoder now. Do you think someone in her family would have wanted to scare me off?"

His head snapped up; his eyes seemed to focus again. "I hope," he said, turning toward her, "she doesn't know that you're any threat to her, even though, right now, you are."

She felt entranced, mesmerised by the depths of his eyes. For once, words failed her. They huddled together, foreheads almost touching as he took her hands in his big, calloused ones.

"Silence suits you sometimes," he whispered, "so I will talk. I see I am not ready for a marriage commitment—to anyone. Barbara and I were far from promised, but I'll have to make my error clear to her and suffer the consequences."

"Emma—"

"Will be disappointed, and I regret that, especially with all she's going through right now. But it's the right thing for me to do. Most people I know will be disappointed, but not you, I hope."

"No."

"Good."

He smiled again to devastate the remnants of her poise. "And that man," he went on, "the one you called down here to help you find clues at the accident scene—he's just a friend?"

"Yes."

"Is there someone else who could perhaps be more than a friend to you?"

"I am starting to believe so—dare to hope so."

"Could you describe the suspect for me, please."

She laughed low in her throat as Daniel pulled her slightly closer so their thighs and hips melded. "He is dark-haired," she whispered, "tall, and entirely too

167

brazen for—for his Amish calling."

"Isn't this like a cross-examination in court?" he asked, his voice warm and soft. "I used to watch Perry Mason reruns on my roommate's TV."

"Is that where all this comes from? That's another sin on your long list of them, Daniel Brand."

"Guilty as charged."

She felt they shared their breathing, slow at first as if they held their breaths, then faster. She could see her reflection in the black mirrors of his pupils. And then, just when she thought he would embrace her, he lifted her into his lap.

"I told myself," he said, "after Tracey, there would be no one else for me outside the faith. Then I decided I would not do this until I made things right with Barbara, but . . ."

He cradled her in his arms; their heads were at the same height. She met him halfway, willing, wanting the kiss she saw coming. Even at the slightest touch of his lips—like in the darkness the other night—she felt a soaring, over-the-hill ride, caught between desire and destruction.

Slowly, almost carefully, he moved his head in little, yearning circles to prolong the kiss; she matched him, slower, even more deliberate, savoring it all. She lifted her free hand to touch, then tangle in the thick hair at the nape of his neck. His fingertips, gentle as the breeze, traced her ear, caressed her cheek and chin and, like a warm, living necklace, lowered to grasp her throat where his warm thumb rested in the hollow there to stroke, stroke her sensitive skin. His hands and fingers felt so strong, calloused and hard, yet so tender.

He began to explore her face again with fingers, then lips, from her pounding neck pulse to the corners of her eyes, then to barely brush her eyelids. She clung to him, shifting closer. Her breasts flattened against his chest, her hip to his hard thigh. With one iron arm around her waist, he grappled her to him, obviously relishing each movement and moment. It went on as their mouths met and held, moved, then melded again. She held to him, her hands holding to his upper arms and shoulders, then clasping his strong neck. Like her, she could tell he was fighting to control himself, leashing his need.

She had not imagined kisses could go on so long and yet pass so quickly. He took and gave, drained her but restoked her roaring sensations No wonder the Amish wed after just a short courtship. If this was what the Amish meant by smooching—and if the outside world found out—everyone would want to be Amish.

His beard stubble scraped her cheek, chin, then throat, as he trailed kisses downward to her fluted collarbones. She wanted that rasp of stubble and slick tongue along her skin, she wanted him to tease and touch and take—

"*Ach*! Dan!"

They jolted apart. Brooke almost fell through his legs. Emma stood aghast just inside the door Daniel stood and steadied Brooke to her feet.

"I—oh!" Emma cried and threw her apron up over her head. She flopped it down, turned, and ran out.

"You'd better go talk to her," Brooke said when Emma dashed out. "The look she gave me, she won't want me. And she's been so down lately, we can't just let her go rushing off."

He went after Emma while Brooke collapsed on the bale of hay. Her hands clasped together, her knees knocking as if she were chilled, she heard Daniel and Emma's conversation in the yard without having to

169

eavesdrop at all.

"Wait, Emma!" Daniel yelled and grabbed her arm. She shook him off and turned her back on him, but stopped near the pile of broken floor tiles.

"Dan, this I can't believe, just can't!"

"I know you like Brooke," he said to her back.

"Now I know you do, too! Dan, you're still a fence-jumper, and that's the way everyone will see it when they cast you out, this time for good!"

"Brooke cares for you, too. It was worrying both of us that we could hurt you—"

"Oh, worrying about me, that's what you were doing, I could tell!" she went on, crossing her arms over her chest.

"I intend to tell Barbara it was too soon—just wrong—for me to court her. You know I haven't spoken for her yet, and wouldn't have been with her half so much if you hadn't tried—"

"Planning for the two of you, I thought I could control that, at least. Some happiness, some order in things I'd find for you and Barbara." She lowered her voice and turned her profile to him. "Right through the roof, that's where Dad's going to go if he gets wind of this."

"Is he going to get wind of it? Why are you here so early?"

"Pointless now, that's sure. On my way to work to see my trusted friend Brooke, thought I'd ask you and Barbara to Saturday supper, and saw you weren't inside the house. Good thing I came when I did, I'd say!"

"Emma, when it comes right down to it, what I do—at least before I join the church—is my business."

"*Dummkopf!* Your conscience has to be that of the

170

community! You think this is still *rumspringa*? But yes," she said and turned to face him at last, "I do like Brooke, but she can't be for you, not for long, Dan. Tell me true. Losing Katie, it brought you and Brooke together, didn't it?"

"In the beginning, yes."

"Famous last words, 'in the beginning.' With what she's doing about the accident, you helping her now? Dan, please tell me."

"I've helped her some and—yeah, I might."

"That roof Dad would go through, you'll bring it crashing down on yourself, on Brooke, too, that's sure. But sometimes, I would sleep easier, I think, if whoever did that to Katie and the kids was at least put away, so he wouldn't do it to others."

Tears shimmered in her eyes. He dared to reach out to grip her shoulder. "Praying," she went on, "about the killer being caught, that I been doing, though not aloud with Levi. Brooke, you still in there?" she called.

Brooke emerged from the shadows of the little barn and stood for a moment with her hand on the latch of the open door. Daniel yearned to go to her, but that would only make things worse. Her eyes looked heavy, her mouth a bit pink and puckered, from what it was obvious to all. And the way the two women were glaring at each other, as if he weren't even here, worried him.

"Emma, she came to me for help," he tried to explain. When neither said a word, he plunged on, "Because in the middle of the night someone shouted at her to leave Maplecreek, someone dressed Amish, who threatened her through a bullhorn."

"Oh, no," Emma whispered. She and Brooke still stared each other down. Daniel kept looking back and forth at them, nervous, not knowing what was coming.

171

Like many things in life, he realized that he might be in the middle, but this was something for womenfolk to solve.

"Emma," Brooke said, approaching slowly, "I'm not sorry about Daniel and me, but I apologize if it has caused you pain or maybe ruined your plans for him."

"It can't come to good for Dan, *if* committed Amish he finally wants to be. But you two have made your own bed and—what I mean is both of you know this, and I—I can't cast a stone. Oh, tongue-tied, that's what I am. But I mean, tell on the two of you, I won't, not unless I'm asked, and then I can't lie."

"Of course not. I wouldn't expect you to," Brooke said as she came even closer. "I hope this won't come between us at the Sewing Circle. When Verna gets back, you won't have to put up with me."

"Put up with you? Cared deep for foolish friends and family before, I have," she said with a little punch at Daniel's upper arm. "On your heads, the two of you, not mine! Besides," she added and her voice broke before she turned to Daniel, "stood up for me before when she thought I was wrong, Brooke has, so now's my turn."

Daniel wanted to ask what she meant, but he knew to leave well enough alone.

"Come on then, Brooke," Emma said, starting away. "It's almost nine. Waiting to get in, workers and customers, too, if we don't get there soon. I'll walk you back, uh-huh."

Brooke nodded and hurried to catch up.

"Danny, to see you so early, what a good surprise!" Barbara greeted him at the back door of her parents' farmhouse with a bright smile and brighter eyes. Always pretty, Barbara Schneider Yoder, he thought, even when

172

she was a gangly girl. Lively, a bit flirty, even possessive—he'd liked that in her at first. But it showed she needed someone steady, someone settled, and that was not him.

"Saw you coming, Mother did," she went on, clapping flour from her hands. The warm, rich, yeasty smell of baking wafted out to curl around him. "Come in, come in."

As he stepped inside, Daniel noted with relief that even if Mrs. Schneider had seen him coming, she was not now anywhere in sight, though two humps of half-kneaded bread dough lay on floured boards on the table. Mrs. Schneider would not be glad she beat a hasty retreat when she heard why he had come.

He cleared his throat. "I have a busy day with furniture deliveries, so I thought I'd stop now." She looked so radiant, so—expectant—that it made things worse. Once before, when he'd left, he had hurt her badly. She had married Chris Yoder on the rebound, as worldly folk put it. Now, especially after her early widowhood, he felt doubly bad to hurt her again. He knew if he had one bit of horse sense—Amish sense, that is—he would just blurt out that he wanted her to be his wife as soon as he made his final commitment to the church this autumn. A good time for baptisms and weddings, just after harvest, his father had said the other day.

"Danny, what is it? You can tell me. Here, sit down, and I'll get you some coffee and a doughnut."

He turned down the offer, annoyed that she still called him Danny as his family had years ago. Only Emma called him Dan instead of Daniel, but never Danny anymore. Did Barbara think he was a child she could lure yet with treats and coddling?

173

"I can't stay. Barbara, I can't stay because I've been wrong to push things so fast between us. Coming home to patch things up, the accident, trying to get my shop ready. You'd think after everything and my time away, I'd know what I wanted from life."

"Losing Katie, I understand, but don't you be fussing it was your return in exchange for her departure, like some of the old folks said. Taking things at your own pace, you've always done that, Danny. And you were like my miracle from heaven, though maybe I've been in too much of a hurry. The Lord can give me patience, uh-huh—patience to wait for something worth having."

This wasn't going well. She came closer and took his arm, leaning her full breast slightly against him. He could feel its pillowy softness even through the layers of clothing. Slowly, he lowered his arm and stepped back. Her touch left the faint ghostly imprint on his arm from the flour.

"I don't know how to say this kindly, Barbara, so I'll just say the truth. Don't wait for me, expect things from me that others expect I can't promise or ask for your hand. As a matter of fact—even though I know it's going to cause me problems with some I love best and want to make happy—"

"Oh, no!" She blinked once and tears clumped her dark lashes. "I thought . . . Emma thought . . . my mother . . . yours . . ."

"I know. I should have made it clear from the first that I wasn't thinking, but was just going along. You deserve a new husband—a family, but it can't be me, Barbara, not now, not later."

"But even the years you were away, I cared for you," she cried, before she clapped a hand over her mouth. "Though I was happy with Chris before he died," she added.

"And deserve to be again. Forgive me, Barbara," he added. "I've already explained things to Emma, and she—she understands."

"Oh, no," she repeated, looking stunned. She came to him and laid a hand on his chest. "Another of the sisters, it's not that you . . . ?"

He cursed himself for flushing hot. "No. I hope you will find a good man and go on with your life."

He opened the screen door, but she came right behind him onto the porch to try to take his arm again. He did not stop.

"Whatever you say, I'll be waiting. After the menfolk build you a shop and you get that house Amishized, when you're settled, you'll need a wife, Danny Brand, and I know—"

"You don't know, Barbara. And maybe I'll never be settled!" He climbed quickly up to seize the reins. "For your own good, forget me—us." He clucked to Bess and, as if the horse sensed his pain, she beat a quick retreat for him. He brushed faded flour handprints off his arms and chest as he turned out onto the road.

When Daddy said good-bye all the way from London across the ocean, Jennifer held the phone for a long time, pretending it was his hand. But it buzzed loud, then beeped. She knew Aunt Brooke was watching, so she hung it up on the kitchen wall. Aunt Brooke had talked to him first, so Jennifer guessed she didn't have to tell anything he had said.

Besides, it was the same. He was busy, he missed her. She didn't exactly believe him anymore. And, even though she wanted to, she didn't think he'd really buy her a horse like he said today, either. He'd said things

175

like that a lot of times, then only got her those fish that got frozen back in Columbus and had to be buried in the flower bed. But now Aunt Brooke was kind of watching her sideways, so she thought she'd better say something to make her feel better.

She was ironing little pieces of her quilt she had stitched together on the sewing machine to make sides of a circle that would turn into a big wedding ring somehow. Mrs. Kurtz had told her she really had to be careful how they went together, so this was just practice to see if she could do the real rings right.

"Daddy said there are still steeplechase horse races in England, like in *National Velvet*," she told Aunt Brooke.

She held her iron in the air, not moving now. "Has he been to one, Jen?"

"No, too busy. Can I go out back to look at the Amish horses at the hitching post? Two buggies and a cart are here, I guess to pick up the quilters."

"All right. Tell Mrs. Kurtz I'll be right down, will you?"

Jennifer told Susie's mother the message on the way out. Sometimes after Daddy's phone calls, she and Aunt Brooke would talk a lot, but not now. Jennifer guessed maybe Aunt Brooke was sad or mad about Daddy always making promises like "see you soon," but then he didn't do it, and just stayed busy and far away. Jennifer felt sad and mad, too, but she didn't want to say so, either.

She hurried out in back and petted the horses. Mr. Bauman and Mr. Detweiler nodded and talked to her. An Amish man she didn't know waited with a real pretty brown horse with two white feet, kind of like the Pi's feet looked in the movie.

"Good horse, old Sam, yeah," the man said to her.

"Oh, it's a boy horse, a stallion."

"A gelding."

"What's that?"

"Better ask your parents."

"I can't, but I'll ask my Aunt Brooke. Can Sam jump?"

"Amish horses not jumpers," he muttered as he climbed up in his buggy. "Want to hold the reins, drive her down as far as the road?" he asked.

"Oh, sure! Thanks!" she said and climbed in.

The last time Brooke had glanced out the window—just a few seconds ago—Jennifer had been talking to an Amish man she didn't recognize from here. Now, Jennifer—and the man and his buggy—were gone.

Reality came crashing back. That threatening voice last night, the fact she had chosen not to tell Jennifer about it so she wouldn't be afraid here among the gentle Amish. But where was she?

Without a word to anyone, Brooke darted down the stairs and hurried through the busy downstairs rooms, her eyes skimming them for Jennifer. She hadn't come back upstairs; she would have heard her. Brooke shouted 'Jen!" down the basement stairs, then ran out the back door. She jagged the entire circumference of the house, shuddering inwardly as she dashed past the place she'd seen the man last night. But in broad daylight with others around, what could have happened?

She loped out to the garage where they kept Verna's car. That reminded her of the stupid search she'd done of the barn down the road. What a mess she kept making of things. Where was that girl?

"Jennifer Reynolds! Jen, where are you?"

On a hunch, she ran down the back lane toward the

pond. And in the distance saw Jennifer, rocking back and forth on her "horse log," talking to it, holding reins made of vines in her hands.

"Thank you, God," she whispered. The child carried such a burden about her parents that she could not bear to tell her about the Amish visitor. She'd just keep her close, watch her better, and tell her only if their unwanted visitor returned. She shouted, "Jennifer Reynolds, there you are! You scared me to death!"

Jennifer saw Aunt Brooke come running. She hadn't see that bad look on her face since before they left Columbus, when she was real scared to let her go off anywhere alone. She'd only come back here after getting to drive a buggy for a couple of minutes. But now, Aunt Brooke only hugged her shoulders hard.

"You said it's okay if I ride my horse," Jennifer protested when she got hold of the Pi again and Aunt Brooke stepped back.

"But you said you were going to look at Amish horses! I saw you talking to that tall Amish man I didn't know, and then you just weren't there when he drove away! Oh, Jen," she said, "I didn't mean to yell. I just didn't sleep very well last night. And I should have known you like to be alone after talking to your father."

"I was telling the Pi I don't believe Daddy anymore. I don't want him to come here, because he'll just leave again and tell lies."

"What lies, sweetheart?"

"Like 'I miss you' and 'I'll see you soon.' Mommy left because she *had* to, but he left because he *wants* to."

Aunt Brooke slipped her arm around Jennifer's shoulders again and sat sidesaddle on the Pi's back behind her. Jennifer pretended to pull the Pi to a stop, but she didn't yell out "Whoa," as she wanted to. Aunt Brooke looked as if she'd been scared enough today.

"Jen, your father misses your mother and you, too, he really does. I believe he is telling the truth about that. The only thing is, he can't face raising a little girl on his own."

Jennifer sighed and patted her horse's neck while she thought about what Aunt Brooke had said. Then she lifted up her leg to sit sidesaddle and hug her aunt back.

"In the movie," she whispered to Aunt Brooke, "when Velvet went to the racetrack, they said something I remember."

"What was that, sweetheart?" she asked, wiping under her eyes, then resting her chin on top of Jennifer's head.

"Her friend said to Velvet, that it's too bad your mother isn't here. You know, because her mother had to stay back at home and not go to the racetrack."

"Yes."

"And then Velvet said, 'But my mother's here, and she's inside me,' like, you know, Velvet still feels her love there," she said, touching her own chest with one finger.

Aunt Brooke was crying again, but Jennifer felt her nod. "Is that the way you feel about your mother, Jen?" she whispered and cleared her throat.

"Sure. I got her inside me and got you outside me. And the Pi and Bess and Mr. Brand, who knows what horses mean to me when Daddy really doesn't."

Jennifer was going to explain that she liked Susie, too, but Aunt Brooke was hugging her pretty hard and her shoulders were shaking, so she didn't say any more right now.

Above the distant desert rocks outside Las Vegas, the

179

sunset painted the sky crimson. Kiki Waldron thought it was a beautiful evening. She reveled in serving as Hank's social hostess when the guests including people from the WWEE offices. It made her feel part of his empire more, although Hank's rule about *no-business-spoken-here* still applied. It was also a great opportunity for her to subtly promote her brothers, Matt and Clay Buckland. Unfortunately, such a party also meant she had to deal with her stepson, Garner, who was so damned condescending—at least out of Hank's earshot—that she could have spit her drink at him. Being with Garner was only slightly less chilling than being with his wife, Sarah, who might as well as have been carved from ice, like the big WWEE logo on the buffet table.

But Kiki felt immensely better when she glanced up to see Matt and Clay across the room in deep conversation without their dates for the moment. Good, she thought. She'd been meaning to get them alone for a little heart-to-heart ever since she'd returned from Ohio.

"Hank, honey, I'll be right back," she told him and left his side for the first time this evening. Speaking briefly to many people, she made her way across the sunken living room.

Kiki was really proud of her brothers, and proud of herself for the way they'd turned out, too. Tonight they looked so handsome—tall and bright with their blond good looks, though she hated those blotchy-flowered, pastel ties instead of the conservative stripes they should have chosen. Sometimes they still needed her for the smallest things, but she was finally learning to let go.

Matt saw her coming and evidently told Clay. When he turned around, his frown made her hope he wasn't drinking too much tonight. Matt got only loud and grandiose when he drank, but Clay got just plain mean.

"Great party, Keek," Clay said, to relieve her mind. "But doesn't the country quilt collection look a little out of place here?" He rolled his blue eyes toward the array of Amish quilts she'd displayed on her two Amish-made racks and draped along the rough stone walls surrounding the freestanding hearth.

"You never did have an eye for interior decoration," she scolded, "neither of you." To assure herself, she surveyed again how the sprawling house and lofty-ceilinged living area complemented the big quilts, as if they were oversize primitive paintings. This great room overlooking the free-form pool and lantern-lit gardens through a back wall of glass seemed to her the perfect setting for the quilts. The white leather couch and long bar, the careful combination of glass, carpet, stone, adobe, and lit shelves of ebony pueblo pots and two Georgia O'Keeffe paintings detracted nothing from the impact of her Amish works of art.

"He didn't mean," Matt put in, "that they aren't beautiful pieces. But if you've ordered more, where the heck are you going to put them all?"

"Now, that's what I wanted to talk to my brilliant, rising-star WWEE projects division brothers about," she said and hooked her arms through theirs to steer them outside toward the pool. Clay's Scotch sloshed down his chin and onto his shirt when he tried to drink and walk, and Kiki pulled out his handkerchief to dab at him.

"I'm all right," he said and snatched it back. "Besides, you know Hank says no business talk outside the hallowed halls of headquarters."

"But I want you two to advise me—on the q.t.—

181

about an idea I have. About the quilts and all."

"To make a few extra bucks you want to sell them instead of Tupperware or Amway products," Matt put in and chuckled at himself.

"Don't tease," she said and smacked his arm. "I want to open a quilt shop/museum in Ohio, maybe in coordination with a sort of Amish village, where visitors could see crafts being made. You know, help the Amish in the process with jobs and all and preserve their unique culture. I think I might even have someone local there who might want to work with me—a woman lawyer, no less."

She felt annoyed by the surprised—or was it shocked?—look Matt and Clay exchanged. "I *can* do it!" she went on. "And I don't want Hank to know until I'm sure I can make everything work. If I can just show him I've got some business savvy—and can promote a project and idea—I'm sure he'll back me on it."

"It's a very possible concept," Matt said, and took a big swig of his drink. "Don't you think so, Clay?"

Darn them, she thought. Were they fighting to keep straight faces when she was dead serious about this?

"We'll keep your secret, Keek—and talk about it later," Clay said and went back inside to the bar again.

"Listen, Matt," she said, unwilling to be put off, "I've got some seed money I can use at my discretion."

"So who's this lawyer?" he asked.

"Her name's Brooke Benton, and she's running the shop where I got these quilts just outside of Maplecreek. It's so beautiful there. I wish you two could see it! One thing we'd need to do, of course, is buy some land in that area. I could ask her to act as an agent and—"

"No, Kiki, listen," he said and grasped her upper arm firmly with his free hand. "Your instinct to keep this quiet is good, and I'm honored you asked us to advise you. It's exactly the sort of thing Hank's got us on lately—acquisitions, sites, theme parks. You're little Amish villages may just be a great idea."

She stood on tiptoe to kiss his cheek. "Thank you, darlin'. Something on a small scale for starters will be fine, and we can go from there, just like we've always done, the three of us."

"Batten down the hatches," he muttered, squinting over her shoulder. "Here comes Hank, and he's got Garner—God's gift to the universe—in tow. Kiki," he said, turning back to her and talking fast, "mum's the word on your idea for now. And don't contact that woman lawyer in Ohio, either, so we can keep this all in the family—the Buckland family. Got that?"

"Sure, Matt," she said, feeling so excited now. "Absolutely got that!"

CHAPTER TEN

EMMA PANICKED THE MINUTE IT HAPPENED. Somehow the plastic bottle of Prozac tipped, and the capsules spilled out to bounce—to clang and clatter, it seemed to her—on the wooden bedroom floor. She had meant to take one to the bathroom with her, but she could already hear Levi's steps, coming from the bathroom, coming to bed, as she shoved them this way and that under furniture with her foot, hoping he would not see one.

But the moment he came in, barefooted, he stepped on one that had evidently skittered clear over to the door. "What's this, Em?" he said, stooping to squint at it. "That pill of yours! It can't be left from before," he announced, displaying the half green, half white capsule between his thumb and first finger. "Emma?"

Lord forgive her, she actually considered lying to him, but he knew she'd been back to housekeeping lately and the floors were immaculate. She only had the will to clean because of that little pill he held, if only she dared tell him so.

"The doctor, I saw him again," she began, clasping her hands before her, "and he said—with my depression—to have the prescription refilled, just once, for a while, was fine."

Levi closed the bedroom door quietly behind him. "A worldly crutch, Em, that's what this is. A crutch for a woman who's got no right to feel crippled with all the blessings she's got. Faith in the Lord, the church, the folk, the family—me. Strength for daily living, all that should give you, not this."

"On all that, I do rely," she said as she watched him twist and crush the pill between his fingers. Powdery stuff came out, sifted to the floor. If he asked for the rest of them, she'd refuse him. If he found them, at least she'd still have the ones she'd shoved under the furniture. But he sat on the end of their bed and patted the place beside him. She went.

"Em, God's will it was about Katie and the baby, too. Accept that and go on, we have to, all of us."

"All of us didn't bear them, tend them. All of us didn't see our younger, best selves in Katie. Right now I need the pills, but I'll get off them soon, husband. How I feel, I can't help that, the black hole of sadness I sometimes can't climb out of."

He took her hand in his, turning it palm up, then covering it warmly with his free hand to sandwich hers in. She could feel the slight grit of the pill powder on his skin. Her hand, herself, she felt caught and trapped.

"Husband, you call me," he said, his words and voice calm with a strength she admired and wanted for herself. However much she saw him as an enemy sometimes lately, she still loved Levi.

" 'Wives, submit yourselves to your husbands,' the Word says. Levi Em, you've got to lean on the Lord and give up those pills. Bodily sick, you're not, for that would make it different, and you'd need a doctor, sure."

"Levi we need our heads healthy, just like our bodies," she protested, sounding much too desperate when she'd meant to match his mood. "And 'husbands, love your wives' so—"

He pressed her hand hard. "You think I don't love you? If I didn't, I'd let you *fress* on pills, on any sort of poison. Emma, no more of those! The bottle of them, where is it?"

As she went dragging her feet to fetch it, she tried to estimate how many she might have kicked into hiding. She felt guilty for her deceit, but he was driving her to it. Get Brooke to take her back to the doctor, tell him the pills fell in the tub or the kids dumped them down the sink or—

"To get these, who took you into the doctor?" he asked as if he'd read her mind. Reluctantly, she lifted the bottle from its hiding place beneath her undergarments, glad to feel it felt so light, because there must be quite a few on the floor.

She didn't look at him as she answered. "Brooke. I asked and, finally, she agreed. I should talk to you, she said, but how you felt, I already knew."

"Our business, our marriage, I don't need her taking care of that for me!" he shouted. "Back to the city, that's where she should go!" As she handed him the bottle, he

185

went on more calmly, "More than get you these pills, that's what she's done, I know it. With all her doings, she's confusing you, pulling you and others away from the proper path, leading others astray."

Emma's hand jerked up. Surely, he could not know about Brooke and Dan! Or, since Levi had heard that Dan had given his regrets to Barbara Yoder yesterday, had Levi jumped to conclusions he must have someone else? He had never liked Dan's independence, always been quick to think the worst—even when he richly deserved it.

"What do you mean Brooke leads others astray?" she dared ask.

"Going after whoever hit our kids when it should be forgiven and forgotten—not forget our Katie, but the sinners that took her. And Brooke Benton's worldly woman ideas, they been rubbing off on you. Em, skilled with the quilts, that you are, but it's been too hard on you, pulling you in pieces, working outside our home."

At least he didn't know about Brooke and Daniel, but she scented where he was going with this, and she wanted to outright refuse and resist. But Levi was the head of the household, and she must have no quarrel with that if she wanted to be Plain People. Besides, she feared he would lose control again: she had never heard him raise his voice as he had just done.

"For a while," he was saying, "at least till Mrs. Verna comes back, especially since you got that extra quilt money and orders to make more, Amos Mary can take your spot at the Sewing Circle."

"But when I'm busy there, I'm better."

"Sure. Better enough to have to live on pills. Now, you listen. Busy enough at home with the quilting, too, you can do it here. When Ms. Verna comes back, when

186

things change, when you are better again, we can think this over. Em, you know Amos Mary needs the overseeing money more than we do, and you'll bring in plenty of quilting to do in the house here."

"But Katie's still everywhere here, Levi. To get out sometimes, it's good for me."

"Get out we will. The end-of-the-year school picnic this evening, you'll enjoy that, sure. Have some of the sisters in for a stitching party. The big auction's coming, and that piece of land up Sawmill for the boys to inherit someday, I want to bid on that so they won't be shoved out of Maplecreek to farm. Levi Em," he said and stood to grasp her shoulders tightly, "that woman is not the sort of friend for you."

Emma wanted to argue, but again she pictured Brooke in Dan's arms. Brooke could be Dan's doom, so why did he want her? And why did she still care for her—even trust her—when Brooke broke all the rules and kept her quest for Katie's killer alive? Levi was right that the sin that took Katie and those kids should be buried, too. Feeling both loved and yet betrayed by Levi, she hung her head and gave herself up to his embrace.

But as she turned her head against his shoulder, even in the dim spill of light from the lantern on the highboy, she saw another Prozac capsule on the floor. Taking his hand, she tugged him toward the bed, however he interpreted her eagerness to get him there. Then he would not step on that precious pill, and she could gather them by feel when she rose early in the morning.

Early Saturday evening Brooke loaded the dishwasher while Jennifer hunched over her arithmetic problems at the second-floor kitchen table. They had made a deal that Jennifer would not put her weekend homework off until Sunday nights anymore, even though the school year at Pleasant Elementary ended in several weeks. Because the Amish children were out for the summer yesterday, Jennifer had decided she could begin her vacation, too. Brooke had given her a lecture worthy of a courtroom summation about the fact they were not Amish, nor was it good to put things off until the last minute.

Now she glanced out the window and saw the square, black top of a buggy pulling in behind the house. Daniel!

But she saw the horse was not Bess. Her regret segued to trepidation, because the man who alighted—though his hat covered his head from this angle—was tall, like her nighttime visitor. Another man and a bonneted woman emerged, too, and the way the woman carried herself with unAmish elegance—that was Ida Brand. So the second man, with the long salt-and-pepper beard, must be Bishop Brand. And since, in place of Emma's presence at work on Saturday, a note had arrived from her husband saying she could not come and he would explain later, the first man must be Levi Kurtz.

Brooke dreaded another reason Daniel's family could come calling: somehow they had learned about her and Daniel—maybe asked Emma, and she had said she wouldn't lie. Then they had probably told her she was not to speak to her worldly friend again. Either that or they were here to serve her with their version of an Amish restraining order to keep her from investigating the accident.

"Jen, I see I have some visitors downstairs. But you stay put, and I'll check those subtraction answers when I come back up. This won't take long."

"It's not Mr. Brand?" she asked, squirming on the chair.

"Not your Mr. Brand, but I see his parents are here."

She wiped her hands and hurried down. Her insides knotted tighter; she recalled the day Daniel and Bishop Brand had come to invite her to Katie's funeral, the day she chased off those obnoxious tourists. But today, there would be no invitations, no chasing this away.

She opened the back door just after Levi knocked; evidently, he refused to use the doorbell. "Hello, Bishop Brand, Mrs. Brand, Mr. Kurtz," she greeted them. "I was concerned about your note, Mr. Kurtz, and I hope Emma's not sick. Won't you come inside?"

"Stopped just a minute," Levi said, not budging. "Now she's off the pills, Levi Em will be better."

So that was it, for starters, at least, Brooke thought. "I know Emma didn't think so," she said, "but I see you do. I'm glad she told you about them, though."

He frowned at her subtle challenge. "But after everything," he added, "she needs rest, to be home with her people."

Mrs. Brand stepped forward, putting herself slightly in front of her son-in-law. "Just for a while, Levi Em wanted you to know," she said with a nod that was probably meant to be encouraging. "Content to stitch quilts at home for now. Asked me to fetch her that list of what patterns that western woman wanted so you won't have to bother to stop by with it. The materials for them, Amos Mary can take those to Levi Em."

Emotions jangled Brooke's thoughts. At least this was not about Daniel, but to lose Emma's friendship hurt. She had feared helping her get the pills would be considered overstepping, but it angered her they would and could keep her from Emma, as if they were two

189

little kids who'd disobeyed. Oh, damn, this was probably some sort of warning sign to stay away from Daniel, too, even if they didn't know one blessed thing about their increasing involvement. At least they weren't asking her to leave, and the implication was that when Verna returned—when Brooke Benton was gone, no doubt—Emma could come back to the Sewing Circle.

"I see," she said. Tears stung her eyes. She knew exactly what Kiki Waldron's prioritized list of quilts read, but she was either going to cry before these people or shout at them if she didn't step away a moment. "The list of quilts—it's right inside, just one minute, please," she said and went in, closing only the screen door. Shoulders squared, she walked into the workroom that sat silent now, empty of dear Emma, who had reached out to her from the first, who had shared Katie with her and been like her Amish alien world sister. But, as she had just lectured Jennifer upstairs, she—they—were not Amish and never would be.

She leaned back against the wall and drew in a slow, deep breath. Breathe deeply in, out, concentrate only on your breathing, relax—advice she had given more than one defense witness before they testified on the stand. The prosecution awaiting her outside could no doubt keep Daniel from her, too, turn everyone against her if they could. She blinked back tears, wiped once under each eye, then went back out.

"Actually, Mrs. Brand," she said, wishing she weren't in jeans and a T-shirt for this interview, "the first quilt the western woman wanted was the same design Emma just brought here to be finished, the Wedding Ring. So I'll understand if she would rather begin the second one on the list, the Bear's Paw. I know after Katie's death, she didn't want to do the Wedding Ring. As you suggested, I can send the fabric over with Amos Mary, although I hope you will tell Emma for me that I will miss her *very much*."

"For sure, I will," Mrs. Brand said and tipped her head to send her son-in-law a cautionary glance around the edge of her deep black bonnet.

"The Wedding Ring, she can do that one again," Levi said, ignoring the look, evidently because he was craning his neck to get a squint-eyed glimpse of a low-flying airplane overhead only Brooke could see without turning around. The others did not pay it the slightest heed. "She's got to let Katie go, accept God's will for her death," he went on, turning back as the plane buzzed away, barely missing the tops of the tallest trees.

Brooke knew not to argue with Levi but she just couldn't let this pass. "Even if she accepts it, that doesn't mean the pain just goes away."

"Don't believe in God's will, do you, Miss Brooke?" Levi demanded, despite the fact that Bishop Brand cleared his throat in obvious warning.

"I do lately, Mr. Kurtz, I really do. Because I used to wonder what I was doing here in Maplecreek when I could have gone many other places to find peace for myself and my niece, and peace is not what I found here. I think it's God's will that I'm here to find out who killed Katie and Gideon and Cora and Ezra, four wonderful kids who showed me how kind and loving the Plain People of Maplecreek—some of them—can be."

"Levi," Bishop Brand intoned before Levi could answer. The younger man looked like he'd strangle if he wasn't able to reply, but he shut his mouth and stood his ground.

Brooke could have bitten her tongue for making the

191

situation worse, but it was too late for regrets—about anything—now.

"That sort of God's will is not our way, Miss Brooke," Bishop Brand said. His eyes, his voice were so like Daniel's that it added to the impact of his presence. "But who is to judge," he added quietly with a nod, "that the Lord God did not give to you this work."

Bishop Brand turned away and climbed back in the buggy as he had that other day. His wife and Levi followed. It took a moment for Brooke to marvel at the fact that, in his own quiet yet commanding way, hadn't Bishop Brand just given her permission to pursue her search—her work? But Levi's voice—at least when he accused her of unbelief—it had sounded like that other voice at night. Hadn't it? Now she wasn't sure. No, it couldn't be. She was momentarily relieved, and yet how could things be worse?

Levi clucked to the horse, and the buggy jerked, then rolled away, its steel wheels crunching gravel. When they disappeared around the corner, Brooke leaned back against the house and lifted her hands to her face. She'd like to explode in tears, but something perversely snagged at her sense of humor, too. In all the world—both worlds, her own and Daniel's—she could never have imagined a more dismal beginning with the family of the man she was coming to love. Yes, love, she was sure of it, however stupid that made her.

Against all odds, against logic, she was falling in love with Daniel Brand! A man who hadn't even been to high school, who believed in Adam and Eve and a real serpent in the Garden of Eden—and maybe, for him, that was her. He distrusted lawyers and, no doubt, thought a man must be the absolute head of his household. And his whole family—all but Emma—all his friends in this entire Amish settlement probably thought she was wrong and worldly and foolish and fancy. She really should, she thought, get herself an insanity plea and have someone commit her before it was too late.

"Aunt Brooke," Jennifer's voice floated down to her, "I see they're gone, and I did my subtractions. Can you check them now?"

Ah, Brooke thought, the voice of reason. This number minus this equals a definite that. Exact answers to problems. Certainly, knowledge, control. And she had someone to love in Jennifer that only a selfish, scared brother-in-law living in England could take away from her. Jeff Reynolds might send support money, but he had no support to give himself. No, she had to give that to Jennifer, even when she desperately needed someone to give her the same.

"Coming right up, Jen!" she called and went back in.

Not a half hour later, Brooke heard a car drive around in back. Nervously, she looked out the window again. Jake's van. She had not known he was coming, but after her confrontation with the Brands and Levi, she could use a friendly face. Jennifer was watching a videotape on the TV in Brooke's bedroom, so she called to her, "Our old friend Jake's here, Jen. I'll bring him up to the kitchen for some of those brownies!"

She went downstairs to greet him, uncertain whether or not to tell him about her Amish harasser. She knew he'd insist on helping out, and she felt bad enough he wouldn't let her pay him for helping trace the hit-and-run killer. And she could not have him down here riding shotgun, so to speak. Jake often carried a gun—an entirely legal one—but that made her as nervous as a live-in man would no doubt make the Amish—and Daniel.

"Hey-ey, country girl!" he said when she opened the door.

"Hey-ey, city boy!" She extended her hand, but he pulled her to him and gave her a hard hug. "Jake, I told you not to drive all the way out here when you got some information," she protested as she stepped back.

"Like we agreed on before, the place grows on you. It's a real pretty drive out, so I know you wouldn't begrudge me that."

Jennifer greeted Jake shyly with a smile and a handshake. They trooped upstairs for pop and brownies, and Jennifer told him all about school. When she went back to watching her video, Brooke showed him around downstairs and they strolled outside. Jake suggested a little walk down the lane, and they went on slowly. She admired a man confident enough to take a walk when it was obviously difficult. Brooke knew she should tell him about her night visitor now when Jennifer could not overhear; yet she hesitated.

"Is your father all right when you come out here for the whole day?"

"Sure, he's still not bed-bound or anything, though he doesn't go out much. You know, he'd really love to see this place. I'll have to bring him out sometime."

"Maybe for a Sunday dinner when things settle down," she said. "I really respect how you've taken him in, when I know that can't be easy on you."

"Like you taking in Jennifer?" he prompted, then went on before she could answer. "So, to the nitty-gritty. First off, I learned the highway patrol has reconstructed the accident, but they're not even telling the press what they learned. Dead end there, pardon the pun. As for the red paint on the buggy, it's from a GM vehicle, which doesn't narrow things down much. Oh, yeah, by the way, your illustrious friend Sheriff Barnes came in while I was looking at the buggy pieces at the gas station. He gave me hell for nosing around," he said and winked at her worried expression.

"Oh, no! But he hasn't called me to say anything."

"Good. That's 'cause I said you told me to keep out of the local police business, that they were handling everything just fine, but that a Columbus TV station, who remained unnamed, had sent me out."

"Jake! And he swallowed that?"

"If he hasn't bugged you again, guess he has."

"I can't believe you!"

"Little lie can't hurt for a good cause. I was just trying to protect you."

"I know," she said. "I *am* grateful."

"Thing is, then when the old windbag drove away and I pretended to set out for home, I U-turned and followed him to his house 'cause I saw he drove a red vehicle. After dark, I got a scraping of his paint—on both his police car and his red family car—and checked them out. Negative match, but it was just a hunch."

Despite herself, Brooke laughed. "What derring-do, Jake Kaminisky! I love it!"

"The guy ticked me off, talking to you like he did! Besides, hadn't you thought of him, too?"

"Fleetingly, but it was too utterly far-fetched."

"You been investigating cases as long as I have, little girl, you'll learn nothing is too far-fetched," he said. "So anything new on your part?"

She studied his eager face. Their eyes held. "Jake, you've done enough already, and I really owe you. But if I need any more lab-type work or advice, I will call."

195

He frowned and looked away. "Give any more thought to coming back to Columbus? It's been a while now. The perp there might have gone on to greener pastures—moved—who knows?"

"I've thought about it some. But not while Jen's in school, definitely not until Verna gets home, and that will be a few weeks yet. Jake, I still feel safer here than home."

"OK, but you just call me if you need me."

"Will do, boss." Again, she almost blurted out about her new problem here in 'safe' Maplecreek. But, telling herself it was for his own good and she could handle things, she took his arm and steered him back toward the house.

Late the next afternoon, when Brooke and Jennifer had packed a picnic to take back to the pond—she assumed they would not be forbidden to walk on the edge of Levi's land, especially on the Sabbath when no Kurtzes would be in the fields—Daniel pulled in behind the house. Brooke was relieved he had caught them as she had just locked the back door and they were heading out with their backpacks full of food. He was attired in his Sabbath best of tailored black suit—a frock coat with its straight, stand-up collars, trousers, white shirt, and black broad-brim hat.

"Whoa!"

"Hello!"

"Hello, ladies."

"You didn't come," Brooke began and walked closer to him while Jennifer fussed over Bess, "to tell me Emma's been exiled from the Sewing Circle, did you? Your family made that entirely clear yesterday."

"So I hear. I had no idea about her medication,

though I'd noticed things. You should have told me."

"I suppose I should have told you or Levi, but I haven't tattled on my friends for over twenty years."

He nodded, looking uncomfortable before he spoke again. "And I came to tell you that I heard in church this morning that Paul Hostetler's left town for parts unknown."

"No! Why?"

He shrugged, then climbed down. "It evidently took his family by surprise. Some think he found a better job somewhere, most say marital difficulties. But I also heard Rhonda Miller down the road has cleared out."

"Oh, dear. Then it probably is marital and not—criminal, though his running could be construed as—"

"That's all circumstantial until proven, madam lawyer."

"Yes, but it would be behavior consistent with someone who runs from a mess he's made rather than facing it—like a hit-and-run."

"True," he said, frowning, leaning one arm on the buggy. He looked so pensive for a moment she wondered if he were thinking that both of them had done the same by fleeing to Maplecreek.

"And, Daniel, I'm feeling a little guilty to think maybe my asking around about Paul is partly what made them take off. I've never seen a place where word spreads so fast without the media."

"Yeah," he said, then shook his head, "there are consequences for everything. Almost forgot," he said. "I've got the back of a borrowed courting buggy just like Gideon's propped behind the seat. Let's put it back behind the garage for now. After dark, I can put it on the back of my buggy and you can handle the car."

"Daniel, I didn't expect that! Thank you!" she cried,

clasping her hands and pressing them to her lips.

She realized that he had thrown in his lot with her to restage the accident. Yet he was still helping her only in ways—like his describing the accident to her—that they could keep secret between them. Would he still be on her side if he had to openly stand up to the Amish for her?

"Verna's big old Chrysler is still sitting in the garage here," she went on, "so I'll use that. She told me to start its engine once in a while anyway and that I could use it if I had to."

"And you have to"

"Yes, I do."

"I understand that now."

"You know, I think your father might, too, just a little. He said maybe God had given me this work."

Daniel looked surprised. "In your world he must mean, because he'd never accept it in his—ours."

She nodded, greatly relieved. Since last night she'd been worried that Daniel's family would tell him he must stay away from her, too. She had no idea how his promised farewell interview had gone with Barbara Yoder, but she was aching to ask.

"How's Emma?" she asked instead. "You didn't get a chance to talk to her alone at church, did you?"

"For a moment. She said"—he lowered his voice so Jennifer would not hear over her continued endearments to Bess—"that you should try to understand that her family came first, and we—you and I—had best be careful."

"And are you being careful? Driving in here on a Sunday afternoon, I mean?"

He shrugged, then frowned. "I worry for Emma, that's all."

198

"Aunt Brooke, please can't we have Mr. Brand and Bess come on the picnic with us? You said we had enough to feed an army, and Bess can drink from the pond. And there's grass for her. I'll bet Mr. Brand likes ham salad sandwiches and pickles and carrot strips and chips and strawberries and pop. *Please!*"

"I guess," he whispered as they lugged the back of the buggy behind the garage, "you haven't taught her much about feminine subtlety."

"I was going to ask you to go along myself. Just so Jennifer and Bess will be happy, of course."

He smiled, squinting slightly into the sun. He'd be so much better off wearing sunglasses, but then, none of them did.

"I haven't been out to that pond since I've been back," he admitted, "and we do have two able chaperones who are also enamored of each other. Let's go."

They lolled a golden hour away, eating, talking, then racing bark boats with cottonwood leaf sails across the pond. They took off their shoes, rolled up their pants, waded, and splashed. Daniel even removed his frock coat and hat and rolled up his sleeves. Still, with his suspenders, he looked too formal for the occasion. On her best behavior, Bess cropped grass while Jennifer watched. Birdsongs gilded the air and puffy clouds sailed the blue sky to make a second heaven above the rustling green clouds of leaves overhead.

"This place reminds me of *Walden Pond*," Brooke told Daniel as they sat, sated, even sleepy, with their shoulders almost touching, leaning against the same huge tree trunk. "That's a real place in a long essay by an American writer named Henry David Thoreau."

"I know Thoreau. I've read his work on marching to a

199

different drummer."

"You have? Yes, that's from *Walden Pond*. I guess I would have picked that part of it for you," she went on quickly to cover her surprise. She was amazed anew by this man; he had read Thoreau. She wondered what other things he had studied, obviously on his own, without being required to do so. That sort of learning—natural, hungry learning—impressed her much more than a man who had been assigned his reading.

"So that's not the part of *Walden* you meant?" he asked, tickling her inner arm with the furry end of a piece of foxtail grass he had been chewing.

"I was thinking of the part where Thoreau says, 'I went to the woods because I wished to live deliberately, to front only the essential facts of life.' I wish that was really why I'd come to Maplecreek, instead of running from things. Thoreau wanted to be sure, he said, when it came his time to die he would not discover too late he had not really lived."

"I've thought that. More than once," he said, looking straight into her eyes. She could see each separate dark eyelash.

"You told me why you came back here, Daniel. But why did you leave in the first place?"

He looked away, a frown furrowing his brow. "I couldn't commit to all the rules and, therefore, to the church. Like I told you, I argued with my father, couldn't bridle my temper—my comments—for the common good. I probably needed to be smacked, but once an Amish child gets past *bletching*—that's spanking—age, none of that. And poor Barbara. She wasn't enough to tempt me to toe the line that time, either, and Emma's arguing did no good."

"I can believe Emma would argue. The two of you are

200

very much alike," she said, but she was secretly thrilled he had said Barbara could not hold him that time, *either*.

"And I had some wild idea I had to get out of here to find myself, though all I ended up seeing was Goshen, Indiana. I studied my craft, audited some courses at the Mennonite College there, went to some concerts and stuff. Of course, I did go to the *real* big city more than once—the great cultural hub of Indianapolis. I've made the grand tour of Elkhart and Shipshewana, too," he said with a laugh.

"But you've never seen Columbus?" she asked. "Some snobs used to call it Cowtown, but it's got a lot to offer."

"Whatever it's got, it doesn't have you right now."

"No, though I keep thinking that, sooner or later, I've got to go back to face the music."

"Return to your life there?"

"Yes. But there are still reasons to stay here for now."

"Such as?" he asked as he reached his hand over in the grass to cover hers. She felt his big warm palm and the strong curl of calloused fingers.

"One, better security for Jennifer and me—at least, I thought so until my mysterious midnight visitor, but I really can't picture an Amish person doing more than giving me a stern warning. Two, finding the hit-and-run killer—and three, I love Maplecreek. And—now you. I mean, at least you and I can get along without quarreling lately," she added hastily.

With his free hand, he reached out to brush back hair blowing in her face. His voice came very soft. "Yeah, I think we can get along. Right now, though, I've got to get home. Jennifer," he called out, "you want to lead Bess back for me?"

"Oh, sure!" she called from her self-imposed sentry duty next to the horse. She patted Bess and stooped to

201

gather the reins. "I might even show her where the Pi is on the way back."

"A tree trunk that's an imaginary horse," Brooke explained.

"Great!" Daniel called to Jennifer and went over to talk to her.

Brooke gathered the remnants of the feast. Even at the mere thought of being alone for a moment with Daniel, her hands shook; she rattled the empty pop cans together as she put the pack on her back, then shrugged out of it again to just hold it.

"We'd better hurry to catch up," Brooke called to him as Daniel strode back toward her. "I still worry about her, so—"

"No talking, no worrying, just for one moment," he said.

He took the backpack from her hand and dropped it. He reached for her and she for him. They lightly leaned together, she on her tiptoes as they kissed once, almost playfully, then pressed powerfully together as the kiss took off and soared them skyward.

He leaned her back in his arms, and she clung trustingly, letting the kiss deepen, letting her hips and thighs tilt heavily into his. She looped her arms around his neck and held tight. He turned them once in a graceful, sweeping circle, as if they would whirl off for a dance across the meadow. But he only pushed her gently against the rough bark of their tree and took her mouth again. For the first time, she tasted his need for her that went far deeper than attraction or even desire. That realization made her downright dizzy.

She wrapped her arms around his waist. His back muscles were tree-trunk hard under his shirt. How she'd love to yank it free, tear its Amishness away. She wished

202

they had time to shed their clothes and their differences, but she felt herself going prickly hot at that thought. She, who used to be so in charge of what she thought was real life, reveled in feeling like a sheltered Amish girl now, falling in love for the first time, mastered by a man, yet knowing her own alluring power. How safe and real she felt held between this man and this tree. Despite his doubts and fears, Daniel Brand was this big oak with his roots deep in the bedrock of life.

Eyes wide, they stepped back to look at each other. She stared up into his eyes, amazed she didn't topple over. He turned them and leaned back against the tree trunk and held her hands in his. With another grin, a lopsided, tremulous one this time, he said, "You're blushing."

"You're panting."

"Your fault."

"We've got to catch up with Jen."

"I know. But we'll find other times—somehow," he said and brushed bark off her shoulders, then intently off her back. She betrayed what he must have been thinking when, like a coward, she brushed the seat of her pants before he could.

He grinned at that, too—and winked. "But I told you I'm willing to help," he said. She laughed, entranced by his lightning quick change of moods. When he walked away to retrieve his hat and coat, she saw his back was peppered with bits of bark, too.

And then, that strange, prickly skin feeling assailed her again—the one she got when she was certain she was being watched, and not by Daniel. She jerked around and squinted into the sun, fully expecting Jennifer had walked back and caught them kissing. No—no one on the path. Guilt—worry that maybe

Emma's boys had sneaked up to spy on them, though there was no sound, nothing. She skimmed the foliage, looked across the peaceful pond. Absolutely nothing. Nerves about kissing Daniel, she told herself, that's all. Residual anxiety from Columbus, apprehension about her late-night visitor.

Scolding herself for her foolishness, she hurried over to join Daniel and brushed pieces of bark off his back off while they walked, then helped him tug his frock coat on. He looked strictly Amish again. She kept glancing through the trees and down the lane, assuring herself they were really alone, the three of them and Bess.

"The moon's not full like it was for the wreck, but it rises tonight about nine," Daniel told Brooke as he harnessed Bess with Jennifer's "help" from Bess's other side. "I'll come over a bit before, and we'll attach the courting buggy to the back of mine."

"Good. That will give me time to arrange for Jen to spend a little time at her friend's, because I can't just leave her alone in the house," she whispered. "And she's not ready to spend nights away from home yet—I don't want her to, either."

"Thanks for the picnic and sharing your Aunt Brooke, Jennifer," he called to the child as he climbed up into the buggy.

"Oh, sure, 'cause you shared Bess with me!"

"An even trade," Brooke heard him say as he grinned again and clucked the horse away.

"I hope we learn something from this idea of yours," Daniel told Brooke as they attached the back of the courting buggy to the rear of Daniel's surrey behind the Sewing Circle that night. "And I just hope we're not headed for a wreck of our own—working together and getting more involved like we are."

"I think this is worth a try—and us, too."

Without looking at her, he cut away the extra wire with cutters from his tool belt strapped to his hips. While Brooke hung the yet-unlit kerosene lantern on the left-side hook of the buggy back, Daniel lifted the heavier battery-operated light and worked on attaching it.

"I keep thinking," he said, "*when* I'm thinking instead of just *feeling* about us, that something will work out."

"You know one thing that helped convince me we're worth a try, even though we can't really live in each other's worlds?"

"I'd say my charm and dashing manners, but that would be prideful," he mumbled around the three nails he held in his mouth.

"It was that Jennifer trusts you and cares for you. You've filled a little of the void her father's departure left in her."

"Then, that's worth—a lot," he said between bangs of his hammer to secure the reflective slow-moving-vehicle triangle she held in place for him.

"I guess we're ready to try this. And Brooke," he said as he lit the kerosene lantern, "I still think we're ready to try us, whatever happens."

"Yes," she said as he blew out the match. "Let's do it!"

Brooke made three passes at their mock-up buggy, while Daniel drove slowly to the fatal site. Each time, she crested the top of the hill at nearly fifty miles an hour before she braked to coast down behind him. Each time, the minute she came over the rise, she could see the buggy clearly below, especially the bright, blinking red light—and the moon was only about half as full as it had been the night of the wreck.

"The only possible thing I haven't realized before," she told Daniel as they finally huddled in his driveway with the car pulled up behind the buggy, "is that, even without being impaired or distracted, someone who didn't know the road could have thought that blinking light was a right turn signal. You know, saw the buggy, but thought that meant a road entered at the bottom of the hill and the vehicle was going to turn off. So maybe they didn't hit the brakes as early as they could have."

"They?"

"It's the way Jake always put it. He or she. I just wish the bastard or bastardette had left a calling card at the bottom of the hill, that's all," she said as she leaned back against the car in exhaustion and frustration.

"*They* probably wouldn't have thrown their calling card out until they got control of themselves later on. I heard that's why the sheriff didn't even look too hard for possible beer cans or bottles tossed out here. *They* would have probably only thought to throw them out much farther on. Then, if they did get stopped, there would be no evidence in the car, but the liquor wouldn't be at the scene, either. Besides, from my vantage point, I saw them back up and go on pretty fast."

"How far down the road before they might throw something out?" she asked as a new thought energized her.

"I have no idea. A ways at least."

"You know," she blurted before she remembered that Daniel knew nothing of her covert search for Paul Hostetler's car in Rhonda Miller's barn, "I saw two liquor bottles off the road in the grass, down by the Miller place."

"What were you doing down there? Brooke?"

"All right, I went to look in the barn for a red car. I didn't tell you, but nothing happened. Except I saw two liquor bottles, expensive Scotch, I think, and one was partly full."

"Once again, it means nothing by itself."

"Haven't you ever heard of fingerprints? Daniel," she cried and got back into the car, "it could mean something!"

"It's pitch-dark. You can't just park on the berm and go fumbling through the grass down there now," he said and reached way in to cover her hand and turn off the engine she'd just started.

"Daniel, this could be important!"

"I said you aren't going down there now, and you aren't going to tie this to Paul again, are you, because the bottles are near the Miller place? I wish you'd told me about going down there."

"The thing is, I remember a trial where the crime lab expert testified that fingerprints don't last long in the elements, and it was raining the night I saw the bottles. I've got to get them!"

When he didn't let her turn the key, wearily, she leaned her forehead on her hands against the steering wheel. "What a mess," she muttered. "But first thing tomorrow I'm going down there and get those bottles if they're still there."

"And give them to the sheriff," he prompted.

"Yes. Maybe I can trade them for whatever else he's found out."

"And you won't go off on your own again where something could happen to you?"

"Promise. I'll just pick Jen up in town, and we'll call it a night." She jolted as his warm hand cupped, then rubbed the nape of her neck. His thumb rode up, then down where her hair began, slightly pressing, stroking the tresses this way, then that. Sensual shivers shook her.

He leaned into the car to nuzzle, then kiss the nape of her neck. "Then," he whispered. "I'll let this be good night, and we'll see where we go from here—in everything."

"Yes," she told him as she lifted her head at last and gave him one quick kiss. "In everything."

When Brooke drove in the driveway with Jennifer a half hour later, her headlights illuminated the pale house. She gasped. She could not believe what she saw. She hit the breaks so the car stopped halfway down the drive.

"Oh, Aunt Brooke. What's that?" Jennifer shrieked. "Should we go look at it?"

"No, stay in this car!" Brooke jumped at the panic in her own voice. Instinctively, she hit the door locks, but they were already down. And, shaking with rage, she just stared through her tears. Everywhere she could see on the shop, house, and garage, horribly painted graffiti, defaced with crudely drawn Pennsylvania Dutch hex signs and five-pointed stars. "Witches' pentangles," she whispered before she realized she had spoken aloud.

When she hit her brights, the obscene lines gleamed the color of the car that hit those Amish kids—the crimson of fresh blood.

CHAPTER ELEVEN

"YOU'RE RIGHT, IT'S BLOOD," DANIEL TOLD Brooke that night as he sniffed at, then touched the horrible goo coagulating along the side of the abandoned plastic bucket by the back door.

Just in case the person had been lurking around, Brooke had driven over to get Daniel's help. He was armed with two of his biggest hammers; Brooke and Jennifer held hands, and they peered into the bucket Daniel illumined with his flashlight.

"Probably chicken blood," he added. "See—a pinfeather."

"Ugh! Like voodoo," Brooke said, "but this is hardly the place for that. And I recognize the message—Pennsylvania Dutch Amish hex signs and witches' pentangles."

"What message, Aunt Brooke?"

"That someone doesn't like me, that's all."

"But neither of those symbols are used in this area," Daniel said. Brooke could only frown and nod.

"Witches?" Jennifer put in. "Like at Halloween? And what's a hex?"

Daniel threw the bucket down in disgust. "Don't worry about it, Jennifer," he told her. "It's probably some sick joke by someone who doesn't even know you."

His eyes met Brooke's again over Jennifer's head. He shrugged, obviously unsure what she wanted to tell Jennifer. "What I don't like," he went on, "is this bucket and the half-finished hex sign by the back door suggests that maybe you drove in while the person was still here. He heard or saw you and took off out back somewhere, probably running toward Levi's place. Without rain lately, I doubt if he'd leave any tracks."

"Toward Levi's place," Brooke repeated, glancing off into the darkness. She felt sick to her soul. Could someone Amish have seen her and Daniel doing the driving test on the road? Then when Daniel went home and she drove into town to get Jennifer, he defaced the house; when they came home, he ran down the lane he knew well. Levi had chickens on the farm. He could have intentionally used hex signs to make her think he wasn't local Amish. But no, she was talking about Emma's husband here—Daniel's brother-in-law.

Or maybe, she began to agonize again, her Columbus stalker *had* found her and was covering his actions by pretending to be Amish—he had pulled off something authentic the first time because maybe he spoke German, but with these hex signs, he showed he didn't realize the Amish were different in various parts of the country. Or could her new tormentor be the person who hit the Amish kids and heard she was asking around and was warning her to desist or leave?

"Brooke," Daniel said, "I'm sure he's long gone, but I'm glad you drove over to tell me." He squeezed her shoulder with his clean hand, while she hugged Jennifer.

"Let's go in now," Brooke suggested more calmly than she felt. "I don't think we need to worry about someone having been inside, since it's all locked up tight and no windows are broken."

"The only other good news is," Daniel said, "I'll bet I can hose and scrub this stuff off by morning and no one will know about it—unless you want to show the sheriff first."

"I don't know," she said as she fumbled with the keys and he took them from her hand to open the door. "If I find those bottles tomorrow and give then, to Sheriff Barnes, I could mention this, but what could he do? Or I could call Jake. I—just have to think about all the pros and cons—about everything. Daniel, will you walk through the house with us—the basement and all first?"

"I planned to do just that," he said as they went in,

clicking on lights to find things completely undisturbed inside. "And in the morning, I'll check around to see if anyone's missing some chickens."

Brooke couldn't sleep and ended up—over Daniel's protests—helping him scrub and squirt the house and garage clean. At three in the morning, they drank hot chocolate and tried to analyze who could be doing all this. He never brought up Levi's name and neither did she, but she admitted to him that sometimes she felt she was being watched. Daniel offered to sleep on the couch, but there were only a few hours before dawn, and she sent him home. "No reason for your reputation to be ruined if someone should find out you'd been here all night," she said.

Over breakfast, Brooke explained to Jennifer as best she could why someone would want to scare her or make her leave. The Amish believed in forgiveness, in leaving well enough alone, she told her.

"Then maybe it's not an Amish guy who painted that stuff on the house with blood, but our old scary person from Columbus."

"There's a chance of that, Jen, but a teeny-weeny one. Still, just so neither of us worries, I'm going to start taking you to school and picking you up like back in Columbus."

Jennifer still had as many questions as she did herself. Though Brooke hated to do it, she cautioned her about strangers again. When they drove to school, Brooke went in and explained privately to Jennifer's teacher, Miss Myers, that because the child's father was somewhat estranged from his daughter, Brooke would appreciate it if the teacher kept a close eye on Jennifer at recess without alarming the girl. She was not to go anywhere with anyone but Brooke. Brooke knew she'd given the woman some misleading information, but she could hardly tell her about chicken-blood hexes and witches' pentangles.

Next, she drove to the Miller farm site where she'd seen the bottles and found them. Yes! Her luck was changing. She placed them in plastic Baggies and took them straight into the sheriff's office.

"Well, you sure are helping me out again here, Miss Benton," Sheriff Barnes told her, though he was obviously as much annoyed as pleased by her find. "Real fancy stuff, like no one around here pro'bly even heard of, this Glenbrae Scotch. You people drink this in Columbus, do you? Thing is, fingerprints don't last long outside, but when I can, I'll get my deputy Tom to call the few taverns and such dare to stay open on Sunday round here. Been laid up with a real bad spring cold, Tom has, but he'll get on it soon as he gets his voice back."

"In other words, you think these were too far down the road and found too late to mean anything?" she demanded, her voice on edge. Damned if she was going to tell a man like this about what she was going through back at the house and expect any kind of civil concern.

"Now, there you go, putting words in my mouth, but I 'spose that's what you lawyers learn to do, isn't it?"

The sum total of everything he said—and his unspoken words—irritated Brooke so much that she drove directly back home and used the phone book to find what places might have been open that Sunday night—and which stocked Glenbrae. No one stocked Glenbrae, but she was in luck; there was only one place open in the immediate area the night of the wreck, the

Dutchman's Keg, over on Deer Run Road.

She almost walked over to Daniel's to tell him what she'd learned, but she knew he'd had almost no sleep from staying and cleaning the house. She couldn't just keep bothering him, especially not in the hours during which he dealt with his people. And she could hardly ask him to accompany her into a bar where some of his Amish friends might see him coming or going.

She really appreciated being able to rely on her rescuing knights Jake and Daniel, but it was broad daylight after all, so it would be safe enough. She was *not* going to be terrorized by that—that pseudo-Amish son-of-a-bitch tormentor, whether he was her original stalker or someone here! And if she hurried over to the Dutchman's Keg this morning, she could interview the waitress there. Meanwhile she felt Jennifer was safe at school, and her workers here would take care of the shop if she just went out for a few minutes.

"Miss Brooke, the postman wants to see you downstairs."

At that voice, even such a soft one, Brooke jumped straight out of her chair, banging her knee on the kitchen table. "Oh, thank you, Amos Mary," she said. "You startled me. You mean Mrs. Neff."

"Sure, Mrs. Neff, the postman," she said and headed back downstairs.

Sally Neff stood at the front door, a letter extended in her hand. "You've got to sign for this one, Miss Benton," she said importantly. "Certified return mail, right on that line by the X."

Brooke recognized the envelope instantly by its buff color and typeset: Stedman & Rowe, Attorneys-at-Law. The address was in Elizabeth's handwriting.

"Thank you, Sally," Brooke said, then thought of

213

something. "By the way, I overheard a customer talking about someplace called the Dutchman's Keg. I thought, if it's some sort of new Amish craft place, I'd better check out the competition."

"The Keg?" Sally said, and shook her head. "That's no place for a lady. It used to be the beer stop of choice for bikers, and I'm talking Harleys, not Schwinns. That's a good one, you going there thinking to find crafts— crafty folks more like."

Sally chuckled to herself as she headed out to do her duty. At least, Brooke thought, there were not going to be any Hell's Angels roaring in late morning when the place wasn't even open.

Still standing in the doorway, she opened the letter and skimmed it. Elizabeth had forwarded this summons from their boss of bosses, Myron Stedman. He was requesting that she come to Columbus for a meeting with the senior partners on Wednesday. They wanted her to return to her position, or they'd be "forced" to replace her.

We all hope you'll come back, Elizabeth had written on one of those attached Post-it notes. *Even Ray McCarron, who is now overworked and wants to have you playing second fiddle so he can rub it in. I know Mr. Stedman said he'd do anything to get you back. Even Judge Prescott asked about you. And if someone's bothering you there, maybe it's for the best.*

"I don't know what's for the best," she said aloud. "But about a lot of things, it's decision time at last."

"Good morning, Mrs. Tammen. Good morning, Mrs. Hermez," Kiki said to Hank's receptionist and his private secretary as she breezed into the WWEE headquarters to meet Hank for lunch. The doors to his big suite stood open, so he was probably waiting for her. She loved to come into the office to meet him, rather than at their favorite restaurant.

"He's out wandering again, Mrs. Waldron," the sweet-voiced, middle-aged Mrs. Hermez said with a smile. She'd been with Hank a long time, but Kiki really liked her, even though she could not get her to call her Kiki. "You know how he is when he doesn't say where he's going, Mrs. Waldron. But you could just sit down and—oh, my, what a beautiful quilt!"

"It's one I picked out for Garner and his wife, and didn't quite get around to giving them when they were over to the house last time. Well I'll just pop in Garner's office if he's there and give it to him before Hank gets back, then. Can you buzz to see if Garner's available?"

Mrs. Hermez buzzed Garner's secretary while Mrs. Tammen, too, admired the quilt. How Kiki ached to tell them all about the plans she was making for a place called Amish Village in Ohio, but until she completed the concept and did some estimations for real-estate outlay with the boys, she wasn't whispering a word to anyone. And, when she finally went public, Hank would be the first to know.

"Yes, Alice says he's in and not on the phone," Mrs. Hermez told her with another sparkling smile.

Kiki walked the wheat-hued carpet hall toward Garner's suite of offices. She was hoping this gift would help to butter him up for what was coming later, because eventually, she'd need his help on her Ohio project.

Garner Waldron was Hank's only child and WWEE's executive vice-president. Kiki had always thought Garner looked aristocratic, as if he should be heir to a centuries-old Bavarian dukedom instead of an upstart American amusement park conglomerate. It was hard to believe he was Hank Waldron's son, because he looked, sounded, and acted more like his mother. With classic features and premature silver hair—and, too often, a silver tongue—Garner at forty-two was just six years older than Kiki and slightly shorter, though he liked to look down on her. Yet she was sometimes certain from the way she caught Garner gazing at her that he would have desired her instead of detested her if their enforced relationship had not been what it was. Maybe, she thought perversely, his taste just ran to statuesque redheads.

"Hi, Kiki," Garner greeted her from across the room when his secretary ushered her in, then stepped out and closed the door behind her. "You don't have the twins in tow as usual?"

How Garner always managed to rile her in so many ways amazed Kiki. She had tried to like him—to win his approval for the boys and vice versa—but Garner ruined everything. She had learned to pick her battles, so she always honed in on only the one or two insults that bugged her most. And now the battle was on again, whether she liked it or not.

"Garner, how many times have I asked you not to call them twins? They're almost a year apart, however much alike they look."

He stayed on the far side of his desk, leaning one shoulder against the panoramic office window behind his desk, and looked out before turning back to her. While she walked toward his desk, he studied her.

"What's that saying?" he asked while she held the quilt tighter to her breasts. "Beware of Geeks—I mean, Greeks—bearing gifts?"

"Not funny. Garner," she said, daring to come clear

216

up to his desk and lean her thighs against its hard edge, "this is an Amish quilt I bought in Ohio I hope you'll take home to Sarah."

"Sure. That's nice of you and Dad."

"Tell her it's called Tumbling Blocks."

He stood his ground to let her put in on his desk like a votive offering. "The blocks don't look like they're tumbling to me," he said, leaning now against the back of his tall black leather chair. He frowned down at the perfectly balanced and aligned design. "They look— stacked," he added and darted a glance at her breasts.

"Let's not set ourselves up for another argument, know what I mean, Garner? I don't see why you and I can't get along for Hank's sake or at least WWEE's."

"As if you have anything to do with the business. But you did mean for the Buckland brothers' sakes, really, didn't you?"

"You know, you're just like a spoiled little boy who's had to get a couple of stepbrothers and throws a fit when your daddy's even a little bit nice to them."

"Judas priest, I don't need you to psychoanalyze me."

"I'm not trying to. It's just that I know how much you mean to Hank, and how much Clay and Matt try to emulate you, that's all."

"Like hell," he heard him say under his breath as she shook her head, turned, and went out.

Garner stared down at the quilt. Ironic she'd brought him that, as if she knew about the big secret project Dad had her brothers on, though everyone was sworn to secrecy for now. He knew Hank wouldn't have told her, though he'd probably let her cut the ribbon—the quilted ribbon—for it, eventually. And if those brothers of hers had let it slip, he'd get them for that. Garish, neon-hued

217

Kiki with country quilts, he thought, and snorted a laugh as he went to stare out the window again. His view swept from the Old Las Vegas Fort to Ripley's Believe It or Not Museum, and that perversely amused him, too. Ah, Kiki Buckland Waldron. She had always been alluring in that cheap showgirl way of hers. Even though she'd sold real estate for years before his dad found her, she'd always be a half-dressed hoofer and nothing more, and they were good for only a one-night stand and then leaving. When she really annoyed him with her let's-be-friends-at-least approach, he always pictured her topless, strutting her stuff, coming straight toward him down some sleazy stripper's runway.

He went to his bar across the room and poured himself some Scotch, though he never liked to drink before lunch. Trust a woman to drive him to it—that meddling, magnetic bitch especially. He supposed he should be nicer to the Buckland boys at least for a while, so when they screwed up with *his* company, he could keep Dad's goodwill while he nailed their hides. He'd play his cards close to his vest, as they said around here, and see what happened with this big new project.

As he went back to work, he found himself stroking the quilt, tracing the edges of the pieces. When his intercom buzzed for an incoming call, he jerked so hard he sloshed Scotch on its perfectly balanced pattern.

"So you really don't recall whether the bottles the two strangers had at their table that night were Glenbrae Scotch?" Brooke asked the Dutchman's Keg waitress, Reba Potts. Reba's tanning-booth skin showed she was somewhere on the far side of fifty, despite her workout queen body. Her bleached blond hair looked as if she'd stuck her finger in a fuse box to style it. And,

218

unfortunately, it seemed Reba might have frizzed what smarts the Good Lord gave her, too. A credible witness on the stand, Reba Potts would never be.

"No," she drawled, chomping on black licorice gum, "didn't out and out see no certain kind of booze. I'd of remembered the bagpiper on the label, like you said. A man in a skirt, wow. But I know they drank their own booze from big bottles. Not some little flasks, they sneaked in, I mean. Drank their stuff like chasers to beer they bought here, see."

Brooke was excited by the fact there had been two bottles and Reba remembered two strangers, however wildly circumstantial this still was. After all, Jake had surmised that a companion in the car could have distracted the driver and that maybe the driver had been elated or in a great mood—drunk or not, on an actual joy ride, Jake had suggested.

"Did they seem to be celebrating any special occasion?" she asked Reba.

"Like a birthday or a raise or something?" Reba leaned on her broom with a sigh that blasted Brooke with the smell of licorice. "No, 'less you want to count they were real glad they bought something or other. Yeah, I remember now. Antique buyers, that's what they said they were, from out west. From California, I bet, 'cause they both kind of looked like Paul Newman. In his younger days, I mean. You know, like *Cool Hand Luke*. Left me a good tip, too, like, five dollars apiece. I mean that's *real* good around here."

"They both looked like Paul Newman? Do you think they were related?"

"Like his sons or nephews you mean? Coming in here?"

"No, maybe related to each other?"

219

"Who knows? Can't even picture their faces right now, only Newman's, how cute and ticked off he could look at the same time."

"And you have no idea what kind of car they were driving? Do you know if anyone saw a big red car in the Keg's parking lot that night?"

"Who knows? This is Billy's place, and he was behind the bar all night. It was dark, and folks come and go, come and go."

"You mentioned the two men were antique dealers. Visiting the area to buy Amish things, I suppose."

"Who knows? I heard it's anything over a hundred years old, and I'm kind of feeling that way this morning," she said, arching her back, though it was her gum rather than her spine she cracked.

As Brooke thanked her and headed out, all she knew was this meant nothing for sure, only more speculation, more dead ends. The antique dealers could be back out west with their Amish booty, never to return. And without solid evidence, there was no way—

She gasped when a hard hand swung her around outside the door in the sharp sun. Instantly, she pictured a leather-jacketed, bearded road-hog biker and tried to knee him. Missing her mark by inches, she kicked the big man hard in the thigh. Amish! Daniel! He grunted and spit out some German she could translate simply by the look on his face.

"You!" she cried. "What are you doing here?"

"I don't need to ask you that, do I? Get in the buggy," he ordered, propelling her toward the side parking lot, even though he limped. "We're going for a ride."

"Let me go. You're hurting my arm. And I drove, so—Daniel, what is the matter with you?"

He half lifted her, half shoved her up into the buggy

220

ahead of him. He climbed up behind her and held her wrist so she could not exit the other side. She jolted against the seat as he clucked Bess away, down a narrow grass lane that ran behind the Dutchman's Keg toward a patch of woods.

"And how did you know I was here?" she demanded. "I'd hate to think you've been watching me!" For one moment, her mind went wild with the possibility he could be her Amish night visitor, but deep down, she knew better.

"Bess could hardly keep up with your car, could she? When Sally Neff delivered my mail, she told me what she thought was a real good joke—that you'd just asked her about visiting the Dutchman's Keg, so when your car was gone, I put two and two together. We Amish can do that, you know. Brooke, just the other night, you promised me we were working together and that you'd let the sheriff handle the liquor bottles and so on. Besides, you could get hurt over here!"

"I am getting hurt! Why the Neanderthal tactics all of a sudden?"

He let her snatch her wrist back. Huffily, she picked her purse off the floor of the buggy and arranged her denim skirt over her knees. "Daniel, I appreciate all your help, really, but I am capable of taking care of myself, you know."

"Yeah, great. That's why you've run to me after both visits by your mystery admirer. And why you've been thinking about maybe going back to Columbus lately."

"As a matter of fact, I'm going back Wednesday to the office. They want me to return to my job."

"And?"

"And I don't know." His voice was edged with bitterness—or was that anger or even fear for her? At least, perhaps he wanted her to stay now as much as he had said he wanted her to leave before. "You think I'd be running again, you mean?" she asked. "I want you to know I did not run from Columbus just because my condo was broken into, not even because I believed Jen and I were nearly hit-and-run accident victims ourselves. What really made me take her and run away was what happened when I was getting ready for my temporary leave of absence."

For some reason, as angry as she'd been when he first grabbed her, she felt desperate to make him understand. She had to smooth things over.

"Go on," he said with a flap of the reins.

"I was clearing out my desk, and a box came to the office for me. I even had my secretary open it, because I thought it was leftover business, so the delivery man was gone when we tried to find him, but later I learned it wasn't any of the regular delivery services."

"And?" he prompted again when she hesitated.

"And it contained a doll from my childhood collection of Barbie dolls—I'm sure you don't know what that kind is—which I thought was stored at my condo in a box in a closet, ever since my mother died. The doll was dressed in a copy of a suit I'd worn occasionally at the trial. But it had stab wounds and red paint splattered on the suit and body—like blood. And it had an old speckled, defaced photograph of me pasted over its face from when I was about Jennifer's age—I used to look more like her than Melanie did. I knew then that whoever had been in the condo had even been into my dolls and my old photograph album. It was as if they had raped my childhood, I know, about my photo album, you're probably thinking 'graven images' . . ."

"No," he said turning to her, "I'm thinking that you

were afraid he meant to harm Jennifer as well as you."

"Yes. I just couldn't stand to tell you that—all of it before."

"I guess there's no way you can really trust me is there, then or now? You didn't tell me you were going to Miller's barn, or here today, either. Our overwhelming differences hit me in the face too often. If you could only step away from the world as I intend to, you'd find some peace. If you could only realize the Amish life offers that peace—"

"Such peace that you've been running from the Amish life for years, Daniel Brand. But as for our differences, you're right there. We're obviously been kidding ourselves about some sort of a deeper, trusting relationship."

"If that's the way you feel, after everything I've—"

"You just wanted an excuse to step back, didn't you? Stop this buggy! Bess, whoa! Don't touch me, Daniel!"

"I just didn't want you to hurt yourself jumping out!"

When he reached for her again, she squirmed free and climbed down. But he clambered down, too. She started down the lane at a half run, but he pulled her around and into the shelter of trees.

"Is this where we are between us after everything we've been through together?" he demanded.

"Look, Daniel," she said, holding up her hands as if to ward him off. "It was crazy—us. Just absolutely insane."

"And that's what made me think it was so precious."

He lifted her almost off her feet and crushed her mouth with his. Shocked, she bowed back in his arms. She wanted to shove him away, to kick, run. But she clung wildly to him, her hands in his hair, then her fingernails pinning his coat to his broad back. She wanted to scratch and bite him, but she pulled him closer and devoured his kiss, the feel, his raw, masculine, outdoor scent.

He thrust her back, but steadied her until she regained her balance. He looked at her hungrily again, studying her so intently, face, body, face again.

"Get in the buggy before I make another mistake," he said. "I'll drive you to your car. I don't know what I was thinking, dragging you out here, being so rough. I only wanted to help and was afraid you'd get hurt."

"I'll walk back. I'd rather. Otherwise . . ."

"Yeah."

In silence now, Brooke walked and Daniel followed her to the Dutchman's Keg in his buggy. She felt self-conscious to have him staring, but she was glad he was behind her since her lower lip quivered and tears blurred her vision.

How could absolutely everything have gone so bad so fast for her here in Maplecreek? Where were peace and safety for her and Jennifer? What had she been thinking of, falling in love with Daniel? And in the end—their end, evidently—the Old Order Amish had not taken Daniel from her, but he was doing that himself. And he was right, of course, wasn't he, and she had to respect that and him? She should be grateful their intimacy had not gone further, and yet she was only sad. Both here and in Columbus, she felt watched, trapped, threatened, and she had only herself to rely on now.

"Good-bye. I'll be fine," she threw back over her shoulder as she unlocked her car door in the empty parking lot beside the bar.

"Above all, take care of yourself and Jennifer, Miss Brooke. And I'm still your neighbor, and I didn't mean you couldn't call on me for help at any time."

She nodded, then shook her head, but did not look at him again. The fading clop of Bess's hooves floated to her. When the buggy turned out onto the road, Brooke just leaned against her open car door; through a blur of tears, she watched the black box on wheels disappear over the first hill. Damn. Jennifer would be so terribly disappointed, too. And as for returning to Columbus versus the allure Maplecreek still exerted on her, she had no idea in the universe what she should do.

She jumped at Reba's sharp voice and the swish swish of broom on the concrete stoop outside the bar. "You still here, honey? You know, I got to thinking, those two fellas looked more like Troy Donahue. You remember him young, like in *This Happy Feeling*?"

Brooke cleared her throat. "Yes, I remember." She got in, slammed the door, and drove away.

CHAPTER TWELVE

ON WEDNESDAY MORNING AFTER BROOKE dropped Jennifer at school, she realized she had plenty of time before setting out for Columbus. She didn't want to seem eager by arriving too early. Neither did she want to give herself time to stop by her condo, not alone, not with all the agonizing she'd been doing about the fact her stalker from Columbus might have found her here or that someone could be following her.

She drove through Maplecreek twice, looping around a back road to make certain she wasn't followed. Because she had not been sleeping well and always felt tired lately, she considered getting a cup of coffee at the Dutch Table Restaurant to keep her awake on the drive to Columbus. Instead she drove by the old Melrose

225

mansion, then went back and pulled into the gravel driveway.

She turned off the engine and sat there for a moment, thinking. Sheriff Barnes—in a somewhat kinder mood—had called yesterday to say the crime lab he used said the Scotch bottles were "clean" of prints. She sighed as her eyes took in the big house and untended grounds.

Despite her problems with people like the sheriff and Levi Kurtz—not to mention her night visitor—she still felt Maplecreek was a friendly place, at least in broad daylight. Even though Daniel had apparently ended their personal relationship, the last thing he had said was that he was still her neighbor and would help her if she needed it. Evidently, most of the Amish felt that way about her so far. Yesterday, Emma's girl Leona had invited her and Jennifer to Daniel's shop raising this Saturday. It would be an abbreviated Amish barn raising, Brooke thought, and she'd always wanted to see one of those.

But it was mostly the fact that the owner of the Scotch bottles had left no fingerprints—or, more correctly, that they hadn't lasted in the elements—which had really made her consider a possible future here in Maplecreek, even after Verna came back to claim her home and business.

Brooke wanted something in her life on which she could leave her "fingerprints," something besides Jennifer, who was really her own person, still Melanie and Jeff Reynold's child, however much Brooke loved her. She wanted something more than learning to make a challenging quilt, even more than her law career, which had once seemed the ultimate goal to her.

And she had also been pondering how the letter from the law firm had said she could be replaced. It astounded her how easily someone else could be plugged into her slot when she had once been so sure it was hers alone. She wanted to have somewhere she couldn't be replaced, a haven for her and Jennifer. Someplace where they weren't, as people said, dependent on the kindness of strangers—even someone as dear as Verna, Elizabeth, Jake—yes, even Daniel—for help.

Slowly, she got out and walked around the big house, picking her way through the too-tall grass. She pictured herself behind one of those old hand push mowers the Maplecreek Amish women used. She admired the ten-foot high door with its graceful fanlight above. She realized that if this house had been deserted in the city, it would be scarred by broken windows and graffiti. She shuddered then, remembering the chicken blood splattered into those grotesque symbols. She looked around to see if someone was staring, but she was alone.

Sun reflected off the windows of the parlor and sitting room, so that she had to cup her hands around her eyes to look in; her shadow leaped inside across dusty parquet floors to the marble mantels as she walked the two wide porches.

Her imagination restored and furnished and peopled the place: white wicker chairs and ferns on this veranda with Jen in one of Daniel Brand's rocking chairs; the plaster molding and ceilings restored to former grandeur; the fine woodwork sanded and refinished—maybe with Daniel's help, if they could only, at least, be friends again. Verna visiting, Emma, too, Elizabeth out for the weekend from Columbus, maybe even Kiki Waldron and her husband clear in from Vegas to relax and unwind by shopping sprees and just watching buggies crop, clop by on the quiet street. Her church friends playing bridge in the Victorian parlor. Jen with a real horse out back to care for in the old carriage house next to one of those handsome Amish-built gazebos. And that beautiful lighted hutch from Daniel's hands in the place of honor in the dining room.

So much work to do everywhere Brooke looked, but when the place was renovated, she and Jen could have two of the bedrooms upstairs and still have four to rent for guests—the sign said six bedrooms. Melrose Manor B and B, she'd call it and maybe at the bottom of that front-yard sign have added in elegant script, *Brooke Benton, Attorney-at-Law.*" That would shake the Amish up, but, whatever they thought of her, other people, both the living and the dead, still needed lawyers for good, honest, important reasons.

Quickly, before she changed her mind, she scribbled down the phone number of the real estate agent in Columbus. It was a crazy idea, but maybe she'd call them or stop by today if she had time.

Stedman & Rowe's suite of law offices looked much larger and yet more crowded than Brooke remembered. Secretaries, paralegals, and associates looked up; some smiled, some nodded or waved; a few called out "Welcome back!" or came up briefly to speak with her as she headed for Elizabeth Crandel's office. She kept a slight smile on her face and called out several names in greeting, but she couldn't help think perhaps someone looking at her right now had wanted her out of here for the terrible publicity she'd brought the venerable firm Someone must have tipped off the man who delivered those bloody dolls when she was here cleaning out her office that last day.

"Brooke, I'm so glad to see you!" Elizabeth cried and hurried around her desk to give her a hug. "I can't wait

228

until you really get back. Mr. Stedman wants to see you in his sanctum sanctorum to be followed by a partners' meeting to work out the details of your return. But let's do lunch after everything to celebrate today!"

"To celebrate our friendship at least. Elizabeth, I'm not sure whether—"

"Ah, there you are," a man's voice interrupted. "My secretary said you'd come in."

So it was to be red-carpet treatment, Brooke thought as she saw Mr. Stedman, "Lord Myron," himself, awaiting her at Elizabeth's door. Brooke could see others beyond him, staring, evidently shocked, too, that he hadn't commanded Mrs. Pickering to summon or fetch her as usual. Just months ago, Brooke would have reveled in this triumphal walk to his office, but somehow, she had changed. Thinking Ray McCarron would really resent this, she skimmed the area, but didn't see him.

As she entered the Georgian elegance of shelved volumes, rich leathers, mahogany furniture, and English hunting prints on the burgundy walls, it seemed a darker den than she recalled. She mentally lightened the place with Emma's quilts and Daniel's warm oak furniture. Poised on a slippery leather chair he indicated, she crossed, then uncrossed her legs. She wished she'd had time to hit the rest room. His wing-back, button-tufted chair gave out a squeak and a sigh as the stocky, sixty-five-year-old founder of the firm sat on the far side of his gleaming desk.

"I feel rather like a father welcoming you back home," he said, steepling his fingers before his mouth and nose. That bothered her because she couldn't read his expression; his gray eyes never indicated if he smiled.

"It seems I've been gone longer than I have."

"I can imagine time drags, away from the vim and vigor of this city and the work you love, et cetera."

"Actually, it's just that so much has happened there—and the more realistic pace of life in the country."

"Realistic? An odd way to put it, Brooke. You will have to tell me more later. All your cloak-and-dagger secrecy about your location has been quite a topic of conversation around here, especially because Elizabeth always takes the Fifth on queries about you. But to business, as I want to have this settled before we sit down with the others. I hope you have missed your calling in life here as much as we have missed your considerable talents."

"When I left, Mr. Stedman, I had the distinct impression that you and the other senior partners were relieved I was taking my so-called talents at least temporarily into exile."

"You're the one who began all this by requesting half days, Brooke. And with those unfortunate, albeit vague threats on your life, I agreed a short leave was best. Besides, I knew it would help you to have a respite with your niece before returning to duties full time here."

"Full time would still be a problem for me because of Jennifer. If I returned, especially if we continued to live outside Columbus for a while, I was hoping that half days—"

"I really cannot fathom how one could defend a client properly with one half the effort and time, but we can shelve that topic momentarily until you and I come to a meeting of minds here."

He was no doubt expecting her to launch into a speech of gratitude or blurt out her excitement to be back, but Brooke merely nodded. The Amish *had* rubbed off on her. Still, although she had not deeply dented her savings account yet, she realized her worldly ambition drove her desire to be earning more than their room and board her Sewing Circle salary provided.

"Brooke, I want us to be perfectly frank. I know I lost my temper at first when Rodney Kistler went berserk. None of that was your fault, but I was simply protecting the firm."

"I realize that and appreciate your support now. But I have come to think the Rodney Kistler disaster was my fault, and I've been trying to come to terms with that. And, as you might suppose, I've also been wrestling with the ethic of defending the client at any cost, which is certainly necessary to—"

"Please, let me go on. In *Ohio v. Kistler*, you did exactly what you were educated and dedicated—Brooke, in your case, what you were born—to do, considering the heritage of your talented father. And you did it well—too well, I suppose. As I said, I was, of course, concerned for the firm, but no matter how Kistler went off the deep end later, your so brilliantly defending him was seen by potential clients as a mark in your favor."

"In this day and age, you might know. No one's willing to stand up and say he or she is guilty of anything anymore. Personal accountability is getting so perverted by the let's-blame-heredity-or-environment excuses. It's hit-and-run for every crime, in a way. I should have known clients would prefer to hire a defense attorney known for successfully defending the guilty, not the innocent."

"Be that as it may, my point is," he said, reaching for a legal-size manila envelope and sliding it slowly across the desktop to her, "the firm has had several inquiries made concerning your defending certain parties in some rather intriguing cases."

231

She saw the picture more clearly now. Lord Myron was inducing her to return, because—with potential clients, at least—her notoriety had made her more desired than detested. If she could get Rodney Kistler off to commit his crime again, they reasoned, surely she could get them off, innocent or guilty. The next words were out of her mouth before she knew she would say them.

"I'm not ready to make a decision on returning, Mr. Stedman. Too many key things are pending in my life— my other life I've begun. I would like to request a continued leave at least until September to see them through."

He pushed the manila envelope closer, so it projected over the edge of his desk. "Four requests, two from quite high-profile, well-heeled potential clients in need of your help, Brooke. One is charged with murder and needs the best criminal lawyer immediately. That could be your first case. The three others have made it very clear they are interested in your representation or at least consultation on their cases. Perhaps you could assist Ray McCarron with those, as I believe I've convinced him what happened in no way has tarnished his so-far stellar career beginnings. You see, your reputation has grown, as have the fees you can command. Brooke, don't frown like that. You know you've geared your whole life toward the courtroom career, and you're good. Your father would be so proud."

"But he'd be prouder of me for taking care of my family first and, right now, that's a seven-year-old who needs me more than some high-profile, well-heeled potential defendants. With the talent you have here at the firm—"

"Which brings me to the unpleasant reality of the

situation. The talent I have at the firm is currently stretched to the limit. I am afraid I cannot allow you to remain at your unnamed rural retreat ad infinitum. Brooke, listen, I could see giving you perhaps until the end of the school year—then maybe take a week or two for a vacation with the girl if you must. But I will need a commitment very soon."

"Perhaps that would be possible—if I could have half time until September. I am sorry I can't commit to all this today."

"You drive a hard bargain, madame counselor. But you will, then, give me your answer as soon as possible?"

"Yes, I can promise that, sir."

"Then, let us postpone our meeting with the partners for another time. And Brooke, if you are still fearful of those threats on your life here in Columbus, I can pull some strings to get you police protection or at least a renewed investigation I am certain we can safeguard you and the child, your condo, et cetera, if you return."

"I appreciate that, Mr. Stedman. I really do," she said as she rose and shook his hand in farewell.

"I'm sure you'll figure out who's harassing you in Maplecreek," Elizabeth told her at their favorite lunch spot, One Nation Restaurant with its lofty panoramic view of the city. "If it's someone Amish, that's a lot smaller pond to find the guilty party compared to this place," she added and swept her hand toward the city stretching away beneath them toward the suburbs. "And, for all you know, your stalker here could have moved or just given up on you. Besides, you're a lawyer at heart. Arguing for what's right is in your blood. You've always been as obsessed on a moral mission as a kamikaze pilot."

Brooke acquiesced with a nod. She took a sip of her iced tea, but only toyed with her luscious-looking strawberry shortcake while Elizabeth delicately demolished hers. She'd been thinking about Daniel, but from her vantage point here in Columbus, he seemed far away. It would never work between them. She felt sobered and wiser now, as if she'd returned to school after summer camp where she'd fallen in love with the lifeguard.

"Penny, Brooke."

"What?"

"For your thoughts. Are you worrying about your condo again?"

"Whether to sell or lease it, you mean? I think I'm going to put it on the market, even if I do end up returning to town. As I said, I just keep wondering the asking price for my dream mansion in Maplecreek."

"I can't wait to see the place. It sounds like something out of *Victoria* magazine. You know, we could petition to get it on the registry of Ohio Historic Places. But, as a real estate attorney, let me advise you to get someone who knows something about renovation to look at it with you before you put big bucks into a place that old. Some of them soak up money like a sponge for years."

"I know, I know. Promise," she said and raised her hand as if she were ready to take the witness stand. "And I'll phone you about the asking price, and you can represent me in the closing if I take the plunge. Oh, Elizabeth, I love that house. Somehow I feel it was meant to be mine, and I haven't even been inside!"

"Not to change the subject," Elizabeth said, "but dish me a little more on what Hank and Kiki Waldron were really like. Now, there's a client I'd love to have. He probably keeps a whole crew of real estate lawyers busy all the time and in style."

"You know, I've thought about it since, and from things Kiki said, it was obvious Hank had been in Lancaster County in Pennsylvania, too. They must really be on an Amish-quilt-buying binge. Didn't you tell me once, though, that WWEE was acquiring theme parks in Ohio?"

"Apparently a rumor without foundation, but I heard they might try to buy out the Sea World parks nationwide, and there's that one in nearby Geauga County, which has Amish in the area, too. So this Kiki is really knockdown gorgeous?"

"Yes, but she was not conceited or plastic. Just the opposite, so I really liked her. And Hank seemed down-home, too, a regular bubba or good old boy."

"Sure, and I'm really Mother Teresa working at Stedman & Rowe in disguise. But, even if the Hank Waldrons are 'real folk,' I'll bet whoever's running WWEE now is the new breed—you know, the know-it-all, slick-and-nasty boys of the world. Sometimes clever, powerful men are deceptive, though. Maybe Hank's totally hands-on—with more than his new wife."

When they were ready to leave, Brooke insisted on taking the check, and they parted with Elizabeth's promise to come sometime soon and look at Melrose Manor. She waved and took the elevator down, while Brooke headed for the ladies' room. Brooke had decided to stop by the real estate office handling the mansion and then Jake's home office to say hello. She had spoken with Jennifer's teacher about her leaving school with her friend until she returned home.

"Home," she whispered to herself. Imagine, thinking of Maplecreek as home! But it was where Jennifer was.

Where she had some friends and many commitments. She wanted to be certain Emma was healed of heartache, and how she longed to settle things with Daniel better than they—

Turning into the hall by the phones, she bumped shoulders with a man who reached out to steady her.

"Sorry! Oh, Ray!" Her colleague on the Kistler case looked as handsome and unflappable as ever. "Whatever are you doing here?"

"I hadn't heard it was now a private club," he said as they stepped apart. He tugged his gray pinstriped suitcoat down as if it had been mussed. "I heard about your royal summons," he added, "but I had a deposition this morning, so couldn't be there to welcome you. Coming back to work?"

"Actually, no. At least not yet."

"We've all missed you, you know. I was really shook for a while about the Kistler thing blowing up. How could you have been so sure he was innocent?"

"An opinion I believe you fully concurred with."

"You're a very convincing person, Brooke, so why are you holding out on coming back? Trying to get a better deal from Lord Myron, or did he tell you you'd be assisting me now and you can't hack that? Still, I can't believe you've had a change of mind about your career."

"A change of mind, yes, but even more a change of heart."

"Don't give me that. A bleeding heart like you would never give up your *Star Trek* path, 'to go where few women attorneys have gone before.' Where have you been living lately, anyway?"

For a moment she stared at him as if she'd blanked out. She still felt startled by him: his sudden appearance, hostile attitude masked by apparent concern, the barrage of questions, and his use of the term *bleeding heart*—that had been in her threatening note. She felt tongue-tied. She told him nothing else, excused herself, hurried to the ladies' room, and locked herself in the farthest stall, sitting on the toilet with her face in her hands.

In just a few hours, this place was making her crazy. She was starting to think everyone she saw could have been her Columbus menacer. Ray McCarron—sure, he was a wild card possibility, but breaking and entering and bloody dolls didn't seem his style, and certainly not chicken blood in the country. So what if he'd used two words from that anonymous note? And earlier she'd even suspected Myron Stedman for a moment. After all, Mr. Stedman had mentioned her condo; he had never been there, had he? He had never shown any interest in his associates' personal affairs. How did he know she even had a condo rather than an apartment or house? He had wanted her to leave town when all this fell apart. To what lengths did he go to protect his precious firm to get rid of her and now to bring her back when it meant profit and prestige? And then he'd given the assurance that he could just 'pull strings' to make those threats simply go away . . .

But her suspicions about a man like Myron Stedman, the founder of the firm, the pillar of the legal community and his synagogue, the patriarch of his socially prominent, influential family was absolutely ludicrous. She knew that. She was letting her previous paranoia swallow her up again. She might as well have accused Elizabeth of being jealous of her success and wanting to get rid of her, too, or Jake Kaminsky or her secretary, Liz. Maybe she should have made the waiter today drink her iced tea or taste her food first to see if it was poisoned, so she could accuse him, too. What was wrong with her?

Luckily, she did not see Ray when she emerged from the rest room. She took the elevator down to the glass-enclosed, suspended walkways, hurrying faster, looking back over her shoulder, especially when she entered the vast, multi-level parking garage. Glancing in her rearview mirror when she could, she was heading north on High Street toward Jake's before she remembered she had wanted to stop at the real estate office and had to turn back and circle the block to find it.

Jake's "Honor-Bound Consulting Firm" was in the lower level of his house on the edge of the northern Columbus suburb of Worthington. His block was zoned commercial; a dry cleaner and a carpet outlet store shared the same small parking lot. Brooke pulled into an empty stall and got out, still feeling shaky from the day's events, even though she'd had a fruitful talk with a realtor, who had promised to drive out to show her through the mansion in Maplecreek.

"Brooke, I can't believe it's you!" Jake called as he hurried out from the back room to his almost bare outer office a secretary no longer staffed. This time Brooke was so glad to see him, she hugged him back. "I'd have killed the fatted calf for you, baked you a cake or something. You all right? Come on in here."

"Your sixth sense is as good as ever," she told him, letting him steer her into his back room, which served as his private office. "It's been a strange day, Jake. But I really wouldn't stop in town without seeing you. Maybe I can say hi to your dad again, too." Brooke hadn't seen the elderly retired city bus driver for at least a year. She felt guilty about not having him and Jake out for Sunday dinner as she had promised, but things just always seemed too busy and risky right now.

"Dad's taking his afternoon nap, so you're stuck with me," he said and winked at her as he pulled out a chair at his worktable for her, then walked away to open a small refrigerator jammed with what looked to be cans of pop and beer.

Quickly, she looked around what he called his "war room," which she hadn't seen for months. Enlarged maps of the city with colored pins stuck in them covered two walls, and phone books from all over filled the shelves. Yet the entire place looked immaculately ordered. Between a fax and printer, a computer screen glowed blue and temporarily blank, as if he'd just cleared it. The fussing over her from an unfussy man touched her: he had politely pushed in her chair for her and now handed her a diet Coke before he sat beside her, leaning forward on his elbows at the small patio-type table. His T-shirt read POLICEMEN'S BENEFIT BALL, MARCH '90.

She told him what had happened at the office and about running into Ray McCarron when she and Elizabeth had lunch. "No wonder you looked rattled. That guy's still high on my hit list of stalker suspects. He had motive and money to hire someone to do the dirty work if need be. But I wish you'd move back to Columbus, Brooke. Enough time has passed and—like I said—I'll nail that jerk—McCarron or whoever—if he ever makes another move."

"We can hardly accuse Ray McCarron because he used the words 'bleeding heart,' though."

"I know, I know. So how's everything in Maplecreek? I was hoping you'd ask me down for a picnic or something."

"We'll do that, Jake." She told him about restaging

239

the wreck—even told him her Amish neighbor, Katie's uncle, had helped her. She explained about finding the liquor bottles and her latest futile attempt to work with Sheriff Barnes. Her imitation of Reba Potts got both of them laughing. Somehow, Jake always lifted her spirits.

"So," he said, "no problems with the neighbors, 'cause you're still working on the hit-run the Amish don't approve of?"

"Actually, I have something else to tell you, but I want you to promise me one thing first," she said and took a steadying swallow of Coke before she put the can back down on its sweat ring.

"Shoot. You know I'm on your side."

"You've got to promise, Jake."

"Cross my heart and hope to die," he said and winked at her, then rolled his clear blue eyes so devilishly it almost made her laugh.

"Because, as you well know from other things I've told you, my relationship with my Amish neighbors is tenuous as times, I don't want you rushing down and staking the place out when you hear this. I mean it, Jake. I can't have a man hanging around the house, so to speak. They'd never understand."

He reached a big hand out to grip her wrist. As he slid farther forward on his chair, the ankle of his artificial leg pressed hard into her, but he couldn't feel it, so she shifted her foot away. "What? Tell me," he demanded.

"I have had two unwanted late-night visits from someone who is either Amish or wants to appear Amish—and who obviously hopes to make me leave Maplecreek or abandon the accident investigation. Or maybe it's my stalker from here, but that's a long shot."

"Two? *Two?* And you never told me—after

everything?"

She held up her hand to stay the coming explosion and filled him in.

"Damn it, I told you to call me!" he shouted and smacked the tabletop with his fist. "This guy spouting Bible verses and cursing you—you sure you didn't get a decent look at him? I could set a trap for him, and—"

"That's just it, Jake. See how you react? I just can't involve you."

"You think I can't be careful and quiet about it?"

"I can't have your van seen near the place, and I know you can't walk far or fast—Jake, I'm sorry. I know you can do anything you set your mind to, but I'm asking you to keep your promise to stay out of this for now. You're one of my best friends, but this isn't like the other mess here in town."

"Why the hell not? Especially, if maybe the guy from here has found you there?"

"I don't think the modus operandi is the same, do you? He has no warped sense of humor like the Columbus stalker with switching the fish and everything. And he's never come inside the way the stalker did here, so I didn't really feel he's violated where we live as the man did here. Please, Jake, understand and accept it, or I won't be able to tell you anything else because I can't have you there—not with my female Amish workers or with the strict Amish morals."

To her amazement, he calmed down quickly after his initial outburst. His ruddy color faded; he took her hand in both of his big ones. "I've got strict morals, too, Brooke. And that includes no one, but *no one*, hurting my lady friend who gave me back my self-respect after—my own car accident. That's another reason I want to keep working on this hit-and-run with you.

241

And I want you to *promise me* you'll fill me in on what happens. You don't want me around, maybe I can work on leads from here. Deal?"

"Deal," she said. "And I'll still ask you for a picnic."

"And Brooke, think about it. As soon as Jennifer's out of school there, you'll be so much better off back here in Columbus."

The big day of his shop raising, Daniel really felt on edge. As far as he was concerned, this outpouring of work—their form of approval and love—by the Maplecreek Amish bound him to them more than baptism ever would. During the growing season, each hour of daylight was precious to these farmers, and yet many buggies came pouring down his lane to build his shop and showroom, so that he could really begin to earn his livelihood among them.

As one of them, he would repay them time and again with the work of his hands over the years, he vowed silently, for it would never do to outright thank a fellow Amish man. As for the neighborhood women, they would be here later—including Brooke and Jennifer. And that fact, after he had told her they were through, unnerved him more than any unspoken Amish commitment today.

"*Sie kuma, sie kuma*! Here they come!" his nephews Isaac and Andy shouted as they spotted each buggy on Sawmill Road. The boys and their friends were in charge of helping to unharness the horses, then staking them out in the back pasture so they could graze during the day before they were hitched up again in the evening. Daniel's parents and Levi and Emma's brood had come early to help; his mother, Emma, and Leona worked to prepare his newly gray linoleum-tiled kitchen for the others who would be here later with more food. Barn, house, or shop railings always meant a frolic with plank tables full of food, but he felt anything but in a frolicking mood.

"Welcome! How are things at your place?" he asked as he strode to meet the Habeggar men, who were unloading saws, hammers, hatchets, and lifting poles from their buggy. They chatted, then went to join the growing group of men, dividing into teams for the myriad tasks. Weather, projected bushels per acre, a sick horse—their varied discussions floated to Daniel as he paced here and there to oversee preparations.

At eight o'clock, fifty-four men went to work on the already laid concrete foundation. Piles of girders, posts, and beams fresh from the Maplecreek sawmill diminished as pieces were constructed on the grass to make the four sides of the building. Then, with eager hands and pointed poles, they lifted and held each side in place until they joined it to the others. To men used to raising massive barns, this mere shop was a holiday.

In an hour a sturdy skeleton stood, its big cross-timbered shoulders and ribs locked together with foot-long wooden pegs driven into bored holes. The tattoo of banging hammers, the singing of saws drowned most conversation, but men moved in a harmony of effort. Some swarmed atop the frame to raise the roof rafters; others nailed the skin of siding to the walls.

By midmorning barefoot women had arrived in buggies, or pulling children's wagons full of *kinder* and food, or just walking. He saw Brooke and Jennifer and nodded to Brooke across the bustle, then tried hard not to look at her again. The women's lighter voices blended with the cacophony of noises. Soon, some came out with welcome pails of water and lemonade with big

243

ladles. Daniel's shirt stuck to his back with sweat; the work felt so good among his fellows, stretching physical and communal muscles in unison.

Barbara Yoder offered him the handle of the ladle from her bucket of lemonade. When he took it, she held on just a moment to make him pull her closer. "A good shop, a good start, Danny, a new life, for sure," she said, smiling at him prettily, letting her thickly lashed eyes wander downward from his face just enough to let him know she still wanted him.

"If things go well, I'll be able to hire an apprentice," he told her, knowing it was not what she wanted to hear. He wiped his mouth with the back of his hand. And then, when she dallied and he turned pointedly back to work, he saw Emma.

She wasn't where she was supposed to be. Across the driveway, beyond the line of parked buggies, she was halfway up an apple tree as if she were a wayward child. Puzzled and worried, Daniel walked toward her, leaving Barbara to go on to the next man. No, Emma was not anywhere near where the *kinder* were, so she wasn't with the young girls overseeing their games. How had his mother and Leona let her wander off right now?

He hurried over and looked up into the leaves where she'd disappeared. She'd been odd lately—sometimes depressed, sometimes normal, sometimes excitable and most alarming, while her housework and meals languished, willing to work only on her new Wedding Ring quilt some worldly woman had commissioned. Leona, Emma's mother, and Levi's mother helped her, covered for her, actually, but what was all this right now? If he didn't get her back to the women and Levi heard . . .

"Emma? What is it? What are you doing?" He had to

244

shout because men had begun to hammer down the sheet-iron roofing and the racket was like giant hail on a tin roof.

"Dan? This bird nest, I'm saving it!"

"From what? Get down here before you fall!"

"No. Up here, I like it, for sure. These eggs, I have to save them, because there is a hawk circling—like one of Levi's airplanes he loves."

He started up after her; she wasn't as high as she looked. But she kicked a foot at him, rustling leaves and skirt in his face when he reached for her ankle.

"Emma! Come on now, or I'm going to get Levi to haul you down!"

"I could care, uh-huh! Besides, closer to Katie this way, you know. Looking down on us, that she is. If I can't go up to Katie, I can at least climb this tree!"

"Oh, man," Daniel said, wiping his sweaty palms on his work trousers before climbing higher. She was bad sick in the head, and Levi refused to have her taken to the doctor. He would have to talk to him again. But for now, he didn't want a scene with Levi furious or her tumbling out of the tree.

"Come on, now, Emma," he said in his most soothing voice for having to yell. She started slowly down, so he stayed put, straddling the crotch of the tree. "That's it, Emma. Leave the nest alone. You're thinking Katie's up there in heaven looking down on us? That's real good, but come on down, now. Good, come on."

"She's up there and so is someone else watching us!" Emma insisted and shoved limbs away with one hand to make a window through the leaves for him. "See?"

Daniel looked up through the opening. A man stood on the rim of the hill; his silhouette made his elbows appear to stick out of his ears. "Just another nosy tourist watching us with binoculars, Emma," he told her as the sun caught the two glass eyes to make them glint before he turned and walked away. "Now, come on, I said."

He startled when she reached down to place two bird eggs in his hand. "And don't let Levi have them for lunch," she said with a laugh. But he saw tears in her eyes, hugely magnified by her thick glasses. Aghast, Daniel let her push past him and drop to the ground. He watched her walk back, scuffing, almost slouching toward the women laying planks on spare sawhorses to make tables. Quickly, cradling the two eggs in his free hand, he scanned the sky, saw no hawk, and climbed up to return them to the nest.

He headed directly over to Levi and explained what had just happened. Levi's features tautened even more; he shook his head. "And if you send her home with Leona," Daniel concluded, "you should know there was a man on the hill watching us, but I don't see him now." Daniel saw Levi look away, not to glare at Emma, not the hill, but momentarily at Brooke.

"Myself, I'll take Em home and come for my tools tomorrow. Walk home, I'll tell the others, because we'll take the buggy. Forgot to feed the chickens anyway, so Isaac said."

"Haven't lost or sold some chickens lately, have you, Levi?"

"On top of this bad foot from the new colt stepping on me, that's all I'd need. Nothing wrong with my chickens," he threw back over his shoulder as he limped toward Emma.

With almost everyone else, Brooke and Jennifer stayed until sunset. After the work was done, people ate again, strolling about or sitting on old quilts in the yard.

Daniel had bought taffy and Tootsie Rolls, and there was a candy scramble for the youngest children. Eventually, the boys brought the horses from the field, and buggies started home to get there before dark. Brooke supposed many still had evening farm chores to do by lantern light.

Despite the fact she had not dared to say much to Emma before Levi had suddenly taken her home, the aura of the day—sharing, working, just being together—lingered in her heart. Even now, she let Jennifer play with Susie and the leftover kids and worked hard, elbow to elbow with the women, cleaning up, packing up. At least she and Jennifer only had to walk over the hill to be home.

"Can I say good night to Bess, Mr. Brand?" Jennifer asked as she and Brooke said farewell to Daniel. He was thanking everyone personally with a firm handshake as they left, and Brooke's hand still tingled with the touch of his.

"She's not in her stall." Daniel explained, "but out in the back field with the others, so maybe you can just make it up to her next time we see you."

"Oh, I guess so," she said. Together, they crossed the driveway and headed up the hill. About halfway up, Brooke heard Daniel's voice and turned back.

"I meant to tell you," he called to her, cupping his hands to his mouth in the gathering dusk, "I saw a tourist—someone standing up there earlier. Let me just bring Bess in, and I'll walk you home."

She almost shouted back, *I'm sure we'll be fine*, but she wasn't feeling one bit foolhardy after the chicken blood the other night. "All right," she called back. "Can Jen help you get Bess?"

Jennifer tore down the hill with a whoop while

Brooke walked back down to wait for them on the edge of the driveway. Everyone else was gone; the new workshop stood sturdily waiting to be filled with Daniel's tools and furniture. Then Daniel and Jennifer were back quicker than she'd expected, running. "What?" she asked.

"Bess wasn't there!" Jennifer called to Brooke as Daniel ran in the barn, then back out.

"Did she somehow wander off?" she asked, rushing toward them.

"Her stake was pulled up," Daniel said, "but I don't think she could have or would have done it. I was hoping the boys brought her back into her stall for me and just didn't say so."

"Could she could get out on the road in the dark?" Jennifer asked. "Bess! Bess!"

"Isaac told me," Daniel said, frowning, "she was the last one left in the field, and I said I'd get her. I just don't know . . ."

"Let's walk home, get my car, and look for her," Brooke suggested.

They trooped over the hill and stopped on the crest to survey the darkening countryside below. Brooke gasped when she saw her place. "Daniel, I left only a single kitchen and front light on, but the entire place is ablaze! Unless Verna's come home . . ."

Holding Jennifer's hands between them, they hurried down the hill. "No paint on the outside," Brooke said out of breath. "The front light's not broken! But both doors look like they're standing open. Oh, no. Oh, no! Someone's—been—inside!"

In the yard, Daniel darted into the garage and emerged with a hoe and garden rake. "Do you still have that phone in your car?" he asked.

"No—I took it inside in case he—someone ever cut the phone lines."

Her knees almost buckled. She thought she would be sick. Just when she had boasted to both Daniel and Jake that her Amish tormentor had not been inside the house—and she'd seen Levi leave with Emma to put her to bed hours ago. And he knew she wasn't home. And what about the so-called tourist on the hill? She began to tremble so violently she could barely hold Jennifer's hand.

"Daniel, you're not just going in!" she said as he started for the house.

"At least to get to a phone!" He thrust the rake in her hand. But then, near the back door, in the spill of light, he bent down to examine the muddy spot where Brooke and Jennifer had washed the car today. "I can't believe it," he whispered. "Horseshoe prints going toward—look, muddy ones up the steps!"

"Bess?" Jennifer asked.

Brooke felt momentarily relieved. "Maybe an Amish prank?" she asked. "Like a sort of strange housewarming prank on the day they built your new shop?"

"No way."

Fear surged back through her. She suddenly recalled that horrible scene from that book about the Mafia. *The Godfather*, that was it, where a horse was decapitated and the bloody head was put in someone's bed to make them toe the line . . .and Daniel with his hoe handle raised like a staff was going in.

"Bess?" he yelled. "Bess! If I find anyone else in here, I'll beat the tar out of you!"

Shaking, her skin icy, Brooke followed, holding Jennifer's hand. *Dear God,* she prayed, *don't let that horse be hurt. Daniel's done nothing but help us, and Jennifer*

249

loves that horse. It would be so much worse than her dead fish. Please, God . . .

Muddy tracks across the kitchen floor and through the hall—of a man's footsteps on the carpeted staircase, too. "You two stay here," Daniel whispered and started up.

"We're coming, too! But wait," Brooke whispered as she closed the wide-open front door and they looked up mud-flecked front stairs. "Even though the tracks are there, let's go up the back way."

Daniel nodded, and they hurried back into the kitchen and went quietly up the narrow stairs, which Brooke seldom used. In the upstairs hall, Brooke noticed all the doors were closed when, but for Verna's, she had left them open. Was the intruder displaying some sort of perverted sense of humor like her stalker in Columbus? *I have something awful hidden here behind door number one, two, or three, and you get to find it to receive your prize . . .*

Hoe handle raised, Daniel opened the first door—Jennifer's room—and looked inside. When Brooke saw it was deserted, she pushed Jennifer into it and motioned for her to stay put and keep quiet. Daniel was already to Verna's door. With rake in hand, Brooke forced herself to head for her bedroom at the front of the hall.

She put her hand to the old brass knob. Her hair prickled on the nape of her neck; she felt queasy. But if the horror was here, she would not let Daniel or Jennifer find it first. Things were escalating in a pattern she recognized from Columbus. Last time chicken blood outside, this time . . . She gritted her teeth and shoved open the door to the lit room.

The shocking sight, the smell hit her hard. She

250

staggered, dropped her rake, and pressed her hands to her cheeks. She leaned back against the door frame for support.

"Bess—is here," she called out, but her voice broke.

When Bess saw Daniel, she rolled her eyes and whinnied, stomping and shifting nervously between the bed and dresser. Jennifer came running, and Brooke held her while Daniel hugged Bess's neck. Trampled manure stained the carpet, Bess had evidently yanked down one of the curtains and broken a bedside lamp, but she was alive and well.

Brooke wilted on the chair inside the door in utter relief. "I can't believe someone got her up all those steps."

"Someone strong and very determined," Daniel said, patting the horse's shoulder. "At least she seems all right. And you?"

Brooke blinked back tears of relief, fury, and fear. "I want to fight back so much, but I don't know how!"

He pulled Bess's rope to turn her head toward the door. "We'll start tomorrow by replacing this carpet with what I'm tearing up at my house. Come on downstairs, Jennifer, because you can hold Bess while I check the basement, too."

"Daniel," Brooke said, following him as he carefully took the horse down the front stairs so she wouldn't turn a leg, "I'm so, *so* sorry to get you involved."

He didn't answer as Bess clambered out into the backyard and shook her head hard as if in relief. "Keep her out of this mud," Brooke called to him, "because I want to measure any human footprints in it."

As Jennifer held the horse, Daniel leaned his hoe against the house and took Brooke just inside the still-open back door. When his hands gripped her upper arms, she realized he, too, was trembling.

"You said you're sorry I'm involved," he whispered. "Don't be. I'm involved in the investigation and with you—in my heart—whether I think it's smart for either of us or not. We're going to have to be very careful now, secretive even. It's probably not just chance that your tormentor took my horse of all of them and let him foul your bedroom."

"Then, you do think it's someone Amish here?"

"Or that man on the hill, who didn't look Amish. Besides, all the local plain men I can think of were at the shop raising."

"About our being involved for more than the investigation," she whispered. "When I went back to the city, I thought I could just keep you out of my mind, but I couldn't. I know it's dangerous for us, but I can't stop now, either."

"Good," he said, though he was frowning. "Good!"

CHAPTER THIRTEEN

ONE, AND TWO, AND SIDE, AND KICK! TURN, STEP, kick, kick!"

Kiki faithfully finished her daily aerobic high-kick routine in the shaded grotto behind the free-form pool. When she'd become a showgirl at the Tropicana at age eighteen, she'd never had trouble with the head-high, chorus-line kicks, because she'd learned them from her mother years ago. Let those snobby cheerleaders at Rockridge High flaunt their legs with splits and jumps; even if no one wanted a damn thing to do with a leggy redhead who came from a trailer park literally on the other side of the tracks, Kiki could outdo them all.

Even her nickname Kiki came not from her own childish attempts to say her name Kathleen, as many surmised, but because she had always said, "Kick, kick, Mama!" as the two of them danced together out behind the trailer. Even Hank and the boys didn't know that little tidbit, Kiki thought as she toweled the sheen of sweat from her skin. There was a lot Hank and the boys would—could—never know.

She went into the pool house to shower because it was faster than going clear into her bathroom, and the boys were coming for lunch. Today they had promised to tell her what they'd found out about purchasing land for her Amish village—and down the very same road as Brooke Benton's Sewing Circle! And as soon as she had the land purchase set, she was determined to tell Hank. Even though her brothers had been helping her with her plans, they were obviously too busy for her these days. That's why they were making this a working lunch during their noon break.

She hoped her little project would make Hank proud of her. Sometimes she thought, as the water sluiced over her skin and she stroked its sleekness, even at Hank's age—and she was no spring chicken, however good her body was—she'd like to have a child who really needed her. Yes, perhaps she should just forget to take those birth control pills and see what happened. Matt always said Hank would forgive her anything. *That* was real love, like her forgiving Matt and Clay for anything at all.

They arrived right on time; Kiki had Claire serve the three of them out under an umbrella by the pool. Although she would much rather have had a salad, Kiki had planned all their boyhood favorites—Reuben sandwiches, taco chips and salsa, and chocolate cake

253

with vanilla ice cream and caramel sauce.

"Would Hank mind if I got some of his Scotch, Keek?" Clay asked. "Don't worry, Matt's the designated driver."

She caught the stern, shut-up look Matt shot Clay, and she hoped they weren't drinking too much. "Sure, if your new responsibilities are really getting to you, go ahead," she told Clay.

"It isn't that," he said, scraping back his chair when she had thought her subtle ploy might make him stay put. "I like the expensive stuff, and goody-goody Garner's the only one Hank ever gives more than one glassful to at a time. Be right back."

"No, he's not drinking too much, and neither am I," Matt put in as if he'd read her mind. He put his hand briefly over hers. "Don't worry about us, Kiki. We're big boys now and in the big time at last, as you always said Dad used to put it."

"Yes, but sometimes his idea of the big time was getting in too deep with his own debts when the dealers were supposed to be clean. You know, sometimes I still think he'll turn up, but after he left Mama like he did—and since she's gone now, partly be cause she never got over his leaving—I don't want him back."

"If he's out there somewhere, I hope he doesn't read the *Forbes* list or see the article on Hank in *Time* or that *Town & Country* you got yourself in. That would bring him back with both blackjack-dealing hands out."

"You and Clay don't feel anything for him, do you—our dad?"

"I feel," he said, wiping his mouth with a napkin and tossing it down beside his plate, "resentment that the bastard left us in the lurch like that. Pure, well-deserved hatred for the selfish coward he obviously was, and—"

"Matt, please! You—you just didn't know him—his good side."

"Right!" he said, sarcastically. "Like the times he knocked Mom and the two of us around, after he'd been drinking. He never raised a hand to you, so what do you know?"

She was sorry she'd opened up the floodgates—the sewer, more like. Even though Dad had left them when the boys were six, the putrid memories still polluted them, and she dare not defend why Dad had held things against Mom and the two of them, but not blamed her. But then, she had her own nightmares, too.

"Matt, listen," she finally got a word in to distract him, "tell me more about this land in Ohio."

"It's included in a big auction of farmland going up for sale this weekend, and we have made arrangements to get it."

"A big auction? How much land?"

"Let's just say enough. You realize this still has to be kept under wraps for now, Kiki. Absolutely top secret. Anything associated with the Waldron name gets out, and land prices in the area could go sky-high."

"Oh, I hadn't thought of that. But I do want to keep things small not to take away from the Amish ambience. I just wish you two could have seen how beautiful it is there, and I intend to help preserve and protect that."

"Yeah, well . . ."

Matt looked around as Clay rejoined them with a cut-glass tumbler filled with Hank's favorite Glenbrae Scotch with hardly any ice in it.

"Going to give us a beginning sociology lecture about the Amish again, Keek?" Clay asked and took a swig. "I think you'd better realize what you want in on is big, bad, bottom-line business."

255

"You're not talking to some ignoramus about land, Clay. And I want to tell Hank soon. Secrets are maybe fine in the corporate world, but not between Hank and me. And I'm going to hire Brooke Benton in Maplecreek for some local legal and—well, social advice. I believe I could trust her."

Instantly, she saw she commanded their avid attention they'd only sporadically bestowed before. Anytime she mentioned Hank, she thought, they were all ears.

"Hank, sure, he'll have to know, but you haven't been talking to Brooke Benton, have you?" Matt asked, his eyes narrowing in that way of his that made her feel stuck in a bull's-eye with more darts coming. Matt was clever, so very sharp that she was surprised he'd never guessed Mama's secret.

"As a matter of fact, she called me to say that several of the quilts I have on consignment have been started. This Amish woman we call the master quilter—they like to stay anonymous—has a good start on my Double Wedding Ring. Let's face it, if I want Amish workers, I can't do anything to annoy them in this project, and I'm sure Brooke Benton can be my liaison to them. Those poor people have been through enough lately with a terrible hit-and-run accident that killed four of their teenagers, including the master quilter's daughter. And you know, Brooke's really sharp because she knew who I was without me telling her, though when she saw me with Hank and all she never let on. Maybe she figured it out later somehow."

She saw the intense look that passed between them, what Garner always called "the twin thing," to rile her. "So why would a lawyer be working in a quilt shop?" Clay asked, turning his glass between his hands before he took another swallow, then got a little coughing fit. Kiki waited for him to stop.

"I asked her that the day we were there, and she said she got burned-out in Columbus and that she and her niece just moved there for a change or something like that. She's really open, and like I said, I need someone local to trust there, so—"

Clay smacked his glass down, sloshing Scotch across the mauve tablecloth. "Trust a lawyer you hardly know? One sitting right on the land we're gonna buy—on that same road? She'll probably want in on all this!"

"Clay, that's enough," Matt said, though he looked angry at her, too. "Kiki, it's just we've been under a lot of pressure at work. We've got to clear things with Hank, that's all. But if it wasn't for Kiki, Clay, we wouldn't even have a shot at the stability and success—the security—we've all been working for, so don't take thing out on her."

"I know, I know. Sorry, Keek," Clay muttered and patted her hand. "The only thing is, once Hank knows, Garner does, too. And we don't need that son of a bitch—and I do mean his mother is a bitch—having any excuse to yank the rug out from under the three of us. See, if our new job on the projects board goes well, the promise you made to Mama on her deathbed to take care of us will be completely fulfilled."

"We'll handle everything, Kiki," Matt said and got up to bend over her chair and hug her. Even though she knew he was manipulating her, she clung to him, then sat back up. "We'll be in touch," he told her.

She watched Clay down the rest of his drink, wondering if he would hug her, too. He patted her on the back, and without another word followed Matt across the patio and through the house toward their car.

257

"You idiot," Clay said the moment they pulled away from the house. "My shins are black-and-blue from your kicking me under the table!"

"A lot of good it did us with you losing your temper like that," Matt muttered as the electronic gates swung open, then closed behind them.

"From what Kiki says, that lawyer lives just over the hill from the accident! And now Kiki's all shook about it."

"Yeah, but we don't know a thing about that. And if Hank won't back us that we've never been to Maplecreek, we still don't know a thing about it because we flew back that afternoon, not the morning after."

Clay shook his head. "And what a morning after. I hardly remember it from all we were drinking that night."

"In your case, *every* night. Days, too."

"Get off my back. I had one drink just now, and you're driving."

"And thinking—that we'd better get someone good around here to become a tourist in Maplecreek to keep an eye on how things go at the auction, even though we've arrange a preemptive bid. And to keep an eye on this lady lawyer friend of Kiki's. You know, just insurance for us, especially if Kiki insists on bringing her in on the deal as consultant or best-Ohio-buddy or some damned thing."

"Hire a private detective? You got someone in mind?"

"How about Morning Rain Chiquito? She owes us big, and no one would suspect a woman tourist. She could visit the quilt shop there easier."

"I don't like it, but then I don't like keeping everything about the Amish World deal from Kiki, either. Why do we have to do this the hard way?"

"Look, Clay, the hard way is the only way I can see. We've got to talk to Hank and let him give Kiki this one little favor before she gets wind of what's really happening. And, above all, we've got to cover for ourselves. Or did you have plans to tell Hank or Garner they'd best pull us from our pet project and send us to Europe for an extended vacation because last time you drove a car you killed four Amish kids and took off? I can just hear Garner now, demanding we be promoted to the state pen."

To Matt's amazement, Clay exploded. With a string of curses, he swung at him, clipping him on the jaw, making him swerve the car. He nosed it against the curb, then pulled it over, trying to hold Clay back. But he flailed away, landing blows on Matt's shoulders and chest like a cornered kid. Matt managed to put the car in park, undid his seat belt, and scrambled out. Clay jumped out his side; with fists raised, he chased him onto the strip of grass under a big electronic marquee. Damn, Matt thought, they were in public view on the edge of the parking lot at the Wet and Wild Amusement Park!

"You're the one who said, 'Drive on, drive on,' you bastard!" Clay roared. "It wasn't my fault those ignorant Amish kids were out in a flimsy black buggy on a hilly black road so late. For all I know, they were drinking, too. They're not saints, so don't blame me! They shouldn't have been in our way, that's all!"

Matt held up his hands, but tried to talk. "That's right, that's right. But you and I have got to hang together or, like they say, we'll hang separately. Those kids should never have been in our way. But now things are getting complicated because of our big project and

Kiki's horning in, and we can hardly go back there ourselves to keep an eye on things."

He still thought Clay might lunge at him. The continued to stare each other down as noisy kids poured out of a newly parked car and gawked at them as they went by. Occasional distant squeals of joy from people on the rides floated on the hot afternoon air. It took the sprinkler system starting to spit water to make them jump off the grass. Yet they stared at each other over the roof of their car, while the sprinklers hissed and traffic crawled by on the Strip. It was only then Matt felt the car reverberating and realized he had not turned off the engine.

Clay slumped onto the passenger seat through the still-open car door. When Matt slid in on his side, Clay said with a deep sigh, "Yeah, all right. Let's go find Rain. We're in this so double deep already, I'll do anything we have to."

"There's Susie over there, Aunt Brooke. Can I go play with her?"

"Yes, all right, but no talking to strangers, even if they have horses," she warned before letting the girl run off to join the Amish children. Brooke kept an eye on her until she was in the middle of a hula-hoop game.

Brooke walked around and saw the farm auction was as good as a country carnival. The place was packed, but then it was Memorial Day weekend, which might allow outsiders time off to visit the area. Amish, local English, Mennonites, and strangers lined up for their bidding numbers, then strolled the grounds among displays of farm equipment, furniture, and household items.

Good—it looked like a treasure trove of antiques, too. She was hoping that would bring out city antique dealers, specifically two who looked like either Paul Newman or Troy Donahue. Her visits to area antique stores and gift shops this week had been fruitless, mostly because the shop workers were Amish and had never seen or heard of any Hollywood actors. She feared, however, she had let too many Amish realize she was still playing detective about the accident they thought should be buried with their kids.

It hadn't been a bad week, though. Her tormentor had not returned, perhaps thinking they were lying in wait for him. And, in a way, they were, for she had bought four motion-detector yard lights to surround the house, and Daniel said he walked over several times a night to survey the place from the hill. If she ever needed him, she was to turn on the light in Verna's otherwise dark room. And finally, she had talked him into taking her cellular phone in case she had to call him for help.

Other things that had picked her up this week were that she and Jen had managed some time with Daniel. Jennifer had drawn a happy face with Magic Markers on her faceless Amish doll instead of the sad one she had wanted to draw before. And Brooke had looked around Melrose Manor with the realtor and had fallen even more in love with it.

Now, in the large Stottlemeyer farmyard between house and barn, people chatted in clumps, planning grand bidding strategies. Amish farmers—yes, there was Levi with them—who hoped to bid on the land itself stood gazing over rolling, fallow fields or toured the rickety-looking outbuildings. On shady spots on the front lawn, Amish women staked a claim for later family picnics by spreading old quilts and plopping babies and baskets on them.

The enterprising Amish had already set up stalls to sell food specialties like wurst and trail bologna sandwiches, shoofly pie, and baked Swiss cheese on a stick. Besides the hula hoops, young girls flung Frisbees and boys played *Eckball*, where they threw a mush ball at people in the middle of four bases to see who would be left untouched at the end of the game. Even a sunflower-seed spitting contest was already underway. Brooke saw Jennifer join Susie in a game of crack the whip.

Brooke looked around in vain for Daniel and Emma, but Bishop Brand huddled with friends near an old McCormick Deering farm machine of some sort. Brooke knew such outdated castoffs were, of necessity, essential implements for the Amish. As she took her place in the growing crowd shaped like a half-moon around the auctioneer's podium, Brooke saw, down the distant back lane *rumspringa* boys racing their buggies in clouds of dust. Would Gideon and Ezra have been there now if they had lived, she wondered.

When the bidding did not start right away, Brooke continued to circulate through the crowd, keeping an eye on Jennifer and trying to spot outsiders. She had invited Reba Potts to be her guest here to help ID the antique dealers, but unfortunately, Reba had plans to meet "someone real special, if you get my drift," in Cleveland for the weekend. Someone real special— that's who she'd like to find here, Brooke mused, and, as tall as he was, why couldn't she see him?

"Hear you been looking at the Melrose place with a Columbus realtor," a voice behind her said. She spun to face Sheriff Barnes in his spiffy uniform, sporting a pistol and club as if he were expecting a riot or rash of crimes today.

"Yes, I think it would make a great B and B," she told him. "I've found I rather like your Roscoe County, Sheriff."

"Shows real good sense. And if you're not just passing through, folks might look on you kinder, know what I mean? Not gonna practice law here?"

"Certainly, not criminal law in this law-and-order place except, you know I haven't given up on the hit-and-run."

"Me neither, no matter what kind of bad looks you gave me over those bottles. Long as you don't overstep, keep handing in things, and tell me if you learn anything chatting with folks—them that's talking to you. Then you and I gonna get along just fine."

She bit back several sharp retorts that came to mind. And, in case he heard it through the twisted Maplecreek grapevine, she considered telling him what Reba Potts had said about the two strangers, but decided not to.

He grinned down at her and tipped his hat back with a big hand. "Glad you learned you catch more flies with honey than vinegar, Ms Benton."

"Just in case we're to be neighbors, call me Brooke."

"Will do," he said, without offering her the same in return. "See you in church." He strolled back through the crowd, almost strutting, as if he were the plantation owner and they were all peons. Still, she questioned the man's sudden change of attitude toward her.

She continued to move through the crowd; the auctioneer's two assistants now carried to the front the earlier numbered items first to go on the block, including copper wall candleholders she'd love to bid on for the mansion—if only she were surer about making an offer for the place itself. Actually, she'd like to ask Daniel to look over its interior with her, the walnut

263

staircase, the molding and woodwork at least, checking for structural problems or even termite damage. She could just picture him, making things for the house, taking care of things there—including taking care of her and Jennifer.

She shook her head to rid herself of that fantasy as she watched cane chairs, heavy stoneware and china, a brass kettle, a wooden icebox, two ox yokes, and boxes of Ball and Kerr canning jars Amish women valued, make their way to the front. A farm auction was the Amish answer to the worldly cable TV shopping channel or clearance sales at the mall.

"The Amish won't get near the county fair, but look at 'em swarming here," the male voice behind her said to his buddies. "I swear, they breed like rabbits. Folks say they make good neighbors, but I get sick and tired of those steel buggy wheel rims cutting up our roads they don't pay taxes on. And their yanking modernization outa their places just lowers the value of the neighborhood, if you ask me."

Brooke wanted to round on the man with a sound defense, but again she held her tongue. She moved away, then looked back at them. You might know, the gas station manager from Maplecreek was one of the men. It sickened her that some people who knew the Amish felt prejudiced against them.

The Pennsylvania Dutch dialect buzzed in Brooke's ears as she edged along the periphery of the crowd. She saw Emma now; how she wanted to go over to say hello, so she could judge how Emma was doing, but too many of the Amish she recognized were right behind them. Later. She would find a way to speak with Emma later when they weren't so much on display.

A stir followed by shushes and then silence descended

as the auctioneer, a swarthy man with an un-Amish, short, trimmed beard, took his place at the podium. He wore a plaid shirt and a baseball cap, so he was hardly Amish. An assistant hefted aloft an ox yoke in each hand, item numbers one and two. Brooke had overheard that the auction built suspense by increasing the size and value of items, until it culminated in the sale of the house, buildings, and fields in the late afternoon. She turned her head to check on Jennifer once more, then stood on tiptoe nearly at the back of the crowd, her eyes skimming the strangers again for someone who even barely resembled a blond, good-looking young English man. No one fit, but, facing her across the way, though she had missed him before in the sea of black broad brims and bonnets, stood Daniel.

She felt a little jolt and crackle race up her spine. Her stomach seemed to fall away, and she blushed, even at this distance with all these people between them. She sidestepped to her left to see him better. Was he even looking at her at all in the press of people? Yes, he must be. She felt his eyes like a physical caress, such a different sensation from when she imagined she was being watched by—the other. Funny, but she had been so busy among the Amish last week at his shop raising, she had not sensed or seen the man on the hill with the binoculars.

The auctioneer began his rhythmic spiel. People thrust their numbers up to bid, sometimes blocking Brooke's view of Daniel, but neither of them looked away. Then it hit her—that voice—or was it just the loudspeaker he used? She jerked her head toward the podium. Yes, tall enough, the auctioneer, with a commanding voice, of course. She could hear him saying now from the depths of the darkness, "Woe to you, lawyers . . ."

She had to get closer to see his face, had to confront him when she could. But she was already sure, very sure who he was. Only, did she know him? He wasn't dressed Amish now as he had been that night. Who was he and why had he wanted her to leave Maplecreek?

At least her luck had changed, she thought, as she left the fringes of the crowd and stretched her strides toward the podium. She might not be able to prove that the auctioneer was the guilty party any more than she could prove Ray McCarron or anyone else in Columbus had threatened her before, but she had found this man, at least. And that gave her hope that maybe, just maybe, she'd somehow find the hit-and-run killer.

Daniel was astounded to see Brooke turn and hurry away, almost at a running pace. They had decided to try to keep their relationship private for now, but, even though this was the most public of places, maybe he could grab her for a minute while everyone's attention was riveted on the auction.

He skirted behind the food booths and caught up with her just before she started into the crowd toward the front. The staccato patter of the auctioneer matched the pulsing of his blood to be this close to her, seeing her, touching her.

"Brooke," he said as he caught her arm to pull her back near the cluster of farm machinery waiting its turn to be sold. "I just want to talk to you, for a min—" His voice trailed off when he saw the strange expression on her face. Anger or fear? "What's the matter?"

"The auctioneer. Is he Amish? He doesn't quite look it."

"He's Mennonite. That's Paul Hostetler's father,

266

Hiram."

She gasped. "I'm certain he's the man who had the loudspeaker outside my window that night. And now it makes sense."

"An-a going once, an-a going twice . . . Sold!" the metallic voice resounded as Daniel tugged Brooke back behind the hulking old hay loader.

"Maybe I've been wrong to insist the hit-and-run driver couldn't be Paul," he admitted.

"I was convinced it wasn't him, too. I thought the fact he left town was coincidence. If he had a guilty conscience, it was for his marital situation and not the accident. But why else would his father go to such lengths to try to scare me if he didn't think Paul was guilty of the hit-and-run? Does Hiram Hostetler look like the man you saw on the hill with the binoculars?"

"He was tall like Hiram and didn't seem to be dressed Amish, but I don't know. His hands with the binoculars were up by his face, so I'm not sure about a beard or hair length. I can't recall if Mr. Hostetler limps."

"Limps?"

"I forgot it until just now, but when the man turned away, he kind of limped."

"Remember I told you one of the footprints in the mud was blurred, while the other one was distinct?" she asked him. "Could it mean the man who stole Bess limped? I'll bet you a good chicken dinner, Hostetler does. He blames me for driving his son away, and he wants me out of here to assure Paul he can come home. And that must mean Paul is Katie's killer, so we're going to have to find him." Daniel saw she was trembling; she folded her arms and gripped her elbows as if to steady herself.

"Brooke, just when are you planning to confront this

man? Surely, not right now."

"Hostetler? Here, today, as soon as I can."

"I'll go with you when you do."

"No you won't. It was your idea to keep a low profile about us, and you're right."

"The sheriff's here. Take him with you."

"And tell him what? 'Sorry, your lordship, that I didn't mention three little incidents, including a breaking and entering, but I've got the guy for you to arrest now?' "

"If Hostetler's the one, he's obviously going to feel cornered, and that could make him dangerous."

"Don't worry about me. I'll go home and get a tape recorder to hide in my purse so I have some leverage with him later."

"He's hardly going to admit to anything."

"Daniel, I've gotten some pretty amazing confessions from people who had a lot to lose by telling the truth. If you'll just watch Jen while I run home for the tape recorder . . ."

"All right, but one condition. Take someone back to the house with you just to be sure. Maybe Amos Mary."

"But Hostetler's the man—I'm sure of it!"

"Just in case. All right?"

She nodded. Daniel squeezed her shoulder; though he wanted to hug and hold her, this was hardly the time or place. Shaking his head, he walked from the circle of tall farm equipment and headed for Amos Mary to ask her to go with Brooke. When he glanced back, it startled him at first, because it looked as if Brooke were stepping from the jaws of those metal monsters.

At first, Emma had kept her eyes on the boys racing buggies on the lane; then she'd watched the girls Katie's age. It would not let her go, this crushing weight of the loss of her children, the loss of herself. She hated the auction, for she grieved for the corpses of the house and barn being stripped of all their insides, their pasts, their very lives. At least the fertile wombs of the fields would bring forth life again, if only Levi and the others who hoped to buy them could make the best offer. Then, craning her neck, she saw Brooke standing off to the side by the farm equipment, staring intently at the auctioneer without bidding on a thing. Brooke had gone home with Amos Mary to get something she'd forgotten, but they were back now.

"Levi," she said, turning to him, "I've got to visit the Porta-John." She hurried off before he could insist Leona or his mother go along, as if she were a child younger than Susie. She was tired of being watched, talked to, helped, prayed for. Nothing lightened her heart, even when she admitted to God it was all her fault that she felt the way she did with all her blessings. Levi was right. She had so much to be thankful for. Yet quilting the same pattern she had done with Katie was the only thing she could stand to do now, even though earlier she could not bear to see the Wedding Ring designs of circles endlessly interlocking. Other than that quilt, even little daily tasks seemed entirely too overwhelming and impossible to be faced or tried.

"Brooke!"

"Emma! I'm so glad to see you. How are you?"

They held hands a moment, like young girls, then realized someone might be watching, and dropped them awkwardly. "Busy working on the Wedding Ring quilt, uh-huh. How's yours going?"

"I've been stitching all those little melon-shaped patches that will make the rings. I wish we could work on them together, as some pieces just don't fit at first. But, Emma, how do you really feel?"

"Off Prozac, that's for sure."

"And?"

"Still missing Katie something terrible. A saying, there is, in *Deutsch*, '*Das heimelt mir an.*' Something it means like 'Memories of old times are painful pleasures.' How I am, that's it, and no one can understand. No one here on earth but maybe just in heaven."

"You don't wish you could—you'd die, do you, Emma?" she asked, gripping Emma's wrist. "I mean, there's so much to live for—Susie really needs you, just like Jennifer needs me. And Leona looks up to you so and tries to help you."

"A joy and not a burden all that should be . . ." she whispered. She repeated the saying in German again and again to scold herself as she walked away from Brooke and went to lock herself in the john for a while, because it seemed to her a silent, private, little coffin.

During the hour lunch break, Brooke sat with Jennifer on their blanket where she could keep an eye on Hiram Hostetler. Unfortunately, he sat with several Amish men and some townspeople, so she couldn't get him alone. She barely ate any of her wurst sandwiches with huge dill pickles, root beer, or shoofly pie, though Jennifer made up for what Brooke didn't eat. Her mind was on her coming confrontation with Hostetler, but the buzz everywhere was that too many outsiders were bidding here, thereby jacking up prices for what to the Amish were daily necessities.

As the afternoon wore on, even the old quilting frame went to the most acquisitive outsider, a red-haired antique dealer people were whispering was either from

270

Pittsburgh or Cleveland. And there was a sleek, black-haired woman who looked American-Indian she didn't know who kept trying to talk her ear off. Finally, Brooke made sure Jennifer was with her friend from school and moved away to get even closer to Hostetler. Jennifer would even go home with her friend, so Brooke felt free to pursue him, though she had no intention of confronting him off on her own somewhere.

Her legs began to shake again as the day wore on, not from fatigue but nerves. Only the buildings themselves and the farmland remained to be sold. The four Amish men, including Levi, who hoped to be able to get part of the sprawling acreage, edged forward in the crowd. It was common knowledge that they were the ones with more than one son coming on who must be provided for so that they were not forced to go into trade, or worse, move away. They had pooled their money to buy the land and would split it amicably later. No one Amish would bid against them; several others would even loan them money for a mere nod if English bidders got in to drive up the price on the land.

"Now, I got an announcement to make to you all!" Hiram Hostetler's voice boomed out through his handheld loudspeaker. Brooke gritted her teeth; she couldn't wait to make her announcement to him that she was on to him. But the opening she'd been rehearsing for him blew right out of her brain with his next words.

"I know this is gonna come as a shock now, folks, but there's been a preemptive bid on the farm that the distant heirs have accepted."

A muted murmur swept the crowd.

"Which part? What fields?" Levi called out.

"Why, all of it, the whole kit and caboodle, and don't

ask me to go naming names, 'cause it's all been done through legal land agents. I don't even know who really did the buying, but obviously it's someone who appreciates prime land and will make a real good neighbor."

"Why weren't we told so we could bid early?" someone else called out.

"Sorry, folks. I didn't even know till today. Honest."

Brooke doubted that the word *honest* meant anything to the man. But this mess was going to make it a lot harder for her to get to him with all the questions and complaining he was going to have to face right now.

But she soon saw she had forgotten the prime tenets of the Amish world: no matter what the affront or injustice, there would be acceptance, forgiveness, and no confrontation. She heard the frowning Levi tell his two crestfallen sons in a wavering voice, "If the warring Philistines stop up the wells for cattle, we move on to new land and dig other wells."

That broke her heart—and infuriated her again. Why couldn't these people protest or fight back? This was consumer fraud at best, because people had been led to believe this was a public auction for the land, too. But it did mean one thing in her favor. She could see Hiram Hostetler was not being bothered by anyone as he headed toward his car in the adjoining field that served as a parking lot. Brooke ran after him, fumbling with her tape recorder in her purse to turn it on.

Only three cars remained scattered among several buggies in the once crowded lot. Hostetler saw her coming as he opened the door; his eyes opened wide, too. He quickly shoved on reflective sunglasses and tossed his loudspeaker on the backseat.

"One word with you, Mr. Hostetler!" she called out

before he could get in.

"What one word is that, lady? I know who you are, and the plain folk hardly hired you to give me flak. Look, it was a couple of corporations whose agents bought the land, that's all I know."

Despite being so intent on her other topic, that admission snagged her interest. "But why would a couple of corporations want old farm buildings and land so far from major cities and transportation arteries? You just led everyone to believe that someone had bought it who would be a good neighbor, as if it were a single purchaser wanting to farm."

"Look, it's been a real long day . . ."

"And could get much longer unless you agree to talk to me. Woe to you, auctioneer, if you won't!"

Hiram Hostetler was a swarthy man with a tanned face, but he blanched visibly at that. "I don't know what in kingdom come you're talking about," he muttered. She edged closer to be sure her little recorder would pick up his voice; from this close distance she could see her distorted form reflected in his mirrored sunglasses.

"I recognized your voice today, Mr. Hostetler. And," the thought suddenly came to her, "since I have your voice on tape from that night, I'd have no problem convincing a judge or jury exactly who harassed me. But worse, that might make someone jump to conclusions that you did it because you heard I was asking around about Paul—and what sort of a car he was driving the night of the Amish buggy wreck."

"Whoa, you're going way too fast for me."

"I don't think so. The thing is, did you believe Paul was involved in the hit-and-run and thought I did, too, so you had to scare me away before I uncovered more evidence? And when you somehow got wind that I was

273

reenacting the accident setting, too, you decided on the grotesque artwork—hex signs and witches' pentangles in chicken blood. But you see, because I was planning to restage the accident, I had in the house that first night you came calling a camera ready with some infrared film," she bluffed, hoping he would take the bait.

"You're lying or you would have accused me long ago!"

"But I didn't see you until today," she reminded him. "And then you had to up the ante, didn't you, by taking Daniel Brand's horse and putting the poor thing in my bedroom."

He slammed his car door and strode toward her. She forced herself to stand her ground. "I don't know what in kingdom come you're talking about—after that first little warning I gave you!"

"With the megaphone, you mean?"

"I only wanted you to know everyone don't think you're welcome to butt in like you have. But chicken blood and taking a horse into a bedroom—you're crazy, lady!"

"And you're guilty just like Paul, and I'm going to prove it!"

"Paul's not guilty, I swear it!" he shouted, banging his fist on the trunk of another car, but, thank heavens, stopping five feet from her. "He's morally guilty, sure, but only of deserting his family—of fornication, getting that good-looking divorcée to whore for him. He didn't kill no Amish kids but tried to help! I thought your asking around about his car would make him bolt from his real delicate marriage, 'cause his wife, Norma, said she'd hold it over his head—say he was involved with the wreck if he didn't give up that other woman. Norma partly brought his taking off on herself, 'cause she
274

threatened him she'd go to you, even though she knew it wasn't true. So he ran with that whore, and I don't know where he's gone, so if you've located him . . ."

That brought her up short. If the man was going to lie, wouldn't he have denied all three incidents and not so readily admitted guilt on the first? But wouldn't it be too big a coincidence if he had only been her first visitor, then someone else had done the graffiti and taken Bess? She had told no one else in Maplecreek but Daniel and Emma about that first visit. But could Emma have told Levi, and he thought he could take advantage of the situation? Her shoulders slumped. Besides, in trailing the man over here, she had seen he had not limped. But even today, she'd seen Levi still did; but Levi was at the shop raising, not on the hill. She felt sick inside again, not half so victorious.

"No, Mr. Hostetler, I haven't located Paul," she told him. "So you thought you'd better scare me away and were willing to disguise yourself as Amish to do it."

"You can't prove I done anything really wrong!"

"As you evidently know, you're talking to a criminal attorney, so let's get real, Mr. Hostetler. Do you think you can continue to be the favored auctioneer in this area—I know you do the yearly big benefit Amish quilt auction, too—if the Amish realize you've been imitating one of them to terrorize people at night? I know they are nonconfrontational, but they do have their ways, believe me!"

"Look, I've had about enough—"

"Then enough said for now. Let's get back to your original admission, that you knew some mystery corporations bought this land and you didn't tell the Amish that, either. I'm going to make you a flat-out business deal, take it or leave it."

275

"What? I'm telling you, I have no control over getting any of this land for the Amish!"

"What I'm asking is that you get me the names and addresses of these purchasing agents and the corporations they represent from the Stottlemeyer heirs. Tell them you need to know to make the sale official or something."

"Why? What're are you gonna do?"

"What I'm *not* going to do, if you get me those facts, Mr. Hostetler, is to publicly accuse you for menacing and harassment. I hope we have a deal. And I'm sorry about Paul's marriage and his running, I really am. Maybe, considering his kids, he'll be back."

He seemed to wilt. So she had hit the heart of it with him. He shook his head and cleared his throat.

"I thought it smelled fishy about more than one purchasing agent and keeping it secret, too. My first thought was all we need is some sort of discount shopping mall here. And what if my contact won't give me the information?"

"Please try. And if you can find out, I think we can let bygones be just that between us, as long as there are no more incidents to try to scare me away from Maplecreek." She knew she sounded strong, though she didn't feel that way. Who had made those other two visits if this man had only been responsible the first time? Or did Hiram Hostetler just not want to be responsible for killing someone's chickens and stealing an Amish buggy horse?

Looking somewhat shell-shocked, he plodded back to his car. Brooke was amazed at how quickly this confrontation had changed its course. Trying to track down buyers of a piece of farmland was all she needed on top of trying to solve the hit-and-run, she thought as she watched the man drive out of the field and turn onto Sawmill.

She nearly dropped her tape recorder she was rewinding when Daniel walked up behind her. "Oh, where were you?" she asked.

"On the floor of my buggy right over there. I couldn't let you face him alone. But I was impressed."

"Daniel, lawyers can be plea bargainers—negotiators and peacemakers—and are not necessarily instigators of contention, you know. But do you think he was telling the truth about only being responsible for the first incident? It sounds like such a coincidence that someone else would start in, but I've seen truth stranger than any sort of fiction when I've investigated crimes."

"You know what else?" he said, almost as if he hadn't been listening. "You've got a streak of Amish in you after all. You forgave that man and got him to help you and his neighbors."

"That remains to be seen. I take it you heard what he's helping me with?"

"Yeah. It's really sad for us if our families have to be broken up for our young people to push on west to get farmland. But it may not be as dire as it sounds. What if some farming partners want rich land, or a particular crop is going to be tested here, or the State University Agriculture Branch at Wooster wants more experimental farmland?"

"But this sounds like multiple buyers."

"I know that's weird. And Hostetler's idea about a shopping mall is way off. Look at this acreage," he said, turning her by the arm and pointing. "It's rolling land with a good-size stream and pond in it, not the best for stores and parking lots. And, let's face it, the stores in Maplecreek and Pleasant aren't that heavily patronized, and the storekeepers there despair of the Amish being so self-sufficient, so who'd put a mall here?"

"You know, we shouldn't be standing out here talking like this," she said. "There are still some people over by the farmhouse."

"You're right. Give me a chance to get home, then leave your car and walk over to see how my shop looks with everything inside. I can show you around, we can talk all this over . . . and do whatever else comes to mind."

They traded taut smiles. Brooke felt both enervated and elated after all that had happened today. She had solved who made at least one of her nighttime visits, and surely that was a good beginning. But who was behind the other incidents—and the wreck?

She nodded. "All right. Jen's at her friend's house in town. A half hour, and I'll be there," she said and turned uphill to get her car.

CHAPTER FOURTEEN

"BEFORE WE TALK THINGS OVER, COME IN AND SEE my new place of employment," Daniel called to her as he stood in the doorway of his shop a half hour later.

Still slightly out of breath from her walk over the hill, she stepped in past him. "Oh, it smells so good in here, all new!"

"I intend to put pine paneling over this drywall when I can afford it and a wooden pegged floor over this concrete. But this is all I need for a start. I just got the furniture moved out here yesterday, partly so I can continue to rip out the wall-to-wall carpet in the house."

"It's a lovely piece you put on my bedroom floor. If I

do buy Melrose Manor, maybe I could buy the rest from you for the bedrooms there. Oh, there's the hutch," she said and went to it, to peer into its glassed door shelves and run her hand along the gleaming finish once again.

"Actually," he said, "I sold the other one that I'd brought from Goshen to a pair of newlyweds from Wooster. That one was just finished last week."

"I don't care if you think it's prideful. You have great talent—you're an artist in wood."

"A gift from God. Besides, my father's good with wood. He's a very talented hand carver, though he forces himself to stick to whittling far less than what he could do. Clothespins, a bird feeder, occasionally a carved and lettered sign. I think I've got him talked into making one for me out front."

Suddenly, it became stunningly silent between them. She saw him approaching behind her in the reflection of the glass as she still studied the hutch. Her body tingled before he even put his hands on her shoulders, then dropped them to gently clasp her waist.

"When you touch my furniture," he whispered, his dark eyes so intense as he turned her around to face him, "it's kind of like you're touching me. I know it's been an emotional day for you, and I don't mean to take advantage of that, but . . ."

The kiss was gentle and reassuring; she was the one who suddenly seemed desperate, who held harder and deepened the kiss and caress of which he took full advantage, before stepping slightly back.

"Maybe we'd better not do this here—all these windows," he whispered, his hands still hard on her waist with his long fingers splayed over the curve of her hips. She nodded, yet only tipped her head back so that his mouth could more thoroughly ravish her jawline and throat.

"We'd hear a buggy," she said, his breath hot against her now.

"Susie just walks over. And you remember Emma . . ."

"I'm afraid you're right," she conceded with a sigh.

"That's why you should come in the house, then." He chuckled. "You can take a closer look at the rest of the carpet to see if you want it."

They walked quickly outside, then in the back door of the house. He led her through the kitchen to the living room, where he'd begun to tear up and roll the thick green carpet.

"Take off your shoes and feel it," he said, his eyes glinting with devilment. In a challenge, he yanked off his own and threw them in the bare-floored corner.

"But I've felt it on my bedroom floor," she protested, laughing. She had wanted to talk over with Daniel all the things Hiram Hostetler had told her today, but now she only wanted to forget all that for a few minutes. She felt entirely reckless as she untied and tossed her shoes.

Like kids, they scuffed around barefoot on the big patch of carpet still down on the floor between the two large rolls of it. Striking strange poses, they pretended to ice-skate; they twirled and giggled and feigned slipping and holding each other up.

"Lovely carpet," she said at last as awkward silence descended between them. "I'll take every bit of it you don't want."

"It feels good on other body parts besides feet, too."

"How do you know?"

"I was pulling it up late last night with not much on."

They sat down on the patch of carpet with a thump. He tumbled her under him and covered her mouth with his again, then peppered hit-and-miss nips and kisses on the soft inner sides of her arms, then her throat.

"Mm, Daniel we have to talk about preventing something."

"Rug burn?"

"No, seriously—I mean, well, losing our heads."

"You want to keep this from being shallow," he surmised, raising his head. "But I feel deep commitment, or I would never touch you like this. However fast this has happened for us, I'm not flirting, not just playing." His intense face hovered mere inches from hers.

He kissed her again; her head spun. She clung in surprise at the hunger of his passion, and then in shock at the roaring rush of her own. At first she thought the distant voice *was* her own . . .

"Daniel! Daniel!"

She gasped as he pushed her against the roll of carpet and pressed her there so they would not be seen from the windows. But hadn't the man's voice come from out back?

"Levi," he muttered, pressing his face into the curve of her throat. He inhaled once deeply, as if he could breathe her in. "I can't believe it," he whispered, exhaling now in a deep sigh. "Emma finds us, then . . ." He lifted his head. "Coming, Levi!"

He got to his feet. Her heart thudded so hard she was certain Levi could hear. Daniel walked to the back door and unlocked it loudly, while she hurried to sit partway up the uncarpeted stairs.

Levi just appearing like this, she thought—if Hiram Hostetler had been her visitor only that first night, perhaps Emma had told Levi and he had decided to take advantage of it to make her leave town. He had

281

obviously been—for an Amish man—extremely hostile to her. And the day of the shop raising, Levi had time to take Emma home, then come back to get poor Bess from the field, and take her up to Brooke's room. Levi knew chickens and horses, and Levi could have made that limping footstep in the mud and had easy walking access to her place, just as he did Daniel's here. Except, she agonized, it most certainly wasn't Levi whom Daniel saw up on the hill that day. And so smoothly breaking into someone's locked home just didn't seem like something Levi would do, did it?

Though Levi and Daniel spoke in their Pennsylvania Dutch, the repetition of Emma's name snagged her thoughts. As usual, Levi's tone was agitated, and she felt sick with foreboding. It was all she could do to keep from running to them, from calling out to know what was the matter with Emma. But she huddled on the stairs until Daniel came back, then scooted crablike down the stairs until her head was even with his.

"I know it's about Emma," she said before he could speak. "She hasn't hurt herself?"

"No—did she tell you she would? Or where she was going if she ran away?"

"No. She ran away?"

"Yeah, and I've got to help look for her."

"But I saw her after the auction. Daniel!" she cried, grabbing his wrist, "this couldn't be something like my harasser taking Bess, could it?"

"No," he assured her. "The whole family got home together after the auction. Levi says Emma kept talking about losing her two sons, too—you know, because they couldn't buy the land. Levi took the boys out to feed the animals; Susie fed the chickens. Emma was starting to fix dinner. Leona was with her, but had to go to the

282

bathroom. And when she came back, Emma was just gone. So far, they've looked everywhere in the two houses, across the fields—even in the pond, because he was afraid . . ." His voice broke. "I told Levi more than once she needs mental help. But now, we've got to find her before she gets beyond that."

"I'll take the car out looking."

"I'm going to take the buggy into town, then toward Pleasant. You know, in case she thinks she's going for more pills or something. I should have told him to have folks look up trees, too. But I did say I'd stop at the Sewing Circle instead of him to be sure she hadn't run to you. She can't have gotten far, since she must be walking. I'm going to harness Bess, and I'll pull up at the back door. You climb in, and I'll take you home, since we should check your place first."

"Yes. Daniel, we'll find her and then—after this—Levi will have to let her get the help she needs." *But*, she *almost added, if he's been tormenting me, now he'll probably blame me even more.*

Daniel started away, then turned back to squeeze her knee. Without another word, he walked out to harness Bess.

The sun was setting in Brooke's eyes, so she had to pull her visor down to see to drive. She and Daniel had checked at the Sewing Circle, but no Emma. Brooke had driven and driven the local roads, but no Emma. Now she berated herself that it had taken her over an hour of that random searching to realize where Emma might have gone—a place she dreaded to look. Yet she turned the car around at a crossroads and headed north.

She gripped the wheel hard as she passed a buggy that got way over on the berm for her. She had passed many in this frenzied hour and wondered if they'd call off the search when it got dark. The whole Amish community was out looking for its one lost sheep, but what good would it do if the sacrifice was that another car hit another buggy? At least each time she'd called out to ask them if there was any word about finding Levi Em, they had spoken to her, so Levi's hatred of her had apparently not spread.

As she drove, she told herself she should have done more to help Emma before, even though they were from different worlds and Levi tried to keep her away. She should have talked to her more when Katie died, when she knew she was still on the forbidden pills, when she saw how strange she was that day she found her just sitting there with that knife jammed in the ravaged grass. Even today when she saw how depressed and strange she was at the auction, she should have helped her.

And why, why had she upset Emma by getting caught with Daniel in the barn in each other's arms? Today Levi would have discovered them if he had just looked in a window instead of calling out at the back door, and then he would have had even more reason to dislike her if he didn't know about them already. No matter how sure Daniel seemed about their increasingly intimate relationship, all that seemed a sort of warning that they were doomed together here in Amish country—if Daniel really wanted to stay Amish.

She saw the wire gate of the Shekinah Amish Cemetery was chained closed, a hint to tourists to stay out, though she'd heard some still entered. Pulling into the gravel entrance, she turned off the engine and got out to duck through the wooden rails. Most of the cemetery grounds lay over the hill, but she could picture

Katie's new-grass grave as she had seen it last when she drove Emma here one afternoon to bring flowers.

Up on the rise, sky high, she sleeps, Emma had pronounced an almost poetic benediction on Katie's life that day. *The comings and goings of her people, she can see over the years, for sure, with a real pretty view of the valley, like watching from heaven.* Now Brooke only hoped Emma hadn't decided that she was going to be with Katie.

Her heart thumping, she strode upward, not staying on the orderly paths, winding her way around mounded turf and modest, identical tombstones. And there, as the crimson sun crashed into the distant western hills, lying prone, face down on Katie's grave, was Emma's dark, sprawled form.

Gripping her hands together, Brooke opened her mouth to call Emma's name, but sound snagged in her throat. She came closer to see if she was breathing, moving, bleeding, anything. Painful memories leaped at her of Katie's body, thrown in the grass beside the road that awful night.

Holding her breath, Brooke stared down at Emma; had she moved or was it the breeze blowing her skirts?

"Emma?"

No movement, no sound. Brooke stepped almost against her body before she saw Emma's broken glasses lay by the headstone. Trembling, Brooke kneeled to roll her over, so afraid she'd find that kitchen knife under her, in her. But before she touched her, she heard a smothered sob.

"Emma?"

"She's not here," came a voice muffled from under the collapsed bonnet brim. "Not here. I called for her, and she's not here."

"Emma, it's Brooke. You're all right now. I'll take you home."

The moment Brooke tried to help her up, Emma rolled on her side, curled her knees tight to her chest, and grabbed her. Brooke went off balance before she righted them, herself on one knee, holding Emma against her as if she were Jennifer. Silent sobs shuddered Emma's body, and they sat that way a long while.

Emma suddenly stiffened and sat back. "Dark, getting very dark, for sure," she said calmly and distinctly. With a sniff, she swiped at her slick face with her muddied apron, leaving more dirt tracks there. Brooke saw she was a mess with snags and rips in her grass-stained and soiled apron and skirt. Her hair spilled lank and loose from her prayer cap; her bonnet hung awry with a leaf stuck in it. Worse, her feet were bare, blackened, and bleeding.

"Lots to be done before bedtime," Emma announced.

"Let me take you home to bed."

"Levi took me home from Dan's shop raising and put me to bed," she said, her face furrowed in a frown. "But then he went off somewhere in the fields to work."

Brooke shuddered and goose bumps prickled her skin. Then Levi could have headed back and taken Bess that day. She bit her lower lip as she recalled now something Verna had mentioned when she'd first arrived: "If you ever lock yourself out of the house by accident, the Amish Kurtz family just back beyond the pond keeps a extra set of keys for me hanging by their back door." And, Brooke thought, her mind racing, the locks had not been battered that day but simply, cleverly picked—or just plain unlocked.

"Emma, come on now," she prompted. Brooke stood and helped her up, reaching to retrieve Emma's glasses, then putting them in her hand, buried in the folds of her dress. Her gaze looked as askew as her appearance, her eyes slightly crossed with her astigmatism.

Arms stiff at her sides, Emma said, "Go back, I want to go back."

"Good, good. I'll drive you."

"Back to how it was before I lost Katie and the baby. But I can't."

"No, you can't go back that way, but you can go home to people who know and love you. The boys, Leona and Susie—Levi, too. Your parents, in-laws, and Daniel. And you know what, Emma? I think Katie would want you to go back for her with a happy heart, since she can't be here. That's one of the gifts Katie always gave people—her happiness and joy of life—and she'd want you to remember that and get better."

"Get better I can't. Never."

"Come on," she coaxed and guided her down the hill. "You know, Jennifer thought she couldn't go on when her mother died and her father left. So both of us went to counseling to help her. And the doctor—it was a woman doctor, Emma—said that even if she never healed, she could learn to go on, to cope, she called it. And Jennifer is doing that, slowly, with some help because she knows I love her, and some others care, too. And you know Levi and the boys love you, as well as Susie, and Leona needs you because she wants to know it's OK with you that she's not Katie."

"Leona, yes, but do you think Levi needs me?"

"Of course, he does."

"But I can't help him because he doesn't understand about Katie—or me."

"After today, I think he'll be ready to try harder. Come on home, and *I'll* tell him he has to *really* understand this time," she said, though the thought of upsetting Levi more was starting to really scare her.

They bent in unison between the fence rails, and Brooke got Emma in the car. When she just sat there, staring but through the windshield, Brooke leaned over her to fasten her seat belt for her. It was then she saw, among the folds of her skirt, the knife in her hand that didn't hold her glasses. It was not the same one from the kitchen that day—oh, not a knife at all, but her long, sharp, bent-handled cloth-cutting shears she must have had hidden under her.

"Can I borrow these scissors, Emma? I'm going to ask Levi if you can come quilt with me. Will you let me keep those for you until we can work on our quilts together?"

Emma gave them up without a word, without interest, and seemed to sleep instantly in utter exhaustion. Brooke thought about wiping her soiled face, but she decided to let Levi see her as she was. It might finally force him to get his wife help, even if it did make him blame Brooke more for her troubles.

Brooke turned on her headlights and, not to jostle Emma, drove slowly toward Sawmill Road. It seemed a dark road home for Emma, just as it had been for Katie that last night of her life. And for Daniel, trying to come back to be Amish. She turned slowly down the lane to the Kurtz farm, trying to plan how to make Levi promise psychiatric help for Emma.

Brooke saw that though the valleys had plunged to blackness, lights gilded the Kurtz farmhouse and *daadi haus* windows. Her headlights silhouetted the numerous buggies parked along the lane. Her heart began to beat hard; if she really stood up to Levi for Emma, what might he do next?

She saw him run out with Daniel and Bishop Brand right behind. She kept the engine running and rolled down only her window a mere two inches. "She's safe! Just sleeping!" she called out her side to them as other dark-clad figures spilled from the house.

"After Daniel checked your place, she came to you later?" Levi called out, peering through the passenger window. His voice came muted to her; she sat still while he futilely tried to open the door. Meanwhile, looking puzzled, Daniel came to Brooke's window. She let them wait until they realized she was not just going to open the doors; Levi hurried around to bend down to her with Daniel.

"What's the matter?" Levi demanded. "Unlock the door!"

"Mr. Kurtz—Levi, Emma's exhausted right now and doesn't need loud voices," Brooke said, twisting in her seat to speak calmly out the crack in her window. "No, she didn't come to me. I found her exhausted and confused, lying on Katie's grave. I believe she's been considering suicide, and she needs medical—mental—help, and that means more than Prozac. I considered taking her to the doctor myself, but I know how much her wellbeing means to you, Levi—that you are her husband and will do what is best for her now. Won't you? Or would it be best if I drove her straight into her doctor's to get her some medicine and counseling?"

"No, no. The same thing Daniel tells me, uh-huh," Levi assured her. "Levi Em, my Emma," he called softly through the narrow space, wrapping his fingers over the top of the plate glass as if to defy Brooke to try to close it. Brooke heard Emma stir, but she didn't wake. Then, when others pressed closer around the car, Levi called in Brooke's window in a controlled, distinct voice, "And

289

first thing tonight, Levi Em, I'm gonna call the doctor. And tomorrow, even if it's Sabbath, I'm gonna ask Miss Brooke to taxi us into the doctor for help for you—medicine and counseling."

Brooke saw tear tracks on his cheeks in the wan kerosene lamp glow from the house. She knew an Amish man's promise was better than sworn testimony on the witness stand. She had won with him here, hadn't she? And wouldn't be afraid to take him into town? Hitting the unlock door button, she leaned over to release Emma's seat belt. Levi ran around the car and lifted his wife out. As he carried her into the house, Ida Brand hurried along at his side. Brooke glimpsed Leona's round face in the thickening darkness before she followed them. Daniel, who had been standing behind Levi, knocked on her window and, surprised to find it still almost closed, she rolled it down.

"Thank God, you found her. And," he added, under his breath "you're two for two today, plea bargaining with Mr. Hostetler and Levi."

"And with you," she whispered. "I'd better go home now," she said louder as others stepped closer. "I'm so exhausted that Jennifer will have to tuck me in."

"Everyone is grateful here, Miss Brooke," Daniel called to her, stepping back among the others.

As she pulled away, Brooke's headlights swung by the row of buggies and the watchful Amish. But this time they—several, at least—lifted pale palms in farewell before darkness swallowed them in her rearview mirror.

CHAPTER FIFTEEN

"HANK," MATT WHISPERED TO HIS BROTHER-IN-law in the midst of the hubbub, "could Clay and I grab a quick word with you in your study? I know you don't like to talk business around here, but it will only take a minute."

"Sure," Hank said with a smile and clapped Matt on the back. "Don't worry about what I think, but if Kiki sees we're missing from the hoopla, then you worry."

Kiki had urged Hank to invite their families for a Memorial Day barbecue at the house; twenty some people were here, including cousins' kids playing horseshoes and volleyball on the side lawn or splashing in the pool. Matt had to admire how Kiki always tried to patch the pieces of two families together—with limited success, despite the big outlay of food, patriotic decor, and booze. Garner and his wife, Sarah, and their two kids were here, but they were all ignoring Kiki— something she herself tried to ignore as if they were just all one big happy American family. Which Matt worried they weren't ever going to be if he and Clay didn't level with Hank soon.

"Thanks, Hank. It will just take a minute," he said as he followed the older man inside.

"Should I get Garner?" Hank asked at the door.

"I'd rather have you decide that after you hear it." Hank raised his eyebrows and led Matt down the hall to his study. It annoyed Matt that Clay was already inside, standing by the window, drinking and looking out. It made it seem they didn't need Hank's permission to enter here or to talk business away from WWEE.

The room was done in earth tones; recessed ceiling lights emphasized two small Remington statues of cowboys; the place was all leather and Navajo blankets. Morning Rain Chiquito, the tough female PI they had sent to Maplecreek, would love the look, Matt thought.

In short, Kiki's new feminine country look had not infiltrated this room yet.

"Actually, Hank," Matt said after he cleared his throat, "what we need to talk to you about is business—and Kiki."

"And Kiki?" Hank echoed, perched nonchalantly on the edge of his large desk. He began to swing one leg like a pendulum.

"Ever since your quilt-buying trip to Ohio," Matt went on, hoping Clay just kept his mouth shut so Hank would not know how much Scotch he'd put away today, "she's had her heart set on owning a sort of quilt shop there evidently, kind of like the one you were in near Maplecreek."

"But in Ohio? Why not open one in Las Vegas? You two didn't tell her about the project?"

"No, sir, we didn't," Clay put in. "We know how to keep a secret."

"She only came to us without telling you," Matt cut in, "because she knew you'd assigned us to the projects division—though she has no idea, I assure you, about Amish World. But we hated to keep stringing her along, Hank—helping her with this so she could make you proud of her when she told you—but not telling her a damn thing, either. Not even that we'd been in Maplecreek."

"She doesn't think she'd be there much to oversee it, does she?" Hank asked with a little smile and shake of his head. He seemed almost amused now; he had stopped swinging his leg.

Matt felt relief flood him. Kiki's power over this powerful man continually amazed him. Hank hadn't gotten angry at either them or Kiki, so he could risk the rest. "I was thinking, sir, we could have her help design

292

and—from a distance, of course—she could oversee the quilt pavilion at Amish World."

"That's probably all it would take," Clay put in, "to keep her happy, but we needed your so-say—*say-so* on it. Keek's really into having us keep everything authentic Amish there, just like the real stuff."

Hank studied them in turn, while Matt held his breath. "Nice work if we can get it," Hank said, "but is Disney's Sleeping Beauty Castle really enchanted? Are the back streets at Universal Studios or MGM really twenties and thirties? Kiki doesn't know the first diddly damn thing about the illusion of things. She's so down to earth if beautifully put together, just like those quilts. But I'm willing to set something up to surprise her— maybe it's not such a bad idea about her input inthe quilt pavilion. Maybe she could even sit in on the planning committee. Let's just invite her to the big board meeting tomorrow where you're going to present everything and give her a little surprise gift of overseeing the quilt pavilion."

"I—we were hoping you'd say that, Hank," Matt said. "Then, things really will be all in the family."

"Speaking of which, I'll handle Garner on this. I have noticed Kiki's need, you see, to be more a part of things. I'm not some old male chauvinist cowboy, and I don't want her to think so. Well, we'd better get back out there, and no one spills the beans to her," he added, pointing at them both in turn. "My girl always did like little surprises."

"Hank, one more thing—about the presentation tomorrow," Matt said. He'd rehearsed this request a lot of different ways; he hoped this came out as well as the Kiki problem. "For a couple of reasons, including the fact we haven't told Kiki we've been to Maplecreek, we'd like to keep our scouting trip there early this month under wraps."

Hank frowned and narrowed his eyes "Garner and several others know. If it comes out later even in the press, what's the difference?"

Matt cleared his throat. Clay, thank God, let him handle this for once. "I think you heard there was a hit-and-run accident the day—I guess it was the night we were there—about a week or so before you decided to look the place over yourself and took Kiki along. Someone accidentally hit a buggy and inadvertently killed four Amish teens right down the road from where we bought the land." Matt swallowed hard; it sounded so loud in his ears.

"And so . . ." Hank prompted, his eyes riveted to Matt's so that he had no choice but to stare him down and not let his gaze flicker. He felt his stomach in his throat; Hank could be like a hawk after a side-winder if he sensed fear.

"We just didn't need anyone thinking any of our people had anything to do with that—in case it got out we were there to case the place. The fallout from a hint of such publicity could kill us there."

"Kill us there," Hank repeated.

Clay, damn him, fidgeted and looked away; Matt could sense it. He stood his ground, his eyes locked with Hank's.

"And since neither of you know anything about this wreck . . ."

"We drove to Cleveland to get the plane hours before it happened," Matt assured him. He tensed his feet so hard in his shoes, his muscles cramped.

"I can see your point," Hank admitted, turning away to walk slowly across the room and open the door. He looked out in the hall, then turned back. "OK, except for Garner, we keep secret Kiki's little part in Amish World until tomorrow. And except for Garner and a few others I'll handle, you two keep quiet about so much as being in Maplecreek when you were."

"Right," Matt said with a silent sigh. Had he pulled this off or not? Had Hank guessed they were lying? But Hank, thank God, knew how much they meant to Kiki.

Brooke had the store open on Memorial Day. The Amish did not recognize it as a holiday anyway, and the long weekend meant a steady flow of customers. Jennifer was home from school, but Amos Mary was teaching her to make an Amish doll—with repeated quiet but firm admonitions she was not to draw a face on this one. At mid morning, Brooke saw the fairly common occurrence of a customer stampede to the driveway-side windows of the workroom.

"Oh, look, talk about a window on the past!" one customer cried to her friend.

"Aren't they just all darling?" another cooed.

Only the Navajo-looking woman who wore the huge squash-blossom necklace—the same woman who had spoken to Brooke at the auction—seemed to disapprove of all the fuss. "Always staring at my people like that, too," she muttered to Brooke as they both went over more slowly to peer out the window. Brooke had thought the woman—who called herself Raine—looked pretty tough with several scars on her brown, wiry arms—but she'd been very friendly, even signing up for beginner's quilt lessons starting tomorrow.

As Brooke bent down to glance out the side window, she was expecting to see that a quilter coming for supplies in a buggy had brought her children, always dressed like miniatures of the parents. But, to Brooke's amazement, today's living tableau was Daniel, helping his father cut Levi's hay field on the hill, while seven—no, eight—boys, including Emma's sons, walked behind to gather loose-strewn grass and arrange the bales to dry in the field. Brooke clasped her hands between her breasts. Daniel was driving a hitch of five blond-maned Belgian draft horses, as if he'd been born to it.

She, too, admired the scene: the power of the big, beautiful beasts, the calm control of the men—and Daniel. Bishop Brand drove the horse-drawn reaper with its hypnotically revolving blades; Daniel followed with the baler, holding the cluster of reins, watching ahead of him for alignment, turning to look behind. The sight struck her as another revelation of the Amish side of Daniel she might never really know—just as she'd probably never really know Emma—or Levi.

Yesterday, Brooke had driven Ida Brand, Emma, and Levi first to see Dr. Marchmont in Pleasant, who had come into his office especially to examine Emma. Then, on his recommendation, they went into the town of Wooster in the next county. There Emma was admitted to the psychiatric ward at the hospital to be treated for what they termed major depression. Despite its being peak farming season, Levi had insisted on staying with Emma, renting a motel room, no less, and Brooke had brought Ida back alone. It had been arranged that someone else would taxi Levi back and forth each day if Emma had to stay more than a week to be stabilized on medication and begin her counseling. Brooke could tell that Levi though willing to do what he must to get his wife back, was still uneasy about English doctors providing counseling. Brooke, however, felt much safer to have him living away from Maplecreek for a week.

296

When Brooke had driven Ida Brand back home, the conversation had been a bit stilted, but Brooke knew better now than to fret over the usual stretches of Amish silence. It perversely amused her that she could not help imagining Jacob Ida, as Daniel and Emma's mother was called among the Plain People, in one of those "I'm over sixty and I don't look it" ads in magazines or on TV. Even more than her regal bone structure, her inherent, unadorned elegance of character had always impressed Brooke. Ida had told her she was very grateful for all Brooke had done for her daughter. Daniel, fortunately, had not been a topic of conversation.

Brooke returned to overseeing the room, but when two other shop ladies came she checked on Jennifer's progress with her doll. Then she went upstairs to look out again in privacy between leafy tree branches as the antique farm machines made pass after pass. Watching Bishop Brand wipe his brow, she thought of something.

She went downstairs and told Amos Mary she was going out for a few minutes and asked Jennifer if she'd like to help. "Oh, sure, especially to see Bess!" she said and followed Brooke back upstairs.

They made a huge pitcher of iced tea from scratch, and poured it and ice cubes into one large picnic thermos. The other one she filled with lemonade made from mix. She knew Emma's boys loved grape Kool-Aid, so that went into a bucket with the rest of the ice cubes. She threw plastic cups into Jennifer's backpack and lugged the pail in one hand and a thermos in the other while Jennifer carried the second one. So they didn't attract a crowd of customers, they went out the back door, behind the garage, then up into the fringes of the newly cut field. It was the Amish women or girls who usually provided their men with drinks, but with

297

Emma gone and Leona watching the house and Susie, this was her chance to make a statement to these people to whom deeds meant so much more than words.

How different the field looked with the tall grasses cut, she realized, however attractively aligned now in fragrant, propped-up bundles of hay. This field had been her and Daniel's special place to meet, to sit and talk—and the site of their first kiss. Now it looked sadly shorn and denuded of its wildlife, though her heart lifted at the thought the barrier between them had been trimmed.

As they walked over the crest, Brooke saw her timing was good. Daniel and his father had stopped the horses partway down the far side of the hill where the big beasts munched stubble. The men rested near Daniel's driveway in the shade of the tree that Emma had climbed last week. Brooke wondered if they had sent the boys into Daniel's house for something to drink or buckets of water for the horses. No one had seen her and Jennifer yet, so they started downhill.

Bishop Brand spotted them first; she could tell when his head turned and he spoke to Daniel. Daniel strode quickly up the hill toward them.

"You are going to earn more stars in your crown with Dad and Levi when he hears," Daniel told them and took the pail and Jennifer's thermos.

"What crown?" Jennifer asked.

"Your heavenly one," he told her as she hurried down the hill toward the horses.

"So how did you and Levi get along in the car yesterday?" Daniel asked. "I know you've been thinking he could have done those things, but it's just not like him."

"You mean his bark is worse than his bite."

"Exactly. Brooke, I'd like to come see you tonight," he said quickly, not turning his head her way. "With Levi gone this week, I'm going to be pretty busy covering for him during the day. Maybe, after Jennifer goes to bed tonight, I can come over."

"Jennifer's going home with Amos Mary for a while tonight while I meet the real estate agent at Melrose Manor at eight. Could you come there to look around afterward? Only, the thing is, I don't want you out on those roads after dark."

"Yes, boss," he said low as they joined the others. "But I'll be there."

Bishop Brand nodded to her; she nodded back. "Tell the boys only water for the horses, Luke!" Daniel called to a skinny lad who turned and ran. "Tell them we've got something better for the rest of us to drink here!"

In typical Amish fashion, they conversed only about the good weather and the fine yield of hay. No small talk or gossip, no agonizing about Emma, no complaining about the loss of the vital farmlands down the road. When the boys lugged buckets up the hill for the horses, Brooke handed glasses around and the men helped themselves from the spigots while the boys dipped Kool-Aid from the bucket.

"Sure good . . . *sehr gut*," they told her in their way of thanking her and assured her that Jennifer could stay and help the boys glean dropped stalks of hay.

When Brooke reached the crest of the hill, she turned to glance back and stubbed her toe on a stone the machines had turned up. In a clatter of pails and thermoses, she went sprawling. As she brushed herself off, she hoped possible observers on both sides of the hill hadn't seen that klutzy move. She gathered her things, but her toe hurt, and she limped as she started off again. And then a thought hit her to make her knees buckle so she sat right down again.

Hostetler didn't limp. Levi did temporarily, but the man on the hill with the binoculars wasn't him. That man had been tall, Daniel said. Could it have been Jake?

Her mind raced: the man who took Bess dragged his right foot. It was Levi's left foot the colt stepped on, but it was Jake's right one that was the orthropedic limb. But Jake? Why, why? Just to get her to come back to Columbus because he missed her? Surely, she was wrong. It was a wild idea, but one she had to consider.

"*Two* incidents?" Jake had shouted at her when she'd told him of her first two unwanted supposed Amish visitations. Had his surprise been that someone was harassing her in Maplecreek or that there were two incidents, because at that point he knew of only one— the chicken blood fiasco? That day in his office, she had told him that at least the menacer was not the Columbus one because her house had not been broken into—and then, it was. She didn't delude herself. Jake could pick a lock if he ever needed to. And they'd taken that walk out by the pond that other time; he'd know where to run back there when she and Jennifer drove in.

"But no," she said aloud, "Jake can't run. I'm being really crazy, just desperate again." But still, she had to know.

She hurried back to the Sewing Circle and phoned him. She had no intention of asking him outright, but maybe he'd give something away if she was careful. Her hand and her voice shook as the phone rang and was answered, but it was Jake's father.

"No, he's not here now, Brooke," the old man told her. "He'll be real sorry he missed you. Took himself a job that keeps him away in Cincinnati at times."

Cincinnati, she thought. At least that was in the opposite direction. If it were true. "Oh, I'll bet you miss him," she said. "Does he have to be gone many nights?"

"Gone most nights this month. But he phones in for his calls, so I'll tell him about this, 'cause it won't be recorded. Usually, they just go on his fancy answering machine, see, but I was waiting for a call back from the pharmacy about my heart pills, so I just picked it up."

"Listen, Mr. Kaminsky, don't bother to tell him I called, because I'd rather just call him back tomorrow—I'm not going to be home this evening if he'd bother to call anyway."

"Sure, all right. Well, I better hang up now so's that call can come in on my pills."

She sat staring down at the phone. Surely, not Jake. Would that mean Jake was her stalker back in Columbus, too? Did he just get off on protecting her, making her feel she needed him? Of course he cared for her, but he'd never shown one sign his feelings were beyond a normal friendship—a light flirtation at times, maybe. If he had been overanxious to help her sometimes, she knew he felt he owed her for getting him the financial settlement. No, all this was so circumstantial. Not Jake. But still, it was a possibility, as strong a one as Levi. One she had to somehow carefully look into before there was another incident. Or perhaps Levi living in Wooster for a while would stop the incidents, indicating Levi?

She put her head in her hands, telling herself she was just losing control again. If only Hiram Hostetler would call her with the names of the land purchasers, she'd get busy on that. If he didn't phone her by tomorrow, she'd somehow get the information on her own.

That evening, after final chores with Levi's boys, Daniel walked from the warmth of the Kurtz barn into the sweet June evening where the breeze cooled the sweat from his skin. When Isaac and Andy went back into the house, Daniel saw his father was still here when he thought he had gone home.

After a day in the fields, they had eaten supper in Emma's kitchen, though other women had brought food in for Leona to dish out. Levi still had not sent news about Emma's condition, but he had said he would phone the Sewing Circle with a message only if there was something important or he was ready to get taxied home. Now Daniel walked over to the north-pasture fence to join his father, who seemed to be watching him, maybe waiting for him with one foot propped on the lowest rail. Without even having to look down, he skillfully carved a clothespin from a small dowel of pine.

"Going to be a pretty sunset, Dad."

" 'Red sky at night, farmer's delight. Red sky at morning, farmer take warning,' " Jacob Brand said, repeating one of numerous traditional *Deutsche* weather proverbs. "A red morning sky for you, my son, that I do not want."

Daniel's pulse picked up its beat. So his father had been waiting for him. He decided to face this head on as he always had—only with calm determination, he warned himself, not a hot temper today as so many regretful times past. Still, his stomach churned in foreboding.

"I take it you mean," he said, picking his words carefully, "that I said at the table I was going to take a look at the place Brooke Benton may buy here in town. That's true, Dad. And I may spend some time fixing it up if she buys it, too."

His father nodded. "Just one more little step, one more, and then you get in over your head and find you forget how to swim. Better read about King David and Bathsheba again," he muttered under his breath as he turned away to gaze out over the orderly green rows of knee-high corn while his hands stayed busy.

"Dad, Bathsheba was married to another man when David desired and took her."

"Married to the world outside our lives, this English woman you care for."

"Born there, raised there, but not married there, Dad. The way Brooke and I feel about each other—it isn't just some fly-by-night thing."

"Your business in that new shop built with Amish hands, going to ignore making your living there now? Hard enough on all of us that you didn't farm, went away to learn a trade."

"It's an honorable, necessary trade, Dad," he said, fighting to keep his voice from rising. "Who knows if you had been born when I was—when the land was getting scarcer around here—that you wouldn't have pursued a career as a carver or made wooden signs. Besides," he went quickly on, holding up his hands to avoid that discussion again, "Brooke will insist on paying me for the repairs I do at the Melrose place."

"And you'd take the money?"

"Not if I can help it, but you've seen how she is when she thinks something's right, just like Mother."

"But," the old man said, turning to him at last with the red glow of sunset reflecting in those flinty eyes like some internal fire, "to my face, you admit it is more than business and friendship for you with this English woman?"

"Look, Dad, I'm not going to lie to you or hide

303

anymore. Yeah, it's more than business or friendship with Brooke. It's grown to mutual admiration and love."

The old man stopped carving and gestured with the knife. "*Ach*, love, admiration. What about duty? What about your precious decision to be one of the Plain People? If really she loved and admired you, she'd let you go. Daniel, my son, to you I am saying I will arrange for you a baptism this next Sabbath. From the traditional after-harvest season for it, I will make exception. You have been away, been in the furnace of the world. You have waited long enough. And then, my son, you will know if this woman cares enough to be worthy of our ways. If she really loves you, as you say, once you are Amish, she must give up the world and become Amish, too, and then I will join you to her in holy wedlock with my blessing."

Daniel gaped at his father. The old patriarch thought Brooke possibly worthy to be Amish? Or did he know she would flee then, once and for all? "But, Dad," he whispered, "that would mean permanent shunning for me if she said no and if I still couldn't do without her."

"The way—our way—you know it well, though you wander off the narrow road yet. But for women, the holy word says: 'Thy desire shall be to thy husband, and he shall rule over thee.' If to be your wife, she will enter in the narrow way—become Amish for you. And if not, *ach*, she is not for you, and should be gone from your life. This way you can test and try her, my son. This Sunday for you, a special baptism, yes?"

In that moment Daniel caught a glimpse of Brooke's dilemma about whether or not to let their relationship go deeper, maybe someday to marry him. She was no doubt torn, even now, when he was not demanding that she be Amish. If he joined the church, grew his beard, became one of them, and gave her this new ultimatum, he was certain he would lose her. And yet, how enticing—if prideful—to dream he could have it all, the Amish people and Brooke as his wife. His father was tempting him to gamble with his future and Brooke's, too.

"You argue like a worldly lawyer, Dad," Daniel dared to say while the old man glared at him. "But I can't be baptized Amish. Not now, maybe never. But it doesn't mean I won't take the best of the Plain People's ways with me, whatever happens."

The old man dug the pocket knife into the fence, as if he could hack it down. "You foolish man. You—"

"I'll go now before we say too much, like we did when I left that other time, because I'm not running from you or what you think are my failures anymore."

"Never again come face-to-face to me, Daniel Brand!" the condemnation pursued him. "No more will I see you, ask you, help you, pray for you, ask the Lord to bless you . . ."

As Daniel walked away, he expected lightning and thunder from heaven. Yet he felt only a strange inner peace that he had done the right thing. And that, when he saw Brooke this evening, he had something very important to say to her.

Brooke walked the silent rooms of Melrose Manor after the real estate dealer drove back to Columbus, saying she could let herself out when she was through. Brooke had told her she would call her soon with her decision, but she felt so torn. Her career and home lay back in Columbus, despite some bad memories there. But here in Maplecreek, dark memories assailed her, too, and she wasn't sure she could see light at the end of either tunnel. Outside, dusk descended, creeping into the rooms like last-minute doubts darkening her earlier exuberant mood as she toured the house again.

It was one thing to leave her job and put the condo up for sale—the same realtor was handling it. But it was something else to purchase this place, commit to fixing it up, and really put down roots among the Amish of Maplecreek. Still, if Daniel said the house looked sound, maybe she ought to take the step.

Jennifer would continue to be her primary commitment; that is, Brooke thought, as long as Jeff let her keep his daughter. Her stomach knotted at the mere thought she might lose her. If she and Daniel could make any sort of plans to build a relationship, she'd talk to Jennifer about it, of course, because this was her future, too.

She heard a buggy and, looking out the parlor window, saw Daniel had decided to drive around her car and tie up behind the house. She walked to meet him on the back veranda.

"A wide back porch, big enough for another swing," he called to her as he came down the garden path. "I don't mean one like Jennifer's new one I made her behind the Sewing Circle, but for two people, adults . . . you know . . ." He sounded as nervous as she felt.

"That would be great. Is it too dark out here for you to check the floor and ceiling here—for bad boards, termites, or whatever?"

He produced a flashlight from the tool belt he wore around his narrow hips. "With no pockets allowed, a man's got to carry things somewhere," he said and stubbed his toe on the top step so he almost stumbled into her. She recalled stumbling on the hill today and how that had made her worry about Jake being her stalker. She wanted to discuss that with Daniel, but she didn't want to upset him with that now. Besides, he might do something rash when she wasn't even certain Jake was guilty in the slightest.

Now she and Daniel stared at each other before he swung the beam around to examine the porch ceiling and floor. "Go ahead," he finally said. "Show me everything."

They were both on edge as they toured the house, first floor, basement, then upstairs. She snapped on lights where she could for him; with his flashlight, he looked around, down, up, into everything possible. They even went up into the attic, keeping close so his beam served to light both their paths. She stood in the dusty dark up there, feeling so close to him, wanting him to turn and touch her while he diligently looked for signs of leaks under the eaves and on the underside of the roof where the long shingle nails poked through. He pointed out areas that needed to be patched or otherwise repaired, and she said she'd make a list of them.

At first she tried to explain how she envisioned furnishing or decorating each bedroom they entered—if she took the plunge to buy the place. But when she talked, he frowned and shook his head; she saw he was listening to creaks and whatever he learned from his tappings on walls. She watched as he peered into closets, knelt to look at floorboards, pressed the side of his face to window frames to see if they were plumb. He opened and closed doors, vents, and registers—even turned on the faucets and flushed the toilets.

They kept getting in each other's way, bumping knees or shoulders. He brushed by her to get in or come out doors; his masculine, outdoor scent bit deep down into her. More than once, in the rooms where she turned on the old-fashioned ceiling lights, she caught him looking at her sideways through narrowed eyelids, at her face and body, and she felt the impact of his glance. She tried to concentrate on the task at hand, tried not just to walk up behind him and kiss him or just block the door with arms outspread to make him touch her. She ached and tingled from wanting him to stop and hold her, especially when he ran his big hands over carved railings, banisters, windowsills, molding, and whispered to himself, "Nice. Built really nice." Now she knew what he meant when he told her what her stroking his furniture did to him.

Finally, standing at the top of the graceful staircase, he pronounced, "It needs work, but I think it's really built to last. It's one beautiful place."

"I'm glad you think so. Now, if I only can find the money for the down payment, let alone enough courage . . ."

Suddenly, somehow, they were in each other's arms. His flashlight thudded and rolled, but they held tight, mouths molded, chest and breasts, even thighs pressing, despite how his tool belt hurt her belly. He pressed her against the wall, and she reveled in his strength. Finally, his hard hands gentled on her, and his mouth drifted from her pouted, sweetly bruised lips across her cheek and down her throat she arched for him as if in total surrender.

"And I came to talk serious stuff," he said finally, leaning lighter against her now, breathing warm against her neck. "Let's sit down right here."

They sat—collapsed, rather—trembling knees touching, holding hands. His tool belt bumped and clinked, and he let go of her to unstrap it before he took her hands again. The house seemed silent but for an occasional friendly creak or sigh.

"I want to say, first of all," he began, "I'll be happy to help with repairs around here."

She felt ecstatic at his offer and devastated he no longer caressed her. "Oh, good," she managed, still sounding out of breath. "I was hoping I could hire you, but I worried about what your people would say. If I buy it and settle down permanently in Maplecreek, I mean."

"Does Jen like this place?"

He had never called her Jen before. His continued concern and care for the girl touched Brooke deeply. "Yes, she thinks it's like a storybook castle. Besides, I told her she could have a horse next year, so she's more certain about it than I am."

He grinned tautly, pressing Brooke's hands tighter in his. "Then, it's back to us. You have to know that though I ran from being Amish—and am realizing that I'm not even now cut out to be baptized Amish—in many ways I am and always will be Amish at heart."

"I know. And I would have to say the same for me— always being English, I mean."

"Right. But what I'm trying to say is I'm not the type—not maybe what you're used to—as bad as I want you, even right now—to just make love to you without intending a serious, deeper union than that. Brooke, I know I'm not doing a good job explaining this. But, the thing is, despite the way I always lose my head around you, I think the commitment of marriage has to come before sex, or at least right along with it."

Marriage! she wanted to scream. How had this gotten to marriage? Talk of sex from him surprised her enough, but marriage?

She must have looked panicked, because he went on in a rush, "I wanted to explain this all rationally, to convince you that marriage is not just a line because I desire you."

"It—I wasn't think that. But marriage to me means trouble with your family and friends again. Besides, I don't know if I'm ready for marriage—with anyone—Daniel. For heaven sake's, I can't even decide whether to buy a house or commit to living here long term."

"I know. I understand."

"Daniel, I do love you, too. But marriage—it's the biggest step, and I just don't know, with so much happening at once—and Jen."

They sat, finally silent for a stretch of time before he fidgeted and spoke again. "Brooke, if your answer is no, tell me now."

"No—I mean it isn't no. Daniel, we've only known each other a short time, and it's been a bumpy road. So much has happened so fast."

He turned to her and took her hands again. "My parents only knew each other for six days before they got betrothed."

"If I say yes or even maybe, will you tell your father?"

"He knows. And you should know," he went on not looking at her now, as if he studied something on the wall, "that he's already shut me out."

"Daniel, not shunning!"

"His own version of it, more than what they've done to you. But I can tell that under his grim looks and the way he clears his throat when you're around, he likes you."

"Oh, sure, he and Levi both!" she declared and tugged her hands free.

"I'll be going right now, to give you time to think. And so I don't put you down on the floor and get your beautiful hair all dusty, and splinters in your bottom, because you deserve so much better. Right now, that kind of convincing—bad as I want it—is not what you need."

Stunned by all he'd said, she nodded as he stood. She amazed herself even now that she had not just told him no, firmly no. *No, ridiculous, impossible!* she should have shouted. *Me, marry a man raised Amish?* But silently, she stood, too, leaning against the wall at the top of the staircase as he hefted his tool belt over his shoulder and bent to retrieve his flashlight. Being with him, laying plans, having hopes—it all seemed so frighteningly right to her. Yearning to touch him, hold him, she gripped her hands together instead.

"Daniel, I have come to admire you more than any man I've ever known."

"That's a nice start," he said, looking suspicious, "but it sounds like a clever lawyer setting up the guilty for the fall."

"I didn't mean it that way. First, I felt curiosity about you, then attraction and admiration and—desire. Now love."

"I just pray that's enough to convince you of what you ought to do, Brooke, that's all."

That evidently *was* all. To her amazement, without another look or word or a good-night kiss, he rapped his knuckles on the banister and went down the steps and out the back hall. The door closed quietly as her legs sagged and she sat again, hugging her knees to her breasts to stop her shaking. She had to lock up here and get Jen, yet she just stared down the steps at the front entrance, replaying everything Daniel had said and searching for the inner key to open the door to her courage that could possibly match his.

That night, Brooke had tucked Jen in her bed and had David Letterman on the TV in her bedroom when the lights went out. She gasped at first, but got hold of herself. It was fairly common for the electricity to go off in the country, but it was usually during storms and tonight had clear skies, if a lot of wind. In fact, she'd been really nervous because the photosensitive cells that made the outdoor safety lights kick on around the house if someone walked in their range had been going on sporadically, evidently from blowing debris. Now, as she looked out, she was doubly upset to see their battery backup packs had not made them come back on.

Pulling a sweatshirt over her T-shirt nightgown, she grabbed a flashlight and checked on Jennifer first. She was fine, breathing with her mouth open and her arm around her new Amish doll Amos Mary had helped her make. Brooke wasn't sure why she did it, but she quietly closed her door and locked her in.

As she navigated her way downstairs with her flashlight, she saw no lights worked in any room, so it wasn't just a switch overload in this big old house. If she were back in Columbus, she would have simply looked out to see if the neighbors' houses were dark, or phoned someone down the block to ask if they had the problem, too, but out here, despite Daniel living just over the hill, she felt really alone. Thank God, she had loaned Daniel her cellular phone so she could call him if need be.

Or if Daniel walked to the top of the hill and looked down, he'd see that the front pole light was out again and come running. Her stomach knotted as she recalled the first night that had gone out, but she chided herself for her fears. After all, she'd changed Verna's door locks as well as put in the sensor lights. There was just an outage at the generator plant down the road, and if the

Amish had used electricity, their houses would be black, too.

She went way down to the basement to see if she could just click on something in the fuse box, but then she remembered that was no good unless it was only a section of the rooms that went dark. Okay, she thought as she headed back up, listening to the wind outside echo her breathing in the silent house, so she'd just phone the electric company, but she knew no one would be there at this late hour.

The phone in the front office was dead—absolutely no sound. Her pulse pounded harder; sweat broke out on her forehead. Immediately, she headed toward the stairs to run up to their second-floor kitchen to get her makeshift weapons and check on Jennifer again.

But she stopped in her tracks, staring up. An Amish man, fully garbed with broad-brim hat pulled low to hide his face sat halfway up the stairs as if just waiting for her. His elbows were on his knees; his hands hid the lower part of his face. He looked huge and dark.

She sucked in a sharp breath. Looking like a crouched statue, he did not move, but just stared down at her.

Her first instinct was to flee, but that would leave Jen upstairs. She tried to lift the light to his face. Her hand shook; her narrow flashlight beam glanced off him, catching only sharp planes and making vast shadows.

"Levi?" she said, her voice so small. "Hiram? "Daniel?"

"You'd like that, wouldn't you—Daniel? Or do all of them turn you on more than me?"

"Jake?" It was Jake's voice; he took off his hat and glared down at her. Her light made his teeth and eyes shine unearthly white. She grabbed the banister at the bottom of the stairs to keep from running, screaming.

Jen asleep up there she had to get to Jen. She fought to keep calm, in control.

"Been shopping for clothes around here, Jake? Why are you dressed like that?"

"Now, you tell me," he said, his voice so whispery, so—crawly. He stood and came down the stairs, looming over her, hesitating slightly at each step to swing his leg down. As he came, he clicked on a big beam of light he shone directly at her to illumine her as if she stood onstage in a spotlight. She squinted and shaded her eyes as she stepped back until she was against the wall of the foyer.

"So you can watch over my place better?" she asked. "Trying to look Amish in case someone sees you?" She had to humor him, though she was certain she knew the worst now. Had his father told him she called and he thought she might be on to him?

"Maybe I'm thinking if I dress Amish, you'll kiss and hug me, too—in the woods out back on the picnic you promised me, but lied. Or kiss me here, or next door in his house, or in your new house I overheard in town you might buy. Didn't want to tell me about that any more than anything else here, did you, you lying little witch? I try to keep you safe," he went on, his voice so strange, so patient but furious—"to give you a chance to be forgiven, and you ruin everything! Didn't even tell the guy who protected you at home about the incidents here until I dragged it out of you!"

"Jake, please, I—"

"*Please*—you know, I do like that word from you. You're gonna get a chance to beg me in a minute, Brooke Benton, so save it. And you're gonna get your chance to please me real good, unless you want me to wake up the kid and let her join this little party we've

314

had so long overdue. I know you locked her room, 'cause I checked when you went down to the basement, but I'm real good at locks—or old, narrow basement windows, too, if need be. You think I can't run fast with this leg, baby? I can do anything, and I'm gonna show you. Now, why'd you go and buy those movement-detector beams outside when they can malfunction with just a little help? You should have asked me what kind to buy—me, Jake, your protector. The ones you bought are about as useful as a modern convenience like a telephone that can go bad."

Her skin crawled, and a terrible trembling began deep in her belly as he shook his head and grinned. Since Jake was willing to terrorize her in person this time, she had no hope he'd just leave her unharmed. He could never afford to have her know and possibly tell someone. Rape, maybe murder—and Jen sleeping upstairs. If she could only keep him talking long enough for Daniel to walk over the hill and notice something was wrong. He said he did that at different times, but it was late now and he had worked so very hard today at the plowing and was probably exhausted. Besides, since he had the cellular phone, he thought she'd call if she needed him.

"Got that quick little lawyer's mind going, right?" he said and yanked her flashlight from her hand. He didn't turn it off but heaved it through the door to the office, where she heard it roll away on the floor. He put his hands on both sides of her, pressing her against the wall in the hallway, leaning into her. He might be missing part of a leg, she thought, but Jake Kaminsky was strong, very strong.

"I talked to your father today, Jake, and he told me about your supposed job in Cincinnati. Eventually, the

315

police will get around to talking to him, to checking you out. You've been around here at night instead of Cincinnati, and you'll get caught. But the charges would only be menacing and breaking and entering so far, so why don't you quit while you can? Your dad's very proud of you, so you don't want to let him down."

"You know, you're making some really fast assumptions here, Brooke. No wonder Sheriff Barnes thinks you're a real troublemaker. You think he's gonna want to help you out here? And I do have a job in Cincinnati, and you're the one who let somebody down. I'm just here to woo you—court you. Is that what the old-fashioned Amish—that Daniel Brand boy next door—calls it when he touches you like this?"

She froze as he slowly moved his hands down, then up under her T-shirt and sweatshirt. Through her panties he grasped her bottom with one hand and squeezed her bare breast with the other one still holding the flashlight. The plastic barrel hurt her and sent the beam crazily out of the neck of her sweatshirt and up into her eyes and his face, so he looked like someone from those horror movies with his features all distorted. Every instinct screamed at her to fight, shove him away, knee him, but she'd never get Jen away before he stopped her.

"Don't try bluffing me with my dad, baby," he went on as his hot breath stirred her hair. She could smell he'd recently used some sort of minty mouthwash. "Never quite got around to asking me and him for Sunday dinner like you said, either. Not planning to, right? Not the one-legged guy who would have laid down his life for you, but you were always too busy with the job, the kid, your causes, then these screwed-up Amish. You had more time for that Rodney Kistler pervert rapist than for me, so you want that kind of guy, you got him now." He pressed his hips and thighs hard into her, so she almost couldn't breathe.

"Jake—about asking you here. I told you I didn't want to bother you—involve you. And I explained how things are out here—"

"No, I'm explaining to you how things are out here!" he said, his voice much louder now as he loosed her, then dragged her by one wrist into the big work area. When she tried to pull away, he twisted an arm up behind her back to make her walk before him. Pain shot up to her neck, but it was nothing next to her fear. He put his big flashlight down on the carpet, then yanked a quilt off a revolving rack so hard it spun. He flapped the quilt partly open and put it like a tent over the light, so it came out muted and diffused. Then he yanked another quilt off and flapped it open in the center of the room, before going down on his good knee to topple her onto her back. He pinned her legs apart immediately, and his weight held her down.

"Now, I'm gonna give you a choice. You can convince me you want me in every way, real bad, or I can just take you down and leave you in the freezer. Like that choice, baby? Remember those poor little fish back at the condo?"

"Jake, I never thought it was you—why?"

"You need me, and never, *never* knew it. But you need me tonight, right now, don't you?"

She shuddered; her teeth were chattering. She had no doubt if he had done all that—in Columbus, here—he would kill her anyway. If only she could be certain he would not hurt Jen. Daniel, please, *please* walk up the hill and see the house is dark!

"All right, that's it for us—for you," he said. "I'm not

317

the one who's doing the begging tonight. It's your turn for that."

"Jake, you never begged, never let me know how—"

"You didn't want to know. Get up Get up and let's get this over with!"

He stood and yanked her to her feet, turning her away to double her arm behind her back again. She went to her knees when he stooped for his light; he merely pulled her up again. No mercy, no time—no sanity. How had this gone so crazy and wrong, and she hadn't known? As he took her by the worktable, she saw the silver gleam of Emma's work shears she had taken from her at the cemetery. If she could just get those in her hand . . .

"Jake, I do care for you, you know that. Please, can't you be more gentle? How can I respond if you're hurting me?"

"Good question," he said, but he stopped for a moment, breathing even more heavily than she was. "How did I respond all those months you were hurting me?" he demanded. "And after everything, you'd rather stay here with the Amish—hating your guts instead of coming back to me. You want to respond, maybe change my mind, show me something?"

She sagged carefully against him and laid her head on his shoulder. "Jake, just give me a chance to explain things—yes, to show you!"

As she talked and pressed her body against him, with her free hand, she fumbled behind her for the shears. She had her hand on the table, but if she could have him only tilt her back a bit, she could reach them. She steeled herself and lifted her head so her lips were just inches from his. She looked into his eyes, feeling she might be sick; she licked and parted her lips, waiting;

he'd have to tilt her back to get to her. When he did so, she leaned her hips against his to make him tip her back even more. The kiss was revolting, wet, devouring, but she had the shears by their closed blades.

He pressed her hips hard against the table. "Gonna pretend I'm your Amish lover-boy," he whispered, "so you can get through this? Brooke, I cared for you, I really did. But I got a long drive clear to Cincinnati tonight, and you had your chances before. Come on, ice goddess, the freezer for you and nighty night."

He yanked her up and forward so hard again, the scissors dropped. She made a little yelp of pain and fear and loss. Her last chance gone, she thought as he marched her to the top of the steps. The freezer, just like Jennifer's fish, he'd said. The same chest freezer where those four kids stood that night to choose their treats before their deaths. Would she suffocate before she froze in that big coffin? Who would take care of Jen when this madman limped away—if he left her untouched?

Jake hesitated at the top of the steps, shining his lights into the blackness. Yet he was careful going down with that right leg of his. He faltered slightly at each step, and, of necessity, to swing his leg down and control the flashlight, he loosed his grip on her arm bent behind her back just slightly.

She took her chance one-third of the way down the long flight of wooden stairs. She kicked as hard as she could at his artificial leg when he swung it down. Then, when he released her to grab for the banister, she clung to it and shoved and kicked at him with all her strength.

His flashlight flew and fell. He toppled, hit, rolled into the blackness. Brooke ran the other way, upstairs, slammed the basement door, latched it, tore upstairs to unlock Jennifer's door.

"Jen, Jen, wake up." But she knew how hard she slept. Despite the pain in her arm, she carried her against her chest, her thin legs bobbing back around her waist. Finally, as Brooke made it to the bottom of the front stairs and fumbled to open the door, Jen woke up enough to wrap her arms around her, too.

Exhausted, shaking, sweating, Brooke started up the hill to Daniel's, just as Daniel ran down it toward her.

CHAPTER SIXTEEN

"DEADER THAN A DOORNAIL," SHERIFF BARNES pronounced as he bent over Jake's prone form to feel for his carotid pulse on his bull neck. The body lay twisted on the basement floor with the artificial leg bent backward under him in a grotesque position. The two lanterns Daniel had brought cast wan light over the scene. Sitting on the basement steps, Brooke looked at her hands clasped in her lap and not at Jake.

"I told you he was gone," Daniel said, bending over the sheriff's shoulder. "I peeked down here and checked before Brooke and Jen came back in the house to wait for you."

Brooke's legs still shook, but at least Jennifer had been put back to bed. They hadn't told her that Jake was dead down here, only that the man who had hurt them in Columbus had been caught.

Brooke had been telling the sheriff the whole story— from the Kistler trial on—the moment he'd stepped out of his vehicle. They'd phoned him from Brooke's phone Daniel had at his house.

"Broken neck, looks like, but we'll have to wait for the

320

coroner from Wooster, and at this time of night, it'll take him a while. You sure you not gonna be sick, Brooke?" the sheriff asked, looking up the stairs at her. He flipped his notebook open and fished for a pen in his plastic pocket, before he evidently realized he didn't have one after being summoned from his bed at one-thirty in the morning.

"No, I won't be sick. It's a shock—a tragedy about Jake, but it's also a relief to me."

"Not being very smart for an attorney, making statements like that to the law, is it now?" he asked, walking to the stairs and leaning his crossed arms on the bottom of the banister. "Makes it sound like you got a motive to kill the guy when there's gonna have to be an inquest, under the circumstances and all. And you realize all this you dumped on me tonight about these incidents should have been told long ago, so I could help you out."

Brooke nodded, dry-eyed now. "I knew that, but I also knew you were busy with the hit-and-run, and I didn't want to take you away from your top priority with something I thought I could handle. And I only mean I'm relieved to know Jake was my stalker in Columbus and here—and to have him stopped—because I feared for myself and my niece."

"Right, I understand that. Folks got no right to terrorize somebody even if they did make a big mistake defending someone guilty in court. Hot damn, I'll bet those fancy city police chewed nails over what you did—maybe the highway patrol boys, too, but this is my jurisdiction here, so don't you worry they're gonna horn in on this. Thing is, Brooke, before I go to bat for you on this with an accidental ruling, I want your word you're not gonna be getting into anything else round

321

here to cause me more surprises—going on with your maverick detective work on the hit-run, nothing."

"Brooke," Daniel said when she didn't answer, "that sounds fair enough."

"Sheriff—and Daniel, I am so grateful to you for your help, but I can't promise anything of the kind."

"I think you'd better," the sheriff said, shifting the foot he had up on the first step.

"I told you the truth, and I'm trusting you to help me, Sheriff. That's all I can do on this. If I wanted to be difficult, I would have said Jake was just here to visit me and fell down the stairs—a pure and simple accident— and not told you all the mistakes I've made trying to judge people's characters and getting it all wrong. But I don't think I'm wrong to rely on you in this, Sheriff Barnes."

"Well, now, you got that right. And since I forgot my pen and didn't write half the stuff you told me down, I'll just make it a short report. Anyone breaks into someone else's house and threatens them gets no slack cut, dead or alive, round here."

He nodded to Brooke, and she nodded back. "And 'specially if you're planning to buy that big house in town and live here, you know I'll be looking out for you. You gonna buy and fix up that place?" he asked.

"I'm really considering it."

"Even though you don't have to be afraid to go back to the big city?" Sometimes, she thought, Sheriff Barnes reminded her of a clever, deceptively down-home attorney.

"Even then," she testified, but her eyes sought Daniel's.

"Good, good," the sheriff said, " 'Course we can't just say on my report that this was an old friend of yours who came calling, 'cause Daniel's folks wouldn't think much of you for having a man in your house that late, even if he did just tumble down the steps going to get something in the freezer with his bad leg and all. Grapevine says you two are getting to be an item, even if the Amish don't care one bit for it. That right?" he asked Brooke directly, as if still testing her.

She nodded again, astounded. Sheriff Barnes was actually taking her side here—her and Daniel's. If only Daniel's family and friends could see things that way, too.

"Sheriff, two more things," she said. "I'll call Verna in the morning to tell her what happened. I will tell *you* the truth, but I'm also going to call Jake's father and *not* tell him the truth about Jake. He thought the world of his son and has a bad heart. That is, unless you think there's any chance this could be blown out of proportion into a well-publicized case."

"Not on my watch," he muttered and turned away to cover Jake's body with a piece of tarp he'd brought with him. "I don't need folks around here thinking I let window peekers and stalkers and such scum loose in my bailiwick."

"Thank you, Sheriff Barnes," she said, "so much."

Kiki Waldron usually drove her own car, but today she had let Hank send Mitch back to their house for her. After she had overseen the packing and stowing of her things in the car, she hitched up her black dress and stepped into the backseat of the white Mercedes. She sat, alert and nervous, as Mitch drove down the curved concrete drive of the estate past the stiff metal sculptures in the saguaro garden. Kiki detested the abstract monstrosities, but she'd been concentrating on redoing the inside of the house Hank's first wife had left, so those would have to go later.

Although Kiki had wanted to breathe fresh morning air before the blasts of heat settled in, she pressed the window button up to avoid wayward spray from the sprinklers hissing at Hank's precious putting green. The electronic gates yawned like vast iron jaws, then clicked closed behind them.

They soon left the secluded suburban Las Vegas neighborhood and edged into the sardine snarl of traffic, heading toward the north end of the Strip. Hank owned only one of these "gambling halls," as her blackjack-dealing dad used to call them, the new Waldron's Western World Hotel-Casino. Kiki always felt vaguely unsettled when she passed the fantastical shapes of the gargantuan buildings. Dormant-looking beasts during the day, though seething inside, they came alive at night as if they'd crawled from the sands with their shifting, slinking whirls of neon limbs to devour those within.

Even though she'd worked for years as a dancer at the Tropicana, she felt uncomfortable on the Strip. Maybe it still seemed too immense a stride from the cramped trailer park, especially after what she'd promised Mama. She could still see the anguished look on her face that last night.

Now Mitch's occasional sly peeks in the rearview mirror bothered her. "The boss know you're coming in dressed like that to sit in a board meeting?" he asked.

"No and I don't want you warning him on the phone. It's part of a little surprise I have for him—with my brothers. We need to make a particular point with the board today."

Mitch looked more puzzled than ever, but he shrugged and that annoyed her, too. She just had to convince everyone she could build a quilting and craft village that was authentically Amish. Still, she wasn't sure this outfit she had researched, then had tailored, was a success, because her face, even sans makeup, didn't look one bit Amish, even in the depths of this black bonnet. But with the quilts, homemade lemonade, and snickerdoodle cookies, she just had to make her point today.

Riding in this car with piles of quilts reminded her of that day Mitch drove her and Hank away from Maplecreek, the day she met Brooke Benton. She wished she could talk to her about this Amish outfit. Brooke was her bridge to the Amish world, her interpreter. Most importantly, Brooke made her feel a part of things, as if she were at least working behind the scenes instead of just being part of the scenery. And despite how Matt and Clay didn't want outsiders involved, she was going to talk to Brooke Benton about her idea as soon as it got approval today.

Kiki knew it wasn't very Amish behavior, but she ordered around Mitch and Mrs. Hermez, Hank's secretary, once they got her things carried into the boardroom. Good, she had twenty minutes to get ready before the onslaught, and she didn't want this glossy onyx tabletop with its geometrically arranged notepads and glasses of water and those big blowups and diagrams to look so business-as-usual.

"Mrs. Hermez, I want to tack up some quilts and use a few more like tablecloths, so if you'd just gather up these glasses and notepads for a moment . . . What are those pictures of, anyway?" she asked Mitch when she saw him staring close up at ones tacked to the strip of cork on the wall.

"Looks like aerial shots of Maplecreek pasted

325

together," he told her, running his finger over the prints as if he were tracing something. "Right, Hank and I drove around the area while you were in the quilt store."

She just smiled smugly to think Matt and Clay had gone to that much trouble for her presentation. "Aerial shots," she said. "And here I've been reading that it's a sin the Amish must confess if they so much as ride in an airplane without the bishop's permission. Our world and theirs are so far apart."

"You mean my world and yours?" Garner said, so close behind her she jumped.

But Kiki was in too good a mood to let him bother her, and anyway, she'd probably need some help from him on her project eventually. She just turned back to her task, though she would like to have kicked him as he bent stiffly at the waist to examine a quilt on the table. His humped-back diamond wedding ring he wore in place of a normal gold band looked so silly against the sweet simplicity of the quilt he touched.

"I hear chain and outlet stores nationwide are getting these so-called handmade things out the door for fifty, sixty bucks a throw," he added to annoy her further. "You'd make a nice Kmart window display in that getup."

She was glad she decided to magnanimously ignore him, because her brothers came in and snapped open their briefcases on the end of the table. Though they didn't say anything about the way she'd softened the room, Matt smiled at her and Clay winked as they took everything in.

"That you under all that, Keek?" Clay teased.

"Can't say that Amish haute couture does much for you, but Hank will love you, anyway," Matt said. He shot a deliberately goading glare at Garner, who quickly

326

took his place at the same end of the table.

But as the meeting progressed, Kiki's euphoria began to waver. She was maybe getting her quilt shop and Amish village, but it was to be engulfed by a huge theme park they called Amish World, a project her brothers had never breathed one word of. As for her passion to keep her little quilt and craft area authentic, more fool she. She felt hurt and furious, not relieved or grateful, despite how pleased Hank seemed that he was throwing her this bone.

"And that's why," Clay was saying to the assembled board members, as he clicked off the overhead projector and the lights came back on, "we need continued cooperation and secrecy until we're ready to make the big announcement. Not that these are the sort of locals to demonstrate or file a lawsuit against us, but we've noticed the Amish are the darlings of the Midwest media . . ."

"What he means," Matt put in, obviously annoyed at Clay's rambling and his continued tapping of the pointer on his palm, "is the Amish aren't just some curiosity sideshow, but are like a living museum, the voice of old-fashioned conscience from our American past."

At least they'd listened to her about that, Kiki thought, but how had everything else gone so awry? Which had come first, her idea for a shop and village or this monstrosity? No, probably Hank was hatching this even before their Maplecreek visit.

"Remember how well the movie *Witness* did in the eighties?" Clay put in, apparently as an afterthought. "The Amish are like a magnet, even to the masses, so the receipts from this park could go off the charts."

"Perhaps," Garner put in, apparently deciding that

he'd better switch from cold shoulder to confrontation. "But *Witness* had cops and killers, movie stars and Hollywood. Don't you think we need to steer clear of the plastic, moving mannequin—the Disney or Hollywood approach?"

Kiki was beginning to feel ill. If Garner agreed with her more than Matt and Clay, she had really been betrayed. And Hank obviously thought she'd be so pleased to be given the damn so-called quilt "pavilion" there. Hadn't any of these men grasped the real essence of the Amish?

She clasped her hands tighter on her aproned lap. The next report concerned the board buying up even more land for adjacent hotels and restaurants, building a temporary mobile home park—that thought alone made her nauseous—until other housing for the workers, to be dressed Amish just as she was today, could be constructed. Heads turned, mouths smiled. Roads would have to be widened, strip malls would go in . . . It seemed to be growing of its own accord, this 176-million-dollar behemoth these men were birthing here.

"So I propose," Hank was saying, "in accordance with the terrific prelim work Clay and Matt have done, that no one set foot back there till we're ready to go public. At various local auctions our agents will get the other land for us and try to buy up some things that will look good in the park and we can then mass-produce to sell—everything made in the heartland of America, too, not China or Taiwan. We'll stress that with good, old-fashioned pride. And our other challenge will be to own enough land so we don't end up with a maverick city like Anaheim or Kissimmee stuck right on top of the park. Clay, Matt, I'm puttin' you in charge of the whole shebang, reportin' to Garner, of course . . ." the words, the growing unease inside Kiki roiled on and on.

Suddenly, she felt outright sick, and she beat a hasty retreat. As she vomited into the washbowl in the ladies' room, she fought to keep alive the soothing memory of those green hills and valleys stretching between Maplecreek and Pleasant. But they kept getting blurred by the hulking crush of garish buildings that looked just like the Las Vegas Strip and trailer courts gone mad up and down the farmhouse lanes.

Brooke kept Jennifer home from school and closed the shop for the day. She was grateful that Sheriff Barnes had forgone the yellow police tape around the place, though he had scheduled separate interviews with her and Daniel, and two criminalists were coming out to examine the basement this afternoon. Brooke explained about Jake to Jennifer as best she could, since she herself still could not fathom how he had been so deranged and appeared to be so—happy and helpful. Jennifer seemed as relieved as she felt, but Brooke could tell that she didn't really grasp what a threat Jake had been last night. Just as well; their lives would be much more calm and normal from now on.

They were going outside for a little walk when Hiram Hostetler called. Brooke wrote down his information, listing three different statutory agents, two in Columbus and one in Pittsburgh, who had purchased sprawling parcels of the Stottlemeyer property. He insisted that no one but the distant heirs who had inherited the property had told him about the preemptive bid.

He apologized again for his trying to scare her off, and she assured him she understood his panic about Paul's delicate state of mind. Yes, she thought as she hung up, she understood a delicate, panicked state of

329

mind *and* wanting to run. She stared down at her scribblings on her notepad.

"But no one is scaring me off or making me run from anything else!" she vowed. She went to assure herself Jennifer was all right and told her she had a few phone calls to make before they could take a walk.

She called the agent in Pittsburgh, who informed her coldly—though, she thought, with a tinge of fear in his voice—that he was "under no legal or moral obligation to divulge the name or names of the person or persons for whom he had acted now or previously." When she tried to pin him down on whether he had bought other local land for this buyer, he hung up. Jotting down *works for someone powerful?* and *may have bought more land*, she shelved that lead for now, in favor of the Ohio ones.

After phone calls to the agents in Columbus, she came up with only one corporation name, T. R. Southwyck, Inc., and getting that was stickier than talking to Ida Brand. Brooke phoned information to get the numbers, then called the secretary of state's office in Columbus and talked to four people there, then two at the state auditor's office. Finally, she had the names of the five major stockholders of Southwyck, Inc.

She could reach only one of them—two had disconnected phones, two were on vacation out of state—strange coincidences, she thought. The man she spoke with told her Southwyck was owned by another corporation called Stetson Western Investors, and he would not divulge so much as their corporate location. She tried the reference librarians she'd work with in Columbus, who called her back after consulting numerous sources. But they could find nothing on Stetson Western. Frustrated, increasingly suspicious,

330

Brooke dialed Elizabeth at work.

"Is this a let's celebrate call on buying the house?" Elizabeth asked. Rustling paper and an occasional mumbled word told Brooke her friend was eating a late working lunch alone at her desk.

"I hope you're sitting down because I have some shocking news I want you to share only with Mr. Stedman," Brooke told her, then explained about Jake.

"I can't—can't believe it! But, you know, when Lord Myron hears the coast is clear for you, he'll really be after you to come back."

"I know. I've got to face it—to decide one way or the other soon." She took a deep breath and told Elizabeth about her relationship with Daniel and his proposal.

"I can't believe that, either," Elizabeth added, sounding breathless. "Anything else?"

"Could you do me a quick turnaround favor on some real estate information?"

"What? Is that all? Of course! But Brooke, I just can't believe you left here to have a quiet life and now all this!"

"I know, but here's the story . . ." She explained everything she knew about the mystery buyers of the local farmland and asked for advice on identifying them.

"I smell a dummy corporation, kiddo. Probably three of them."

"Me, too. But I'll bet all threads lead through the labyrinth to the same monster buyer. Something strange is going on here."

"I'll get back to you as soon as I can. And, Brooke, please take care of yourself—Jennifer, too. Oh, by the way, I don't suppose you have a fax machine there?"

"Are you kidding? The phone downstairs is still one you dial. At least it's not a party line, and I'm just lucky to have it working already after Jake cut the wires. Whatever you discover, Elizabeth, please just call, and if you have any problems, let me know and I'll come to town to do the grunt work myself."

Brooke looked out the window at Jennifer pumping her legs to get the most height on her new swing Daniel had put in for her in the backyard. Now that the girl had hopes for a real horse of her own next year, she had ridden her imaginary mount the Pi less and less. She realized how far she and Jennifer had come as she glanced over at her once overwhelming quilt project.

She had handled the daunting choices of fabrics; the laying out and cutting of the pieces; their careful sewing and pressing to make the pattern fit. Still, it was in apparently disrelated segments: she had to integrate it all with the background, then stretch it on a frame to layer, quilt, and bind it. Everything was coming together for her life, too, maybe for her and Daniel. If she had only been able to solve the hit-and-run! If only, she thought for one moment, Jake had admitted to that, too, but that was a crazy idea. And now, if she could only discover who was buying big chunks of Amish land and why.

She hurried out to push Jennifer on her swing. "Want to take a turn, Aunt Brooke?"

"Maybe in a minute. I wanted to talk to you about something else about—Daniel."

"He said I should call him Daniel, too, not Mr. Brand anymore. We get along great."

"That makes me happy, because I like him a lot, too."

"I already know that!" she called back in her high arc, then the next time down to earth, scuffed her feet to begin to break her momentum.

"Jen," Brooke told her as she helped the swing slow then stop, "the truth is I love him, and he loves me. I know this may seem a little fast, and we haven't told anybody else but you this yet."

"It's not so fast to me—but it's a secret from the Amish?" she asked, wide—eyed, whispering, loving to share secrets.

"For now, but we don't want it to be. The thing is, Jen, Daniel asked me to marry him, and in my heart I want to but I'm afraid in my head because it would be such a big step for me and you, too. Do you know what I mean?"

"Would we live at his house or in our new house? And where would he sleep? We've got lots of bedrooms in the big house."

So much for plumbing the depths of emotion here, Brooke thought. Jennifer was being practical to the core. And to her dismay, Brooke realized these were questions she, too, should have asked.

"I—we didn't talk about it, but we'd have to live at the big house if we buy it. And, you know when people are married, Jen, they sleep in the same bedroom—even the same bed."

The girl put her arms around Brooke's waist and looked up into her face; Brooke hugged her back, swaying them a little. "But you didn't say yes?" Jennifer asked.

"The thing is, you can see how different Daniel and I are from each other."

"Is that bad? Susie and me are different. Especially, boys and girls are different. You and Daniel both live here and like the same people and don't like the same ones bad people like Jake and the one who hit Katie and the kids."

"Well, yes, that's true. But I'm telling you all this, Jen, because you are the most important person in my life, and if and when I do get married, then you would have to share me with Daniel. But I would never stop loving you. If we did become a bigger family, there would be more people to love, that's all."

"Then Daniel would be right in our house to teach me all about horses. It's OK with me, but I guess you can't decide, huh?"

"I guess," Brooke said with sigh, "that's about right."

"Would you have kids of your own for me to play with and baby-sit? How soon?"

It occurred to Brooke for the first time that Jennifer could become Daniel's ally in some things. "I don't know. But Jen, you've made me realize that Daniel and I have a lot more to talk about, when he made it seem so simple. You know, I think I want to tell him yes, but so much is going on right now, that I need a little more time—and courage."

"Don't be afraid, Aunt Brooke. You never wanted me to be afraid, even when all kinds of bad things happened. 'Cause I had you, you said, and don't forget that you have me."

Daniel offered to stay the night, sleeping downstairs, but Brooke was no longer afraid, even if the basement did give her the creeps. In her exhausted state, she was certain she could sleep. But she heard something outside. Wheels in the drive, a voice? She bent low to look out her bedroom window.

A car—a stretch limo. It looked huge, compared to the boxy buggies, even the cars, that came calling here. The only person she could even vaguely picture getting out of a thing like that was Kiki Waldron. But no—

white, curly hair, the too-loud voice of a hard-of-hearing person too stubborn to wear a hearing aid. And how many elderly women could you look down on and see boobs as well as shoulders? Verna! So she had been much more upset than she let on when Brooke had phoned her today.

Brooke hurried downstairs to meet the airport limousine. "Why didn't you tell me, Verna? We would have picked you up!"

"With everything else, I hardly wanted you two out after dark, dodging those demented truckers on the interstate and driving clear to the airport in scenic Cleveland. Didn't know if I could get tickets this fast. Anyhow in Maine, didn't want to outstay my welcome," she explained in a rush as they hugged while the driver put her suitcases on the steps. "And I knew," she said in Brooke's ear, "with all the terrible goings-on, you could use me."

"Verna, I'm so sorry about everything happening here at the house."

"You should have called me the minute the first thing happened, and I'd have given them what for!" she said.

Verna paid the driver while Brooke lugged the bags in. "I'm so glad you're home. I'm afraid, though, Jen's asleep like a rock, but she'll be thrilled in the morning. I've got so much to tell you."

"More than what I already know?" she demanded, looking astounded. "My girl, I thought you had a funny tone in your voice every time you mentioned Daniel Brand today. Is that it? Well, is it?"

"Yes, Verna. You've got the best radar I've ever seen. That's part of it."

"*Part* of it? All right, Brooke Benton, as soon as I go to the toilet, I want to hear it all, every bit."

Brooke was both excited and appalled when Elizabeth called her back the next day. When she hung up the phone, she hurried down to talk to Verna. Brooke could tell she was happy to be home. She had not taken one day off but was back among the customers in the shop, even helping Amos Mary with the beginners' class today. Right now, she was showing Raine how to use a quilt maker's leather thimble.

"Excuse me, Verna, but I've got to run over to tell Daniel something about the land buy." She had to talk louder than she wanted so Verna could hear in the buzz of the room.

"Go ahead, dear," Verna told her. "You've got over an hour before Jennifer is out of school, and I can pick her up if need be."

"No, I'll be back by then. How is your nine-patch square going, Raine?" she asked the woman. She had such big, blunt-fingered hands, Brooke wondered how she was handling the needle.

"Good, really good, Brooke," Raine told her as Brooke headed out.

She was out of breath when she crested the hill. Running down toward Daniel's place, she almost lost control and tumbled. His back door was closed; she dashed for the workshop and saw him through the window, bent over, intent, planing a tabletop, luckily alone. She knocked on the door and rushed in. His head jerked up; he straightened to his full height, then started toward her.

"Brooke! What's wrong?"

"I just learned something that could tie to the hit-and-run because it gives us some new suspects we can pursue."

"What are you talking about?"

"I asked Elizabeth to help me trace the buyers of the Stottlemeyer place, and I know you don't need all our problems around here complicated by my going off on another 'worldly lawyer's binge' to stir everyone up, but—"

"Just tell me. Don't you see, I've burned my bridges here, and I'm with you on the Katie quest, on anything?"

"Yes," she said, still breathing hard as he led her over to a newly sanded deacon's bench and sat them down. "Daniel, the new owner of the Stottlemeyer land—and some other parcels out behind it, maybe others if we'd check it out—is someone I know about, Hank Waldron and his amusement park company. You know—his wife Kiki bought those quilt racks from you the day they visited here. I can't reason this out any other way but that his huge conglomerate WWEE is going to build some kind of Amish Land-orama here, an Amish Disneyland!"

Gaping at her, he grabbed her wrists so tightly she flinched. "They—they can't. If it were really big—like that—it would mean traffic jams, more outsiders—I mean we want visitors, but not hundreds of thousands!"

"The utter pillaging of whatever remnants of Amish privacy remain," she said. "It wouldn't only be the next generation like Levi's sons who would be dispossessed, not just four innocent kids who would be victims of a crash."

He lifted his big hands to cup her shoulders; his heavy touch weighed her down. "Brooke, are you sure about this?"

"I'm afraid so. I traced one so-called corporation to a name, and Elizabeth's contacts traced that to Las Vegas

337

that's where WWEE's headquarters are. And then she had someone trace the names we found on one board of directors back through two more dummy corporations—you know, front men. And we finally hit two names that matched two men on the WWEE board of directors."

"Oh, man. Oh, damn!"

"It all came flooding back to me then, little things about Kiki and Hank's visit that day that makes terrible sense now. Hank Waldron here in Amish country was weird enough, but he was probably looking over their future purchase. And Kiki said that Hank had told her that Pennsylvania's Amish country was already too touristy to *bother with*, but that Ohio was relatively untouched with lots of tourist interest, since this area was between Columbus, Cleveland, and Pittsburgh. *Good for business*, as Kiki put it. Daniel, I really liked her, but every time I tried to get her to tell me how she found our shop, she changed the subject. I should have smelled something rotten from the first!"

"Yeah, I guess so. I feel sick. And not very accepting and forgiving."

Now she wrapped her hands around his wrists. "That's why I thought we—I—somehow, have to warn your father."

"Oh, that'll be good since he's not talking to us—me, at least. He'll be devastated," he said, standing now to pull gently away from her touch, his shoulders slumped. He began to pace back and forth past the open window. "But he'll just turn the other cheek—all of them will."

"Not with this. This means their ruination at least in Maplecreek, the raping of everything beautiful and best that belongs to the Plain People here!"

He turned back toward her and stood for one moment. "Brooke, you still don't understand. They'll

338

just move on, if it takes every dime they have, every tear the women can shed, every wayward son and daughter like me they're forced to leave behind. Some worldly people doing this to the Amish, as you said, it's just like their hitting Katie and the kids all over again, only bigger."

"But that's the thing. I think this outrage could be linked to the hit-and-run. Surely, there were operatives here to look over the land, strangers to the area who might have been out driving on Sawmill past 'their' land at night. I may even have a lead on them—the two blond men who told the barmaid they were antique dealers celebrating some big buy, probably the two who dropped those two Scotch bottles, either while they drank a toast to their deal or which they tossed out the window after they hit the buggy. Through this WWEE opening, we have a possible new lead on the killer!"

"You're not going to Las Vegas?"

"Not yet. But if I have to."

"All right. I'm ready to do whatever it takes to fight this—this obscenity."

Quickly, he pulled her closer, pressing his lips in her tumbled hair. They just held tight, very tight.

"I told you *never* call me here at work," Matt said into the phone and lowered his voice, even though he was alone in his office next to Clay's. "Where are you calling from?"

"The pay phone at the gas station in Pleasant," Morning Rain Chiquito said. "Don't jump down my throat till you hear what I've got. About a half hour ago, I was taking my quilt lesson at the shop, and lady lawyer comes in and says to her friend she just got news on the land deal and has to go tell the Amish guy in the next house, uh, Daniel Brand."

"*Our* land deal?"

"You sent me out here to find out about someone's new garden plot?"

"Go on." Matt fought to keep calm; he twisted the phone cord around his fist and held it tight.

"So I said I felt I was getting the flu or something, hopped in my car, drove past said house, parked in the entrance to a field, and went around the back of the place. The door of this guy's workshop was open, voices inside, so I stood outside an open window and heard it all. Lady lawyer's on to you big time, and wants to tell some Amish people. She's got someone working for her who traced the buys—and probably the hit-run to some WWEE operatives—two of them—blond guys whose Scotch bottles have been found and who have been traced to a bar around here. Matt—you there?"

"Yes, I'm here."

"You didn't tell me about a hit-run. I had to learn all about it here."

"We don't have anything to do with it, but we can't be linked to it or the big land project's down the sewer."

"Something else. The quilt shop was closed yesterday and word in town says a male friend of lady lawyer's fell down the basement steps and got killed, the same guy evidently the boys in the garage here say was trying to trace the hit-and-run driver earlier for lady lawyer. And I did find out that she moved to Maplecreek because a big case blew up back in Columbus, and she got hate mail and who knows what else. Now that I've got the flu, I can drive into Columbus and check all that out if you want."

"Listen, Rain, you mentioned Brooke Benton's niece before, how close the two of them are. Is she around

340

much?"

"Oh, no, you don't, whatever your thinking. The kid's only seven and probably knows zilch."

"And can still know zilch when this is over. But we have to put the skids on Benton somehow, without having her disappear herself."

"I owe you two, but whatever you're thinking, not that much."

"It would just be a matter of detaining the girl for a little while—long enough to make sure Benton backs off."

"Then, you two better get your tails out here and take care of things yourself!"

"Rain, listen, I want you to stay put at your motel in Wooster until I call you back. But if someone came there to help you—take her off your hands right away and cleared out of that area with her while you stayed behind for a little while so you would never be suspected—"

"Not unless that someone was both of you! Then, if anything goes wrong, you two can take the fall—for all of it. You're not talking to some stupid squaw here, Matt Buckland!"

"Like I said, go sit tight by your motel phone. I'll call you back soon."

CHAPTER SEVENTEEN

DANIEL SEEMED AS NERVOUS AS BROOKE ON THEIR way to confront his father that evening. They bumped noses when they kissed in the shelter of the buggy after they waved good-bye to Jennifer and Verna.

"You're sure your father's home?" she asked.

341

"Yeah. Probably just finishing up his supper. I thought it might help to have my mother around because she's torn about all this, and you'd be surprised how she can soften him up at times."

"I'm not a bit surprised. I greatly admire your mother, and I've come to see Amish women have more power than anyone knows."

He grinned tautly. "I just hope she has a chance to know and admire you over the years, and the power to convince others to do the same."

"At least it's probably cheered both your parents to hear Emma's coming home next week. Levi's made great strides to agree to attend her follow-up counseling sessions and to accept the fact they put her back on medication for a while. I just wish you and I could give her a homecoming gift of not only finding whoever killed Katie, but also telling her the mystery buyer has withdrawn. Daniel, all of that's worth working for—worth any sacrifice!"

"You're starting to sound Amish at the strangest times," he said and shook his head when they turned up the lane.

As they had decided was best, Brooke went to the house and knocked while Daniel got out but waited off the big porch. Ida appeared through the mesh of the screen door. "Oh, my," she said and went back for her husband. "*Jacob, komm!*" they heard her cry. She returned with him, following him out onto the porch. It both amazed and angered Brooke how Bishop Brand seemed to glance right through Daniel, while his mother, unfortunately, ignored him, too.

"A friend of Levi Em, you are welcome here," Bishop Brand informed Brooke. "Come calling, Levi says to you, Miss Brooke, see his Levi Em after she gets settled in a bit, but come alone."

"I am grateful to you and Levi for that kindness, sir. However, I believe it is as wrong to keep Emma from her brother as it was to keep her from me earlier. But I am here today not as Emma's friend or even as your son Daniel's very good friend."

Ida looked lightning quick from Daniel back to Brooke. Brooke thought it was joy or love that flitted across her fine features before she composed her face again.

"I'm here as a neighbor," Brooke went on, "and as a concerned citizen of Maplecreek to inform you, because you are bishop of the church here, that the purchaser of the Stottlemeyer land your people should have had— and several other parcels that have gone piecemeal to supposedly different buyers—have all been purchased by the same source and for a very nefarious reason."

She jumped at Daniel's string of German so close behind her. Too late, she realized she had used too unusual a word for them, maybe too long a sentence, and Daniel was explaining, though neither of his parents looked at him.

"That land," she went on when he stopped speaking, "has all been purchased by a big business from out west that builds theme parks. They evidently intend to build a huge amusement park around an Amish-Americana theme on the land with rides . . . restaurants . . . stores, parking lots," she floundered when they both stared at her with puzzled frowns.

"A country fair?" Ida asked.

"More like Disneyland, Mother. Big and brazen," Daniel put in, this time in English. Again, Ida's eyes darted to Daniel, then her husband, who had not moved but to clench his jaw.

"Jacob," Ida said, gripping her hands over the waist of her apron so that her fingers turned white as sausages, "tourists times ten, I think."

"Times ten thousand," Daniel added.

"*Ach*! 'For they speak not peace,' " Bishop Brand said directly to Brooke as if Daniel did not stand five feet from him. " 'But they devise deceitful matters against them that are quiet in the land.' "

"Against this big business, he speaks Bible truth—not against you, Miss Brooke," Ida put in.

"Bishop Brand, I realize," Brooke said, "your philosophy—your belief is simply to accept hard times as God's will and move on, but I am not willing to see Emma's sons and others like them who would love and till the land and preserve Amish ways dispossessed—sent away. I realize I am not acting for you and you have no use for lawyers, but I wanted you to know that I am going to file a civil suit in the state of Nevada—something like a restraining order—with Mrs. Verna as sole plaintiff for now. Plaintiff means it will be on her behalf against this company called Waldron World Entertainment Enterprises."

When she saw Bishop Brand was listening intently, she went on, "My first thought was a class action suit—one in behalf of many people here—but I know the Amish would ignore it and, I'm afraid, other locals would fight it. People who own borderline businesses in town might be only too happy to have this place get more traffic and business, and non-Amish farmers would love to sell fields and meadows for hotels and parking lots. Then I thought about using the media and general public outrage, but that is a last resort."

She could only hope his listening meant some sort of approval. "If that doesn't work," she plunged on, "I'm

344

going to claim the park and new development will break the Clean Air Act, and if that doesn't work, I'll try something else. I regret this will probably stir up newspaper and television coverage, but I believe this blatant lie about promoting what's best about the Amish by actually ruining the Amish has to be stopped."

She almost shared her suspicions that some sort of WWEE land scout might be tied to Katie's killer, but she restrained herself. "Thank you for hearing me out on this, Bishop and Mrs. Brand. If you want to warn the others about this, it is up to you. And—I understand that you cannot accept certain things—like this worldly lawsuit or my not just accepting Katie's death—or the love and respect that has grown between Daniel and me. Daniel, I guess we can go," she said as she took his hand.

"*Ja*, go" was all Bishop Brand said in farewell, though Brooke saw his eyes were glassy with tears as he turned away. And perhaps, she even dared to hope, he had meant, go and do your best.

At dusk when Bess pulled the buggy behind the Sewing Circle, Verna and Jennifer came out to meet them. Jennifer had flour all over her shorts and in her hair; she proudly handed up still warm and fragrant chocolate chip cookies to them, while Verna extended a white padded envelope.

"It came special Federal Express," she said. "From Elizabeth, so I thought you'd want to see it right away."

Daniel slit it open with a pocket knife. Her hands still trembling from facing his parents, Brooke pulled out several pieces of paper; a small one fluttered away, which Jen ran to retrieve.

Quickly, Brooke scanned the names of WWEE's

board of directors, then went down the longer list of corporate officers and division heads. None leapt out at her but Garner Waldron's, who was obviously related somehow. She'd check him out first, hoping she could trace his or any of these names to a hotel or B and B or car rental, a purchase of Glenbrae Scotch—anything to prove they were in this area around the dates of the hit-and-run.

And she was going to get Sheriff Barnes's help on this. It was time to tell him about WWEE's purchase if he hadn't smelled it out already. She knew exactly how to assure his help: she would show him the recent *Time* magazine article she had photocopied at the Wooster Library, which mentioned not only that big theme parks always brought in some crime but that WWEE preferred to have its own internal police force in addition to the local one.

"Here's the picture you dropped," Jennifer said, extending it to her.

"Oh, it's Kiki and Hank Waldron at their wedding reception," Brooke said, "a society photo from *Town & Country* magazine. Look, Daniel, this prematurely silver-haired man is labeled as Garner Waldron, Hank's son. Does he look familiar to you?"

"Hardly," Daniel said; then Verna took a peek, and Jennifer had to see it. Brooke couldn't place him, but she was sure she'd seen him somewhere—and then it hit her. That callous, brazen man who had driven up to the accident site in the sportscar when she was with Sheriff Barnes—the one she'd tried to trace through the IDZRVIT license plate. Even as she explained it to Daniel and Verna, she knew where she would start her investigation anew tomorrow morning: back in Ken Champion's car dealership near Cleveland, trying to establish that Hank's son had also leased a large red GM car the day of the accident to look over that prime farmland for WWEE.

"And these two, who look like twins, are Kiki's brothers, Clay and Matt Buckland," she said, squinting to read the small print. "Wait a minute! I just saw their names in this list under WWEE's special projects division. Yes, here! Three suspects!"

"Can you prove they were here, too?" Daniel asked.

"I'll bet I know who can. I've got to go talk to Reba Potts, that waitress at the Dutchman's Keg. These two look like a young Paul Newman or Troy Donahue— don't they, Verna?"

"Well, I guess, but so what?"

"That's how Reba Potts described the outsiders who had drinks the night of the wreck, so I've got to run right over there. If she identifies them, we'll really have some ammo—Kiki Waldron's brothers in charge of special projects, and Hank's son just happening by the wreck site!" She knew she was going too fast, but she was ecstatic as she hugged each of them.

"You just be careful," Verna said. "You know what I mean about you, out of the frying pan and into the fire . . ."

"Can I go this time?" Jennifer was asking.

"No, but I will be back in time to tuck you in. I've got to get my car keys!" she called back over her shoulder as she raced toward the house.

"I'm going, too!" Daniel shouted after her. " 'Whither thou goest,' as my dad would say!"

"What kind of a ghost is that?" Jennifer asked. "And if you two talk about getting married, can I help plan the wedding?"

When Brooke emerged from the Dutchman's Keg, she signaled Daniel with the V for victory sign. He, to her amazement, gave her a high-five before he kissed her.

"She identified them, and she'll testify!" she cried and hugged him hard in the front seat of her car. "I can establish they were here the night of the accident, drinking, bragging about their big deal, lying about who they are, and who knows what I'll find out about Garner tomorrow. After I get Jen to bed, I've got to really make some plans. And as soon as I get that restraining order, I'm taking a little trip to Las Vegas!"

"Alone? We'll see about that."

"It would be strictly to take legal action. I'm afraid I'm even going to have to give up my relationship with Kiki, but I can't imagine she knew anything about this. And then, Daniel, when it's over, we can get back to us."

It was nearly dark; she drove slowly, however triumphant she felt. But she pulled into Daniel's driveway and stopped the car beside his house. "Did you forget Bess and the buggy are at the Sewing Circle?" he asked.

"No. It's just I wanted one moment for us before today ends and I get going with all this tomorrow." She turned out the lights but let the motor idle and turned to him. His hand tousled her hair, then caressed the slant of her cheek. Despite the console between them, which hurt her hip, she leaned toward him to hold tight. They kissed until they were breathless.

"This is our celebration for today," he murmured, his mouth against her temple, his breath warm in her ear, "and a promise—of even better times to come."

Something dragged Jennifer from deep, dark sleep.

348

Aunt Brooke's hands on her? Over her mouth and eyes. Was that man back again in the house and they had to keep quiet? But, no—Jake was gone for good and Mrs. Spriggs was back and Daniel might be kind of her new father. But why was Aunt Brooke lifting her, carrying her, hurrying?

Jennifer tried to hold to Aunt Brooke's neck, but her hands were caught—taped together. She could not open her eyes or her mouth to ask—to cry—or scream. They went down the stairs into more darkness, hurrying.

It was not Aunt Brooke at all because her arms were so thin and hard and her breasts were smaller. The woman bumped Jennifer's leg into something; she heard her open a door and felt the rush of night air. Were they outside?

She heard the woman close the door quietly; then they were running, bouncing. A long way outside because leaves and branches whipped Jennifer's bare legs. Out of breath, the lady—gasping.

She heard the jingle of keys, and her leg pressed cool metal before she was put on the floor of a car. Again, she tried to scream but her voice sounded like "*Mmmmmm. Mmmmm!*"

Why didn't this woman at least say something? Now she was taping her legs together, too. A blanket or towel came down to cover her. Then two car doors slammed, an engine started, humming to make the floor vibrate under Jennifer. Her head jerked back as the car pulled away. Tears burned her eyes and crying caught in her throat to choke her.

It was a long car ride. Had she been asleep? Jennifer heard whispering, a woman's voice, maybe two men. Her eyes felt pasted shut with tears, and the tape was

349

still on her mouth and eyes, her wrists and ankles.

A man who smelled of liquor—she knew that smell from Daddy—leaned close into the car to lift her out and bounce her once in his arms. He talked to her in a kind of a growl that didn't sound like a real voice, so he probably didn't want her to know who he really was.

"Just relax, kid, and things will be OK. Just a little plane ride now."

"*Mmmm!*" Jennifer said and tried to kick, but that was not a good idea, because he squeezed her real hard and said to shut up. She counted each step up they took. If it was into an airplane like he said, it didn't seem like many steps—only six. She hadn't been on a plane before, but the pictures she'd seen looked like more than these steps. If she could get to a phone and call Aunt Brooke, what good would it do to tell her the plane that she flew in had only six steps?

She was really scared she would be flown far away from Aunt Brooke. She used to ask God in her prayers if she could go on a plane ride, but she meant to see Daddy in England, not this. Now she only wanted to stay in Maplecreek.

"Sit down," another man's voice said, a whispery voice. She didn't hear the woman anymore. Someone kind of pushed her back in a soft seat, but her legs didn't touch the floor. "I'm going to fasten your hands in the seat belt, too, and don't pull them out. You have to go to the pot, you ask, and I'll take you."

No way, she thought, she was going to let a man take her to the bathroom blindfolded, if that's what he meant. She wondered if all airplanes had pots instead of toilets. She did have to go, but it was maybe because she was so scared. That was why her stomach hurt, too. And tears kept burning her eyes and making her nose run.

When she heard the big roar and felt the fast liftoff, Jennifer tried real hard to picture just being in the buggy in the sunshine behind Bess's brown, bouncing back with Daniel and Aunt Brooke beside her.

The next morning Brooke got out of bed, jammed her feet in scuff slippers, and went down the hall to wake Jennifer. Her cheap *Beauty and the Beast* alarm clock must not have gone off again. Besides, Brooke wanted to tell her niece she felt bad she hadn't gotten back in time to tuck her in as she'd promised last night; she had tiptoed in to kiss her after she'd been asleep. At least she was content to know that Jen was getting more secure all the time and Verna had said she'd read to her, just as Brooke would have done.

Yawning, Brooke looked through the open bedroom door. Jen was up. Her bed looked as rumpled as Brooke felt. But if they both didn't hurry, she was going to be late for school, even though Brooke was still running her in by car instead of having her ride the bus. At least today was Friday, so if Jennifer was tired, she'd have the weekend to catch up. As for Brooke, she was heading for Columbus today and hoped to have a restraining order prepared so she could go out west this weekend and be in the WWEE offices first thing Monday morning.

But the bathroom was empty and dark. Now, why didn't Jennifer wake her up? Just because Verna was home and could cook breakfast? Were the two of them in cahoots to let her sleep in after all she'd been through?

"All right, you two . . ." Brooke began as she poked her head in the kitchen. "Verna, where's Jen?"

"Not up yet."

"But she is. Why would she go downstairs?"

They called and looked. Verna yelled upstairs to Brooke as she hurried back upto Jennifer's bedroom, "Don't worry. The back door's unlocked, so she's just gone out!"

But Brooke sensed something was wrong. Maybe it was just living too long in fear, but something was wrong. It wasn't like Jen. It just wasn't. Her bed sheets were never thrashed in waves like this. And then, under the new blank-faced Amish doll, amidst the mess, Brooke saw the piece of paper she'd missed before. Shaking, she reached for it carefully, as if it would burn her.

She stared down at the boldly printed words until they stopped swimming. They seemed to shout at her: IT HAD BETTER BE THE END OF ANY MORE PRYING—ON ANYTHING—OR IT WILL BE THE END OF THE KID. NO POLICE! IF YOU'RE GOOD, I'LL TAKE GOOD CARE OF HER. SIT TIGHT. BE IN TOUCH LATER.

Her legs collapsed, and she knelt beside the bed. "Verna! Ver—na!"

The old woman came running. "Someone—took her, just took her away somewhere!" she cried pointing at the note. "Don't touch that. It might have fingerprints."

Verna ran to call Daniel, since he still had Brooke's cellular phone. Brooke stumbled to her feet and ran through the house, just in case Jennifer was here, in case there was some clue, some hint of what had happened. Looking under beds, peering into closets, she discovered something: someone had spent some time in the linen closet. The lowest shelf had been removed to allow space for someone to lie or huddle in here, evidently curled up on a quilt. Could the kidnapper have been

352

secreted in the house while they locked up and went to bed? That's how this had happened with no warning and no break-in, only a walk-out in the dead of night through the back door with Jen.

Daniel arrived out of breath as Verna read the note aloud to him, leaning over where it lay on the bed. Brooke's head spun; they spoke to her, but she wasn't sure what anyone said. She heard a muffled scream as she pressed her hands to her mouth. The scream—it was her.

Verna tried to hold her, though she was sobbing. "No, no, it can't be, can't be! She has to be here!" Daniel ran outside, looked all around, clear back to the pond, he said.

"No! No, not Jen, not Jen!" became Brooke's baffle cry. She knew she had to act, but fear froze her. Time blurred, she wasn't sure what she said or did.

Verna sent the workers and customers away again and closed the shop without telling anyone why. "I wish we could ask them to help us," she told Brooke. "Amos Mary was there, and she could mobilize the Amish for a search. Raine was there, and she's got her own car."

"We can't get outside help now—not yet," Brooke said.

Brooke stayed by the phone, fighting panic, waiting for a call while Daniel and Verna searched outside the house—garage, yard, fields, back lanes, desperately driving separate cars slowly up and down the roads, looking for any sign of strangers in case the kidnapper had taken Jen on foot to a car awaiting him somewhere.

Brooke began to pace, trying to stay sane. The kidnapper would call with further directions; he would have to call, soon, now, damn him! She would promise him she would never practice law again, pursue no investigations, move away—anything if he just gave Jen back. *Anything*! Nothing else mattered, not Melrose Manor, not her future with Daniel, not catching Katie's killers, or the demise of the entire Amish world. If she lost Jen, she'd never love anyone again, never survive.

"We'll find her and bring her back!" Daniel promised, even when he and Verna returned empty-handed with no trace of Jen to report.

Brooke's panic twisted to bitter anger at herself, at them, at everyone. "I'm not like all of you Amish! I won't just accept this, never, never!" she shouted to Daniel.

"I said, we'll find her!"

She saw tears mat his eyelashes when he blinked, yet she pounded his shoulders and chest when he tried to pull her to him until he let her go. She could not bear to look at Verna, slumped over the kitchen table, head in her hands.

Brooke lost control. She tore her hair, knocked over a chair, kicked it, and hit her fists against the wall harder than Daniel had. She paced again, her palms pressed to her forehead, seeing nothing and no one except Jennifer, out there somewhere, terrified that she was alone and deserted again.

"Why doesn't he call?" she demanded. "She doesn't deserve this. I'm the one who got into everything!"

"Brooke, I never imagined . . . in my house . . ." Verna said. "And since no one broke in and I'm sure the doors were locked, I'm at a loss."

At a loss . . . her voice seemed so far away. Verna and Daniel—everything—was a black-and-red smear of frenzy. Brooke remembered to tell them what she had seen in the linen closet, then leaned into the wall again; Daniel came close but did not touch her. Her mind replayed scenes she had tried so hard to shut out: Melanie, a frail shadow in her bed at home, reaching out her white hand, saying, "Brooke, please be there for Jen, because she's going to need a mother." The Amish kids dead and dying on that black night road, that bleak day the Amish buried Katie, and Emma facedown on Katie's grave.

Now she knew Emma's tearing panic and pain at Katie's death. She had been so brave, even though that was the torment of loss without hope. And yet, at least Emma knew Katie did not fear or suffer, and that was torturing Brooke now about Jennifer.

"Not Jen!" She shoved away from the wall, her arms wrapped over her head as if she walked through a driving storm. Never had she acted like this, but she could not find control. Feelings churned in her so fierce that she ran to the sink, bent over, sure she would be physically ill. She only dry heaved, again, again, gasping, with Verna's arm around her shaking shoulders.

Finally, she collapsed in the kitchen table chair to which they guided her. And, head in her hands, she found she could begin to reason as well as feel and fear.

"I should never have thought we were safe here in Maplecreek," she told them. "But when I was able to explain the incidents—Hiram Hostetler and Jake—I got careless." She still refused Daniel's touch and the coffee Verna offered. Finding and saving Jennifer was her burden alone, because she loved her more than life.

Brooke's stomach heaved again, but she fought for control; her legs shook and ached, though she stood to walk again; her contact lenses burned, but she had no time for anything—anything, but finding Jennifer. "No, not Jen!" she whispered one last time, but now, climbing from the black depths, she began, with Daniel and

Verna, to put the pieces together. And, for Brooke, they fell together into only one pattern.

"Unfortunately," she said, "I think Jen's kidnapper is tied either to the WWEE mess or the hit-and-run, and that leads us to one possibility."

"You've ruled out Jennifer's father?" Verna asked.

"It's not Jeff, but that's another reason not to call the police. In a case like this, they might assume he had someone snatch her and leave the note as subterfuge, which I don't believe for one minute, because Jeff could take her anytime he wants and I couldn't stop him. If we called in the police, they'd phone him and he'd go crazy and never let me have her again, when he obviously doesn't give a damn about her. A hit-and-run father, that's what he's been, and he doesn't deserve her."

"Still," Daniel said, "you're going to have to tell him."

"I will if this doesn't work. Verna, will you stay here in case someone calls with a ransom demand or a message? I don't think that's what this is about, but if the kidnapper wants me, say I'm sedated or in shock or grief. Tell him to give you the message, and I will call you every hour here, so don't panic if the phone rings. And seal Jen's bedroom and the linen closet off with everything just where it is in case we are forced to use the police—if everything else—fails."

"You're going to try what?" Daniel demanded. "If what else fails? You're still going to Las Vegas, aren't you? Then I am, too."

"All right, but you know—this might change things for us. If I lose her . . ." Brooke took a sip of coffee before she realized it was stone cold. Her mind raced, but she sagged momentarily against Daniel, who put his arms around her and kissed the top of her head. But even his strength was no comfort now.

She started upstairs to pack a few clothes, then turned back. A hundred pieces of a plan bombarded her at once to make her almost dizzy. "Verna, I'd like to trade cars with you so Daniel and I can sneak out in case we're followed, but I'll take my car phone with me to call you. And, if he's willing," she added, looking at him now, "could you give his hair a trim, so he doesn't stand out?" Bless them, they both nodded.

"And if you'd get my Wedding Ring quilt off the frame," she went on, "I've got a use for that, too."

Jennifer was so exhausted she slept sprawled on the back car seat where two men had kept her after the long airplane ride. After the highway, the man who didn't smell like liquor drove now on such a bumpy road it kept jolting her awake. She wished it was an Amish road, but it was somewhere hot and dry and dusty, that's all she knew. When the car stopped, she did not want them even to touch her, but the one with bad breath carried her in some house anyway and laid her on a soft, lumpy bed.

"You're in a bedroom in a house in the desert, kid, with the windows boarded up and no phone. After you hear the door close, you can take that tape off your eyes, mouth, and legs, but you gotta put on a cloth blindfold we've got here each time before you're fed on a tray. There's a slop jar in the corner for a toilet and a change of clothes for you in a paper sack."

He rolled her over and pressed her facedown into the bed. "Do what you're told, or you'll be out with the lizards and the coyotes," he said, still in that awful, growly voice. He cut her wrists free with big scissors, then walked out and slammed the door. She heard a key turn in the lock.

She rolled over, sat up, and finally managed to get off her sticky blindfold. She saw the one little lamp was off and boards covered the only window. But light coming in around the boards hurt her eyes, and she blinked and squinted.

It was an old-time room, but not a nice one, not dusted even, with dirty walls and a beat-up, dark-wood dresser gray with dust and cobwebs in the corners and this old brass bed that sagged. But she saw the bed had a messy, spotty quilt on it she could wrap around her. She touched it, petted it as though it was a spotted horse, over and over. That quilt, more than anything, made her wish so, *so* bad that she was safe at home.

CHAPTER EIGHTEEN

ON THE LAST LEG OF THEIR FLIGHT TO LAS VEGAS, after a long wait in Chicago, Brooke and Daniel completed their plans and tried to boost each other's spirits. The flight seemed endless, the airline food dry and plastic, but they decided they had to eat to keep up their strength. Brooke knew she must try to be sharp when she faced Kiki, but she could not sleep because she kept seeing Jen, hearing Jen:

Don't be afraid, Aunt Brooke. You never wanted me to be afraid even when all kinds of bad things happened. 'Cause I had you, you said, and don't forget that you have me . . . I got my mother's love inside me and yours outside me, Aunt Brooke.

Now, she tried to send Jen her love and strength, out there, down there, wherever she was.

"Brooke." Daniel's voice startled her. "The woman on the airplane loudspeaker said to put these trays in the

358

back of the seat because we're landing. The waitresses strapped themselves in up there. But I can see we're still real high up, so how can we land now? Do jets do it different from crop planes?"

"We'll take a long approach in first," she told him. She berated herself, realizing how bold he'd been to fly for the first time when she'd done next to nothing to inform or reassure him about it. But there had seemed no time for that, for anything but desperate plans.

Now, as the plane banked, she saw they were chasing the sunset and knew she would have to wait for morning to face Kiki. But tomorrow was Sunday; could she get her alone? At first when she figured out WWEE was buying Amish land, she had thought she should avoid Kiki, but now she needed her. She only hoped she was not off with Hank on some weekend jaunt, and they would have to wait longer.

She leaned over Daniel in the window seat to look down as far as she could. Stark shadows already huddled in the sandstone clefts and canyons; bland beige stretches of desert sand darkened to grays and blacks. Daniel pressed his nose to the window while she inserted her credit card in the seat-back phone to call Verna once more before they landed.

"Bright lights are moving everywhere under us!" he said, his voice awed. "And there's a strip of tall buildings up ahead with real bright lights—so many!"

"And Jen's down there somewhere. Please, God, let her be down there somewhere, waiting for us, and safe."

"Yeah," he whispered. "Amen."

Brooke insisted on driving the rental car, because she was more used to traffic. The streets were thick with cars, limos, taxis, and tour buses crawling out of

359

McCarran International, past the university, toward the Strip. And Daniel had been right about bright lights. Brooke had never seen Las Vegas, either, and pictures, even moving ones, had not captured the reality—or fantasy—of Glitter Gulch. Though they both gawked, it annoyed her that traffic was only going about thirty, as if everyone were just cruising their Saturday evening away without a care in the world.

"How much farther to the hotel?" she asked him. He didn't even click on the dome light, but lifted the car-rental map spread over his knees to read it by outside lights.

Immense hotel-casinos with decorative themes—Roman, Egyptian, Medieval—seemed to rotate by, all draped in sweeping, spraying, sizzling lights in crayon-box colors, luring people in to stay or eat or gamble. Hot pink, cobalt blue, sun orange, chartreuse, magenta, lipstick red, and tangerine cascaded and swirled against the ebony or eye-blazing white backgrounds of signs. At the Flamingo, neon rings filled with pink champagne bubbles fizzed sky-high. In front of the Mirage a massive volcano spewed red lights, flames, and smoke. Brooke felt shell-shocked by the change from Maplecreek—and her chances of finding Jennifer here, in all this.

"The Waldron place is in the next block, on this side," Daniel told her. "Brooke, I never imagined this. Are you sure we're smart to stay at Hank Waldron's place?" he asked again, even as they turned in. Huge, moving figures of a cowboy and cowgirl twirling six-shooters and lariats guarded the entrance to Waldron's Western World Hotel-Casino.

"It's the last place they're going to look for us if things get rough, and I switched credit cards with Verna.

Which makes you Mr. Dan Spriggs, in case anyone asks."

"Yeah, but I still think we should just try a place at random," he said as they parked under the registration sign and the Stetson and chaps-clothed valets jumped to roll a brass, carpeted luggage cart their way. Luckily, Brooke thought as she undid her seat belt, she had seen from their brief ride that Vegas had all kinds of visitors, so surely Daniel would blend in here, even if he were probably the first and last Amishman to visit.

They registered, dumped their things, then located their car in the vast, multilevel parking garage. They thought they had memorized the map, but got lost twice locating the WWEE office building. It loomed all glassy curves, some windows lit, seething with reflections. They checked where all the entrances and exits were—they weren't sure why—then headed out to the most upscale suburb Brooke had ever seen. They drove by the fenced, gated Waldron estate several times, once again checking side streets for escape routes in case they needed them. Brooke would phone Kiki early in the morning. If she didn't tip her off that something was amiss, maybe she could get in to see her.

They stopped at a McDonald's to check a phone book to locate where Garner Waldron and Matt and Clay Buckland lived, but none of them were listed. Near midnight, Brooke and Daniel returned to the hotel and grabbed a sandwich in the Last Chance Saloon Coffee Shop. Brooke kept staring at everyone who passed, even though she knew she would not see any of the Waldrons from Kiki's wedding photo among the gamblers. She began to feel closed in here, trapped by the eternal pulsing, throbbing beat of the place, for everything seemed to be open twenty-four hours in this windowless, clockless, massive saloon.

She held tighter to Daniel's arm as they cased the gigantic, busy structure. Even inside, as it did out on the Strip, the noise, the lights bombarded them like strobes piercing the brain: stairs and banisters glittered, walls twinkled, bulb-lined mirrors glared, thousand-light chandeliers hovered over them. They walked through hives of banging, clanging slot machines and video poker screens.

Waldron's Western World Hotel-Casino included 2,400 rooms in two buildings linked by skywalks; three casinos named Silver City, Golden, and Dodge; two pools; many restaurants; numerous bars; countless shops; a big showroom for the all-cowgirl western review; and a chapel.

They thought they would share a peaceful moment in the chapel, but when they opened the door, it was not private or quiet. It turned out to be a wedding chapel where, even at one-thirty at night, three couples stood in an anteroom waiting to be wed as if they were in a checkout line at Kmart. Only one couple wore traditional bridal attire. The first pair in line were coiffed and dressed as Elvis imitators in matching, rhinestone-studded white silk jumpsuits, though Brooke thought the taller one was probably a woman. The two who looked like *Star Trek* aliens laughed at their obvious surprise and called after them, "June's a monster wedding month, you know!"

"This whole place is like a monster," Daniel muttered as the chapel door closed behind them. "But it's not going to devour us or our Jen!"

At ten the next morning, Brooke drove through the gates of the Waldron estate. Her heart beat harder than

362

it ever had in court, but then she had never pleaded for the freedom—the very life—of her own flesh and blood before. She wore a beige pantsuit and navy V-necked silk blouse, trying to strike a balance between looking casual but deadly serious. Her Wedding Ring quilt clasped in her arms—at first glance, it looked completed, but needed a border and hours of final quilting—she got out of the car and went up to the front door to ring the bell. She heard it chime musically, muted within.

So far so good, she tried to buck herself up. Kiki had said Hank was golfing and she would be happy to see her—though Brooke had sensed surprise and then hesitation in her voice. But why hadn't Brooke called from Ohio before she flew out here? Kiki had asked. For all Brooke knew, she might be walking into a trap. But Kiki was her only way to really get to her brothers and WWEE.

When no one answered the door, her stomach clenched even harder. She rang again, wishing desperately that she and Daniel had not had that last-minute argument over the fact she thought it best if he didn't even wait for her in the car. They had compromised: he would not wait back at the hotel, either, so she only hoped his walking back and forth on the curved road that circled the estate would not draw undue attention from Waldron security or the neighbors.

Kiki answered the door herself. "Brooke, how wonderful of you to stop by to see me on your vacation and show me how your quilt's coming along!" Despite that effusive welcome, Brooke thought she looked wary as well as curious. Brooke had only called her a half hour ago, hoping that even if Kiki had time to alert Hank or

363

her brothers, she could have a few minutes with her before they got here. She had wanted to call her much earlier this morning, but she had to keep up some semblance of normality, so Kiki wouldn't bolt or panic before she could present her case.

Garbed in a lemon silk jumpsuit and paisley obi belt, wearing a necklace of chunky amber, her red hair tumbled loose, Kiki seemed as brightly colored as the Strip, but her vitality and animation did not reach to her face and voice. "Oh, that's quilt's looking real fine, and I can't wait to see mine. So, how's the master quilt maker who had that breakdown after her daughter's death, anyway?"

That set Brooke back. She hadn't expected Kiki to bring it up. But didn't that indicate she must know nothing about her family's involvement in the hit-and-run, she reasoned, as Kiki led her through the sprawling house to the lofty-ceilinged living area.

"She's on medication and getting counseling—her husband's attending the sessions, too," Brooke replied, choosing her words carefully. "Her husband, you see, was part of the problem."

Kiki's green gaze slammed into Brooke's at those words, even as she indicated she should sit on the white leather couch facing a huge, freestanding, central flagstone hearth and long bar off to the side. Brooke bit back the desire to scream out accusations, especially because she could see from here, sitting on shelves of the bar, several bottles she could not read but recognized as Glenbrae Scotch, flaunting their bagpiper and bold print. What if it wasn't the Buckland brothers, but Hank Waldron himself, maybe even his son, Garner Waldron, who had driven the death car? But no, she must have figured this right.

By lawyer's instinct, she rejected her long-rehearsed opening statement with all the evidence about the Amish land sale, which then linked to all the evidence about the hit-and-run. Instead, she simply spilled the quilt free over their legs and began, "Kiki, I came to get advice and help from you."

"What? Listen, making one of these is not up my alley. But you don't mean that kind of help, do you?"

"I liked you from the first, Kiki, and thought you were genuine, and as different as we obviously are, I felt an affinity with you."

"I felt the same way about you," Kiki said, but she didn't meet her eyes now. Perhaps her flattery had made her self-conscious. How much could she know? About the betrayal of the Amish? Dear God, not of Jen's abduction!

"So, I'm just going to respect you enough to spit this out and not play games. My seven-year-old motherless niece, Jennifer, my ward, whose father has more or less deserted and entrusted to me, has been abducted."

"Oh, no!" she cried and clapped both hands over her mouth, before dropping them to grab Brooke's. "And you've come to me for money the kidnappers want?"

"I have come to you to help me get her back, but not that way."

"But what can I do? I mean, Brooke, I'm so sorry, but what are you doing here? Haven't you called in the police or FBI?"

"The abduction note instructed me not to. Kiki, Jennifer is the only family I have, so I am absolutely desperate and will do whatever I must to get her back— anything!"

"That's so awful! I do understand." She crossed her arms under her breasts and rocked slightly. "I'd do anything for my two brothers, and I raised them myself after my mother died and Daddy left, so they're like my sons, too."

"But, Kiki, your brothers and the others who have a lot to lose if the WWEE Amish land deal—"

"Land deal? You know about that already?"

"Yes. My point is, Matt and Clay and your stepson, Garner, are adults now, responsible for their own actions, and my niece is just a child. I have something to explain to you. Please, just hear me out."

She did not start with the land deal, since that had seemed to alarm her; she was afraid she'd throw her out and they'd never get beyond that. She began with the night of the accident and painted for her, with specific details, the portrait of the possible culprit: cowardly but bold, as Daniel had surmised; someone who didn't know the road, who was out for a joyride of sorts, Jake had said—maybe a person who had someone else in the car to distract him.

She told her—without using the name of the place or waitress—about Reba Potts's willingness to testify about the two young blond, good-looking men drinking Glenbrae Scotch that night in the tavern—and about the twin bottles found on the road. At that point—a tactic she'd learned from watching her father years ago—she glanced dramatically at the pertinent evidence on the shelf above the bar. Kiki kept her silence; her beautiful face was frozen, sullen, even stubborn, but tears glazed her eyes and she bit her lower lip hard.

"And, Kiki, from your wedding photo that appeared in *Town & Country*, this witness identified the men in the bar as Matt and Clay Buckland. And I myself briefly met your stepson, Garner, in Maplecreek just after the accident—he was driving by to check out the scene. At first I suspected him, but I don't think so now. Does it make sense to you that he was there checking up on your brothers?"

Brooke saw Kiki's expression had changed at the mere mention of Garner's name, but she plunged on. "And in case you haven't guessed by now, I've traced the sale of a lot of would-be Amish land back to WWEE—and we know that your brothers are also on the projects committee to create some sort of Amish-rama amusement park."

"Amish World," Kiki whispered to give Brooke her first glimmer of hope Kiki might help her.

"Amish World, then, Kiki, listen, I'm not here to insist your brothers be arrested, but to trade Jen's life—and the four lives of those Amish kids I can prove in court they hit and left dead and dying on the road—for theirs."

Kiki got up, walked to the sweep of windows overlooking the pool, and turned away to lean her shoulder there. "About the land," she cried, "I didn't know until this week, I swear to God, I didn't."

"All right, I believe you," Brooke said, rising and coming to stand behind her. "But the land deal only interests me right now because it leads me to who took Jennifer. Of course, if you admire the Amish as you've said, in helping me get Jennifer back safely, you could also try to stop this theme park. Kiki, I'd help your family and company build that obscenity in Maplecreek myself, pour the concrete over those beautiful meadows, force the Amish to staff the damn place—*anything* if I thought I could get Jennifer back safe and sound!"

Kiki spun to face Brooke. "But because you're desp'rate, you're jumping the gun!" Kiki insisted. "Even if my brothers were in on the land deal or were in town when that accident happened, they would have no reason to kidnap your poor little niece!"

"Of course, they do! Somehow they learned I'm investigating the land deal and the hit-and-run, so I could ruin them. Kiki, believe me, I can convince a jury it was your brothers, but by then, Jennifer could be dead. It's one thing—isn't it?—to make money from the souls of dispossessed, gentle people who can make quilts like we both love? But it's something else to have to face up to the deaths of four Amish kids—and maybe"—her voice broke and she blinked back tears—"Jennifer's, too. Please, Kiki, do what's right here. Talk to your brothers now, the minute I leave, because what I'm offering today will be gone tomorrow."

"Offering? What're you offering?" she cried, starting to pace. "You want to ruin Matt and Clay at WWEE— ruin their entire lives! They've worked so hard to get where they are with Hank and that selfish, stupid Garner, they'd do anyth—" she got out before she turned away again. Her shoulders slumped and began to shake. She put a hand to the glass to steady herself.

"Kiki, I imagine the men in your life don't share much with you about the business. But I am trusting you, offering this deal to you. If your brothers or anyone else returns Jennifer unharmed to me today, I will not pursue the kidnapping and homicide charges. And, if anything happens to me, my law firm will file and pursue this for me."

Kiki wiped tears from her cheeks; when she put her hand back on the glass door, it left a smear. "Also," Brooke went on, "partly so that there is no possible linkage of your brothers or WWEE to the Amish land sale, which will in turn link them to the hit-and-run, you have got to talk your family into selling that

368

property at a fair price to the Amish."

"I knew—I wanted that, but it's too far along."

"No it isn't because nothing's public, and even then Waldron World could make the magnanimous, altruistic gesture. What I can do to your brothers and WWEE means they have to listen to you, even now. It goes against my grain to let criminals off, Kiki, but for Jen and the Amish, I can forgo if not forgive. Real forgiveness is what the Amish want—Amish justice where judgment and punishment belong to God. This time, I'll trust God—and you—on that."

Finally, Kiki nodded and turned to face Brooke.

"I'm leaving directions here," Brooke said, going over to her purse to take the paper Daniel had written. "This is a cellular phone number that will reach me so I know where to pick Jennifer up, safe and sound, today, soon. Don't try to trace me or let anyone be so foolish to try to find me. I have numerous backups," she bluffed, "whom WWEE will not like dealing with because they don't offer plea bargains—they just arrest and indict and convict. And, Kiki, make sure that whoever is behind this atrocity does not have second thoughts later, but leaves all of us in peace when it's over."

Brooke turned and walked away, just as the maid came in, carrying coffee for two on a tray. She opened the front door herself before the maid, who scurried after her, could reach it. She got in, started the car, and drove down the driveway, hoping, praying this would work. She locked her doors, fearing the gates would not open, that an armed guard would run out to stop her, but they buzzed and swung wide. She spotted Daniel almost immediately, leaning out of breath against a palm tree.

"I had to hurry over that fence and run when I saw

369

you walk out of the glassed-in living room," he told her, panting as he jumped in beside her. "Luckily, those fences aren't electrified, though I know from cattle fences how to kill the voltage if I have to. Jennifer's not in the pool house out back or in the garage or shed, and—like you said—they'd be stupid to have her upstairs where she could hear something."

"You didn't say you were going to climb their fence and get on the grounds!"

He shrugged. "You might have needed me. All right, let's circle around, then change drivers, and we'll see if she sends for her brothers or runs to them."

"I believe she'll at least contact them. I just hope they don't panic—so this could backfire. But I think this plan is our only chance."

"Kid!" the growly voiced man called at the door so loud Jennifer jumped. "Get that blindfold on, because I'm coming in. And hurry up! Is it on? It better be!"

"Yes," she called out, her voice shaky. It was a real bad sign, she thought, that the man was yelling.

Sitting there scared, she heard him come in the room and stop by the bed where she sat.

"I'm going to tie you up again. We've got to move you."

"Just take me back to Maplecreek!"

But he pushed her facedown and tied her wrists and ankles, tight again like that lady had done when she took her away from home. His breath smelled like drinking again. He taped her mouth and eyes, too. When he went back out, he didn't close the door all the way, because she could hear his words to someone, real upset and not whispering this time.

"I'm never listening to you again, Matt. That's all we

370

need—Kiki demanding to see us about the land deal. You created a monster listening to her little quilt shop idea, and I don't like it!"

"That message from her has been on our machine since late morning, so we can't keep ignoring it. She says to meet her at McCluskey's old store, so I say we go or it's going to look funny. Besides, she sounded shook. But I think we'd better lower the kid down the old well while we're gone, just in case something is really wrong, like Kiki or Hank's on to something. Besides, there's always the outside chance someone will come around here like we did years ago. And would you quit your damned drinking for now?" he shouted, and she heard glass breaking.

"You bastard! I just don't like Kiki out in this area when she never sets foot here anymore!"

"So? Neither had we until we remembered this place."

"All I can say is everything with this kid is on your head if we have to get rid of her!"

"Hitting four kids is on yours, so you can just finish it with this one if we have to! And I'll do all the talking with Kiki, so just hold it together, will you? I can handle her, always could."

Most of their words blurred in Jennifer's head after she heard they were going to put her down a well. They were going to put her into water? But she'd never swim all tied up like this, never even get her breath with her mouth taped! She tried to keep tears from squeezing out because that would make the water in the well much, much worse.

It was near sunset and Kiki felt frenzied waiting for Matt and Clay. A message on her machine at home said they'd be here late afternoon—as soon as they could.

She waited in her car before the derelict, concrete-block convenience store almost directly across the rural road from the entrance to the Happy Haven Trailer Park where they had grown up. Scrubland and desert stretched all around, crisscrossed by sporadic, dusty roads leading into the hills past some abandoned houses they'd explored as kids. She hadn't been back here for years and hated the place, but it was the only really out-of-the-way area she could think of for this desperate gamble to impress upon Matt and Clay how serious she was.

Her hair jammed up into an old baseball cap of Hank's, huge opaque sunglasses obscuring her swollen eyes and ravaged mascara, she got out of her car when Clay's sports car wheeled in next to hers. Funny, but they had come from the direction of the desert, not town. And she noted Matt was driving again. Her stomach churned at maybe knowing why, at seeing the two of them for the first time through different eyes.

"What's the problem, Keek?" Clay asked. He looked more frazzled than she did.

"Where are you two coming from?" she countered with a sweep of her hand at sand and sagebrush.

"Just taking a ride—temporary escape from the pressures of the job," Matt put in, striding toward her. "Thought we'd take a look at the old neighborhood we've all made it out of—together, thanks to you, Kiki. I don't know what we would have done without you."

"I'm not buying that crap anymore, Matt."

"What's your problem?" he demanded, grabbing her upper arms. "You're still mad about the Amish thing? You're getting your quilt shop, aren't you? Not telling you everything before the board meeting was the only way we could go, so—"

"A lot you haven't told me lately," she said, hitting his hands loose. "Now, you two listen to me! You'd better stop this whole Amish avalanche if you don't want to get buried under it!"

"Keek..."

"I mean rot in jail in Ohio for four counts of vehicular homicide. It looks to me like Clay was driving, but you were an accomplice, Matt."

"What in God's name are you talking about?" Clay shouted and raked both hands through his hair.

"But it's worse than that, isn't it?" she demanded, feeling so sure but so sorry now. "An accident on a dark, hilly road is one thing, but running and never taking responsibility? And if you or anyone you know dared to abduct that little niece of Brooke Benton's..."

Her voice trailed off in horror, for she saw then they were guilty, *really* guilty. Their heads snapped sideways like mirror images, so they could look at each other. She knew the worst then: but could they have actually done this thing themselves and not just hired someone else? She felt nauseous; her legs shook.

"I'm just the messenger here," she told them more quietly now. "The deal is, the girl gets returned safely today to avoid charges like homicide, kidnapping, transportation across state lines—"

"You're sounding like a smart-ass lawyer," Matt said, his voice coldly calm now. "You been talking to that Brooke Benton when we told you not to? Did you call her and tell her about the land deal?"

"No, she figured it out and came to me."

"Now? Lately?"

"Since you've arranged to have her niece taken and told her not to bring in the authorities, you mean?" Kiki shouted. She sniffed so hard her sinuses stung; she swiped at tears under her sunglasses.

"Well, whatever happened," Matt said, amazingly controlled, "the thing is, Kiki, we don't have any girl to give back and don't know a damned thing about it. If you don't know us better than that after all these years—"

"I haven't known you at all, or at least been willing to admit it! Selfish, greedy users—bastards! You want to know why Daddy knocked you and Mama around—because you were such mean little buggers, he thought you weren't his! And when she died, Mama said it was true, but she wouldn't tell me who your father was. I was Daddy's, but you weren't, and I felt so sorry for you. All these years my love for you and my promise to Mama to take care of you blinded me, but no more!"

"Come on, Clay," Matt said, "let's go. She's hysterical and she'll do anything she can to sabotage us with Hank. Might as well literally go get in bed with Garner, Kiki, because he's wanted that for years. Still, I can't believe you'd sell us down the river."

"Right now," she shouted, "there's a little girl being sold down the river, whose father left her and whose mother died, and I know how that feels. Here!" She produced Brooke's directions from her slacks pocket, hurrying after them. "This is the number to call to tell people where to come get this child named Jennifer Reynolds. The police aren't involved—yet—if you take care of this tragedy right now."

Clay's eyes were huge, Matt's narrowed to slits; neither of them reached for the paper. "We don't have the kid, and we didn't hit those Amish teenagers we read about, Kiki," Matt said, daring to stare deep into her eyes, even when she whipped off her sunglasses. "Our only tragedy is lies and betrayal by the sister who

374

said she loved us. Come on, Clay. it's getting dark, and we've got work to do before tomorrow."

Kiki saw Matt's chin quiver; Clay could not look at her. They got in Clay's car and slammed their doors in unison. The tires spewed gravel as they took off toward town. Still blinking back tears, Kiki squinted into their drifting dust as down the road she saw a man jump out of the car she'd noticed there before the boys arrived. Its hood had been raised in distress; she had assumed it was deserted. But now, even in the deepening dusk, it hit her that it was the model and color that Brooke Benton had arrived in this morning.

She stared at it: the man slammed the hood, jumped back in. A woman was in the passenger seat, bending down. The car made a quick U-turn to squeal away in the direction the boys had headed. So Brooke and someone else had followed her out here? Could she have lied and the police were already involved? If so, she had to warn Hank and get help from him.

"We're dead if we stay around here," Matt said as they sped down the road.

"Especially if that kid talks. Everything's ruined because of Keek and that lawyer."

"Just shut up so I can think. I'm going to circle around the back way to the farmhouse; we'll throw debris and the old furniture down the well to cover the evidence we put there and just keep driving. We'll get a plane out from Reno. We can be in Europe, access our money by tomorrow or the next day. How could all of this have happened just from driving down a dark country road?" he said and sucked in a sob as he turned off the paved road onto a dirt one, rough as a washboard.

"They're not heading back toward town," Daniel said as he, too, turned onto the narrow road that seemed to go straight into the black mountains up ahead. "At least the dark might cover us if we don't turn on our headlights to follow them."

"With that dust trail they're leaving, we can stay back so—they won't see us. Ah!" she cried out as they hit a pothole that bounced and jerked them despite their seat belts.

In raw reds and golds, the sun sank behind the ragged stone horizon ahead of them. Brooke gripped her hands together so hard that her fingers went numb. Some twenty miles out from the city, now only a silver glow of lights as night descended, they raced after the dust trail of the Buckland brothers' sports car. The rough road shook their bones and jarred their teeth as Daniel pushed their speed to fifty-five, then sixty-five, much too fast for the conditions. He hunched over the wheel, intent, concentrating fiercely on keeping the car on the road without headlights. She steadied herself with hands on the door and dash, but she trembled even worse inside.

Five miles, ten. The road rushed at them; night thickened. In her worst memories, Brooke saw again that other night, their first together, when they raced toward town together, trying to save Katie. And now they had to find Jennifer, and those men were their only hope. Perhaps, she thought, she had made a mistake not to get the police involved, or was misguided to trust Kiki, to trust her own instincts after she'd been so wrong about Rodney Kistler and Jake Kaminsky—even poor Levi. She'd been living in fear for so long, she almost didn't believe there would be a happy ending for her,

Jen, Daniel, Emma, even the Amish.

"If it gets darker, I'll have to hit the lights, even if they see us," Daniel said. "This road runs straight, but —" Another pothole jarred them, but he held them on the road.

"If they're not going anywhere specific, but just running for it, we can't lose them!" She clicked on the dome light to try to read the map she'd been studying the long, hot hour they'd watched Kiki down the road, praying she was waiting for her brothers. But now the car was vibrating and bouncing too hard for her to read the map to see where the Bucklands might be headed. She crumpled it up and heaved it in the backseat.

"As I recall," she said, "there's just a few roads out here, all two lane, probably unpaved like this one. The thing is they drove up to that old store from the other direction, not from the city so they could have already been out here instead of in town."

"Brooke, look! They must not know we're back here. They've finally put their lights on, and they're turning right again."

The shifting dust trail—none ahead, some to the side—proved Daniel's words, too. At this crossroads marked only by a route sign, the sports car had turned right onto another unpaved road. When Brooke looked behind them when they turned, she saw another car— this one with headlights on too—following them through their own dust. She craned around in the seat and squinted to see better.

"I think that car behind us might be Kiki's, small and white."

"Are you sure? I haven't been looking back."

"Could she and her brothers be in cahoots to set up a trap for us? Lure us out here and sandwich us in or lose us—leave us out here somehow?"

She shuddered even as she said it. She wondered if they could get help if they called 9-1-1 in this godforsaken-looking area. But how much explaining would it take to get the police out here and where should they tell them to come?

"Hang on. We're turning right again!" Daniel shouted.

"Circling back toward where they met Kiki? But why?"

"To lose us before they head back to town? Or maybe they have Jen out here somewhere. Brooke, I've got to turn on our lights, too, to stay on this road. I've dropped far enough back to not be blinded with the dust, but it's too dark now."

"Go ahead. If they look back, they'll see Kiki's anyway."

"I don't see them anymore—their dust, either!" He slammed the steering wheel with his fist and pulled over on the narrow dusty berm.

"Keep your lights on or Kiki might just slam into us. Hit your warning blinkers, too! She helped us once before—I think."

They gasped and ducked in unison as a big tumbleweed came out of the dark, hit their car on the passenger side, bounced off, and blew away. The car behind them pulled up behind—yes, Kiki. Brooke could see her silhouetted in her own headlights when she got out.

Brooke unsnapped her seat belt and unlocked the doors, but Daniel pulled her back and hit the locks closed again.

"What if she has a gun?" he demanded. "The Bucklands could double back, or be out here in this dark. What if Kiki's in with them, and it's a trap?"

"I just believe in her, Daniel. I have from the first, even though I've been wrong about some others. And what else are we going to do?"

"I saw you!" Kiki shouted through Daniel's window as he rolled it partway down. "Oh, it's you, the Amish man. Brooke, I saw you chase them, and I followed to help," she added, looking in.

"We lost them!" Brooke said, leaning over Daniel. "Do you know where they could have gone?"

"One possible place out here, just a little farther. We used to play there when we were kids."

"That's it," Daniel said, hitting the steering wheel with both fists. "That's where they went to make a stand—maybe with Jen."

"Or else," Brooke whispered, her mouth close to his ear, "they're lying in wait for us there, and she knows it. But I *do* trust her."

"Where?" Brooke called to Kiki. "Can you take us?"

"Follow me. An old place we used to call the ghost house. It's had squatters on and off, but I just thought —"

"Let's go!" Daniel shouted.

They waited until Kiki roared by them, then followed. She slowed right away as if looking for the place. Did she really know where it was out here?

"Brooke, if she just drives in and traps them there, they might panic and do something rash."

"Panic more than they evidently have now? Something more rash than taking Jen? Look, she's signaling. And turning!"

"Good, she's not driving all the way in. Your friend Kiki either has more brains than I thought, or she's really setting us up good. Let me get out with her, and

379

you stay here locked in, ready to call or go for help."

"But if Jen's there, I can't. You stay here, please, Daniel! And hit your lights, because they've probably already heard the cars if they're here. Then, if I don't come back, get help! Or if the Bucklands are here and take off, follow them in case they're fleeing with Jen or could still lead us to her. I only hope this chase hasn't ruined everything."

Kiki, too, turned on her brights from where she had stopped ahead of them down the dusty, weedy driveway. But someone had driven in here recently, Brooke thought, because the ruts were deep, the scrub grass smashed down. Daniel maneuvered so the headlights crisscrossed Kiki's to bathe the old house in a double beam of light. If the Bucklands had driven in here, Brooke told herself as she got out shaking, they had pulled way around in back. Could they be armed?

The old house reminded her of a building from a ghost town, although several windows, looking newly glassed, reflected the headlights; the ones upstairs gaped blank-eyed under sagging, frowning eaves.

Although Kiki had the only flashlight, a small one, she led Brooke into the house through the unlocked and partly broken front door. They bumped shoulders when the light caught two glowing eyes before a rat skittered away. Her dark search of the Miller barn jumped into Brooke's memory; it had ended in utter defeat.

She saw two rooms here were furnished with spartan things that looked somewhat new; two cots, a card table, two chairs, a white plastic cooler. They looked inside: melted ice, some French onion potato chip dip. Brooke realized she'd been expecting Glenbrae Scotch or at least drink cans. Where would they have thrown their empties?

The bedroom on the first floor had an old bed that had been made up with a sagging mattress with a single, mussed sheet and dirty quilt that looked as if a small form had lain there. Brooke gripped her hands hard between her breasts.

"Jennifer? Jen, are you here?" she called, her voice shaky.

Like children themselves, Brooke and Kiki held hands to go upstairs. The first two stair treads over floorboards creaked; the next several were missing.

"No one's been up here for a long time," Kiki whispered and they backed down.

Then came the rush of revving engines outside, the squeal of tires, the blur of headlights—twice. Brooke leaped to the window.

"They were somewhere out in back!" she shouted. "Daniel's going after them!"

Her carefully controlled frenzy swelled and spilled over. She felt so alone, abandoned, as Jennifer must have. Afraid, so afraid, even of Kiki. If just one of her brothers had drawn Daniel off, and then the other had stayed behind to join Kiki here in the house to settle things once and for all—

"Should we take my car after them, too?" Kiki's voice made her jump. "I called home on my cell phone when I figured where Matt and Clay might have been before they came to meet me. Hank wasn't there, but Mitch said he'd find him and send some help out here, maybe even a chopper. It shouldn't be long now."

"Let's go out in back and see if there are any signs they took Jennifer with them," Brooke managed, but her voice sounded so small. She wanted to cry; they were so close and yet so far. Daniel could be killed out there, chasing them in the dark and dust. And Jen—

"Looks like they were parked out here by this old well," Kiki said and motioned Brooke over, shining her weak beam into car ruts. "You know, we used to throw pennies down there and make wishes we'd all be happy and rich when we grew up," she got out before she leaned her hands on the old, broken adobe-concrete base, and cried.

Daniel kept his eyes on an imaginary line in the middle of the Buckland brothers' dust; he saw no markings on the road—not even a road. It was like driving into a black blur, a vortex sucking him to destruction. But if those bastards had Jen with them, he had to save her. Katie was lost to him, hit and thrown into earthly oblivion, but not Brooke's niece, too, not sweet Jen. Not that night of nightmares over again.

He gripped the wheel to stop its shuddering—his, too—and pressed the accelerator harder, harder, flooring it now; he glimpsed a taillight. Were they braking, turning off? No, it must be a slight lift in the angle of the road, the beginning of the mountains. Like the kids in the buggy that last night on the road, up and over a rise, and then what lay below?

Funny, but his life did flash before his eyes. The lovely times, pretty views, the people, the leaving—then Brooke and Jen when he came home again.

The wind must be better up on these rises, he thought. It yanked the dust off to the side so he could see their lights before they swerved into a new turn of blackness. He had to catch them now, force them over before they climbed into the mountains' twists and turns. He did not want to fall into an abyss with one wrong move.

His tires squealed; he almost fishtailed off the road on

his first turn up into the foothills he didn't know and couldn't see. His shoulder muscles ached, his hands cramped as he hunched over the wheel; the lighted dashboard was a green blur of dials and lights. To think he'd vowed he'd never drive again when he came home that night he'd first met Brooke. He'd begun to live again when he met her, and he didn't want to die.

Her shoulders shaking, Kiki sucked in great breaths as if she dry heaved. Despite her own agony, Brooke approached the well to put a hand on Kiki's shoulder and leaned over her to attempt words of comfort that would not come. And then, in the silence of the desert night, broken only by wind rattling and rustling things and Kiki's quieting sobs, Brooke heard something else. Something murmuring like water down in the well.

She seized Kiki's flashlight and played it down into the black water. No, it was a dry well. But—something white—a leg? Another sound breathed from the depths. Damn this flashlight, so dim, the well so dark. But the beam caught and shimmered on a blond blur of hair, a sprawled leg, a small face, tied twice with the white slash of taped blindfold and gag.

"Jen? Je-eeennnn!" her voice echoed desperate and hollow.

"*Mmmmm*," the sound came, sudden and piercingly sweet. Movement rustled something in the well and shook Brooke to the depths of her being. Gooseflesh prickled her arms and her stomach cartwheeled.

"Jen! Jen! Kiki, it's Jen! Drive your car up and see if the headlights will reflect down the well. Jen, I'm here! Daniel came, too! Don't be afraid! I'm here! Hang on, sweetheart!"

Kiki's headlights barely reflected down the well but

enough to see the small body bent and trussed at the bottom. Brooke swiped tears away to see; she gasped in big breaths.

"I'm here, Jen! Coming down for you! Daniel and I came for you—everything's all right!"

"You can't go down there!" Kiki cried and grabbed Brooke. "It's too far! They must have lowered her down with something! You'll hurt yourself and her, too! We can find something to—wait! Listen!"

Brooke pressed her hands to her mouth, then between her breasts. Kiki loosed her and stepped back to stare up into the vastness of black sky. Yes, the distant chop, chop of an aircraft, its roar, then a big beam burst over them before the helicopter tilted away to land in the distant field. Brooke blinked away temporary blindness as four men ran over, one with a thick rope over his shoulder. Their golden lantern beams burst down the well to drown the darkness. Brooke pressed in between their big shoulders, calling Jennifer's name as she bent over the well; behind, Kiki shrieked a cheer and clapped her hands.

"Get back, now, ma'am, and I'll go down real careful."

The men's voices blurred in Brooke's brain. Deep-voiced orders to one another, the rope tossed in. Dear Katie had not been saved, but Jennifer's life would be her legacy. Brooke wanted to hug the man going down, help him, but Kiki held her back. His footsteps—his cleats—scraped strange echoes from the depths; his voice sounded hollow.

"It's all right now, honey," he was saying. "Everything's all right . . . right . . . right I'm going to take off your blindfold and gag, then put you over my shoulder and take you up real careful like . . . like . . . like. Here, now, okay, kay . . . kay."

384

By tying the rope to Kiki's steering wheel, then slowly backing the car away, the three other men hauled them up. Draped over the man's back, Jennifer's bottom, back, head, then limbs, still tied, emerged into the glare of lights. When she tilted her head to look at Brooke, her face was tear-streaked, filthy—and absolutely beautiful.

Brooke helped to lift her down and took her into her arms like a baby. Jennifer felt so good to Brooke, trembling, cold, but so solid, so real. Brooke collapsed on the ground, cradling the child on her lap. Even before the men cut Jen's bonds, she held her tightly. Her face was slick with tears against Jen's as her mouth pressed in her tangled hair and she whispered, "It's all right. I love you, love you," until those words, too, echoed in her heart. Then she remembered.

"Thank you—Kiki, too," she said, looking up at the circle of faces, nestling the top of Jen's head under her chin. "But there's someone else who needs your help. My friend Daniel—out there where—"

"Yes," Kiki said and stepped forward to grasp Brooke's shoulders. "He's in a tan car chasing a red Jag, driven by—by the ones—who abducted this girl. They went west down this road toward the mountains. Can you call it in, because this child should be flown to the hospital, and I've got to call ahead to my husband so he can take care of everything."

"No," Jennifer spoke her first word not smothered by sobs. "I can't go anywhere till Daniel's here, too! Please go help him like you did me!"

By his headlights—perhaps by starlight, too—Daniel half saw, half sensed a flat place before the next turn. He was really on their tail now, pushing it for all it was

385

worth, wanting to stop them but knowing he could not let them crash that car. If Jen were in it—in the trunk. He had to make his move now!

He could hear his father's voice from so far away—no, close inside him: *Sitting in the driver's seat of an English man's car in town again, so's I hear. Forbidden, boy, verboten, ja, that it is . . .*"

He pushed his front left fender against their back one and tapped, then banged their small bloodred sports car. In the driver's seat . . . *forbidden.*

The bad thing here was that he was on the outside of the turn, pushing in, crowding them. Shove them over. Make them stop. Save Jennifer. But with one wrong move, he's the one who would go off the road and over.

"Jennifer! Jenn-i—fer!" his own shout banged and roared through his brain as the red car swerved away and rolled over once to stop, right side up, against the cliff face.

Daniel braked hard, skidded sideways almost to the edge of night. His head jerked forward; his seat belt kept him from the windshield, but his forehead hit the steering wheel. He put his arm on the seat behind him, craned his neck, and backed up.

He staggered out of the car onto the road. Clear, crisp air burned deep into his lungs. His legs shook so hard he collapsed to his knees in grit and cinders, stunned, his eyes closed, for one moment back home in his parents' house, praying hard for Jen.

He shook his head to clear it. Sounds, lights pulsated, pounding behind his eyes. He got to his feet, swaying, so dizzy, confused. At first he thought the golden beam and roar in the heavens above signaled the end of the world for him, and he felt deep regret.

He ran to the Bucklands' car in the shaft of sun, and

saw them battered but alive. But no child, front seat or back. "Where is she?" he shouted. "Jennifer! Jen!" He yanked open the dented door and grabbed the keys from the ignition. His hands were trembling so hard, he could barely unlock the trunk. It gaped dim and empty, no Jen. He stood, swaying, his feet wide apart, and wrapped his arms over his throbbing head.

But then the hovering angelic voice like a loudspeaker from above called to him. "The girl is safe, the girl is safe. She's with her aunt. We have her."

Tears streaming down his face, he lifted it toward the light and smiled, for he knew now this was not the end of his world, but a new beginning, fresh and sweet and good.

AFTERWARD

THE NEXT AFTERNOON, TWO LAS VEGAS detectives delivered Daniel, Brooke, and Jennifer to the airport after they had given their statements. They had spent the night in the hospital, Jen for a checkup, Daniel under observation for a concussion, and Brooke keeping watch over both of them.

Luckily, Brooke had thought during her all-night vigil, the Buckland brothers had not been brought to the same hospital, or she would have gone after them tooth and nail. But today, she knew, though the three of them would testify against the Bucklands later, like the Amish she had to get on with her life.

Early boarding for their flight home had already been called when Brooke spotted Kiki. As ever, she stood out from the lines and clumps and blur of other people.

"Daniel, there's Kiki! And Hank. Maybe you should take Jen and board the plane."

"No, neither of you is getting out of my sight until we're home. I'll wait right here, and you just nod if you need me. I see she's got your quilt."

She did indeed. Brooke had intended to leave it with Kiki as a sign of friendship and gratitude, especially because the police said Kiki had made a statement naming her brothers in the kidnapping plot. Now Brooke saw Kiki had covered the quilt with clear plastic and cradled it in one arm like a baby. She also carried two large framed photos under the other arm. Hank stood back; he stared briefly at Daniel, then looked away, his head down, as Kiki came slowly toward her.

"We just had to find you," she said as she approached, still looking tentative. "I called to find out there was a flight to Columbus this afternoon. I guess you heard Matt and Clay will go directly from the hospital to jail until they're arraigned. They're luckier than those Amish kids they killed."

"We want to thank you and Hank—whatever powers that be—for keeping all this out of the papers for now."

"It will hit when they get arraigned and go to trial. But it's the least we could do—Daniel being Amish and all. I'm partly here because we wanted you to know the return of the Amish land will be kept out of the press, too."

"Kiki, the detectives told us it wasn't your brothers who took Jen from our house, but they were waiting in a car in Columbus for her. A woman who dared to pretend to be a Sewing Circle customer has been arrested, named by one of your brothers."

Kiki nodded. "You must hate the Waldrons—and this place."

"It's the place I got Jen back and more than that," Brooke said. She almost told Kiki she had decided on marriage and a new life, but she looked so tragic that Brooke didn't mention her own joy. "No, Kiki, I don't hate you or this place, and I'm trying not to hate your brothers, because it's not the Amish way, or mine now, either—at least that's one of the things I'll be working really hard on."

Biting her lip, Kiki nodded. She wore no makeup, but it did not mute her beauty, only heightened it to see her suffering. Dark half-moons set under her eyes; her mouth dragged down at the corners. When she extended the quilt to Brooke, Kiki gripped her hand.

"I promise you, Brooke, the Amish can have that land real cheap. Hank's letting me oversee it personally and maybe work more with future acquisitions, with my real estate background and all." She cleared her throat, looked down at the floor, then back up. "The board has to vote on it, but Hank and Garner will tell them they figured the backlash from Amish World publicity would be too bad. Will you act as the transfer attorney when that land is put back on the market? It'll be real soon."

"Gladly! Kiki, you've done wonders," she said as another announcement came for boarding the plane. "I can never thank you enough for helping us to get Jennifer back. And I am deeply sorry about the pain your brothers have caused *you*."

"Oh, it's me who should be saying that. Here, almost forgot something else to seal the deal, Hank says. These are two aerial shots of the farmland we're releasing." Without looking at the photos, Brooke leaned them against her legs.

"Kiki, I'll let you know when your quilts will be ready. I'm sure Emma—the master quilter—will soon finish yours like this. Are you all right—with Hank and all?"

Her eyes widened in obvious surprise, then glossed over slowly with tears. She nodded jerkily. "He loves me—for me, not just because—you know," she said with a dismissive gesture at herself.

"I know," Brooke said and squeezed her hand again. She lifted the photos and joined Daniel and Jennifer in line. But before they walked through the gate to board, Brooke turned back once more; Hank had his arm around Kiki and was steering her off down the crowded concourse, her red head almost resting on his shoulder.

Because the local Amish refused to attend, the congregation today was small, sadly so for such a happy day, Brooke thought as she started down the aisle on her own. It didn't really bother her that she had no one to give her away, for she had made this major, life-changing decision on her own—with Jennifer's approval. At least Emma and Levi had come, though they sat way at the back and evidently did not dare to bring their children. But Verna and some church friends were here, Elizabeth was her maid of honor, and Jennifer was her flower girl. That would have to be enough for now.

Daniel awaited her, looking so serious, but with his eyes alight with love. Next to him and the minister stood his best man, Paul Hostetler, who had returned to reconcile with his wife. He and Daniel had renewed their boyhood friendship, so Paul's little family sat up front, for Daniel had no one else to support the groom, either.

And so, six weeks after getting Jen back, Brooke became an almost happy August bride. Jennifer, however, ecstatic about the wedding—and the new horse back in the Melrose Manor barn with Bess that was *her* wedding gift—did too good a job of strewing rose petals, so that people's hair and not the aisle was littered with them. Emma had given Brooke and Daniel the Wedding Ring quilt she and Katie had meant for Daniel's nuptial bed, but Brooke had decided to drape the altar with it today. She stared at it during the service, her eyes shimmering with tears; an errant rose petal had even gotten that far.

But it was a lovely service. Daniel's Amish Sabbath suit and Brooke's old-fashioned candlelight satin Victorian gown seemed a beautiful blend. She felt quietly content, and that was joy, wasn't it? Still, how desperately she wished she could be accepted here among Daniel's people.

Outside in the late morning sun, the wedding party and guests piled into Levi's Amish buggy or Paul's car. Before they pulled away from the church, Emma came to kiss Brooke's cheek and hug her. "Sisters-in-law, almost as good as sisters, uh-huh," she said. Brooke's heart soared, for Emma seemed happy today. Now, with a girlish grin, she waggled her fingers at Brooke from her seat beside Levi in the buggy across the small parking lot.

Brooke wasn't certain if Levi was here because he had finally forgiven her, wanted to please Emma, or was thrilled with the two framed aerial shots of the recently released farmland. She and Daniel had given him the photos, which he had proudly hung in his barn, as fancy and forbidden as the airplanes he still stared at in the sky. She wondered what Levi would say when he heard Emma had volunteered to go with her into the city next week and help pack up her condo for her move into Melrose Manor. They had just closed on the deal last week, and there was so much to do. Already she had plans to expand the place to make at least eight guest bedrooms and add on a tearoom—hopefully, to be built by the local Amish if Daniel could get them to agree.

Brooke held to Daniel's arm as he clucked Bess out onto the road toward Maplecreek with Levi falling in behind and Paul bringing up the rear. It was a happy, bright road home today, she tried to convince herself, despite the problem with Daniel's people.

The jogging pace, the jingle of the harness, and clop of Bess's hooves soothed away her disappointments of the day. Through Levi, she had sent word to Bishop Brand that the Amish World farmland would soon be for sale. Evidently, that was not enough to make him even begin to accept his prodigal son or his worldly wife.

"I just wish your parents and the others would have agreed to come at least for punch, cake, and ice cream back at the Manor," Brooke said. "Verna and Emma have worked hard on the reception, and it's going to be on plank tables in the yard, so they wouldn't even have to step inside. Wouldn't it be great if they were waiting there for us, even though they're all supposedly busy elsewhere?"

"Don't get your hopes up, not on that," he warned.

"I know. We'll just build on what we can get over the years. At least your father didn't tell Emma and Levi they couldn't come."

"Temporarily—for Emma's sake," he muttered. "But we may not be able to rely even on them after today. But I promise you we are going to celebrate big time, in bed and out, all the rest of our days," he whispered to her. She wondered what was coming next when he winked at her. "I've got something for us tonight for a very special toast," he explained.

She smiled back at him. "Such as?"

"Such as Amish wine," he told her proudly.

"*Amish* wine? And I thought I knew all about the Plain People!"

"My favorite kind, dandelion—Dan the Lion—Emma used to call it. I made a big batch earlier this month and didn't tell you."

"You did? In other words, it doesn't have to age to be good?"

"Age? You mean like vintage? I don't know. Everyone likes it so it gets drunk up fast, even if it's supposed to be medicinal, too. My grandfather taught me to make it. When I lived at home, I used my mother's big porcelain stew pots, but this year I just stirred it up in my bathtub. I swear it's one of the reasons people were glad to see me back, so maybe I can get some of them to visit when they know we've got it. No one likes to admit it, but it's quite an aphrodisiac, too, not that we need that. But it's been responsible for helping young, skittish wives conceive their first child around here. Brooke?"

She was not certain at what point in his explanation she had begun to laugh, but she couldn't stop. Nerves, she thought. Still the shock of everything that had happened so fast. The joy of the beauty of this place and this man, the disappointment of keeping him apart from the family he—and she—cherished and admired despite their differences.

"Daniel—look," she cried and pointed, sobering suddenly to wipe tears from her cheeks. "A whole row of buggies coming down the hill toward us. You don't think they meant to come and just got the time wrong?" she asked as Jennifer stood and leaned on their shoulders from the backseat.

"No way. They're probably making a point of going

right past the house, right past us to someplace else. But then maybe my mother . . ."

They recognized the bishop's buggy as the first. At least a dozen others strung out behind that like black ducks in a line. "I can see his long silver beard," Jennifer cried. "I always thought Bishop Brand would make a really good Santa Claus!"

"Daniel—if they snub us," Brooke said, "I'm going to call out a greeting, anyway. And I don't want you to start any sort of argument with him again, not on our wedding day at least, no matter what he does or says."

"The pity is you and my mother are so much alike," he said and shook his head. "And she may never get to know it."

Brooke sat erect, feeling defensive and yet desiring their approval. She kept her hand boldly through his arm, however much the Amish frowned on open emotional expression, even between husband and wife. She felt him stiffen on the seat beside her and feared a bad beginning for them all.

The buggies neared; the space closed. "*Guten Tag, Herr und Frau Brand!*" With a wave and a smile, Brooke dared some of the very sparse *Deutsch* Daniel had begun to teach her. Both pairs of old eyes snapped left. Bishop Brand nodded deeply, and Ida Brand smiled broadly, and then they passed.

Brooke breathed again. "You don't know it," Daniel said, his voice exultant as he hit his knee with his fist, "but that was almost a public display of affection from them!"

They continued to call out greetings in German to the other buggies they passed—Daniel's brothers Moses and Mahlon and their families, cousins, and neighbors. Emma and Levi's brood were in their big surrey with

Isaac proudly handling the reins; grinning, they waved to Jen and she waved back. After the last one went by, Brooke and Daniel laughed, hugged, and laid plans to dare to invite his extended family, and Amish neighbors, the girls who worked in the shop—all of them—to the housewarming when they had the place expanded. The Maplecreek Amish might have made their point about keeping separate today, but surely there would be other times.

As they kissed each other and Jennifer cheered, Daniel and Brooke let Bess find her own way. They didn't even mind when cars of tourists passed and gaped or honked—not today. Finally, he turned the horse into the driveway of the house, and then they saw. Brooke gasped and climbed down the moment Daniel reined in. He swung Jennifer down and hurried to catch up with Brooke, his mouth as wide in disbelief as hers.

On the front porch steps and railing were draped and spread at least ten—no, twelve—Amish quilts. The ones on the porch held perfectly piled, neatly aligned Amish bounty like a blessing: jars of jellies, golden honey, ruby strawberry preserves, a rainbow array of canned fruit, cakes, bread, cookies, a basket of hand-carved clothespins, a beautifully made deacon's bench, three big down pillows, another Amish doll for Jennifer, and several big white aprons. And, against the steps leaned a large, wooden sign someone had carved that read:

MELROSE MANOR
<<<<<>>>>>
BRAND FAMILY
Bed &Breakfast & Tearoom
Amish Furniture &
Attorney-at-Law

AUTHOR'S NOTE

All of the characters in this story are fictional. The settings, except, obviously, Columbus and Las Vegas, are also figments of my imagination, although I created specific places in Maplecreek loosely based on real locations.

I do not intend this story to promote the use of the drug Prozac: it does have dangerous side effects for some people, although it is a great help to others.

I would like to thank the following people for lending support or advice. They answered many questions for the book's background research concerning such things as farming, the law, and small-town hospitals and police departments. If there are any mistakes in research, they are mine and not those of these people who generously shared their expertise: David Harper; Nancy Armstrong; Laurie Miller; Julianne Moledor, M. D.; Don Love; and Don Harper. Also, the Columbus Crime Lab and Columbus Burglary Squad and the Ohio Farm Bureau.

For assistance and advice in shaping the story, to my wonderful agent, Meg Ruley; my editor, Hilary Ross; and special consultant John Paine.

Especially, my gratitude to the Amish of Holmes County, Ohio, the little town of Charm, and the Helping Hands Quilt Shop and Quilt Museum of Berlin, Ohio. Also, Yoder's Amish Home, Millersburg, Ohio. These private people probably cannot and will not know how much help and inspiration they were to me. Like a fine Amish quilt, the quiet people in the land may be admired, even displayed at times, but they still choose to keep their borders.

—KAREN HARPER
April 6, 1995

Dear Reader:

I hope you enjoyed reading this Large Print book. If you are interested in reading other Beeler Large Print titles, ask your librarian or write to me at

Thomas T. Beeler, *Publisher*
Post Office Box 659
Hampton Falls, New Hampshire 03844

You can also call me at 1-800-251-8726 and I will send you my latest catalogue.

Audrey Lesko and I choose the titles I publish in Large Print. Our aim is to provide good books by outstanding authors—books we both enjoyed reading and liked well enough to want to share. We warmly welcome your ideas and suggestions for new titles and authors.

Sincerely,